Love
Remains

Love
Remains

KAYE DACUS

BARBOUR
PUBLISHING

Cover design: Lookout Design, Inc.

Published by Barbour Publishing, Inc., P.O. Box 719, Uhrichsville, OH 44683, www.barbourbooks.com

Our mission is to publish and distribute inspirational products offering exceptional value and biblical encouragement to the masses.

 Member of the
Evangelical Christian
Publishers Association

Printed in the United States of America.

Dedication/Acknowledgment

To Kevin Cloud, Sergeant, U.S. Army, and Joshua Lesley, Senior Airman, U.S. Air Force, for your bravery and devotion in volunteering to put yourself in harm's way for us. We can never thank you enough.

Prologue

"You'd think she won the lottery or something." Katrina Breitinger glared at the woman flouncing by, nose in the air.

"She'll be lording it over all of us until someone else achieves the same feat." Lindy Patterson crossed her arms and blew a lock of blond hair from her eyes.

"One would think she'd be mortified that it happened when she's still so young." Celeste Evans craned her neck to continue watching the woman in question.

Helen Bradley made a derisive raspberry sound. "Young, my foot! You know she's had work done."

"The least she could do would be to stop coloring her own hair." Maureen O'Connor touched her professionally hued auburn tresses. "Hers always looks so brassy."

Trina clicked her tongue, feeling slightly guilty. "Listen to the five of us. Standing here being catty about someone in church."

"You're right. Someone might overhear us and tell her." Lindy looked over both shoulders.

"We sound just like teenagers. It's unbecoming of us to speak ill of someone else." Trina set her lips in a firm line and looked at her four companions.

"To *speak* ill of her, but not to *think* ill of her?" Lindy, Trina's best friend since high school, winked.

"You know what I mean. Honestly. We're over eighty years old, and we're still acting like sorority girls." Trina raised her hand to signal her husband, who'd just entered the back of the sanctuary.

"But what are we going to do about *her*?" Helen jutted her chin toward the object of their ire.

"There's nothing we can do. Until one of our grandchildren gets married, she'll keep taunting us with the fact that she'll have great-grandchildren before we do."

Lindy grabbed Trina's arm. "That's it!"

"What?" Maureen asked.

"All of us have grandkids who're getting up into their twenties and thirties. High time they should be getting married." Lindy pulled the rest of the girls into a huddle.

"Don't remind us," Helen wailed.

"No, listen. We make a pact. Since each of us prides ourselves on knowing our offspring well, we're going to be very picky about whom our grandchildren choose. So we narrow the pool."

Trina stared at Lindy, following the train of thought to the next logical step. "We set our grandkids up with each other's grandkids."

"Exactly! We take the guesswork out of finding suitable partners for them."

"But how—?" Celeste's question was cut off by the organist beginning the prelude.

"We'll work that out later—we'll talk about it at coffee on Thursday." Lindy stuck her right hand into the middle of the circle. "Who's with me?"

Trina hesitated only a second before placing her hand on top of Lindy's. Celeste, Helen, and Maureen quickly followed suit.

Lindy looked around at each of them, beaming. "I hereby dub us the Matchmakers."

Chapter 1

The sharks were circling.

Bobby Patterson had been at the party a total of three minutes. But half that time was all it took for the smell of fresh blood to circulate among the single women.

"Hey, you must be Bobby. Patrick told us you were coming. I'm. . ." (fill in the blank with a female's name).

He shook hands, smiled, greeted, laughed, introduced himself, and promptly forgot the names of the couple dozen women who continued to circle around. . .as if there weren't a couple dozen other guys out on the back deck supervising the few men in charge of the grills.

"Diesel Patterson!" The masculine voice boomed through the room, and Bobby started to relax.

"Mack Truck Macdonald." He accepted Patrick Macdonald's hand for a vigorous handshake, which turned into a back-slapping hybrid embrace. A *bro-hug,* they called it back in California. Here in Nashville, Tennessee, he wasn't so sure. Having been gone for sixteen years, he had a lot to relearn about his hometown.

"I can't believe you actually came back, man. When you left the day after graduation, I thought you had shook the dust of this place off your feet for good." Patrick led him through the large gathering room and the open french doors to the expansive deck attached to the back of the house.

"I thought it was for good, too. But, you know, once your parents and grandparents get to a certain age, it's nice to be nearby." The edge of annoyance caused by the excessive female attention began to dissipate when Bobby was once again surrounded by men. Quick surveillance gave him a count of twenty-two men, in their early twenties to early forties, well-dressed—though they all wore jeans or shorts, they were high-end and new-looking—and with only a slight diversity in ethnicity, just as the women had been.

"Hey, y'all." Patrick raised his voice to get the attention of the majority of the guys standing around drinking sodas from red plastic cups and cans. "This is Bobby Patterson, my high school football buddy I was telling you about. He's just moved back to Nashville and will be looking for a church home, so let's make him welcome tonight and convince him he wants to rejoin Acklen Avenue Fellowship—because we could really use him on the softball team next summer."

After Bobby met a few of the guys, Patrick cuffed his shoulder. "I'll leave you to it, then. I've got to go back in and help in the kitchen."

"Thanks, Mack." Peripheral sightings informed him the women had grown tired of the segregation and were infiltrating the formerly all-male encampment outside.

One of the men standing near Bobby nudged the guy beside him. "Hey, pressure's off us. New meat." He jerked his head toward Bobby but grinned at him. "The gals in this group are great. . .once they get used to a guy. But don't worry. We'll try to protect you as best we can."

Bobby returned the guy's smile—he'd identified himself as Steve—and stifled his frustration. One of the reasons he'd left California was that the undercover work he did for the California Bureau of Investigation made it impossible to become an active member in a church, to be a part of a community, to meet someone.

Yeah, that last one was laughable. Ever since leaving New Mexico fourteen years ago, the possibility of meeting someone he'd want to spend the rest of his life with had been pretty much nil.

"So, Bobby, what brought you to Nashville?" Someone—the guy with the mole on his jaw. . .Chris—handed him a can of soda.

Though already the Saturday before Labor Day, the heat of summer lingered on, so Bobby really didn't care what flavor the drink was, as long as it was cold and wet. "I'm an agent with the Tennessee Criminal Investigations Unit."

"Oh, yeah?" The pronouncement drew quite a bit of interest. "Like. . .are you out there busting the drug dealers and murderers and stuff?"

Bobby shook his head. "No, I leave that up to guys who have a higher threshold for excitement than I do. After two tours in the Middle East, I prefer chasing the guys who commit crimes from behind desks— fraud, conspiracies, political corruption, and stuff like that."

As he suspected, the others picked up on the mention of war and his involvement in it. "What branch?" the former marine asked. Had to be former—wasn't in great shape, but still wore the jarhead haircut.

"Army—infantry. You?" Might as well get it out in the open.

"U.S. Marine Corps, baby." He raised his sleeve to show the USMC tattoo at the top of his bicep. "Did my tour five years ago. Afghanistan."

"I got back six years ago. A year in Afghanistan and a year in Iraq." To keep the conversation from turning to politics—as it had always done when the topic of the war had come up out on the West Coast—he cast around for another; his gaze came to rest on the orange baseball cap of the slender twentysomething across from him. "How're the Vols looking for this year?"

It turned out to be the perfect diversion. With the University of Tennessee's first football game of the season tomorrow, the entire group surrounding him jumped into the conversation—and warded off all but a few of the hardiest women—until the grillers announced the meat was finished and carried the pungent platters, piled high with hot dogs and hamburger patties, through the crowd and back into the house.

Bobby's new acquaintances ushered him inside. The forty-some-odd people all crowded into the house made it feel much smaller than before, even when split between the family room and living room.

He turned to Ryan—only to find the former marine had been replaced by one of the generic-looking females he'd met on his way in. She smiled up at him expectantly.

"Restroom?"

Her expectation fell into disappointment. "Past the kitchen and to the left."

"Thanks." His hands had been touched by so many people tonight that he wasn't about to use them to touch food that was destined for his mouth until he had washed them.

Unlike the houses he'd been looking at online, most of which were new or recent construction, the kitchen in this older home was cut off from the rest of the house by walls. Not the best setup for holding parties like this. Something to consider as he planned to get involved in the singles group at whatever church he decided to join and would love to host gatherings.

He rounded the corner and headed down the hall between the kitchen and dining room.

Someone zipped out of the kitchen, mitt-covered arms laden with an aluminum pan so full it sagged in the middle.

Both of them stopped short—and Bobby jumped back as a wave of baked beans sloshed over the side of the pan.

"I am so sorry!"

Bobby, who'd reached out to steady the woman, froze at the familiar voice. He dragged his eyes up from the mess on the floor to the face that had haunted him for fourteen years.

"Zarah?"

The horror at almost spilling an entire pan of baked beans on someone dissipated into frigid shock upon discovering the near-victim of her clumsiness was the one person she'd never expected to see again. Zarah Mitchell tried to regain her balance, both with the pan of beans and with her own emotional equilibrium.

"I'm so sorry," she repeated, not knowing what else to say. She'd always run the risk that she might one day see him again—she'd known that when she moved to Nashville fourteen years ago. But why here? Why now?

"Whoa! What's the idea?" Patrick's voice came from behind and above her. "Oh, good. I was hoping to introduce the two of you."

Zarah couldn't tear her eyes away from the vision in front of her—terrified he was real and terrified he was a figment of her imagination—until he reached out to take the pan from her.

"No introductions necessary, Mack. Zarah and I met each other a very long time ago." Giving her a tight smile, Bobby turned and carried the pan to the dining room. Zarah's chest tightened, and it had nothing to do with the relapse of pneumonia that had landed her in the hospital again for four days this week.

Bobby Patterson. Her first love. The man she compared all others to. The reason her father kicked her out of the house the day she turned eighteen.

She risked taking a deep breath, filling her lungs only until a coughing fit seemed imminent. She turned to face Patrick. "I–I'll get something to clean this up." She skirted around him and slipped back into the kitchen. But with five other people in the small space, relief was not to be found.

Pulling the roll of paper towels off its holder and grabbing the trash can, Zarah set about the task of cleaning up Patrick's beautiful new wood floor. Fortunately, not much had spilled; unfortunately, that meant it didn't take very long to clean up.

A shadow blocked the light, and she looked up. Patrick towered over her, arms akimbo, a dishrag hanging from one hand. "I was about to get that. I sure don't understand why you feel you have to act like a maid every time you come here."

"Not a maid." Zarah wiped up the last of the bean sauce and tossed the wad of towels into the trash can. She used the edge of the can for leverage as she got back up on her feet. "As your co-leader in this group, when we're at your house, I think of myself as the hostess. And when a good hostess spills something, she cleans it up. She doesn't leave it for someone else to do."

"Which I understand. However, I just visited you at the hospital three days ago. You don't need to be down on no floors cleaning stuff up."

"I appreciate your concern. But I'm fine. And I should know. This isn't the first time I've made a comeback from pneumonia—you know that, too." She turned to pick up the trash can to take it back into the kitchen, but Patrick snatched it out of her hand.

"Yeah, I know. This is the second time in four months you've landed in the hospital because you were too stubborn to take care of yourself after the first time your mule-headedness landed you there."

"I promise I'm fine." Instead of following Patrick into the kitchen, she continued down the hallway to the guest bathroom. Finding it empty, she entered and locked the door behind her. It didn't take long to wash the stickiness from her fingers. Once her hands were clean and dry, she leaned against the marble countertop and stared at her reflection in the mirror.

After all these years, after everything she'd lived through, seeing Bobby Patterson standing there made it seem like no time had passed—though he seemed taller than she remembered and much larger and more muscular at thirty-four than he'd been at twenty.

Why hadn't Kiki warned her Bobby was coming home? As his grandmother's best friend for more than sixty years, Katrina Breitinger knew everything that happened in the Patterson family—most of the time before the rest of Pattersons knew it. Zarah pulled her cell phone out of her pocket and slid it open to tap out a text message to her grandmother. Kiki knew the whole story, so Zarah could not understand why her grandmother wouldn't have given her some forewarning that the man who broke her heart was in town.

She exited the bathroom just as someone else was about to knock on the door. She plastered on her best I-am-fine smile and made her way down the hall to face the specter of her past.

With almost fifty people gathered in the main living areas and on the deck of the seventeen-hundred-square-foot house, avoiding Bobby turned out to be relatively easy. All she had to do was stay in the kitchen. But she couldn't hide in there all night. She had obligations. Grabbing the bottles of diet and regular soda out of their ice bath in the sink, she went out to circulate.

As expected, in the living room where most of the younger women sat around talking and eating, there was one main topic of conversation: Bobby Patterson. How tall he was. How cute he was. How muscular he was. How square his jaw was. And most ridiculous of all, an argument over whether his eyes were blue, green, gray, or hazel. Zarah could have answered the question for them. His eyes were blue, green, gray, *and* hazel, depending on the lighting and what color he was wearing. Tonight, dressed in a maroon polo shirt, his eyes probably looked hazel. In the brief time her gaze had been locked with his, the color of his eyes had not been her primary concern. But oh, how well she remembered the deep, dusky green they were the few times she had seen him in his army dress greens.

She moved from the living room into the den, where more of the guys were gathered. Off to one side stood Patrick and Bobby. Neither had plates in his hands, so she assumed either both had eaten already or, as Patrick was wont to do, they were waiting until everyone had been served before getting their own food. As a visitor, Bobby should have been one of the first people to eat tonight. But it didn't surprise her that he would wait. He was just that kind of guy.

Bobby suddenly looked away from Patrick and caught her watching him. She sucked in a startled breath, which caught in her fluid-filled lungs and triggered a coughing spasm. A couple of people standing nearby turned to ensure she was okay until Patrick made it to her side. It took awhile for her to be able to breathe enough to tell him she was fine. Patrick tried to make her sit down, but she refused; as a leader in this group, she knew people looked to her for strength and support. She could not show any vulnerability.

So they wouldn't see how weak and shaky the coughing spasm had left her, she carried the empty soda bottles back to the kitchen. It was all she could manage to pull the appropriate recycling bin out from the pantry and toss the empty plastic bottles into it. A couple of big black trash bags slouched on the floor in front of the sliding glass door that connected the kitchen to the deck. She sank into one of the chairs at the kitchen table and stared at the trash bags for a moment. As soon as she caught her breath, she'd get back to work.

After what felt like a long time, Zarah forced herself to stand up. She pulled the red drawstrings at the top of the bags closed, tied them, and shoved them with her feet under the table—which was where Patrick always put them during a party. She put a fresh bag in the large trash can and hooked another onto the knob of the pantry door—both of those would be full soon, too. With every muscle in her body weak from fatigue and exhaustion, she trudged to the sink, slipped on the pair of pink rubber gloves she'd given Patrick for his last birthday, and started washing the empty serving dishes and utensils that had already been brought in from the dining room.

"I thought I might find you in here."

Patrick's voice startled her, and she dropped the heavy metal pan she'd been scrubbing with a *clank* against the dishes still in the sink.

"Don't sneak up on me like that. You want to give me a heart attack on top of my pneumonia?"

Patrick laughed his signature booming laugh, erasing the concerned scowl from his expression. "Come on. Everyone's wondering where you are."

Yes, much as she didn't feel like it, she should be social at this thing. Building relationships with the younger women was the only way she would be able to mentor them and teach them to treat single men like brothers rather than prizes to be competed over. She understood the desperation that many of the young women felt; she'd felt it herself in her mid-twenties when the majority of her friends from college got married. Thank goodness, though, for Flannery and Caylor. At one and two years older than Zarah, her former roommates were also still single. The three of them, best friends since Zarah had moved into their apartment her junior year of college, shared all the agonies and joys of unmarried life together—something many single women did not have: a shoulder to cry on, listening ears, and more than one person who understood where she was coming from.

"Zarah, come sit with us." A group of older single women waved her over to join them. Uncomfortably, she eyed the space they made for her on the sofa, knowing her size-fourteen hips would never fit in that narrow gap.

The boom of Patrick's voice reverberated through the house, though Zarah could not make out what he was saying. But as more people flowed into the room, crowding it even further, the intent of his announcement became clear. He herded the last few people into the room ahead of him, then made his way through the crowd at the perimeter to stand in the middle, a stack of papers in his hands.

Zarah groaned. Patrick and his games. While she appreciated the fact that his seemingly endless supply of mixer games had helped them build this singles' group from a Sunday school class of about eight to the vibrant active group of almost sixty they had now, she personally hated playing these games. And he knew it. Which was why he'd come and gotten her out of the kitchen—because he loved to torture her.

The papers passed from hand to hand around the room as Patrick gave the instructions. People Bingo, he called it. The point, he said, was to learn new and interesting facts about other people in their group. Each of the twenty squares had hobbies, activities, places, and stuff like that written in them; and they were each tasked with going around the room and finding someone who had been there or done that. When two of the ladies on the sofa, who enjoyed these kinds of games and usually won them, jumped up to participate, Zarah sank down gratefully into the space they vacated. Until her tired muscles hit the soft cushions and pillows, she hadn't realized how much they were knotting up.

She wanted to close her eyes, to let the exhaustion she'd been holding at bay all day at work and all evening carry her away. But she couldn't; she had to pretend she was having fun playing Patrick's game.

So with great effort, she pushed herself up off the sofa and joined the melee. She read through the list of items needing to be matched to people.

Born on the East Coast. Knows how to knit. Still has their appendix and tonsils. Has been skydiving. Knows karate. Has been to Las Vegas.

Her eyes fell onto the box in the middle of the far right column: *Served in the military.*

She glanced around the room. As far as she knew, the only two people in this room who had ever served in the military were Ryan and Bobby. She made a beeline for Ryan.

She avoided the cluster of women—both young and old—who used this as an excuse to converge on Bobby and find out whatever they could about him. The great thing about such a cloud of admirers was that they created such a buffer, it gave Zarah the confidence to move freely around the room without worrying about another unexpected tête-à-tête with him.

But she did catch snippets of his answers to some other questions. Yes, he'd served in the army for ten years, achieving the rank of sergeant. Yes, he had been stationed overseas during his ten years, including two tours of duty in the Middle East. No, he had never been to Vegas, even though he'd lived within a few hours' drive when he'd been posted at Fort Irwin. No, he had never been skydiving, unless repelling out of helicopters in his air-assault training in the army counted for skydiving. No, he had been born right here in Middle Tennessee.

"No, I've never been married."

Zarah looked down at the sheet trying to find where that question came from, but could not find a box labeled *Has ever been married.* She shook her head; the audacity of some of these women.

Bobby continued speaking. "But my grandmother keeps nagging me to introduce her to my fiancée."

Chapter 2

$\mathscr{B}$obby watched Zarah out of the corner of his eye as he made the outrageous statement. Though he hadn't thought it possible, she lost what little color she'd had in her face before swaying and grabbing the back of the club chair she stood behind.

Okay, maybe the joke hadn't been that great of an idea. Patrick had mentioned Zarah had been sick recently, but he hadn't said with what or how severely. Bobby began to think that whatever it was had been pretty serious. Zarah looked like she was about to collapse.

"Oh, so you are. . .engaged?" a voice asked from the gaggle around him.

Bobby wanted to go to Zarah, to explain to her, to support her and comfort her. But his honor—or was that his pride?—wouldn't allow him. He drew his focus back to the women in front of him. "No. It's just my grandmother's way of hinting that she thinks it's high time for me to get married."

He couldn't be certain Zarah heard him. And he berated himself both for making the joke and for caring whether or not she heard his explanation. She was the one who had run away the day before he planned to propose to her. Her father's explanation afterward—that Zarah had confessed to secretly dating Bobby and that she no longer wanted to see him—had not rung true, but that never factored into the indignation, wounded pride, and anger he felt every time he thought of her. Which had been often, considering he carried her picture with him throughout his entire military service—including tucking it in the inside of his helmet to have it near him at all times throughout his tours in Afghanistan and Iraq.

Bobby put all his acting skills to work in continuing to play the game and pretend he was having fun doing it. Shortly after his boneheaded remark, he looked around the room again and was not surprised to find no Zarah.

True to their word, just when Bobby was starting to feel overwhelmed by the laser-focused feminine attention, the guys infiltrated and created a bulwark around him. Some even started flirting with the girls. He'd be interested to see how the dynamic changed in the Sunday school setting. If that and the Bible study class were as much of a meat market as this pre–Labor Day cookout, he might exercise his options and enlist elsewhere.

He spent so much time answering everyone else's questions that he only had a few squares filled out when a woman hollered "Bingo!" and brought the game to a merciful close.

With Patrick's attention tied up in verifying the woman's answers, Bobby slipped out of the room. He shouldn't allow himself to worry about Zarah, but he couldn't help it. She hadn't looked good before she'd slipped out of the room. He needed to make sure she was okay. He tried to blame it on the six months of intensive training as a medic between his two tours of duty, telling himself it was only her health he was concerned about. But he'd never been a good liar, not even to himself.

The hallway blocked much of the noise coming from the den, allowing him to discern the sound of running water and dishes and utensils clanking together. Of course. When everyone else was gathered together having fun, Zarah would be in the kitchen cleaning up behind them. It was what had been expected of her growing up, so it shouldn't surprise him to discover she was still at it all this time later. It was what she'd been doing the first time he met her.

He leaned against the doorjamb and watched her for a moment. She'd twisted her shoulder-length curly brown hair into a knot at the back of her head, which she had secured in place with the red pencil bearing Patrick's company's logo that they'd all used playing the game. Though it looked like she had put on twenty to thirty pounds since the last time he'd seen her, he couldn't say it did anything to affect her attractiveness—in fact he found her very feminine curves more attractive than ever. He was not surprised by the fact she wore cropped jeans that covered her legs down to midcalf, revealing only a few inches of ankle, when practically every other woman at the party wore shorts—even the few women who were larger than Zarah. She'd always been overly modest.

After a few swipes at an encrusted glass casserole dish with a scrubber, she paused, braced her hands against the edge of the counter, and leaned heavily against it. Bobby straightened, about to make his presence known, when Zarah's knees gave out. He crossed the kitchen in three strides and caught her around the waist before she crumpled to the floor. All it took was one touch to determine she burned with fever. Half under her own power, he got her to one of the kitchen chairs.

"I'm fine," she rasped.

"I can see that."

She'd always hated it when people humored her. She hated it even more when anyone tried to take care of her. Ducking his head to hide his smile over those remembered facts, he reached for her arm, pressed the tips of his first two fingers to the inside of her wrist, and looked at his watch.

"Your heart rate is elevated; your pulse is thready; and though I'm no human thermometer, I'd venture a guess that your fever is hovering somewhere between 102 and 103."

"I'll be okay." Her breath rattled in her chest with each aspiration. It sounded painful.

"Patrick told me you've been sick recently. He probably told you you're not going to get any better unless you stay home and rest, just like your doctors should have told you." He tried to keep his tone detached, professional, so she wouldn't feel like he was hovering. The one way to ensure she would do exactly what she was not supposed to do was to hover. Reverse psychology used to work pretty well with her; but in this situation, if he told her she should do more work in hopes she would do the opposite and go home, it would backfire—she would do the work.

"Why are you here?" she whispered. "I thought you were living in California and that you were happy there."

He shrugged. "I decided to move back to Nashville." No way was he going to tell her the full reason why he decided to move back.

Her eyes drifted closed for a long moment, and her breathing became more ragged. He gently shook her shoulder. With what appeared to be great effort, she opened her eyes, and it seemed to take even more effort for her to focus on him.

"You just sit here for a second. I'll be right back." He was rather surprised no one had yet come into the kitchen. In his experience with parties like these, half the party took place in the kitchen. He supposed these people were so accustomed to Zarah doing everything for them that they felt no need to come in and offer to help.

He assigned his indignation to his innate sense of justice and fairness. Surely there could be no other cause for it.

He didn't hear Patrick's voice over the din of the crowd, so finding him took a little longer than he expected. He finally located him out on the deck. Bobby inserted himself into the group beside Patrick and waited for the first pause into which he could interject himself. "Mack, can I get your help with something in the kitchen?"

Patrick's thick, blond eyebrows practically met over his nose when he frowned. Thankfully, he didn't ask for details but excused himself immediately from the group and followed Bobby back into the house. When they rounded the corner into the hallway, Bobby was appalled to hear the water running and dishes clanking together again. Had the woman absolutely no sense whatsoever?

Apparently not. She once again stood at the sink washing dishes. The shimmying motion of the fluid material of her blouse exhibited her tremors—whether from the fatigue and exhaustion, the fever, or a combination of factors, he couldn't tell.

As soon as Patrick saw her, he let out a grunt and crossed the small space to her, put his hands on her shoulders, and steered her away from the sink. "I thought I told you to take it easy tonight. This doesn't look like taking it easy to me." Patrick's frown grew fiercer. His left hand moved from her shoulder to the side of her neck to her forehead. "Okay. That's it. You're going home."

"But I feel fine—"

"I never thought I would accuse you of being a liar." Patrick straightened and looked around the kitchen. Bobby looked around, too, wondering what his friend sought. Patrick answered the unasked question when he stepped around behind Zarah and picked up a purse from the floor under the table. He reached into the small black bag and withdrew a key ring containing a car key, a house key, and a couple of plastic tags with bar codes on them. "Where did you park?"

"Up near the stop sign." Zarah propped her elbow on the table and leaned her head heavily against her fist. She reached her other hand out toward Patrick. "I'll take it easy. I promise."

"You need to go home because I don't want you making anybody here sick with whatever it is you have." Patrick dropped the small black purse into her outstretched hand and crossed the kitchen to the pegboard beside the door that looked like it probably led to the garage. He pulled his keys off a small hook. "And you may not feel bad now, but how are you going to feel when everybody at this party comes down with whatever you have?"

Bobby stared at his friend for a moment. While on the surface the words sounded harsh, humor glinted in Patrick's eyes. Bobby wondered how long Patrick and Zarah had known each other for Patrick to be able to push her buttons like this.

Worry filled Zarah's pale face. "I don't want anyone else getting sick." She stood up—too fast. She staggered, trying to catch herself on the table, but missed.

Standing beside her, Bobby did the only thing he could: He wrapped his arm around her waist and drew her into his side to keep her from falling over. It was the second time tonight he'd held her in such close proximity, and it was the second time tonight he felt like his skin had been branded by the touch. But it was only because of her high fever. Yes, that was it.

"You're not staying, and you're not driving yourself home. Diesel—"

Bobby looked up just in time to catch the keys that came sailing toward him.

"You drive her in her car, and I'll follow you to bring you back. I'd offer to drive, but that little tin can she drives just don't fit me." Patrick grinned at him. "And since you're such a puny guy, should be okay for you."

At six-foot-three, 210 pounds, no one would dare call Bobby *puny*—except Patrick, who had three inches and at least thirty pounds on him. But if Zarah's car was that tiny. . . "Maybe someone else ought to drive her. Someone she knows better than me."

Patrick shook his head. "Naw, man. Once she gets to feeling better, she'll be embarrassed enough that you witnessed this. If we bring anyone else into it, she may never show her face again. Either that, or she'll kill me."

"I can hear you." Zarah's voice sounded muffled, and Bobby realized he still held her up against his side. She pushed herself away from him, and as soon as she was balanced with one hand holding the edge of the table, Bobby released her. "I'll drive myself home."

Patrick laughed and crossed his arms across his massive chest. "Oh, yeah? Prove it. Stand here in the middle of the kitchen floor for two minutes without falling over, and I'll let you drive yourself home."

Letting go of the edge of the table was probably not the best idea in the world. But Zarah was already embarrassed enough at showing any signs of weakness in front of Bobby. She was thirty-two years old; she could take care of herself. She was no longer the weak, emotionally abused teenager whose emotions he'd toyed with so long ago.

She released the table, ignoring the way her head spun. She'd been living with this for four months, off and on. She could get through tonight. Although, she now wished she had taken her boss up on his offer to cut short her workday today. He had come into her office this morning, told her she looked pale, and reminded her she was still supposed to be on short-term disability and not back at work.

She could do this. She ignored the ripple-and-wave effects of the floor and stepped out to the middle of the room. Turning her back to Bobby, her eyes found the photo she'd taken of Patrick with the small group he'd taken on the advanced-trail hike at Fall Creek Falls last October. Though Patrick had pleaded and cajoled, and even offered to wash and detail her car, nothing would have convinced her to step out onto the suspension bridge—even though she now felt like she was standing in the middle of one. She struggled to keep her eyes open, fought the chills, and kept her breathing shallow to stave off another coughing spell.

Sleep would be so nice—curled up in her bed, warmed by the thick featherbed topper on her mattress below and the winter-weight comforter wrapped around her. She could almost feel the covers wrapping around her and pulling her down into their soft, warm depths.

Lights flickered past her eyes. How had she gotten in the car? To her left, a large silhouette filled the driver's seat. She almost laughed. At five-foot-eight, she had to sit with the driver's seat all the way back just so her knees didn't hit the steering wheel when she moved her foot from the accelerator to the brake pedal or worked the clutch.

Patrick couldn't even sit upright in the late-nineties model Honda Civic—Bobby's head pressed against the fabric roof liner.

When she opened her eyes again, she stared at the front of her own house. The 1911 brick cottage was cute, even in the dark and illuminated only by the headlights of her car and Patrick's. Either she'd forgotten to turn the porch light on or the bulb had burned out.

She rested her heavy head on the headrest, then lolled it over her left shoulder to look at the man in the driver's seat. Her driver's seat. With Bobby sitting in it. Something that had been building inside her was very near to exploding.

"I have to get out of the car." She fumbled for the door handle and practically spilled out onto the driveway when the door gave way more easily than she expected. She made a mad dash for the front door—though it felt like wading through three feet of mashed potatoes—and fumbled in her purse for her keys.

A familiar jangle behind froze her in mid-motion. Of course. Bobby had driven her home; thus, he had her keys.

She turned and snatched them from between his thumb and forefinger. "You shouldn't be here."

"I can't just walk off and leave you without seeing you get safely inside." Bobby leaned his shoulder against the brick porch pillar.

Patrick ambled toward them, hands in pockets, whistling. Zarah dropped her voice—not that she had much of one left. "You don't understand. I don't want you here. It was. . .we were. . .just one of those things. But that was then. This is now. I've moved on with my life."

Bobby glanced over his shoulder and lowered his voice as well. "I haven't told anyone, if that's what you're worried about. People will only know as much as what you've told them."

Patrick stepped up onto the porch, took Zarah's keys from her hand, and proceeded to unlock her front door. When she didn't move, he took her by the shoulders and steered her into the house. Once inside, he turned her around to face him. From this angle, she had a clear view of Bobby, still leaning against the pillar as if he had not a care in the world.

"If I see you at church Sunday, I'm going to be very unhappy." Patrick squeezed her shoulders until she looked up at him. "And if you won't listen to me, I'll call Trina Breitinger. Because I know you won't ignore your grandmother the way you ignore me."

"But what if I'm feeling better Sunday?" Zarah tried to give Patrick a flirtatious smile, but she wasn't sure if she was successful.

Patrick heaved a dramatic sigh. "I suppose there's nothing really I can do to stop you. But I'm serious: I will sic your grandmother on you if you look the least pale or feverish."

Zarah was good with makeup, and she was pretty sure she could avoid letting Patrick feel her forehead in public. "Agreed."

"Are you sure there's nothing you need? I can fix you some. . .tea or something." Patrick moved toward the kitchen, but Zarah stopped him with a weak hand to his chest.

"No, but thank you. You know how I feel about people hovering."

She stole one last glance at Bobby then ushered Patrick out the door. Though speaking to Bobby was last thing she wanted to do, she had to be polite. "Thank you for driving me home. I'm sorry you had to leave the party, but I'm sure it'll still be in full swing when you get back."

Bobby gave her a tight-lipped smile and nodded his head. She'd forgotten how that expression emphasized his broad chin and large, square jaw. She closed her eyes, trying to stop the memories from flooding in.

She waited until they were both in Patrick's car before closing and locking her front door. The questions, the memories, the pain brought on by Bobby's sudden appearance tonight crashed down on her. The tremors, which they had attributed to her fever, increased tenfold as she allowed herself to experience a rush of emotions now that no one else was around to see it.

Her tired, aching, chill-wracked body wanted to melt into a

puddle right here on the living room floor. But she could not let that happen—she would not let Bobby's presence make her lose everything she'd gained during the last fourteen years. She had worked far too long and far too hard to become a happy, independent, self-reliant person.

Chapter 3

$\mathcal{I}$n the kitchen, Zarah filled the kettle with water, put it on the stove, and turned the burner on high. Then she went back into the living room, found her purse on the floor where it had fallen off the sofa, and pulled out her cell phone. She glanced at the antique clock atop her entertainment center. Good. Barely eight thirty. She pressed the button to make the number pad show up on the touch screen, then pressed and held the two. CALLING KIKI scrolled across the screen.

One ring, followed by, "Zarah, dear? Is everything all right?"

As if she didn't know. "Why didn't you tell me?"

"Tell you what?" Her grandmother sounded genuinely surprised.

"Bobby Patterson. Why didn't you tell me, first of all, that he was back in Nashville and, second of all, that he would be at the singles' cookout tonight?" The kettle started whistling, and Zarah trudged into the kitchen to pull it off the burner. She grabbed a tea bag out of the jar of herbals, tossed it in a mug, and poured the steaming water over it.

"He's at the party?"

"He will be as soon as he and Patrick get back there. I. . .started feeling bad, and Patrick insisted they drive me home." Zarah carried the blue ceramic mug into her bedroom, pulled a pair of flannel pajamas off the dresser, put her phone on speaker, and started changing.

"Are you okay? Do I need to come over and take you to the emergency room again?" From the tone of her voice, Kiki sounded like she was halfway to the car already.

Zarah's head spun when she bent over to pick up her discarded capris from the floor. She staggered over to the cedar chest at the foot of her bed and sat to pull on her pajama bottoms. "No, I don't need to go to the emergency room. They told me I might continue to run a low-grade fever over the next several days. And you're avoiding my question."

"I knew he was coming back to town, but I was not certain when. Lindy told me a few weeks ago that he accepted a job at the TCIU and would be moving back. I guess she didn't think to mention he'd arrived when I saw her yesterday morning."

"That still doesn't explain why you didn't tell me he was moving back to town." She donned a Vanderbilt University sweatshirt over her pajamas and pulled on a pair of thick wool socks she usually wore only in the winter and then only if it snowed.

"I thought, maybe if you just ran into him. . ."

"What? That it would be easier on me if I just ran into him out of the blue?" She turned the overhead light off and climbed into the bed. "Because believe me, it wasn't easy all."

"But if I had told you, if you had been forewarned that there was even the slightest chance he might show up at a singles' event or church, you would have gone back to being a hermit, just like that first year you lived here."

Zarah stopped fussing with pillows behind her and sank back into them. She picked the phone up off the nightstand, switched it back to normal mode, and pressed it to her ear. She wanted to deny what Kiki said, but a little voice in the back of her mind told her it was true. If Kiki had told her Bobby was coming to Nashville—moving here to live—Zarah would have done whatever she deemed necessary to avoid him. Even if it meant locking herself in her house.

Her head, chest, and throat hurt too much to think about this tonight. "Does Lindy know? About Bobby and me, I mean."

"No. She knows you two knew each other when he was stationed at White Sands, but she doesn't know he's the reason your father kicked you out of the house."

"Thank you for that." It was probably the only thing Kiki had never shared with Lindy Patterson since they first met in high school more than sixty-five years ago.

She snuggled into the featherbed mattress-topper and pulled the thick comforter around her. Moving the phone to her other ear, she reached for the mug of tea on the nightstand. . .and realized she'd left it on the dresser. The cold expanse of floor between the bed and the dresser, though just a few feet, looked like the miles Roald Amundsen had to trek across Antarctica to get to the South Pole. She glanced to her right. The water bottle still had enough left to take the heavy-duty decongestant that would knock her out for the next twelve or so hours. Thank goodness tomorrow was Saturday and she could work from home on her own schedule.

Reaching for the bottle apparently loosened something in her lungs, triggering another coughing jag.

"I really wish you would come stay here and let me take care of you."

Zarah curled up in a ball on her side, covering her mouth with one tissue, dabbing her watering eyes with another, the phone lying on her ear and cheek. She took shallow breaths until the spasm eased. "Thanks, but I'd rather die alone. Besides, if whatever I have is still contagious, I don't want to pass it on to you and Pops. Especially Pops. He hasn't fully recovered from that staph infection he got after surgery."

"Don't let him hear you say that. You may not have noticed it, but he believes he's a spring chicken again, now he's got new knees." Kiki hollered something at Pops in the background. "Are you certain you don't want me to come over and bring you home for the weekend? I'll make your favorite: chicken and dumplings, with the dumplings baked separately and served on the side so that they aren't the least little bit soggy."

Zarah laugh-coughed. "Don't make me laugh. I love your chicken and dumplings, but I'm afraid even that isn't enough to entice me. You know how I feel about being babied." It had taken her a couple of years to say anything to Kiki about how much it bothered her to have someone make a fuss over her whenever she was sick. A retired pediatric nurse, Kiki hadn't taken the news very well.

"Well, you call me if you need me—even if it's the middle of the night. I can be there in less than ten minutes."

"I'll do that." Moisture escaped Zarah's eyes again, only this time it wasn't an involuntary reaction to her coughing. She didn't deserve to have anyone love her the way Kiki and Pops did. Which made her all the more thankful for them and the way they'd taken her in when she'd had nowhere else to go.

"You try to get some sleep now. And don't work too much this weekend." How well Kiki knew her.

"The sleep, I'll guarantee. The work. . .I missed almost a week at the office, and I have my meetings with the Metro Council and the state senate committee coming up. I have to be prepared."

Kiki made a noise that came through the phone like an annoyed grunt. "There's more to life than that job, Zarah."

"I know. There's teaching and the singles' group." And between the three, she had almost no seconds in her day left unaccounted for. "I'll try to rest as much as I can. Patrick said if I show up for church Sunday, he'll sic you on me."

"Good for him. He's such a nice boy. I don't know why—"

"Don't start, Kiki. Patrick and I are just friends." She'd always thought it was because they were so different—but since Bobby had walked into her life, every decision she'd made since he chose his career over their relationship plagued her, forcing her to doubt every attraction she'd downplayed, every man she'd rebuffed—there hadn't been very many—every man she'd made walk away from her. Had it been because she didn't like them or because of Bobby?

"Good night, Kiki."

"Good night, Zarah. Sweet dreams."

Zarah ended the call and tossed the phone onto the stack of books on the nightstand. She'd thought she was over Bobby, thought he was out of her system. So why did all those old feelings come back as soon as she saw him?

And now he knew where she lived. Maybe it was time to think about moving.

"Bobby? Is that you?"

Bobby came back down the two steps he'd taken up toward the guest bedroom on the back side of the house and went through the mudroom into the kitchen. "It's me, Mamm."

His grandmother, Melinda AnneMarie Mansfield Patterson—alias *Mamm*—sat at the kitchen table, a multicolored floral scarf tied around the blond hair she'd spent an hour at the beauty parlor this morning getting "set." A delicate china teacup sat on its saucer near her right hand while she worked the newspaper crossword puzzle with her left. She watched him walk around and take the seat across the corner of the table from her.

"How was the party?"

He tipped the chair back on its hind legs and hooked his fingers together behind his head. "Fun. It's a big group—you're right."

"Meet anyone interesting?" Mamm's blue eyes took on an unusual glint.

Bobby let the front legs of the chair down slowly and crossed his arms. "Do you know someone named Zarah Mitchell?"

"Of course I know Zarah. She's Katrina and Victor Breitinger's granddaughter." Mamm picked up her teacup and took a sip, then made a face. She stood and crossed to the sink, where she dumped the contents. "Want some tea?"

"No thanks." He turned sideways in the chair and hooked his arm over the back of it. "So. . .you know who Zarah is—she's the granddaughter of one of your friends. But do you *really* know who she is?"

Mamm slid the kettle forward on the ancient gas stove and turned the front flame on high. She leaned against the countertop. Dressed in cropped jeans—much like Zarah's—flip-flops, and a short-sleeved blouse, Mamm could have passed for a woman twenty or thirty years younger than the eighty-three he knew her to be. She even had pink toenails with little rhinestone designs on the big toes.

"Are you trying to tell me she's an undercover superhero or something?" Mamm winked at him. "Ooh, is she Wonder Woman? I always suspected she might be."

He rolled his eyes and fought against smiling at her. "No, Mamm. What I mean is: When you sent me to that party, knowing full well that Zarah Mitchell would be there, did you know that she and I already knew each other?"

The kettle shrilled, and Mamm turned to get a fresh tea bag and pour the water over it into her cup. A perfect stall tactic. He'd interrogated too many people over the years not to recognize such a typical method of trying to gain oneself time to formulate an answer. And as with all of them, he waited. People with guilty consciences hated long, uncomfortable silences.

Mamm carried her teacup back to the table, and from the matching china bowl in the middle of the table, she added two sugar cubes. Bobby hadn't known any companies out there made sugar cubes anymore. He was tempted to grab a handful of them and eat them like he had as a child, but with everything he'd eaten at the party tonight, he'd already sentenced himself to several extra hours at the gym next week—once he joined one.

"What's a five-letter word for *slip past*?" Mamm picked up her pen again and tried to be convincing with her act that she was more interested in the crossword puzzle than in their conversation.

Bobby didn't buy it. "I asked you a question. Did you encourage me to go to that party tonight because you knew Zarah Mitchell would be there?"

Mamm pulled her reading glasses off her nose and let them dangle by the bejeweled chain around her neck. "You've only been back in town three days. I told you that the reason I thought you should go was because you would see people there you already knew."

"I thought you meant Patrick Macdonald and the few other people I went to high school with who are still around." Unable to resist it any longer, he reached for the sugar bowl, extracted a cube, and put it in his mouth, where he held it between his back teeth as it dissolved.

"If I knew of any specific reason why you would not want to see Zarah, then I might not have encouraged you to go. But since no one will tell me anything more than that you and she knew each other when you were stationed at White Sands, I had no way of knowing you wouldn't enjoy seeing her again after all that time. Did I?"

Bobby scrubbed his hands over his face, then leaned his elbows on the table. "Well, some things are better left in the past."

"See? That's exactly why I didn't know any better than to send you to one of Zarah's parties. Because there's not a lot about your past—at least the years you've been gone—that you're willing to share with anybody."

He had to hand it to her—she had a point. Though he and Zarah had clandestinely dated for more than six months, he could only remember once mentioning to his parents he'd gone out with someone while he was stationed in New Mexico. He had not mentioned her name. And he had never told them he intended to ask her to marry him, because they would have tried to talk him out of it. And they would have been right. Twenty and eighteen were too young to get married. Not that he'd even had the chance to ask.

"Suffice it to say, Zarah and I knew each other well for a brief period of time, but it ended with some hard feelings." Bobby picked up another sugar cube, but this one he held between his thumb and forefinger. "What do you know about her?"

"I know she came here to attend Vanderbilt. She studied history, and I believe she has her PhD." Mamm tapped her pen against her chin. "Yes, as a matter of fact, I do remember Kiki and Victor feting her when she received her doctorate."

He supposed it was nice to know she had gone on and accomplished the dream she had left him for. "And what does she do now?"

"She works for a local history museum or historical society or something." Mamm shrugged. "I'm not certain precisely what she does or where she works. All I know is it has something to do with history."

Preservation of historic sites had been something of a passion of hers back when he'd known her.

"So does this mean you aren't going to go to church with us Sunday? I've been telling everyone you're going to be there." Mamm looked so crestfallen, so sad, he couldn't bear to disappoint her.

"No. I'll go with you Sunday. I'm not going to let some. . .trivial incident from the past interfere with my getting involved in what seems like a great group of people." Between the way the younger single women had checked him out tonight and the presence of a few of his high school classmates he'd like to reconnect with, becoming an active member of Acklen Avenue Fellowship—the church he grew up in—would be a great way to create the opportunity he'd wished for since leaving New Mexico: to show Zarah he'd moved on, had made something of his life.

Mamm patted his hand, reminding him of the sugar cube he still held. He put it in his mouth. Yes, showing Zarah he had far exceeded her father's dire predictions for this juvenile delinquent's future would be sweet.

He stood, then bent over to kiss his grandmother's cheek. "Evade."

"Do what?"

"A five-letter word for *slip past*: evade." He grinned. He'd missed hearing people say *Do what?* instead of *Sorry?* or *Pardon?* or *Huh?* when they didn't understand the first time. He squeezed his grandmother's shoulder before slipping past her to continue on up to the guest room he was occupying until he found a place of his own.

Mounting the stairs, he whistled an old Johnny Cash tune. Though he hadn't been too keen on the idea of staying with his grandparents for weeks, perhaps months, while he searched for a place, closed, and moved, tonight's talk with Mamm made him almost glad Mom and Dad had sold the house he grew up in and bought a luxury condo in one of the new mid-rise buildings in midtown Nashville—a luxury condo with more than three thousand square feet and two guest bedrooms that were far too small for him to consider staying in. At Mamm and Greedad's house, he had the whole second floor to himself, almost.

He stepped into the back bedroom and turned on the light. Maximus, the Great Dane, thumped his tail against the denim patchwork quilt covering the queen-size bed. Yes, he had the second floor *almost* to himself.

"Dude—off the bed." He snapped his fingers. After a few more thumps of the tail, Maximus complied, though slowly. And once down, the massive dog took time to stretch and yawn, sniffed Bobby thoroughly to see if he'd been anywhere interesting, and then ambled out of the bedroom, nails clicking on the hardwood floors. "Go see Greedad."

Maximus cast him a glare over his shoulder before continuing down the hall to the front staircase.

Bobby shook his head. Dogs. While having one around the house provided more safety against break-ins, he wasn't sure he could live with one. Especially not one the size of Maximus—who answered to nothing but his full name.

He pulled the denim quilt off the bed to reveal a nice, colorful one with an actual pattern to it underneath. Mamm had explained when Bobby chose this bedroom that Maximus liked to take naps in here occasionally. But as the room at the back corner of the house, it was farthest away from Mamm and Greedad's room on the opposite corner in the front of the house downstairs. Though Mamm always stayed up late, Greedad was a firm believer in early to bed, early to rise. Bobby usually was, too, but just in case he decided to stay out late sometimes, he didn't want to disturb his grandparents' sleep and make them regret their decision to ask him to stay with them.

Perched on the side of the high, antique four-poster bed, Bobby pulled his shoes off, then carried them to the closet.

In short order, he completed his nightly rituals and soon climbed into the bed. As soon as he turned out the lights, Zarah Mitchell's face formed in his mind's eye. Still beautiful after all these years. Still stubborn and unwilling to accept help from anyone. Still disdainful of him—well, she hadn't been feeling her best tonight, so her real emotions toward him had yet to be discovered.

Now he understood why God had so adamantly pushed him into returning home to Nashville. He had to show Zarah Mitchell not only that he'd moved on with his life, but that he was also ready, willing, and able to meet someone new, fall in love, and get married. He might even be magnanimous and invite her to the wedding.

Chapter 4

$\mathcal{Z}$arah checked her reflection one last time. The extra makeup added the right amount of color to hide her sickly pallor. Even though she felt much better this morning, after taking it easy and limiting herself to only working six hours yesterday, she still looked sick—and Patrick would be true to his word and cause a scene if he didn't believe she was completely well.

She glanced down at the prescription bottles lining the countertop beside the sink. Stuff to take at night. Stuff to take during the day. Decongestants. Expectorants. Antibiotics. Ibuprofen drug for the lingering headache and other sundry pains. Ever since the upper respiratory infection she'd developed after the seemingly unceasing rain in April and May, she couldn't remember more than a few days this summer that she hadn't been sick.

And she was tired of it. Her own blue eyes stared back at her from the mirror. Did she really need to force herself to go to church this morning when instead she could put her pajamas back on, climb into bed, and stay there the rest of the day? Kiki would probably even make her some chicken soup—with the baked dumplings on the side.

Guilt overrode any thoughts of indulging her laziness. Here she was, a perfectly capable thirty-two-year-old, thinking about creating more work and worry for her eighty-two-year-old grandmother. Besides, after this relapse, which included spending four days in the hospital, she'd already missed the last two Sundays. The records were probably a mess. And she needed to follow up with anyone who'd visited during her absences—because no one else would have thought to do it since she hadn't reminded Patrick to get someone on it.

With her Bible and spiral-bound sermon-notes journal tucked in the crook of her left arm, she grabbed her purse, keys, and sunglasses off the table by the front door. After checking to make sure she had at least half a pack of tissues in the small handbag, she got in the car—and felt like she was sitting in a hole. The backrest was halfway into the backseat of the small sedan.

Her skin tingled. Bobby—he'd driven her car last, and leaning the seat back must have been the only way he'd been able to fit into the compact vehicle. She readjusted it, once again weighing the merits of crawling into bed and staying there. Forever.

No. She would face him eventually. Might as well be today. Just like taking off a bandage—best to do it quickly to cause the least amount of pain.

She checked the clock. Good. She had enough time to stop for coffee. And God must have thought it was okay, too, because someone pulled out from a parallel spot on Twelfth Avenue South just as she drove up to The Frothy Monkey. With no traffic coming, she hung a U-turn in the middle of the street and slipped her car into the vacated spot.

Several people she knew from the neighborhood greeted her from their tables on the front porch. She pushed her glasses up to the top of her head, shoving her mass of curly hair back away from her face.

A few minutes later, she fought to get the glasses untangled from the snarls of hair with one hand while holding her large, sugar-free, fat-free caramel latte in the other. Mission accomplished, she waved at her neighbors and turned the car around in the middle of the road again to go to church. For the thousandth time, she wished Becker's

Bakery hadn't gone out of business. For the first couple of years she lived in the 12 South area, it had been the perfect place to stop to get pastries to take to church or work. Of course, she loved the table and chairs she'd gotten for her back porch at the furniture store that had moved into the old bakery building after Becker's closed, but she missed the ease with which she used to buy snacks for everyone.

This area had changed so much, just in the fourteen years she'd lived in Nashville. What must Bobby think of it, coming back to a city nearly half again the size it was when he left? She was still surprised by some of the changes that had happened, seemingly overnight, especially in areas like the Gulch and the Demonbreun Avenue corridor.

Though traffic on Wedgewood was minimal, she got caught at the light at Sixteenth Avenue South, giving her time to enjoy a few sips of the latte. Last April during the Country Music Marathon, her cousin and his band had played on a stage set up in the median triangle here, between Belmont University and Music Row. She wished she'd felt well enough to walk over and hear them play. Even after fourteen years, her maternal aunt and cousins still felt like strangers to her. Of course, only the oldest of her four cousins, Lee, lived here—he'd just started his sophomore year at Belmont.

The light changed, and she continued on past the college. Turning off before reaching Hillsboro, she wound around a couple of secondary streets to Acklen Avenue. Usually, she parked on a side street, nearly a full block away from the large church. Today, however, she indulged her laziness and found a spot near the small parking lot at the rear of the church. Must not be too many people in the early service for there to be this many parking places available near the building.

Halfway up the stairs to the Sunday school classroom, she paused, wheezing, chest heavy. If she started coughing now, it would sap her of what little strength she had to try to make it through the morning. And she couldn't collapse again, not in front of Bob—Patrick and everyone else.

Her low-heeled black pumps echoed loudly against the tile in the empty corridor. As she expected, the singles' classroom—which had been made large enough to accommodate them by the removal of the walls between three regular-sized rooms—was empty. With it being Labor Day weekend, she didn't expect more than half their normal number to show up.

The Sunday school director had already dropped off their attendance sheets. In a way, Zarah was glad they got new record sheets each week. That way, she didn't have to see if someone had messed up the job that had been hers almost from the first day she'd attended this church. She pulled out the basket of name tags from the metal cabinet behind her welcome desk and started laying them out on the table on the far end of the room by the coffee station.

"What are you doing here?"

She cringed at Patrick's tone and volume but rearranged a few name tags to put them in alphabetical order before turning. "I'm feeling much better."

Patrick slammed two half-gallon jugs of orange juice down on the beverage table hard enough it was a miracle the tops didn't pop off and spew the sticky liquid everywhere. "Just because you have your voice back—"

"And no fever and no headache."

"—doesn't mean you're better." He grabbed her head—one hand wrapped around the back, the other covering her forehead and eyes. "You don't feel overly hot."

"I told you I don't have a fever." She'd forgotten just how fussy he could be. She should have remembered—she'd wanted to kill him after she'd twisted her ankle two years ago hiking in Gatlinburg, he'd hovered so much.

"What's this, an exorcism?" Flannery McNeill's voice floated into the room.

Zarah pushed Patrick's hands away. "Yeah, Patrick is trying to exorcise my pneumonia away." She handed Flannery her name tag. "I thought you were going to Birmingham for the weekend."

Flannery made a face that would have twisted anyone else's features into ugliness. But not Flannery McNeill with her big hazel eyes, high cheekbones, patrician nose, and full lips. She couldn't do ugly no matter how hard she tried. She set the five doughnut boxes she'd carried in on the table. "One of the senior editors quit Friday—with a book due to the printer by Tuesday that wasn't ready to go. I was at the office until one in the morning Friday night and then didn't get home until almost midnight last night. But now all the changes are made and all that has to be done is for the designer to prepare the electronic files and upload it."

"Sounds. . .fascinating." Patrick rolled his eyes.

"Thanks, Mr. I-Hit-Things-with-a-Sledgehammer-All-Day." Flannery propped her fist on her hip.

"Face it, Ms. Wordy Girl. The work of a building contractor will always be more interesting than the work of an editor. Plus, no one feels like they have to watch what they say—or the way they say it— around me."

"As if you'd ever be bothered by speaking improperly in front of me."

Zarah chuckled and returned to setting out the name tags. The constant bickering between the two of them had bothered her when she first met them, until she learned that not only had they grown up together—same church, same neighborhood, same schools—but in their World History class in high school they had been assigned a project on Scotland, based on their last names. Upon discovering the clans Macdonald and McNeill had been bitter enemies in medieval times, they'd taken to bickering with each other whenever possible— to make their ancestors proud.

Oh, she should forewarn Flan—

"What are *you* doing here?" Flannery's voice carried a note of surprise and disdain.

Too late.

The beautiful, icy blond pinned Bobby with narrowed eyes. When he'd made the decision Friday night to attend Acklen Ave. on Sunday, he'd never considered she might still go to church here.

"Flannery. You're looking well."

She crossed her arms. "I asked you a question."

He mimicked her stance. "I'm here because this is the church I grew up in, and it's the church I plan on attending now that I've moved back to Nashville."

Flannery's eyes went back to their normal roundness, now filled with surprise, and she turned toward the far right end of the room. Bobby looked, too. His heart bumped against his ribs. Even with her back turned, he'd recognize Zarah's mass of curly hair anywhere.

"Zarah, did you know about this?" Flannery demanded.

Zarah's shoulders raised and lowered—then shook as she stifled a cough. She turned. Not quite as pale as Friday night. But dark circles dug trenches under her eyes—she looked like she could use a solid month's sleep. "Yes, Flan, I knew."

"And you're. . .okay with it?" Flannery's tone dropped almost to a whisper.

"I'm sure I don't know what you mean." Zarah's expression clearly warned the other woman to lay off.

"We'll talk later."

Patrick's head swung back and forth between the two women. "What are y'all talking about?"

Zarah patted Patrick's arm—and a flash fire of jealousy surged through Bobby before he could snuff it. "Don't worry about it, Patrick. It's nothing."

And there, in one word, he had Zarah's opinion of everything that had happened between them as young adults—*nothing*. It had meant nothing to her then; it meant nothing to her now.

"Diesel, help me put the chairs out." Patrick seemed to take Zarah at her word.

Bobby gladly pitched in with the manual labor of moving forty chairs into a circle in the center of the large room. It gave Zarah and

Flannery a chance to have a private conversation as they finished laying out the name tags.

Zarah and Flannery McNeill—friends. Figured. He wasn't sure if he should be flattered or offended that Zarah had sought out people from his past to become friends with when she moved here.

"Started your house hunt yet?" Patrick asked, pulling Bobby's attention away from the women.

"Not yet. I wanted to get my feet on the ground at work first. I finished all of my certifications with the state last week. This week will be my first on the job at the unit."

"Any particular area you're looking at?"

"I'd kinda like to stay around here. This is the area I grew up in; it's what I'm most familiar with. The office is off Briley Parkway, northwest of downtown, and it's only a ten- to fifteen-minute drive from my grandparents' house—but that's without traffic. I want to give it a week or two of morning and evening rush hour to see what it's going to be like."

"Thinking about a house or what?" Patrick pointed at chairs as he counted them.

"Nah—too much maintenance. I love my parents' condo—but I can't afford something like that. I've been noticing all the new condo and townhouse developments along Hillsboro, Music Row, Demonbreun, and West End. I'm thinking about maybe getting into one of those. I realized a pretty good profit on my place in LA, so I've got a budget that will go a long way here."

A gasped, "No!" from Flannery caught Bobby's ear, but he refused to turn. He wasn't being egotistical in his belief they were talking about him. Flannery's reaction to his arrival pretty much guaranteed it.

He continued talking real estate with Patrick, finding out how much Patrick had paid for his house in Green Hills—and barely hiding his reaction to the mid-six-figure number. The area had always been upscale; apparently it was even more so now. Thursday, he'd had to drive down through the heart of Green Hills, past the mall and

Hillsboro High School, to a multi-use retail and office building to get his car registered and his Tennessee license plate. At eleven o'clock in the morning on a weekday, traffic had been horrible—akin to what he might expect in the shopping district on the Saturday before Christmas.

Not only did he not want the maintenance a house required—yard work, exterior, roofing—he wanted to be close to one of the interstates. Easy on, easy off—meaning easy to work. After four years spending an hour to ninety minutes sitting in traffic every morning and evening to go about twenty miles to get to work, he was ready for an easy commute.

"I can hook you up with my real estate agent—she's a member here, actually. She'd have been at the party Friday night, but she was going out of town for the holiday weekend. She did me a huge favor getting me in to see my house literally five minutes after the listing went public."

"Thanks. I'd appreciate that."

People started trickling in. Patrick stopped trying to get the chairs arranged so that there was the same amount of space between each one and went over to the side table and made coffee.

Zarah moved to stand beside the small desk just inside the door. She greeted everyone by name, offered to get them coffee or orange juice, and, as they mingled, brought each one his or her name tag and beverage of choice. The only people who didn't let her serve them were the ones who wanted to doctor their coffee with the powdered creamer and sweeteners.

Bobby observed in horrified fascination. Didn't these people remember that Zarah had been in the hospital recently—and that just Friday night, she'd been so sick he'd had to drive her home? A few people asked her how she was feeling, but those were the women he'd tagged as forty-plus, most likely divorced, and almost certainly moms. But the younger people—those he estimated to be no older than Zarah's thirty-two—were the ones who took advantage of her subservient nature, who seemed to find nothing amiss in her acting like a restaurant hostess rather than a member of this group, an equal of everyone here.

He remembered all too well the Thanksgiving dinner at General Mitchell's home when he'd mistaken Zarah for part of the catering staff her father had hired in to cook and serve the meal. He also remembered asking her a few months later if she ever got tired of always doing things for others and allowed herself to have a selfish moment. Her answer had been no. Apparently, it was still no.

"If y'all will take a seat, we'll get started." Patrick's voice boomed over the din of conversations.

Zarah quickly wended through the crowd, the coffee carafe in one hand, a jug of OJ in the other, refilling people's cups. He shook his head. If she did it in the middle of the lesson, he might have to reconsider his decision to become a member of this class. He couldn't watch her debase herself like that every week—even though he wasn't allowing himself to feel compassion toward her. Not after the way she'd treated him.

There were just enough chairs for everyone—well, for everyone except Zarah. But she sat down at the desk and started marking the attendance sheet. She'd probably bring her chair over when she finished.

He sat so that he could just see her. After a few minutes, she took the roll sheets and put them in the plastic box on the classroom door, which she then closed. She stood just inside the door a moment, looking over the circle—and apparently noticing no empty chairs. Not even Flannery had thought to save her a place.

Zarah went back to the desk to get the chair—no, wait, what was she doing sitting down over there again? Sure enough, she opened up her Bible as if she was going to sit there, apart from the rest of the group, for the entire lesson.

Bobby clamped his teeth together. How could these people be so insensitive to someone who did so much for them?

As soon as Patrick finished his introduction and asked a discussion question, Bobby scooted his chair back, creating a wide enough hole in the circle to accommodate another chair. He ignored the questioning looks from everyone else, pulled another chair off the stacks lined up against the wall, and put it in the gap. He then went over to the desk, picked Zarah's Bible up off it—careful not to lose her place—cupped his hand under her elbow, and escorted her to the extra chair.

Her face went from sickly pale to eight-hours-in-the-sun red in a flash, and her eyes glittered with extra moisture, making Bobby's triumph empty. He hadn't just embarrassed her, he'd mortified her. In front of her friends and acquaintances. But he refused to back down—or to let her act like an unwanted appendage rather than a vital organ in this body of believers. He opened his Bible and returned his attention to the lesson as if nothing had happened.

Something odd caught his attention, and he turned and looked at Flannery. She smiled at him and gave a slight nod of her head.

He refused to acknowledge the gesture. If Flannery were the good friend to Zarah she'd acted like earlier, she would have done what he had long ago—and every week before now—to show Zarah they wouldn't tolerate her hiding in a corner.

Not that he cared. He would have done that for anyone, not just the first—and only—woman he'd ever loved.

Chapter 5

Uncertain she would be able to face anybody in the singles' group ever again, Zarah sought out her grandmother as soon as the worship service ended. She waited until Kiki finished her conversation with Lindy Patterson, not wanting to give either of the grandmothers any reason to discuss or speculate about any past, present, or future relationship there might be between her and Bobby.

Kiki wrapped up her conversation with Lindy as soon as she noticed Zarah waiting in the wings. "Zarah, darling, you look tired." Kiki pressed her cool, dry palm to Zarah's forehead.

It was all Zarah could do to refrain from pushing Kiki's hand away. "I thought maybe I could join you and Pops for lunch, since I haven't been able to spend much time with you recently."

Kiki pushed Zarah's hair back from her face before returning her hand to her side. "What about lunch with the singles' group?"

"I'd really rather spend time with you. If that's okay. But I don't want to be an imposition." Zarah hugged her Bible and sermon-notes journal to her chest.

"Why do you always think you are going to be imposing on us? You are our granddaughter, our flesh and blood. We want to spend time with you. We want to be able to show you how important you are to us."

50

Zarah refused to get emotional. She'd spent far too long not having the strength to adequately police her reactions over the last four months—had found herself crying over greeting-card commercials—and now she needed to start rebuilding those barriers.

"You happen to be in luck—I got industrious and put a pot roast in the slow cooker this morning, so you'll definitely get us all to yourself, with no waiters to interrupt us." Kiki waved at someone over Zarah's shoulder.

"Is there anything I can stop and pick up on the way over?"

"No. I have everything we need. And you know I always make too much food for just Pops and me."

"Thanks, Kiki. I'm going to run home and change clothes, and then I'll be over." Zarah left her grandmother to talk to all her friends and slipped out of the auditorium through a side door unmanned by a church staffer or volunteer shaking hands.

"Zarah—wait! Where are you going?"

If it had been anyone but Flannery, Zarah would have pretended she hadn't heard and gotten in her car. She set her Bible atop it, forced a smile, and turned. "Hey, Flan."

"What is going on with you today? I mean, I know it's a shock to see him again after all that time, but since you already knew he was here—or was it because of the whole chair thing in Sunday school? I would have saved you a seat, but I know you prefer sitting at the desk instead of in the group—especially since you've been sick and have to get up and leave the room if you start coughing."

Zarah touched Flannery's arm, and Flannery stopped talking. "I have never been so humiliated in my life. He just couldn't leave well enough alone. I know everyone was laughing at me afterward."

Flannery's pencil-darkened brows knitted together. "What are you talking about? Everyone felt guilty for not being the one to do it themselves. Zarah, Bobby saw what none of the rest of us did—that you made yourself into an outsider, and that we've all accepted it and let you stay outside the circle instead of being part of the group. A lot of that is my fault. I know you don't like to be pushed, and I didn't want to be the one to push you to change the status quo."

Zarah crossed her arms and leaned against her car. "I happen to like the status quo. I'm happy with it. I don't want people making a fuss over me."

Flannery rolled her eyes. "Including you in the group in Sunday school isn't making a fuss over you. Bobby did exactly what you would have done if it had been anyone else who didn't have a place to sit in the circle."

Because she wanted to stay angry at Bobby, Zarah tried to ignore the logic and truth of Flannery's statement. "I was happy where I was."

"Come to lunch with us. We're walking over to Boscos."

Zarah's mouth watered at the thought of her favorite Sunday brunch dish there—a prosciutto and artichoke omelet. "I can't. I'm going to Pops and Kiki's for lunch."

"Then how about you and I get together for coffee this afternoon. Portland Brew at three?"

"Make it four, and I'll be there." Zarah let Flannery hug her before they parted. Funny how, when she couldn't stand being touched by anyone, a hug from one of her closest friends did actually make her feel slightly better.

At home, Zarah quickly changed into a pair of lightweight cotton capris and a T-shirt printed with a design that looked like a watercolor of a Paris cityscape. Someday, she might actually visit the City of Lights, but for now Music City would have to do.

Leaving her subdivision, she drove south several minutes, past the small James Robertson University campus, and turned left into her grandparents' neighborhood. One of the things she loved about this area was the canopy of trees shading the streets and the big old houses—something her neighborhood, almost equally old, lacked.

She pulled up in front of a large, dark red, foursquare house and parked on the street in the shade of an old silverleaf maple tree rather than in the sunny driveway. She let herself in through the carport door and was greeted in the mudroom by the decadent smells of perfectly roasted beef and baking bread.

As soon as Zarah stepped into the kitchen, Kiki handed her a glass of iced tea. Zarah thanked her and then crossed the large kitchen to the table, where she bent over and kissed the top of Pops's head.

"So, you haven't keeled over and died on us, huh?" Pops snapped the funnies section of the paper to straighten the drooping corners.

"I've decided to linger." Zarah sank into the chair beside him. It didn't matter how long she'd lived in Nashville or how many times she sat in this kitchen, she could never forget that her mother grew up here—that her mother had eaten at this very table, had probably sat in this chair, had laughed and cried in this room, and had stormed out of this house almost forty years ago to elope with Walter Mitchell the night before he shipped off to Vietnam. If Kiki and Lindy Patterson hadn't been trying so hard to get Zarah's mother and Lindy's son together, Zarah's mother would never have made the biggest mistake of her life.

Zarah shook off the welling memory of the terrifying fights her parents used to have, unable to understand how two people who fought like that in private could put on such a show of being the perfect couple in public. Just like everything else in history, nothing she could do now would change it. She could only learn from it and move forward. She picked up the Op-Ed section of the newspaper and quickly scanned the titles of the pieces from the syndicated columnists before flipping it open to the center where the local opinion pieces were located alongside the letters to the editor.

"That one columnist really doesn't like you." Pops didn't bother looking up from the comics.

Zarah didn't have to ask what Pops meant but looked at the right-hand side of the two-page spread:

MITCHELL'S WHITE WHALE

An expensive, illogical, and self-destructive quest. You might think I'm referring to Captain Ahab and his ill-fated hunt. But this is no work of fiction. Dr. Sarah Mitchell of the Middle Tennessee Historic Preservation Commission has far surpassed Melville's Ahab with her manic search for a Confederate battlement which no other historian or archaeologist will confirm ever existed. . . .

"The least he could do would be to get my name right." She closed the newspaper section, folded her arms atop the table, and rested her chin on her wrist.

"Sort of makes you wonder what else he's getting wrong if he can't even get your name right." Pops reached over and patted Zarah's back.

"I mean, there has to be other stuff going on in this city that's more important than the fact I got a couple of injunctions to stop development down on that riverfront property."

"Sounds to me like he has a vested interest in getting that property reopened for commercial development." Kiki clanked a wooden spoon on the side of the slow cooker and put the lid back on. "Why else would he always be railing against you?"

The columnist had started his tirades against Zarah and the commission about four months ago. The second injunction had stopped the developer from tearing down three flood-damaged old houses, clear-cutting the land, and building another strip mall, and it had benefited the neighborhood by stopping construction of something that would have lowered the home prices in the area. "Dennis has contacted the newspaper and told them we would be happy to have someone come out to talk to us about the site and about the research. I think this columnist hasn't bothered because it makes a convenient subject—so he can gripe about it when he can't come up with an original idea for his column."

The oven timer buzzed, and Kiki pulled out a small pan of yeast rolls, filling the room with a tantalizing aroma merely hinted at before. Zarah pushed back from the table and stood.

"What can I help with?"

Kiki shook her head, opened her mouth as if to speak, closed it again, and turned to pull the pot roast out of the slow cooker. "Why don't you grab the plates and silverware and help Pops set the table while I finish up with this?"

Zarah didn't bother keeping her smile to herself. After all these years, she had finally trained her grandmother not to insist Zarah do nothing and act like a guest. Zarah selected three different-colored plates from Kiki's massive stoneware set along with a three-piece flatware service for each of them and carried them into the dining room. Even though she would have been perfectly happy eating lunch at the kitchen table, Kiki would insist—no matter how many people or how few, whether related or not—that guests should not eat in the kitchen.

Pops brought in place mats and cloth napkins which he set at the places at the end of the table closest to the kitchen. Zarah set out the plates and silverware.

"How was the party Friday night?" Pops rested his forearms on the back of the head chair and watched her finish setting the table.

"I didn't enjoy it as much as I thought I would. I wasn't feeling well and had to leave early." While she knew Kiki would never lie to Pops about anything, she trusted Kiki to keep her promise of confidence. Pops knew the whole story, all about her past with Bobby, but she wasn't sure she was ready to tell anyone else about Bobby's role in Friday night's fiasco.

Over lunch, topics of conversation stayed on safe grounds: the newspaper columnist, Zarah's job, books they had read recently, and updates from Kiki and Pops about other family members. Though she actively participated in the conversation, during lulls or when she was listening to one of her grandparents speak, her imagination drifted to Boscos, picturing Bobby there, surrounded by at least ten of the pretty, flirtatious, twentysomething girls from the singles' group. Even if Zarah wanted him back—which she didn't—she would never stand a chance against those girls. She had no delusions about her looks; her eyes were such a light blue they sometimes appeared to have no color at all, while her nose was, according to her grandmother, a throwback to Kiki's Greek ancestors. Zarah didn't know if that were true or not; all she knew was that it was too big, too pointy, and had been the source of much amusement for her classmates in elementary school and middle school. Kiki said it made her unique. Of course, having pretty much the same nose as Zarah, she would say that. Bobby was the only boy she'd ever known who said he thought she was beautiful and didn't suggest she get a nose job. But with the way things ended, she couldn't be sure he truly meant anything he had said to her.

Zarah and Pops insisted Kiki sit at the kitchen table while they did the dishes and cleaned up the kitchen. Kiki kept them entertained by reading tidbits from the Lifestyles section of the newspaper.

Though both Kiki and Pops entreated her to stay, just after two o'clock Zarah said her good-byes and left, feeling better than she had in weeks.

Bobby knelt to tie his trainers tighter after his warm-up stretches. He was as quiet as possible descending the stairs. With Greedad dozing in his recliner in the living room and Mamm listening to an audio book while she knitted in the den, Bobby didn't want to disturb the somnolent atmosphere of the house by crashing down the stairs the way he usually did.

Maximus jostled Bobby at the door, obviously assuming Bobby was going to take him for a walk. Bobby considered taking the long-legged monstrosity with him but then remembered Greedad's complaints that when he took Maximus out, he spent half the time being dragged and the other half trying to drag the 130-pound dog. Not conducive for the kind of hard run Bobby needed today.

By the time he managed to shove Maximus far enough back from the door to get out, he'd already had a pretty decent workout, gotten his pulse rate up, and broken a sweat.

With no particular destination in mind, only a desire to clear his head, Bobby headed northwest through the neighborhood of gridlike streets. He noted several five- or six-unit condominium developments along with several town house–style duplexes which had obviously been built to replace smaller, older homes like those that surrounded them. He made a mental note of several for-sale signs, but even though his sense of curiosity led him to want to tour the condos and duplexes in this area, he was pretty sure he wanted to try to get into one of the newer buildings in midtown or closer to downtown. Not only would they have better amenities, but they would be more like what he'd grown accustomed to in Los Angeles. Especially if his parents' three-thousand-square-foot penthouse condo was any indication of the kind of quality he could expect—not that he could dream of affording something like that.

Eventually the steady rhythm of his feet pounding the pavement worked its magic. Rather than a confusing jumble of images, memories, questions, and thoughts, his consciousness seemed to stretch out in front of him like the road ahead. Tuesday on his way to work, he would put in a call to Patrick's real estate agent. Then, he would focus on gleaning what he needed to know to make his transition into his new job go as smoothly as possible. As for church, and the people he had encountered there, he didn't need to think about that for six more days. He shuddered, interrupting his study rhythm, at the memory of the young women at lunch today. He'd felt like the fatted calf thrown to a pack of ravenous wolves. One would have thought he was the only unmarried man at the table of twenty. Actually, one would have thought to he was the only single man in the whole of Nashville—or even Tennessee.

He had hoped, upon discovering his home church had such a large singles' group, that finding a wife—the next step on his life's journey—would be easy. He hadn't planned on Zarah's presence making that completely impossible. Seeing her again after so long—seeing that she was more beautiful now than she had been at seventeen—these generic, bleached-blond Stepford girls would never be able to compete with her.

After about an hour, with thunderheads approaching from the west, Bobby headed back toward his grandparents' house. The first few splashes of rain helped his cool-down efforts considerably as he made his way up the driveway at a slow jog.

He grabbed a quick shower and then pulled on a pair of khaki shorts and a blue polo shirt, but was only able to find one of his pair of favorite leather flip-flops. He had a sneaking suspicion that if he ever did find the second one, it would have some pretty big teeth marks on it. He tossed the single thong into the bin with the rest of the shoes he hadn't needed yet and pulled out a different pair. Yes, not only would he call the real estate agent first thing Tuesday morning, he would let her know to look for properties with owners who wanted to close quickly. If worse came to worst, he might even be willing to rent for a while. He loved his grandparents; but, after just a few days, he was ready to be back in his own—dog-free—place. His cell phone beeped, indicating he'd missed a call while he was out and someone had left him a voice-mail message.

"Robert Patterson, this is Captain Carroll from the TCIU. I wonder if you might be available to come into the office for a few hours this afternoon. We have a new fraud investigation case we want you to take the lead on, and we'd like to bring you up to speed so you can hit the ground running on Tuesday. Please give me a call at your earliest convenience." Bobby scrambled to find pen and paper and ran the message back twice to write down and double-check the phone number Captain Carroll left.

Excellent. Even though he'd been hired as a special agent in charge, he'd worried that he might get stuck with either administrative work or acting as a support person on someone else's investigation for a while—exactly what had happened to him the last few months he was in California. Whatever this new case was, he would put all his efforts into closing it quickly and showing Carroll the kind of asset he would be to the unit. With no family of his own and, as of yet, no outside commitments, he could devote almost all his time and energy to the investigation.

These bad guys had no idea what they were in for.

Chapter 6

"So you had absolutely no forewarning that he was going to be there?"

"None whatsoever. I walked through the door, and—bang!—there he was."

"Excuse me, but I'm the one who actually dated the guy fourteen years ago." Zarah couldn't help but be amused by the interchange between Caylor and Flannery. When the gorgeous redhead had shown up just moments after Zarah arrived at the coffee shop, Zarah knew she'd been betrayed. Of course, she had almost suggested that Flannery call and invite Caylor to join them. After all, the three of them were best friends. And Sunday afternoons were pretty much the only time they could get Caylor out without Caylor experiencing a guilt complex over leaving her grandmother home alone with no means of transportation, since Sassy couldn't drive anymore.

"But I knew *you* would've been shocked to see him, Zare." Caylor flashed her megawatt grin at Zarah. "I was more curious about Flan's reaction to seeing him." Caylor's turquoise eyes twinkled.

"Seriously though," Flannery interjected, "why do you think he's come back to Nashville after all this time?"

"You're asking me?" Zarah held her hands out in front of her. "If

I could read that man's mind, my life would have turned out much differently." If she'd known from the beginning that he'd never intended to do anything other than toy with her, she never would have agreed to sneak around and disobey her father's direct order that his daughters were not, under any circumstances, allowed to date enlisted men.

Caylor and Flannery continued to gaze at her as if somehow, miraculously, she would come up with an answer for them. "Flan, you've known him a lot longer than I have. Why do you think he came back?"

Flannery shrugged her delicate shoulders. "Why does anybody do anything?"

Caylor threw a wadded-up napkin at her. "What kind of answer is that?" She pushed her coffee mug back and leaned forward on the edge of the table. "Why does anybody move back to their hometown? I've never met this guy, but I can't imagine his intentions in moving back to Nashville are evil or malicious. And he grew up here. From what Flannery said, it sounds like all of his family is here. I think since we're close to his age, we can all understand if he came back because of a desire to be close to them. He probably spent his twenties being wild and free, but now he realizes it's time to grow up and start acting like an adult."

"The problem with that scenario," Zarah said with a sigh, "is that in being closer to *his* family, he'll be closer to *my* family—because his grandmother and my grandmother are best friends. And you know how much they and their closest friends—including your grandmother, Caylor—like to throw parties where all of our families are invited."

Flannery pulled her hair out of its haphazard ponytail, finger-combed it back, and secured it so that half of it stayed tucked up in the band. "There's only one solution then."

"Oh yeah, what's that?" Zarah crossed her arms and leaned back in her chair.

"You're just going to have to find some absolutely fabulous guy to start dating, so you can show old what's-his-name that you're completely over him and that you're capable of landing someone a hundred times better than he is."

Caylor made a face as if considering the merits of the plan.

Zarah shook her head, staring at her two friends. "And where, exactly, am I supposed to find this paragon of manhood?"

"You just leave that up to me, sweetie." Flannery patted her hand.

Zarah hoped her expression showed her friend just how insane she thought Flannery was. She could count the number of dates she'd had since moving to Nashville on two hands, with a couple of fingers left over. And most of those had been in college. It wasn't as if she hadn't been attracted to anyone since Bobby—she had, but he had turned out to be more interested in that year's Miss Tennessee. And, as her father had always said, no man in his right mind would choose a fat girl over a slender one. If it hadn't been for her father's bootcamp-like diet and a training regime he had put her on at age fifteen, not even Bobby would have been able to pretend to be attracted to her.

"I guess that means I'm going to have to join the gym again." She groaned and rested her chin on her fist.

"Why? I told you I would see to finding you someone. Trying to meet someone at the gym is too chancy."

Zarah almost laughed at Flannery's expression of wide-eyed innocence. "I don't mean to meet someone at the gym. I mean I need to go to the gym to work out and try to lose about fifty pounds."

Across the small table, Caylor made a raspberry sound. "Puh-leez. If you lose fifty pounds there'll be almost nothing left of you. Besides, you know good and well I'm at least twenty pounds heavier than you. So what's that say about me?"

Zarah rolled her eyes. "I seriously doubt you weigh more than I do, but you're also almost four inches taller than me. When I look at you all I see is someone who has curves in all the right places. When I look in the mirror, all I see is fat."

"Yet you know I wear the same size you do. So if you see yourself as fat, how can you not see me as fat?"

"Because you're tall. You carry it better than I do."

Caylor's expression sobered, and she reached across the table to squeeze Zarah's hand. "No, that's not it. It's because I didn't have a father who called me fat when I wasn't. But if you're serious about joining the gym, I'll join with you. Even though I think I'm pretty fabulous just the way I am, taking off a couple of pounds would give me a great excuse to splurge on a bunch of new clothes."

"And don't forget the shoes," Flannery added, grinning. "You realize that if I'm going to start setting up Zarah on some fabulous dates, that means it's time for a makeover. Because you can't wear a business suit out on a hot date. And it has come to my attention, Miss *Thang*, that your wardrobe is entirely too serious."

Caylor nodded, chewing on her bottom lip. "Flan's right. If you're going to make this Bobby guy jealous, suits and separates aren't going to cut it."

Zarah shook her head, laughing. "You guys know how I feel about too-short and too-low cut. Not happening."

"Nobody said anything about making you into a hoochie mama." Flannery's emphatic statement drew looks and guffaws from the college students at the nearest table. "All I'm saying is that we have to break you out of the professor look."

"Hey, now!" Caylor playfully smacked Flannery's shoulder. "I resemble that remark."

"Now, now Professor Evans. You know I wasn't including you in that sweeping generalization, for all that you are a tenured professor. Actually, you have a few things in your wardrobe that I'd love to see if we can find—or borrow—for Zarah. And we've got to do something about that hair."

Zarah self-consciously touched the frizzy curls resting on her shoulder. "What do you mean *do something about* it?"

Flannery narrowed her eyes and gazed at her as a sculptor might study a slab of marble. "I think it's time for something drastic and dramatic. I'm seeing short hair."

Caylor grimaced. "I don't know, Flan. You're the one who forwarded that article to us last year about the survey that proved men are attracted to women with long hair and intimidated by women with short hair." She cocked her head and touched the flipped-out ends of her artfully messy, short hair.

"Exactly my point." Flan smacked her hands down on the table. "Short hair is a sign of confidence, and we want Zarah to appear as confident as possible."

Nervousness rose in Zarah's chest. "There's a huge difference between *appearing* confident and *being* confident."

"And how would you know?" Flannery raised her brows. "You neither *appear* nor *are* confident. You never have been in the entire time I've known you."

Though Flannery's words were harsh, Zarah could not take offense at them—they were too true. At least, in her personal life. The only time Zarah had ever experienced confidence—since Bobby anyway—was with history, with her studies in college and her work in research since. If cutting all her hair off could give her that sensation about herself—if it could make her as confident and vivacious as Caylor—she'd consider it. However, she had a feeling it would take more than just a haircut. And it was going to take more than just a haircut to deal with the Bobby situation.

Bobby closed his umbrella and shook off as much water as he could while waiting for someone to buzz him into the building. He turned at the sound of footfalls slapping against the wet pavement behind him.

"You must be Patterson." The stocky African American man lowered his umbrella in the protection of the awning above and extended his right hand. "Chase Denney."

Bobby shook the man's hand. "Robert Patterson. But everyone calls me Bobby."

Chase pulled out his ID badge and slid it over the reader beside the door. With an electronic beep, the door unlatched. Chase pulled it open and motioned Bobby to enter ahead of him. "We'll have to see about getting you a key card today, though it's unlikely with everyone arriving at the same time on Tuesday you'd have to wait out the rain to be let in."

From the front lobby, he was pretty sure he remembered his way to the captain's office, having been escorted there on the several interviews he'd had as well as the meeting Friday to complete his paperwork and migration of information from the California bureau. He was glad he didn't have to rely on his memory, however, once he followed Chase through the labyrinthine corridors to a small conference room on the third floor.

The captain and three other men were already seated at the round table when Bobby and Chase entered. Captain Carroll stood to shake Bobby's hand and introduced him to the others. Bobby shook hands all around and worked to commit the other agents' names to memory.

"Agent Patterson's area of expertise with the CBI was investigating fraud cases with businesses as well as government agencies. A new fraud case has come to my attention, and I believe Agent Patterson's experience makes him the perfect person to lead the investigation." Carroll opened the thin dossier in front of him.

"It has been brought to the unit's attention that members of a government agency might be misusing their legal oversight abilities in real estate dealings for personal gain. Permission to open a case just came through, and we need to hit the ground running on this one—otherwise I wouldn't have called you in on a Sunday afternoon." Captain Carroll began explaining the evidence already collected.

The case summary piqued Bobby's interest. It sounded similar to a couple of real estate fraud cases he had handled in Los Angeles. Nothing like starting a new job with something familiar.

Captain Carroll picked up a remote control. Bobby shifted his chair so he could see the projection on the screen behind him—a land-tract map of Nashville. Along the north side of the Cumberland

River east of downtown, two large tracts of land were outlined in red. If Bobby remembered correctly, that area was residential with homes at least as old as those in Belmont and Green Hills.

"This is the parcel that is of most concern to us right now. You'll need to go back into the agency's land acquisitions and zoning applications to see if anything raises a red flag."

Bobby leaned forward. "What fraudulent activity is suspected?"

Captain Carroll seemed impressed by Bobby's simplistic question. "When a tract of land like this comes on the market and is rezoned commercial, someone at the agency requests an injunction against any purchase or development of the land, supposedly to give the agency time to go in and survey the property. The value of these two tracts of land in the four months they've been under injunction has dropped considerably."

Bobby turned to look at his new boss. "So we're thinking they find a valuable piece of land, stop development on it through the agency, wait until the property's value bottoms out, drop the injunction, and buy it cheap?"

Carroll nodded. "Something like that. That's what we want you to find out."

"I assume the agency's records are public?"

"Public, and on record at the Tennessee State Library and Archives. I expect you will want to spend part of your day Tuesday down there looking into it."

Bobby vaguely remembered a high school field trip to the state library. But as a sixteen-year-old jock, the idea that the dusty old place that stored the records of the state government going back more than two hundred years might one day hold valuable information for him had never crossed his mind. Back then, he had been so focused on the dream of playing professional football, as his father had, that he paid little attention to anything other than football. But then he had been arrested. . . .

Carroll was still talking. ". . .agency makes monthly reports to the

Metro Council budget committee and quarterly reports to the state senate's budget committee."

Though most people would find it tedious, Bobby actually enjoyed investigating government agencies—there were always more records, meaning a longer paper trail, giving him more points of access, a greater understanding of how the agency worked, and, usually, lots of evidence. "Are they completely government funded?"

Carroll looked down at the dossier. "Not entirely. The majority of their funding comes from state and local government, but they also have plenty of federal and private grant money—and they do tons of fund-raising."

"Is there any evidence that any of those monies have been embezzled or used in the improper purchase of any of this land?" Only through great effort did Bobby stay seated. He was so anxious to start this investigation, he wanted to be on his feet, headed out the door to start.

"Add that to your questions-to-be-answered list." Carroll laced his fingers above his head and stretched as if they'd been meeting for hours already. "I figured this would be right up your alley, based on cases you closed in California. Sounds like you're eager to get going."

Bobby shrugged. "It's been a few months since I've had an active case."

"Understandable. And that's why I wanted to bring you in today, so you can have tomorrow to formulate a plan and come up with the list of resources you might need—as well as determine if you believe this case is prime for covert infiltration."

Bobby pressed his lips tightly closed and ran his knuckles along his jaw. He had made the decision to leave California not just to be closer to the family but also because he was tired of the isolation and deception necessary to work undercover. Yet he did have the experience necessary to do it, and maybe that was why God had brought him here. Even so, it could be problematic that he had already told a couple dozen people he would be working for the TCIU.

Captain Carroll clicked the remote and the projector turned off. Bobby turned his chair square to the table again.

"So, are we talking. . .environmental group?" Bobby pulled a pen out of the inside pocket of his sport coat and slid the brand-new legal pad someone had been thoughtful enough to put on the table closer to take notes and start jotting down questions.

Carroll shook his head. "Sadly, no. We couldn't make your first case with us that easy. It's the Middle Tennessee Historic Preservation Commission."

Bobby wrote the agency's name at the top of the page, frowning. Something about that sounded vaguely familiar, but he couldn't put his finger on it immediately.

"I will have my secretary make you a copy of the file before you leave this afternoon, though it doesn't contain much information. There are two people we are especially interested in investigating. The first is the agency's director, Dennis Forrester. Undergraduate degree in civil engineering from the University of North Carolina. Worked as a city planner and zoning official in several places for the first twenty years of his career, then must have gone through a midlife crisis because he moved to Nashville and went back to school to pursue his graduate degree in historic preservation at James Robertson University. He's been the director of the commission for going on ten years now. We will need to look into his financials, because he seems pretty well-to-do for someone who's been the head of a government-funded nonprofit agency for that long."

Bobby started a list of actionable items under Forrester's name down the left side of the page. He drew a line down the middle. "And the other person of interest?"

Carroll looked down at the file and frowned, thumbed through a couple of pages, then flipped back to the beginning of the file. He turned to call for his secretary over his shoulder. "I seem to be missing a page from my notes, but I have some of the pertinent information here. If I recall, the person's title was assistant director and senior preservationist. Um. . .let's see. . .oh, here we go. Bachelor's in history from Vanderbilt; master's and PhD from Robertson, and all in six years." Carroll's secretary stepped into the room. "Julie, I'm missing the page on—"

The middle-aged woman handed him a sheet of paper. "I saw it sitting on my desk just as you called for me. Sorry about that."

"Not a problem. Thank you." The secretary left, and Carroll looked down at the page. He frowned. "Looks like there's a typo on this. I'll get her to fix it before she makes you a copy of the file. Okay. Says here the assistant director and senior preservationist is named Dr. Sarah Mitchell."

Bobby's heart dropped into his stomach. That was why the name of the agency seemed familiar. "Sir, is the first name spelled with a *Z*?"

Carroll looked down at the page then up that Bobby in astonishment. "How did you know?"

Bobby thought he might be sick. "It's not a typo, sir. Her name *is* Zarah."

Carroll rocked back in his chair. "Do you know her? Should I assign this case to someone else?"

With every fiber of his being, Bobby believed in Zarah's innocence. But he had seen far too many assistant directors and vice presidents thrown under the bus and convicted of crimes perpetrated by their superiors to let someone else handle this case. "No, sir. I want this case."

Chapter 7

$\mathcal{A}$nd that's why we live in Nash*ville* and not Nash*borough*. Because during the lead-up to the Revolutionary War, we didn't like the British, but we did like the French. So they changed the settlement's name to the French *ville* rather than the British *borough*."

Zarah looked over the group of homeschooled children. Ranging in age from four to late teens, it was hard to gear her regular talk on Nashville's history toward one end of the spectrum without either totally confusing or totally boring the other. However, she was starting to lose all of them.

"Who here has ever heard of David Crockett?"

Eyes lit up, hands flew into the air. She could always reel them back in with Davy Crockett—though they weren't necessarily always thrilled to learn that the "King of the Wild Frontier" wasn't nearly as glamorous as the TV shows and movies made him out to be.

Zarah continued the educational tour of the small museum that took up the entire first floor of the Middle Tennessee Historic Preservation Commission's building. Now that everybody was back in school, she would have one of these field-trip groups to entertain and try to teach something at least once a week until Thanksgiving. She had learned over the years to structure these types of instructional lessons much differently than how she taught the students in her adjunct Tennessee History class at the community college, which was also different than the Middle Tennessee History Seminar she taught at James Robertson University. The good thing about the pre-college school group tours of the museum was that she had no homework to grade afterward.

Dennis hadn't been extremely happy to see her this morning. But as long as she remembered to not take deep breaths—which cut down considerably the number of coughing spells she had—everyone seemed to believe her when she told them she was feeling better. And, after spending the day yesterday with Caylor and Flannery sunning herself beside the pool at Caylor's grandmother's house, she really did feel better.

Besides, the last thing she needed was to spend any time alone; no sooner had she gotten home from spending time with the girls Sunday evening and yesterday, than thoughts of Bobby filled her mind. What was he doing back in Nashville? Why had he come to Acklen Ave. when he most likely knew she would be there? What did he want from her? And could Flannery really find some good-looking hunk of a man who would deign to be seen in public with Zarah just to make Bobby jealous?

She led the group over to the Civil War display and started talking about Tennessee's secession, the Army of Tennessee, General John Bell Hood, and the Federal occupation of Nashville for most of the war. After the thirty seconds it took the students to look at the displays of uniforms, battle flags, ordinance, and weaponry, their attention waned. Time to pull out the big gun.

"How many of you have ancestors who fought in the Civil War?" Zarah smiled and glanced around at the students. The three mothers with them looked at each other questioningly, then encouraged the children to raise their hands. Zarah doubted whether they actually knew or just assumed—but such an assumption for a family whose roots went back more than 150 years in this country was a safe assumption to make.

"Three major battles took place right here in Middle Tennessee. Does anyone know what those battles are called?"

One of the smaller children's hands went up.

Zarah inclined her head toward him and motioned at him with an open hand. "What's your name?"

"Benjamin."

"Hi, Benjamin. What's the name of a Civil War battle that happened in Middle Tennessee?"

Benjamin tapped his small forefinger against his pursed lips as if pondering the question. Then his eyes lit up and his face brightened into an *aha* expression. "The battle of Murfreesboro!"

One of the older boys, obviously Benjamin's older brother, guffawed. "You're such a dufus. There is no such thing."

Even as the older boy's mother grabbed him by the shoulder to silence him, Zarah smiled at the crestfallen Benjamin. "Actually, Benjamin is correct; there was a battle of Murfreesboro, only that isn't the name it's commonly called anymore." She studied the young boy's face, and he seemed to be following along with where she was going. "Do you know the other name of the battle, Benjamin?"

Benjamin nodded his crew-cut little head. "The battle of Stones River."

In this little boy, Zarah could see herself at the same age. "Do you know why it has two different names?"

"Because the Southerners named battles after cities, and the Yankees named them after nearby rivers or creeks." Little Benjamin flashed a conspiratorial grin at Zarah.

"That's right, Benjamin." She looked around the group. "Even to this day, some of the most famous battlefields are known by one name given to them by the North and another name given to them by the South. For example, the Battle of Bull Run is still called the Battle of Manassas by many Southerners. Now, who can name the other two Middle Tennessee battles?"

She finally managed to coach the kids into coming up with the battles of Nashville and Franklin. From the multiple eye rolls she received when she started talking about some of the dates of each of the battles and their importance in the outcome of the war, she suspected they had already been on field trips to the Stones River battlefield and some of the historic sites around Franklin where they did more in-depth lessons about the battles. But now, the big gun was primed and she was ready to take aim.

Zarah moved over to the enlarged copy of a sepia photo of a handsome young man in a Confederate uniform standing beside an equally beautiful, seated young woman in a hoop-skirted gown, her thick, fair braids arranged in a very Germanic coronet atop her head.

She always felt like Vanna White whenever she used her open hand to draw people's attention to the photo. "This is Zander and Madeleine Breitinger, my ancestors. As with many people from that era, they were not born in this country but had been brought here by their families when they were very young. Zander's family, the Breitingers, and Madeleine's aunt and uncle, who took her in when she was orphaned as a baby, all settled just north of Nashville—in what is now known as Germantown. Back then, it was mostly still farmland. When Zander was a young teenager, both of his parents died of typhoid, and Madeleine's aunt and uncle took him in.

"This is Zander and Madeleine's wedding photo, taken in May 1861—three days before Zander left for the war. From 1861 through early 1864, Madeleine received somewhat regular correspondence from her husband. She, in turn, was able to get most of her weekly letters through to him, including the letter informing him of the birth of their son, Karl Alexander, in the spring of 1862.

"In mid-1864, the frequency of Zander's letters slowed until they finally stopped coming. Madeleine was convinced her young husband was still alive, though her family and friends tried to get her to accept that he was most likely dead. Every morning found her down at the telegraph office waiting for that day's casualty reports to be posted. Every day, she returned home without the satisfaction of a letter from her husband or the confirmation of her worst fear."

Zarah paused a moment, partially for effect and partially to gauge her audience's interest in the story. From the expressions on every face, all of them were eager for her to continue.

"In that cold, rainy late-November of 1864, the war came almost to Madeleine's doorstep. When Madeleine heard of the fighting in Franklin, she left two-year-old Karl with her aunt, packed all the medical supplies she could find into her saddlebags, and rode south toward Franklin to try to find Zander. But when her uncle figured out what she had done, he went after her, finding her just before she stumbled upon one of the fiercest pockets of fighting of the battle. Their route home had been cut off, so her uncle took her to a nearby farm where they rode out the Battle of Franklin in the root cellar, listening as bullets and cannonballs from both sides peppered and pounded the house above them."

After so many years of telling this story, Zarah should have been able to do it without any emotion; but her throat tightened, and her eyes started stinging. She swallowed and was about to take a deep breath when she remembered it would make her cough. Instead, she pressed her short nails into the palms of her hands and continued.

"When the fighting stopped, Madeleine was frantic to get out to the battlefield and try to find Zander, but her uncle would not let her leave the house until he knew it was safe. The few paltry medical supplies she had brought with her were needed in the Confederate field hospital, as were her nursing skills. What she saw in that field hospital in the aftermath of the Battle of Franklin made her believe for the first time that Zander was most likely dead."

An audible sniffle came from near the back of the group where three young teenage girls stood huddled together.

"Madeleine, her uncle, and the friends they had taken shelter with worked nonstop, through the night and the next day, tending the wounded and comforting the dying soldiers from both sides. Before then, Madeleine's prayer had been that she would find her husband alive. After that experience, she prayed only that his death had been swift and painless and that he had not suffered the way these men were suffering. Having worked more than a full day with no rest and little food, Madeleine collapsed from exhaustion and grief. Ensuring their way home was clear, Madeleine's uncle brought her back to Nashville, where two weeks later they once again found themselves in the heart of the fighting. Madeleine, her aunt and uncle, and baby Karl sought refuge in the underground icehouse and watched as their home burned to the ground. The fighting had been so intense all day that they never knew which side had torched the house.

"With nothing left and no hope that Zander would ever return, Madeleine agreed to travel back to Germany with her aunt and uncle."

"But what about Zander?" burst out one of the teenage girls. "Why didn't she wait for Zander to come home?"

"He better not be dead!" piped up Benjamin's older brother.

"He's going to go find her, right?" Little Benjamin looked quite concerned over the fate of people who died long ago.

"Shush," one of the mothers said sharply. "Let her finish the story."

Zarah tried to keep from smiling too much at the reaction she always got at this point in the story. "Madeleine returned with her family to Bavaria, but she left her heart behind in Tennessee. After the war, she no longer laughed, and she no longer danced. She barely spoke at all. She would, however, spend hours writing in her journal—writing long, grieving love letters to her dead husband. After several years, when she seemed over the worst of her grief, her family encouraged her to remarry—if not for her sake then for the sake of her child, now eight years old. Though she agreed to let men court her, not one suitor could make her forget her love for Zander."

Zarah reached under the display stand she stood beside and pulled out another reproduction of a sepia photo, this one of a young man by himself in a fine suit with a thick shock of blond hair like his parents'.

"This is Karl Alexander Breitinger at eighteen. It was time for him to attend university, and he decided he wanted to return to the land of his birth, America. Madeleine, who had never forgotten her adopted homeland, sent him off with her blessing and with the original of this photograph"—she motioned to the portrait of Zander and Madeleine behind her—"in his pocket."

She returned the picture of Karl to its shelf. "Having heard the stories of his family's life in Nashville, Karl made his way to Middle Tennessee to find out if anything remained of the farm they'd left behind. With a map drawn by his great-uncle, Karl made his way to where the farm had been. Expecting to find a pile of burned-out rubble obscured by more than fifteen years of overgrowth, he was shocked to find a large white farmhouse looking exactly the way his mother and great-uncle and aunt had always described their home. Because his great-uncle still owned the property, Karl felt no hesitation in knocking on the front door to find out who had built this house and was living on the land he would one day inherit."

Throughout the group, reaction was mixed. A few faces—including those of two mothers and young Benjamin—wore knowing grins. Others wore looks of concerned consternation, feeling something of what Karl Breitinger must have felt upon seeing the house.

Zarah relaxed her expression into neutral, so not to give away the ending, and continued. "Karl knocked on the door and waited to see who would answer. He was about to knock again when the door opened to reveal a young woman. Karl introduced himself as the owner of the land and asked to speak with the master of the house. The young woman invited him in. As soon as he entered, the strange feeling that had started upon seeing the house from the outside grew as he realized the interior was just as his mother had described it. The young woman took him into the study in the back of the house, where an older man in a wheelchair sat at the desk. As soon as the man looked up, Karl knew who he was. After eighteen years, he finally stood face-to-face with his very own father."

Zarah cleared her throat of the emotion that tried to work its way up out of her chest. The story of a son's reunion with his father always reminded Zarah of her own broken relationship with her father.

"With the wedding portrait to prove Karl's identity, the reunion between father and son was joyous. Karl learned his father had been captured by the Northern army at Chickamauga and sent to the Rock Island military prison in Illinois for the remainder of the war. By the time he was released and managed to make his way back to Tennessee, Madeleine had already been back in Germany for several months. However, none of their neighbors knew what had become of them; so when Zander returned, he was misinformed that Madeleine, Karl, and the aunt and uncle had died in the fire. Even though he lost his leg in the war, as a memorial to his beloved wife and the baby son he'd never met, Zander rebuilt the house just the way he remembered it.

"Using some of the money his great-uncle had given him for school tuition, Karl booked passage for himself and his father across the Atlantic to reunite his parents. When they arrived in Bavaria, it was to discover Madeleine bedridden, so ill she couldn't speak. Her uncle informed them that as soon as Karl left for America, Madeleine had stopped eating and seemed to lose the will to live. All that long night, Zander sat by her side holding her hand and talking to her almost without pause. Just before dawn, Madeleine stirred, opened her eyes, and spoke Zander's name.

"Seeing her beloved, the one she had pined for, Madeleine rallied. Though she never returned to full health, with Zander always at her side, the last five years of Madeleine's life were the happiest she'd ever known."

Most of the females in the group sniffled audibly, which Zarah always took as a sign she'd done her job well. The story did not really teach children anything specific and about the battles of Franklin and Nashville; but she'd received so many letters and e-mails from visitors, telling her how much they had enjoyed the story of Zander and Madeleine, and how they'd chosen to research their ancestors' involvement in the Civil War to see if they could have a story like that to tell. It was usually the only thing out of the hour-long tour that most of them remembered.

After passing around the box of tissues she kept hidden on the shelf beside Karl's picture for this very moment, she continued the tour—though many pairs of eyes continued to drift back to the portrait of Zander and Madeleine Breitinger.

Throughout the rest of the tour and as she bade farewell to the students who now looked upon her fondly rather than with skeptical trepidation, a strange sense of disquietude shrouded her like an icy blanket. Always before when she'd related the story of Zander and Madeleine, she'd walked away with a sense of melancholy over the happy reunion of Zander and Karl, putting the rift between her and her father into Technicolor relief. Today, however, though she still felt a touch of sadness at her broken relationship with her father, it was the reunion between Zander and Madeleine that struck her the hardest. Her great-great-great-grandfather and grandmother had been exactly the same ages when they married as she and Bobby had been when their relationship had gone up in flames.

The difference was that Zander had actually loved Madeleine and married her, not walked off and left her on her own to face a father who'd always hated her and the consequence of his discovering their secret relationship: being kicked out of the house to face making her own way in the world with no parental support.

She thanked God every day for her mother's parents.

Returning to the Civil War display, she stood under the portrait of Zander and Madeleine. Their love for each other had remained true through eighteen years' separation. Zarah prayed she might one day find a love like that, too.

Chapter 8

$\mathcal{A}$fter spending Tuesday morning getting all his appropriate documentation, identification, and computer passwords—as well as meeting seemingly everybody in the large office building—and after a rather long lunch with the five other special agents in charge in the Middle Tennessee division, Bobby finally found himself alone in his small, plain, but very private office.

He turned on the computer and logged in to make sure his passwords all worked. He looked at all the icons on the desktop and moved his mouse to hover over one. He might as well start working while he had a few minutes to himself. He double clicked the icon and typed in another password to get into the unit's proprietary search engine. For all that it had been supposedly written for the TCIU, the look and layout of the interface was almost identical to the CBI's program.

Hopefully it would give him better information than what he'd been able to find available publicly on the Internet yesterday. He moved his hands to the keyboard as soon as the search box came up, but then he hesitated. In the six years he'd worked as an investigator, he had never before experienced the feeling of guilt over looking into a person-of-interest's background. His left pinkie finger touched the

Z key, but he didn't press it.

Yesterday he'd spent several hours online searching for information on Dennis Forrester. He'd garnered enough details to put together a pretty impressive résumé for Forrester, as well as a schedule of speaking engagements from the past two years. Forrester was something of a philanthropist, his name popping up in news articles and blog posts lauding him for his donations of money and time to certain charitable organizations around Nashville—everything from the rescue mission and food bank downtown, at which he volunteered regularly, to his "generous" donations to literacy organizations and Humanities Tennessee in support of reading programs and book festivals. The more Bobby read about Forrester's philanthropy, the more questions arose in the back of his mind. Where was all this money coming from?

What he found online about the Historic Preservation Commission had not brought him at all closer to forming any conclusions or generalizations about the agency and how it was run. They held an annual black-tie fund-raiser—he had done his best to ignore the photos of Zarah in a floor-length burgundy gown that, though covering her almost completely from neck to toe, did nothing to hide her curves—and tried to concentrate only on what he could gather from the text of the articles and blogs covering last year's event.

In addition to ignoring the few photographs someone had managed to surreptitiously take of Zarah—he would never forget how much she hated having her picture taken, even *back then*—he also ignored the search results that linked to several editorials that had appeared in the local newspaper over the past few months disparaging Zarah over the land injunctions in question.

If he couldn't bring himself to investigate Zarah, he needed to tell Captain Carroll and let somebody else get moving on this case. But it nauseated him to think of anybody else digging into her life and background in the detail they would need. Even though he still resented her and what she had done to him, he could not let her be exposed like that to a total stranger.

Chickening out, he typed Dennis Forrester's name into the search box and set the computer to work finding information on Zarah's boss.

He looked up at a knock on the open office door. Captain Carroll stepped into the small room. "Am I interrupting?"

Bobby stood behind his desk. "No, sir."

"Good. The director stopped by unexpectedly, and I'd like you to meet him." He motioned for Bobby to follow him.

Either the captain's presence on this floor was an unusual sight, or everyone had decided to take this opportunity to check Bobby out. He could feel the gazes following them as they walked down the aisle between the cubicles at which the administrative and lower-level investigative staff sat. Captain Carroll led him to an elevator Bobby had not seen before, which took them up one floor and opened across the hall from a nondescript door. Swiping his key card through the reader, Captain Carroll opened the door and ushered Bobby in to what turned out to be the captain's office.

A well-dressed, African American man—mid-fifties, right at six feet tall, between 170 and 180 pounds, and wearing what looked like a class ring from one of the service academies—stood and approached Bobby from the small table in the corner of the room, right hand extended.

"Agent Patterson, welcome to the Nashville branch of the Tennessee Criminal Investigations Unit. I was just reading the recruitment report on you. Your background is impressive, and I know you're going to be a great asset to the TCIU."

Captain Carroll joined them and made a formal introduction, and Bobby sat down at the table with them. He wondered if every new agent got to meet the unit's director on his first day on the job. He had a feeling this did not usually happen.

"I understand Carroll has given you the Preservation Commission case."

He hadn't realized he needed to bring the case file with him. "Yes, sir. It seems very much like several cases I handled in California."

The director nodded. "Yes, I saw that in your file. By way of full disclosure, there is something you need to know about this case. I do not expect it to influence in any way how you choose to handle the case. But you should know this information up front." The director bent down and pulled a file out of his briefcase. He opened it and took out a photo and a piece of paper and put them on the table in front of Bobby.

Bobby's breath caught in his throat when he looked down at the picture. Unlike the couple photos he'd seen online yesterday, this one showed Zarah in a royal blue dress that not only showed her figure to perfection but her arms and legs as well because it was sleeveless and knee-length. She stood in the middle with Dennis Forrester to her left—Zarah stood several inches taller than Forrester—and the director to her right. She gazed directly at the camera, smiling that shy, innocent smile that had drawn him in when she was a young woman.

Who was he kidding? It would still work if he let it.

Wait. This was a picture of Zarah and Dennis Forrester with the unit's director, who had his arm chummily around Zarah's shoulders. He finally slid his eyes over to the second item that the director had put in front of him: a tax receipt for a five-figure donation to the Middle Tennessee Historic Preservation Commission. A tax receipt with the director's name on it. Bobby's diaphragm twisted into a knot. This was not good.

"As you can see," the director said, "it could be construed that I have a conflict of interest in this case. I bring this to you at the onset of the investigation so that everything is out in the open and aboveboard, and so we're clear that I will not interfere in any way with your investigation of the commission. If you deem it necessary to interview me, I swear to be cooperative and forthcoming."

"Thank you, sir. I appreciate your honesty, and I will try to not involve you in the investigation unless absolutely necessary."

A few moments later, Bobby found himself on the other side of that nondescript door, breathing deeply to try to ease the tension in his shoulders and back. He wished this facility had a fitness room. He'd give just about anything for a go at a punching bag right now. What had looked like a plum assignment at the perfect job was turning into what could possibly be the worst case of his life.

Zarah kicked her shoes off as soon as she walked in the door. The flats had a cushioned sole and had always been among her favorite shoes, but for some reason today they decided to start rubbing her little toes. The sandwich and cup of yogurt she ate before leaving work to teach at the community college had not stuck with her very long. If she wasn't saving up to buy a new dishwasher, she would have stopped somewhere for carryout on her way home, since she let class out half an hour early. But she couldn't justify the ten or fifteen dollars to buy food cooked by someone else when she had plenty at home.

Rather than create an abundance of dishes to wash by hand, she filled the teakettle with water, put it on the stove, and went to the pantry to pick out a pack of oatmeal from one of the boxes on the top shelf. She was still trying to choose between apples-and-cinnamon and raisin-date-walnut when the kettle whistled. She grabbed the packet of maple-and-brown-sugar-flavored oatmeal and shoved the pantry door closed, thinking again about how she needed to take Pops up on his offer to come rehang the door so it would close properly. As Kiki— who had encouraged Zarah to buy one of the brand-new townhouses down the street—said, she got what she paid for. The 1911 brick cottage had cost her half what one of the duplex units would cost, and she loved the original character and the privacy afforded by not sharing walls with anyone. But it brought with it all the problems inherent in buying an old house, even one that had been as extensively renovated as this one had: doors sagged and swelled, the original hard-pine floors creaked, the water pressure wasn't great, and a few of the windows were slightly drafty.

But it was hers—her very own, in her name—and no one else's. She had done that. She had purchased a house all by herself. She had refused her grandparents' offer to give her extra money for her down payment so she could afford something more expensive; but even though they had initially been hurt by her refusal, she finally led them to understand that she needed to do this on her own to prove to herself that she was a grown-up, that she could take care of herself, that she was finally independent—and deep down, that she could try to prove to her father she had made something of herself, even without his support.

She poured the boiling water into the instant oatmeal and looked around her kitchen and breakfast room. Small but well appointed, with granite countertops and brand-new black appliances—well, the refrigerator, stove top, and wall-mounted double ovens had been brand-new when she'd bought the house five years ago, but the previous owners had been forced to sell before they could afford to replace the dishwasher, too.

She filled a glass with water from the refrigerator door and carried it and the green stoneware bowl of oatmeal to the table. Using a dish towel for a napkin, she ate with her right hand and flipped open her laptop with her left to check e-mail and read her favorite online newspapers.

She almost choked on a wad of the hot, gooey cereal when she clicked the arrow to go up to the next e-mail and the computer opened a message that contained an automated request from Bobby Patterson to join the singles' group's e-mail list. She and Patrick were co-moderators of the automated mailing list manager, but Patrick only checked his personal e-mail account once a week—on Saturdays. She had three choices: She could leave this for Patrick to deal with on Saturday—but he usually ignored these requests because she always took care of them when they came in; she could delete it and pretend she'd never seen it; or she could be the forgiving Christian she claimed to be and approve his request.

She grumbled under her breath. Why was she the one who always got stuck having to do the good, right thing? She knew everybody at church called her a Goody Two-shoes and considered her a prude. She'd lived with that all her life. It was just the way she was built, she supposed. Even in college when she decided to try to break out of her good-girl shell, she had not been able to walk through the door of the nightclub. Everything her father had ever said to her or about her, every rule he had ever imposed came flooding in as she had stood there listening to the thumping of music and smelling the foul odor that she later discovered was a mixture of alcohol and cigarette smoke.

Flannery and Caylor had helped her break out of her shell a little at a time, taking her to places like the Bluebird Café, Douglas Corner Café, and Fido—restaurants and coffeehouses to hear some great local bands and expose Zarah to what it really meant to live in Nashville, Tennessee. But there were still some lines Zarah refused to cross. And ignoring someone's request to join the singles e-mail list was one of those lines.

She moved the mouse to hover over the correct link, closed her eyes, and clicked APPROVE.

"Lord, that better have earned me a jewel in my crown." Her appetite now ruined, Zarah dumped the half-full bowl of oatmeal in the garbage disposal and washed the bowl and set it on the drainboard.

Rather than return to the computer to risk seeing any more e-mails that might make her want to take permanently to her bed, Zarah went into her office, pulled the stack of quizzes from tonight's class out of her bag, and sat down to grade them.

At nine o'clock on the nose, the time she usually left class, she turned her cell phone on. It immediately started chirping, announcing a backlog of text messages. Students asking questions about the assignment she'd given (she texted back, clarifying that their papers must be at least ten pages long and the works cited had to include at least five sources not found online). Patrick wanting to know if she would be okay with leading one of the small-group breakout discussions during Bible study tomorrow night (she was always happy to help in whatever way she could).

Kiki called to check up on her. Zarah spent fifteen minutes assuring her grandmother she was fine; yes, she ate supper; yes, she would get plenty of sleep; no, she didn't need Kiki to bring her a pot of soup. As soon as she hung up with Kiki, one of the young women from the singles' group called to cry over her breakup with a guy she shouldn't have been dating in the first place.

During that phone call, Zarah got the majority of the quizzes graded, as the frequently heartbroken young woman did not need much more than *hmm*s and *oh really*s from Zarah. After the girl spilled everything, she thanked Zarah for helping her feel better and ended the call. Zarah shook her head and set the cell phone down, then rubbed her sore ear. She graded the last two quizzes, interrupted by only one text message—a mass text from Patrick reminding everyone what chapter of their book they were supposed to read for tomorrow.

Feeling it safe to leave the phone sitting on her desk for a moment, she returned to the kitchen to retrieve her laptop so she could record the grades online. If she didn't post them tonight, she'd be getting texts all day at work tomorrow from students wanting to know why they weren't showing up yet.

The phone, with the ringer turned to the lowest volume setting, nearly vibrated itself off the desk before Zarah realized it was ringing once again. She caught it before it tipped off the edge of the desk. Caylor's name and number scrawled across the touch screen.

"Hey, girl." Zarah slid the phone open, exposing the keyboard and turning on the speaker-phone feature. She set the device beside the laptop and pulled up the appropriate Web site and logged in.

"Hey, yourself. Hope it's not too late."

Zarah checked the clock in the bottom right corner of her computer screen. Eleven fifteen. "It's before midnight, isn't it?"

"That's what I figured. I'm grading my sophomore American Lit class's first test. It's going to be a tough semester."

"Same here—with the Tennessee History class at the community college. Haven't given the first quiz at Robertson yet." She created a new line item in her online grade book and started entering the rather depressing quiz scores. "What's up?"

"I'm just calling to see if you're really okay."

"I haven't had a single coughing spell all day."

"That's not what I mean. I was thinking about our conversation Sunday afternoon. I know that this whole Bobby thing has to be harder on you than you're letting on. Even though you tried not to show it when we first met way back when, he broke your heart, and I know you secretly hoped he'd come back for you someday."

Zarah pulled her fingers off the keyboard and pressed them to her closed eyes. Caylor had the bad habit of seeing much more than she should. As not just a professor of literature but also a multi-published author, Caylor constantly studied the people around her.

"Zarah?"

"I'm still here. And yes, when I was still young and naive and hadn't cottoned on to what he'd really done to me, I did hold on to a false hope that he would come to his senses and 'rescue' me—that he would prove that everything my father told me about him was wrong. But he didn't. He never truly cared enough about me to find out where I ended up or try to get in touch with me."

"But he's here now. Maybe. . ." Caylor's voice, soft to begin with, drifted off.

"Maybe what? Maybe he's changed his mind after all this time? Or maybe he's found something else he thinks he can gain by trying to seduce me again?"

"Sed—what?"

Zarah had to laugh at the shock in Caylor's voice—Caylor, of all people, to be shocked by the word *seduce*. "Okay, maybe that doesn't have the right connotation. But he dated me in order to. . ." What had he gained by dating her? Her father's rules for dating couldn't have been clearer: Zarah and her sister were forbidden to date enlisted men. "You know, I don't even know why he dated me—except maybe he thought dating the general's daughter might get him some kind of special attention or favors."

"You think he dated you to get in good with your father—for what? Promotion? Transfer? But you said you told him pretty soon after you started dating how your father treated you. Why do you think Bobby continued dating you for so long after that?"

"I have no idea. I mean, why did he end the relationship by telling my father about us, instead of just dumping me when he found out my father didn't like me and didn't want me dating an enlisted man?" Zarah tapped her thumbnail against her front teeth. "Why wait until right before he knew I'd be moving away for college anyway?"

"Bobby knew you'd be leaving?"

"He knew I was planning to leave for college after I graduated. I had already been accepted to summer school at Vanderbilt. Of course, I was depending on my father to pay for my travel and housing, as he'd said he would do. Instead, I got a few hours to pack up what I could carry and two hundred dollars for a bus ticket anywhere but there."

"Thank goodness you had your mother's address book—and that your grandparents still lived in the same house. I hate to think what might have happened to you if you'd gotten here and hadn't been able to contact them."

Zarah shuddered. "I know. Me, too."

Caylor was silent for a long moment. "So, back to my original question. Are you okay?"

"I—" No. She could lie to herself, but she couldn't lie to one of her best friends. "I don't know. I thought I'd forgiven him a long time ago, but seeing him again dredged up a lot of pain and anger I thought I was finished with. I just wish he would leave me alone."

"What is the worst that could happen with him here now?"

"The worst?" Pain tore at Zarah's throat. "The worst thing that could happen would be for him to fall in love with someone else, and I would have to watch it."

"So Flannery's right. We're going to have to find your Mr. Right first. Then it won't matter what Bobby Patterson does."

Chapter 9

Bobby hadn't attended Wednesday night church since he graduated from high school—and he'd only gone before then because his parents had made him go whenever he didn't have football practice, trying to keep him on the straight and narrow. So when Patrick told him about the Bible study he led after the church's Wednesday night supper each week, Bobby wasn't certain he would attend.

So what was he doing here now?

"Bobby, hey!"

He was pretty sure the blond in the business suit had been at both the cookout last Friday and lunch Sunday, but for the life of him, Bobby couldn't remember her name. She looked too much like several other women who'd also been there. He inclined his head toward her.

"Hello." He shifted his Bible into his left hand and shook hers.

"Lyssa Thompson." She flashed him a toothy grin. "If you're anything like me, it'll be awhile before you can remember everyone's names."

He was pretty sure he wasn't anything like her, but he didn't bother to mention that fact out loud. Extracting his hand from hers, he glanced around the room for Patrick. . .who happened to be in deep conversation with Zarah and a couple other people.

Of course Zarah would choose exactly that moment to glance around the room, too. Her face froze as soon as her gaze locked with his, and then her smile faded when she glanced to his right and saw Lyssa Thompson standing slightly too close to him. Zarah turned her attention back to Patrick, but Bobby couldn't help but be affected by the all-too-brief encounter.

She was jealous. His ego and pride flared up. Yep. She was jealous and hurt that it appeared he was *with* Lyssa Thompson, not trying to figure out a way to extricate himself from her.

Good. She deserved to be hurt—just like she'd hurt him.

Guilt punctured his pride. It didn't matter what she'd done to him; he shouldn't revel in anyone's being injured—emotionally or physically—by anything he did or appeared to do. Though he wasn't certain why he felt God was calling him to join this church, to be part of this singles' group when Zarah was here reminding him of his past, he knew beyond a shadow of a doubt that both he and Zarah needed to move on, needed to forget whatever had happened between them way back when and focus on building futures—separate futures—without the bitterness they both obviously held for each other.

He allowed Lyssa to reintroduce him to some of the folks he'd met before as well as to several people who'd been out of town for the holiday weekend. He made a point, though, when Patrick called the room to order, of sitting with some of the guys instead of beside Lyssa. He didn't want *anyone* getting the wrong impression.

Patrick opened with prayer then invited everyone to open their books to chapter four. Bobby glanced around. Everyone in the room had a copy of the same book—everyone but him. Why hadn't Patrick forewarned him? He had a copy of it at home—he'd studied it on his own during an especially isolating case in which he hadn't been able to attend church lest he risk blowing his cover.

Someone tapped his shoulder and handed him a book from behind. He glanced around to thank the mystery benefactor—but

Zarah turned and walked away as soon as he took the book from her grasp.

After giving an overview of the themes and spiritual issues raised in the chapter, Patrick used an old sports technique and had everyone number off from one to six to determine which small group they'd go into for the discussion part of the lesson.

Bobby carried a couple of chairs over to where group four was told to assemble. He sat and looked across the circle—and Flannery McNeill glared back at him.

He tried to keep his expression neutral. If Flannery wanted to have a go at him, she wouldn't get any help from him.

After a quick whispered exchange with Zarah, Patrick joined them. "If y'all will turn to the discussion questions at the end of the chapter, we'll get started."

It didn't take any coaxing to get the group talking about the theme of the chapter—developing confidence in one's identity as a Christian. Bobby was impressed. Patrick had this group well trained. Though a few of them started out answering the questions by flipping back through the chapter and reading passages they'd highlighted as the "correct" answers, they quickly diverged from the safe ground of what was printed in the book into expressing personal beliefs and opinions—without having to be prompted to do so.

Somehow, the discussion veered onto the subject of self-worth and self-esteem.

"If someone's really a Christian, a genuine, sold-out believer," Lyssa Thompson raised her voice to gain the small group's attention, "they wouldn't have low self-esteem or problems with self-worth. If they're really a Christian, they will have all the self-confidence they need. After all, that's what the Bible says—that our confidence is found in Jesus."

Flannery glared at Lyssa. While Bobby didn't agree with the Barbie Doll look-alike, he didn't think her statement glare-worthy.

"Yeah," Patrick drawled, looking somewhat consternated. "The

Bible says we can be confident in our salvation in Jesus and because of what He did for us. But it doesn't say that becoming saved means we'll suddenly be confident in everything we do."

"No, that's not what I said. We'll still have questions when we face decisions, like job changes and other life-changing events. But if someone's saved, they won't have such low self-esteem that they're afraid to participate in things like witnessing or evangelism or outreach."

Flannery slammed her book closed. "The Bible says we all have different gifts and talents. Some people have the gifts of"—Flannery looked like she was censoring words to find something appropriate for this venue—"gifts that require. . .boldness and brashness and the ability to talk to just anyone. But not everyone is called to do that. It's just like Paul wrote: The whole body can't be just a mouth. Some people are gifted differently—to be quiet and work in the background and do all of the piddly little things no one else wants to do so that someone who's called to *outreach* or *evangelism*"—Flannery's somewhat snarky tone of voice put invisible quotation marks around the two terms—"doesn't have to deal with all of the details." Her hazel eyes shot flames at Lyssa.

Patrick cleared his throat, but Flannery wasn't finished.

"And you also have to look at what someone has been through in her. . .or his life. For example, someone who's been emotionally abused is going to be affected by that for her—or his—whole life, no matter how strong of a Christian they are. If they were told often enough they would never be good enough, would never succeed at anything, it's something they may never get over." Flannery's gaze shifted briefly toward Bobby—and the effect was just like the time he'd fallen through the ice and into the pond behind his great-uncle's home in northern Minnesota. . .in January.

Did Flannery think he'd said those kinds of things to Zarah? After all, that was obviously to whom she was referring. What kinds of stories—lies—had Zarah told about him?

Patrick took advantage of Flannery's pause to regain control of the discussion. "Yes, abusive relationships are quite damaging, and the affects linger. And Flannery is correct: We are all gifted differently and have different personalities. It isn't for us to judge someone else's calling or their relationship with God. Now, the next question. . ."

Everyone in the group appeared relieved at Patrick's change in subject and jumped all over each other to answer the next question.

Whether or not Flannery believed he had emotionally abused Zarah, something wasn't quite right in this group. While everyone seemed to rely on Zarah, to depend on her for things to run smoothly, it seemed very few people had any respect or feelings of true friendship for her. Her constant self-deprecation probably didn't help. Just as Patrick had trained them to actively participate through his leadership style, Zarah had trained them to think as little of her as she thought of herself.

Flannery might think Bobby responsible, but he'd seen and heard the way General Mitchell treated his younger daughter. He'd heard him call her a "fat cow" and "useless for pretty much anything." He'd done his best during the six months they dated to try to offset the horrible things the general said to her—and had apparently been saying to her all her life. That was why Bobby couldn't understand how Zarah could have chosen her father over him.

Could Dennis Forrester have seen her weakness and figured out how to exploit it for his own gain?

Bobby clenched his back teeth together. He couldn't go undercover. But he had access to Zarah—in addition to a past with her—that provided the perfect opportunity to try to find out what was really going on.

He was going to have to make her fall for him again—or at least become friendly toward him—without getting hurt by her a second time.

"Don't forget, if you're planning to go see *The Music Man* at JRU two weeks from Friday, get your money to Zarah tonight." Patrick's voice boomed over the din of voices and shrieks of chairs being shoved across the tile floor.

Zarah, on her way toward the door and escape—from Bobby, from Lyssa Thompson, from everyone—stopped and took a deep breath.

In college, Flannery and Caylor had started teasing Zarah for having a third ear—one that could hear every single conversation going on around her while still allowing her to concentrate on the conversation she was in. Sometimes it was a blessing. Other times, like tonight, it was a curse; she'd heard only too clearly that Lyssa had started in again on her diatribe against anyone—Zarah especially—who wasn't as extroverted as she thought he or she should be. And of course Flannery had taken the bait. At least this time, Flannery hadn't called Zarah by name when trying to defend her.

Three people wrote Zarah checks for their tickets to the drama department's fall musical presentation at JRU. With Caylor playing the role of Mrs. Paroo, Flannery and Zarah had decided getting the biggest group possible to attend on opening night would be one of the best gifts they could give her. Zarah had requested a block of twenty-five tickets be set aside for them—and so far, she had sold vouchers for seventeen of them: thirteen adults and four children. She would be taking Kiki and Pops—along with Caylor's grandmother, Sassy—to the Saturday matinee performance the next day.

"Want to go grab something to eat?" Flannery hooked her arm through Zarah's when the last ticket buyer walked away.

Zarah lifted the antique pendant-watch that hung from the long chain around her neck.

"It's only eight thirty. I hoped we could chat. I have something I need to tell you." Flannery cocked her head. "I know there's no way you left work early enough to make it here for supper at five thirty. So, come on. Let's go eat."

Zarah heaved a dramatic sigh. "Oh, all right. But somewhere cheap."

"I know. You and your dishwasher. I wish you'd just take the money out of your savings account and go ahead and buy the stupid thing. But then, all I'd be hearing about would be replenishing your savings account. It's always something with you." Flannery pulled out her buzzing cell phone and started tapping the screen. "How about Fido?"

"Fine." Zarah knew better than to try to continue conversing with Flannery once the phone came out. Between calls, texts, and e-mails, the device kept her so tied to work that Zarah could only laugh when Flannery accused her of working too much. So she'd best not mention she had a ton of work to do tonight on the Metro Council and senate committee reports.

"I'll. . ." Flannery's pale brows knit, and her lips pursed. She looked up at Zarah. "I'll see you there in a few minutes. I have to go make a call." She started dialing and had the phone to her ear before she made it out the door.

Shaking her head, Zarah put the checks for tickets into her wallet and dropped it into her carryall. The leather bag had turned out to be one of the best hundred dollars she'd ever spent, even though she'd agonized over parting with the money three months ago when the messenger-style book bag she'd carried ever since college had finally disintegrated. Not only did the leather tote look more professional, but with its three compartments and myriad of smaller pockets, she was no longer frustrated by the lack of organization of all the stuff she had to carry around with her. And the new, smaller laptop Dennis had insisted on upgrading her to fit in it perfectly.

"Have room for one more?"

Hollow dread filled Zarah's chest—Bobby was inviting himself to supper with her and Flannery? She swallowed hard, then turned. Bobby stood a considerate few feet away, hands behind his back as if in an at-ease stance before a superior officer. She slapped a smile on. "One more?"

"At the musical."

"Oh, of course. Tickets are fifteen dollars." She crossed her arms— then realized the implication of the closed body language and dropped them to her sides.

"Cash okay?" Bobby pulled a sleek black wallet out of his back pocket and extracted a five and a ten.

"Yes. That's fine." She took the cash from him, careful not to touch it anywhere in the vicinity of his fingers to minimize the risk of touching him. What she thought would happen if they made incidental contact, she wasn't certain. She just didn't want to find out.

She pulled a ticket voucher out of her bag and handed it to him. "I'll be getting the actual tickets next Thursday night and will exchange one for the voucher later."

"Thanks." He tucked the slip of paper into his wallet and returned it to his pocket. Instead of walking away, though, he hesitated.

"Was there something else?" Zarah felt as uncomfortable as he looked. Good, he should be uncomfortable standing here in front of her, knowing what he had done to her.

"I just wanted to say. . .I think we may have gotten off on the wrong foot the other night. Since it looks like I'm going to be moving my membership back to this church, I don't want there to be any"— he scratched his cheek—"weirdness between us."

This time, she didn't care what it looked like or what message it sent when she crossed her arms. "Weirdness between us?" She pressed her lips together and frowned as if considering the statement. Nervousness over saying anything to him sped her heart, but growing anger quickened her tongue. "Now why would there be any weirdness between us? I can't imagine. Yes. We knew each other a long time ago, but that was a long time ago. Lots of things have changed since then. I don't know about you, but I've moved on from that and can't really see the benefit of allowing things said and done during childhood affect who I am now and whether or not I'm living a happy and productive life."

When had she become such a proficient liar? Moved on? Ha. Not hardly. But she kept her expression as neutral and friendly as she could make it.

"Oh. Okay. I just thought. . .well, it seemed like things were. . . rather uncomfortable between us the last couple of times, and I wanted to be sure everything was okay between us."

She smiled and shrugged. "Why wouldn't it be?" Running in quickly on the heels of the initial flash of anger she experienced, regret, sorrow, pain, and remorse grabbed her throat in a vise grip. She needed to get out of here before she showed him any signs she wasn't completely in control.

He mirrored her shrug. "As I said, I just wanted to make sure we were okay." He backed away a few steps. "I guess I'll see you Sunday, then."

"Guess so." She flung the straps of her carryall onto her shoulder and fled the classroom, not slowing down until she reached her car, parked in the lot across the street from the church in front of a vacant restaurant building. She blamed the tears leaking out the corners of her eyes on the wheezing and coughing the quick retreat had caused.

She had to pull herself together before she saw Flannery. For as much as the girl was one of her best friends, Zarah didn't trust Flannery to keep the peace with Bobby if she knew just how anguished Zarah continued to be at the very sight of the man.

He seemed taller now than he had been when she'd known him—and given that he'd turned twenty during the months they'd dated, that shouldn't be surprising. He'd measured in at six-foot-one back then, but he must be at least six-three by now. He hadn't lost his football player physique, either. And his brown hair was longer—by at least a quarter of an inch—than the army-standard buzz cut he'd sported then.

Was it possible for a man's jaw to get squarer over time? Then, it had imbued her with a sense of security in the strength he'd offered her. Now, it gave him an air of stubbornness and obstinacy.

She shook her head and started the car. If he wanted to whitewash the past and pretend nothing ever happened between them, she could play that game. There were plenty of other people in this large singles' group whom she didn't particularly care for, but with whom she made an effort to be polite and friendly. He could go right into that category.

Zarah didn't see Flannery inside Fido when she arrived, but hungry as she was, she went ahead and ordered rather than waiting. Flannery would have done the same thing. She'd just found a small table in the middle of the crowded coffee shop when Flannery came in, phone still to her ear.

Flannery acknowledged Zarah, then went to the counter and placed her order, not even bothering to remove the phone from her ear. She had perfected the art of doing everything one-handed, but only because she hated using the wireless earpiece that came with her phone—she didn't want people to think she was talking to herself, she'd said.

"Tell him a deadline is a deadline—and he's already six months past his. Remind him he signed a contract to write the book, and that we've already paid him a goodly amount of money for it—and as his agent, you know what that means. Listen, I'm going to have to talk to you about this tomorrow, after I have a chance to sit down with Jack and discuss options." She flashed Zarah a smile. "You, too. 'Bye."

Zarah made a show of looking at her pendant watch again. "Quarter of nine at night and still working? My goodness, Flan, can't you ever just leave your work at the office and not let it follow you everywhere you go?"

"Oh, whatever." Flannery laughed. "I only rag you about it because we're both the same way—we love what we do, and we do what we love. Eighteen or twenty hours a day, sometimes, but isn't it worth it in the long run? Besides, that agent is out on the West Coast; it's only a quarter of seven out there."

They chitchatted until they got their food. No point in having that interrupt a more important conversation.

"Have you thought any more about it?" Flannery asked.

"About what?"

"The haircut—the makeover."

Zarah rolled her eyes. "I've thought about it. But you know, no matter what you do to me on the outside, I'm still going to be the same person inside. I'll just be even more self-conscious about the way I look if everyone's making a fuss over me making changes to my appearance."

Flannery looked like she wanted to protest, but a few seconds later, she shrugged.

"So what did you want to tell me?" Zarah touched the spoonful of soup to her lip, then lowered it back to the bowl to let it cool a few more minutes.

"I wanted to tell you. . ." Flannery squinted and screwed up her face. "Wait, it'll come to me." She poured both ramekins of dressing on her salad. "Oh, yeah! I've found a few candidates to set you up with."

Anxiety did away with Zarah's appetite. "Really?"

"Don't sound so thrilled. I thought you were excited about this— about showing Bobby Patterson up." Flannery pulled out her phone, used her thumb to press a couple of icons on the large screen, then turned it toward Zarah. "This is Tom. He's one of my authors."

"Not the one whose agent you were just yelling at, I hope?" The black-and-white head-shot photo showed a thirtysomething man with curly hair, dark-framed glasses, and a pinkie ring on the hand fisted at his chin.

"Of course not. He has a mole on his chin, and he hates it—that's why he's covering it up in the picture. And he likes history—he's written a couple of historicals." Flannery turned the phone back around to face her. "They didn't sell very well, but still, he wrote them."

"And you. . .you talked to him about me? About going out with me?"

"No, not yet. I wanted to run my list by you before I approached any of them."

"Wait. . .what? You have a *list*? I thought this was just one or two guys for one or two dates." Her pulse throbbed loudly in her ears. As uncomfortable as first dates always were—especially blind dates—the idea of going out on more than just a couple horrified her.

"Zare—do you want to move forward or not?"

She took a long sip of her flavored water before answering. She did, didn't she? Steeling her nerve, she set the bottle down. "Yes. Bring on the list."

Chapter 10

"So, who has any progress to report?" Katrina Breitinger set her triple espresso latte down on the table and slid back into her chair. The regular Thursday morning coffee get-together was the perfect place to plot and plan.

"Progress?" Celeste Evans asked.

"Our pact, remember? To get at least one of each of our grandchildren married and giving us great-grandchildren before. . .a certain other person in the Keenagers group." Lindy Patterson leaned forward. "I can't say there's been much movement on my front—my grandson has only been back in town for a little more than a week. But he has decided he's going to rejoin Acklen Avenue Fellowship. He's already been to a couple of the singles' events."

Trina traced the edge of the cardboard sleeve around her cup with her thumb. Yes, Bobby Patterson had indeed been to the singles' events, much to Zarah's consternation and dismay. She'd at first thought that Bobby's coming back to Nashville now, just when she'd made the agreement with her friends to work at getting their grandchildren settled down, had been providential. She'd hoped God had brought him back so that he and Zarah could mend things between them.

With the way Zarah reacted to seeing him, it was obvious she still held strong feelings for him. Trina just wasn't certain if there was anything but bitterness and unforgiveness at the root of her granddaughter's emotions. "My granddaughter is going to be a hard nut to crack."

"Caylor is open to dating, but she doesn't get too many offers." Celeste's granddaughter lived with her.

"You should start working on her to get her to attend Acklen Avenue," Lindy suggested. "There are many fine young men in the singles' group."

With the way Lindy's blue eyes twinkled, Trina figured her friend thought of Bobby as a potential match for Celeste's granddaughter.

"She gave up so much of her independence when she moved in with me five years ago that it seems unfair to ask her to give up what little individuality she has—going to a different church— to come to Acklen Avenue with me, too."

"What about the young men at her church?" Helen asked.

Celeste shook her head. "It's too small. She says she prefers it that way, but it makes me wonder how she's ever going to meet a man. At least there are a few prospects at the college. Not that she'll admit to it. But I hear a few names mentioned from time to time. Between teaching and the committees she serves on and participating in the drama department's presentations, it seems like her whole life is wrapped up in that place."

"Zarah spends most of her time at work, too." Trina swirled the remaining liquid around in the bottom of the cup. "She loves it, but I worry about how much of her heart and soul she pours into that job—I don't want her to burn herself out and not have anything left to give when the right man comes along."

"All my grandson does is work," Maureen O'Connor chimed in. "I think the only reason he takes the time to go to church is because there are so many prominent people who attend Christ Church— important clients or business contacts."

"At least he still attends church," Helen commiserated. "My oldest grandson no longer goes—and last time he spoke to his parents, he told them he's involved with a woman considerably older than him. His parents suspect it's one of the other professors at the art college where he's an instructor—and this woman thinks religion is for the ignorant and uncultured. They're worried if the college's administration finds out that they're dating, he'll lose his job. But he wouldn't listen to them."

"It's hard," Trina joined in, "when a child strays—my heart still aches for my older daughter, as I'll never know if she returned to the faith she had as a child before she died. But we have to hold firm to God's promise that once someone is in His hand, He'll never let them go—no matter how far afield they stray."

The other women nodded.

"Speaking of far afield"—Lindy tried to inject smiles back into the somber group—"it's time we scheduled another family get-together. October is always a good time—the men can watch football, and it'll still be nice enough for all the ladies to sit outside and chat."

"We'll need a weekend when there's an away game for Vanderbilt," Helen said. "Gerald got season tickets this year."

"I'll send y'all an e-mail with possible dates, and we can figure out the weekend with the fewest conflicts for everyone in our families." Trina winked. "Or at least for a few key grandchildren."

Chapter 11

Let me guess—you were up all night working on this." Dennis Forrester looked up from the packet of paper in front of him on his desk.

Zarah stopped rubbing her neck. "No. . .not all night." Just until 4:45 this morning. Then she'd sent it to print and collapsed into the bed for an hour and a half.

"What time did you come in this morning?"

"Not until about seven thirty."

"Oh, you were late, then."

"Sarcasm doesn't become you, Dr. Forrester." She rolled her head from side to side. "Would you rather I just threw something together at the last minute and do an incomplete job?" She tried to put a teasing lilt into her voice, but she was just too tired to be successful. Besides, they had this conversation every quarter when she put in a little extra time to get the senate committee report written.

"In case I don't say it often enough, I do appreciate all the time and effort you put into your job. I receive more positive comments from the council members and the senators on your thoroughness and the accessibility of the information you provide in your reports. Not to mention the photos, charts, graphs, and maps."

She pressed her lips together in the closest approximation of a smile she could muster. "Thanks."

"I got a call from the head of the senate committee this morning. There's been a little bit of a shake-up and some reassignments going on, and he wanted to let me know that there's a new member on the committee. So you may want to be prepared to get a little more detail in your report than usual and to answer some basic, fundamental questions that everyone else on the committee already knows." Dennis looked through a few more pages, turning the stapled stack sideways to look at one of the maps.

Zarah resisted the urge to rub her forehead. A new senator on the committee always meant a spate of questions about things the senator could have learned for himself—or herself—just by going back and reading past reports. It almost always meant the meeting would last twice as long. She might need to rearrange her schedule for next Thursday.

Dennis muttered to himself as he continued reviewing the report. As expected, when he got about three-fourths of the way through it, he stilled, reread the page several times, and then looked up at Zarah.

"Are you certain you have enough evidence to back up your claim on the historical significance of the riverfront property?"

"The specimens coming in from the field are promising. I haven't been able to be as hands-on with discovery as I would like, but from what the team has shown me, I'm very optimistic." Every time she thought about the archaeologist and students out researching the riverfront site for evidence of the earthen-work fort that was rumored to have been there during the Civil War, she wondered how she ever allowed Dennis to talk her into taking the position of assistant director—which meant no fieldwork, little lab work, and enough paperwork to choke a humpback whale.

Sometimes she thought she'd give just about anything to go back to being simply one of the several researchers who worked for the commission. Of course, having been the assistant director for almost three years now had brought her to the attention of other organizations—like the National Archives in Washington DC. She still wasn't quite certain what she wanted to do about the message the director of research had left on her cell phone yesterday, asking her to call him back about a position there. While she didn't really want to leave Nashville, she couldn't shake the idea that this out-of-the-blue job opportunity might be God's way of putting her in a position to reconcile with her father and stepmother.

"Well, if you're ready to take the heat on the riverfront property, go for it. It's your baby." Dennis flipped through the final few pages of the report and then set it aside. "How do you feel about taking a trip to Washington in a couple weeks?"

Fear coiled in Zarah's stomach. Had Dennis somehow heard that the archives wanted her to come in and interview for a job? "Washington DC? What for?"

"John from the American History Museum called. Someone died and bequeathed them a ton of family photos and documents. Apparently the family is from Nashville, and the bequest includes a lot of Middle Tennessee Civil War items that aren't dated or marked in any way. They aren't certain of the historical connections or significance of most of it. He asked if I could send you up for a week to sort through it all and see if there's anything significant they could use in a Civil War display they're planning."

Excitement and interest replaced the fear in Zarah's belly. "I'd love to go. Is there any possibility that we might be able to get what they don't want?"

Dennis grinned at her. "I knew you would ask that, so I asked John. Once you sort through it and discover what's there, if there's anything you think would be beneficial to the commission, John and the museum's legal department will work with the family to find out if they will allow the items to be transferred."

Excited anticipation over the idea of getting her hands onto documents and photos unseen by historians before now replaced her earlier disappointment over not being able to spend time in the field.

And while she was up there, she could arrange a trip to the National Archives as well as try to see her father and stepmother. With a few weeks' notice, surely they would at least be able to schedule to get together for dinner or something.

"I can already see your wheels turning, Dr. Mitchell. Just remember, the museum has first dibs on everything in that collection."

Zarah laughed. "But what's important to us might not be important to them."

"And who knows, the letters might contain references to your great-great-great-grandfather that could fill in some gaps in your research for your book." Dennis's brown eyes twinkled.

"I am not writing a book." Zarah emphasized each word. "It's just a paper, and it's only for my own benefit and entertainment."

Dennis raised his thick, dark eyebrows. "Really? How many pages is this paper?"

Zarah rolled her eyes. "About 150 pages—single-spaced."

"And if one of your students turned in a 150-page, single-spaced paper, would you accept it as a *paper*?" Dennis chuckled. "When you get ready to try to have your book published, let me know. I have some connections."

On her way back to her office, Zarah thought about Dennis's last remark. That he had "some" connections was a vast understatement. For someone who had spent the first twenty or so years of his career working as a city planner, and the last ten as the director of a historical preservation nonprofit, Dennis Forrester knew people in the highest echelons of just about every industry out there—from museums to publishing to education to Hollywood. If they needed something done, he knew someone who could do it for them. But it wasn't for her to question how; it was for her to be grateful when Dennis's seemingly endless Rolodex provided the name and contact information of someone who could make the impossible possible.

She dropped into her desk chair. Was it possible Dennis knew someone who could alleviate her Bobby problem?

∞

"Thank you so much for agreeing to meet me after hours." Bobby shook hands with the short, dark-haired young woman. Finally, someone from the singles' group who didn't look like a lingerie model wannabe. Not that this gal wasn't pretty; she just seemed much more real, more natural, than all the other girls at the church. Well, almost all the other girls at the church.

Stacy Simms had a firm grip for someone so petite. "It's my pleasure. I'm only sorry we couldn't get together before now." She grinned, showing slightly crooked front teeth. "You sounded somewhat desperate in the message you left Monday evening."

Bobby grimaced. "Don't get me wrong, I love my grandparents. I just need—"

"You just need a place of your own. I understand, and that's what I'm going to help you do." She looked up at the building they stood in front of. "I think this place has everything you're looking for. And because this is a new building and it's an unsold unit, the developers want to close quickly."

Bobby glanced over the marketing flyer she handed him. Two bedrooms. Fabulous amenities in the building. Balcony. No fireplace— too bad. Granite and stainless in the kitchen. Underground garage parking. Stacy was right; it did look like everything he wanted. Could it really be that simple?

The concierge at the front desk greeted Stacy by name. One of the four elevators opened immediately for them. She hit the button for the sixth floor, and the doors slid closed.

"You must show a lot of units in this building," Bobby said.

Stacy's curtain of straight dark hair flowed over her shoulders and spilled down her back when she craned her neck to look up at him. "I do. And I live here, so they know me pretty well."

"Well, there's a ringing endorsement for this building." He shifted his weight, moving him slightly farther away from Stacy. While she was an attractive woman, and obviously single from her membership in the singles' group and the lack of any kind of ring on her left hand, he knew from experience and many years of observation that business relationships and romantic entanglements did not go well together. Besides, there had been something in the tone of Patrick's voice in the few brief comments he'd made to Bobby about Stacy that made Bobby want to keep his distance on his friend's behalf.

As soon as Bobby walked into the condo, he realized he'd forgotten to look at one very important piece of information on the marketing sheet. "How many square feet is this?"

"The interior has 675, and almost 100 more if you include the balcony. Plus you'll have a storage unit in the parking garage. It comes with one parking space, and you can buy a second parking space for an additional ten thousand."

Bobby turned sideways to slip past the bar chairs that half blocked the entry hall between the front door and the living room. The kitchen, to the left of the front door, was indeed granite and stainless—but just looking at it from across the bar that separated it from the hallway made him feel claustrophobic.

"As you can see, everything is high-end. From the black granite countertops and backsplash to the dark walnut cabinets to the stainless appliances to the travertine floor."

Bobby decided not to interrupt Stacy's well-rehearsed sales pitch of the condo. Even though on paper this apartment had almost two hundred more square feet than his studio in Los Angeles, all his square footage there had been open, loft-style, and felt much larger than its five hundred square feet. The research he had done online showed him he could get something twice the size for less money than the asking price listed on the marketing flyer for this shoe box.

The bedrooms were tiny—he was pretty sure the bed in the master bedroom was actually full-size and not queen-size. But it didn't matter, because he could still barely move around it in the room.

"So? What you think?" Stacy set her large leather planner on the end of the kitchen bar.

"It's very nicely appointed. The bathroom was great. But it's just a little small for me. How far out from downtown am I going to have to go to get at least a thousand square feet?"

Stacy didn't do a very good job of hiding her disappointment, and it made Bobby wonder if she got some kind of discount or special perks from the developer for selling units in this building. "Not too far. Though it will put you in midtown rather than downtown."

"That's fine. I think I'd rather be in midtown than in downtown, as long as it has good interstate access."

Stacy picked her portfolio up and moved toward the front door. Bobby opened it for her and then waited in the hall until she locked up. She opened her planner and rummaged through it while they waited for an elevator.

"Here's one you'll probably like." She pulled out another marketing flyer and handed it to him. "This is not for the exact unit that I'll take you to look at, but it's in the same building. The flyer is for a one bedroom, but the one I want you to look at is a two-bedroom plus study. I know the smallest one-bedroom has just over nine hundred square feet, so the two-bedroom must be at least twelve to fifteen hundred, if not bigger. I heard the owner is facing foreclosure—so they should be open to a quick closing."

In the lobby, Bobby studied a fine-art photo of the Nashville skyline while Stacy arranged with the agent for the other listing to be able to stop by and see it tonight. One really good thing about people desperate to sell—they were usually pretty amenable to dropping everything at the last minute for a showing.

He turned at a tap on his elbow. Stacy tossed her sable hair over her shoulder. "They'll be ready for us to view it in half an hour. With traffic, it'll take us a good ten or fifteen minutes to get there. I can show you all the amenities first, and then we can go see the condo. That sound okay?"

"Sounds great. Where exactly are we going?"

"Just south of Hillsboro Village—the condo complex is right on the corner of Hillsboro and the 440 Parkway. Stay on Broadway all the way down almost to I-440—you know Broadway becomes Twenty-first Avenue and then Hillsboro Pike, right?"

If she was taking him to the building he thought she was taking him to. . . "Yeah, I know exactly where you're talking about."

"There are several units for sale in the building, which explains why this one hasn't sold. It's almost nineteen hundred square feet, it's on the top floor, has downtown views from a panoramic balcony, *and* it comes with a two-car individual garage."

"Really? And it's in my price range?"

"Near the top, but still in it. Ready to go?"

Bobby followed her little blue BMW down to the area of town where he would really rather be. She did indeed pull into the guest parking lot of the building he'd been eyeing ever since he came back to town.

Though it wasn't a high-rise, the sprawling complex surrounded an enormous, beautifully landscaped courtyard. The workout room contained top-of-the-line equipment, and he could picture the singles' group having a get-together in the party room.

He was almost ready to put in an offer before even seeing the condo.

Stacy's phone beeped. "Text message from the agent—the condo is ready for you to see."

The fourth-floor unit turned out to be on one of the corners. Bobby's hopes rose even higher. From what he could see from the outside, the corner units had magnificent balconies.

"Here we are." Stacy opened the door.

Bobby stepped into the hallway. Hmm. . .a narrow, enclosed hall was not what he'd been expecting.

"The door to the right"—Stacy opened it—"is the office."

It wasn't huge, but it was big enough for a desk along one wall and bookcases on the others. The entry hall angled. An opening to the left revealed a dining room—an actual dining room—and directly across from it, a good-sized kitchen with stainless appliances and dark granite.

"There should be"—Stacy opened the door in the angled wall beside the refrigerator—"a walk-in pantry."

Excellent. Now he could actually keep more than a couple days' worth of food in the house. The double doors to the left of the pantry revealed a full-size washer and dryer.

"Do all of the appliances stay?"

Stacy checked something on her smart phone. "Yes. All appliances stay."

"It seems rather closed off. Is there the possibility that I can take down some of these walls? I'd love for the kitchen and dining room to be open to the living room." From the hallway, he had seen part of what turned out to be a magnificent view of midtown and downtown, and he could only see a sliver of it through the opening over the kitchen sink. The corner of the building was anything but a corner—it was round, giving a panoramic view with floor-to-ceiling windows and glass doors on either end in the fan-shaped living room.

He wanted that view—and he wanted to be able to see it from all of the main living areas of the condo.

"I'll check to see if renos are an option." Stacy tapped on the screen of her phone.

While she was busy checking on that for him, Bobby found what he hoped was the second bedroom—not huge, but adequate—and guest bathroom. On the opposite side of the living room. . .yes, this was the master bedroom. The current owners had a king-size bed in the room, and there was still plenty of space to move around. And the master bath was one of the nicest he'd ever seen.

Renovations or no renovations, this was it. He'd be happy here.

Stacy was still doing something with her phone when Bobby rejoined her in the living room. "How much?"

She looked up and gave him the asking price.

"Comps?"

"Hang on." Apparently she had an app for that on her phone, because within minutes she gave him the sales price of several other condos in the area and one in the complex that had sold in the past three months.

She looked up from the phone. "Sounds to me like they're trying to make a profit on this place instead of get out of it what they owe the bank."

Bobby's decision was made. "Write up an offer for fifteen thousand under asking."

"Are you sure you want to start that high? I think you can get it for way under that."

"According to the comps you just gave me, that's a fair price for this unit. Fifteen thousand under, and thirty days for closing." Given the sparse furnishings in the place, it didn't look like they'd need much time to pack up.

She pulled a form out of her planner and filled in the appropriate information.

He read it to verify she'd written in the numbers and date he wanted, then signed it.

"I'll call the other agent and fax this over tonight. I'll ask for a reply by noon tomorrow." She extended her hand. "Congratulations, Bobby. I have to say, you've been one of the easiest clients I've ever worked with."

He shook her hand. At her age, she couldn't have worked with that many. "Thanks."

Long after Stacy drove off, Bobby sat in his car, staring at the building. If all went well, a month from now he'd live here. No more worrying about disturbing his grandparents. No more hints about finding a girlfriend. No more living out of plastic bins. No more Maximus.

His phone started playing "Rocky Top," the song he'd picked for Patrick, a die-hard University of Tennessee fan. "Hey, what's up?"

"What're you doing tomorrow night?" Patrick asked without preamble.

"Friday night? Hadn't planned on anything. Why?"

"We're pulling together a guys' night. We try to do it every so often—get together for some male bonding time. Zarah just reminded me that the girls are doing their thing tomorrow night, so I figured it would be a good time for us to do something, too."

Gee, thanks, Mack. Bobby had gone almost two entire hours without a single thought of Zarah. He'd planned to call Patrick to see if there was anything going on with the singles' group this weekend—the idea of sitting in the living room watching TV with his grandparents, while scintillating, didn't really appeal. The only reason he hadn't yet was the knowledge that if there was a get-together, Zarah would probably be there. And while he still hadn't been able to bring himself to do the background check on her, the idea he was going to have to do it, and soon, made it hard for him to think about facing her.

"A guys' night, huh? Sounds great. I'm in."

Chapter 12

$\mathcal{Z}$arah wandered through each room in her house one more time just to make sure she hadn't missed anything. Though the gathering had been announced as beginning at six thirty, she didn't expect anyone to show up much before seven—except Flannery of course.

At 6:25 on the nose, the front door opened, and Flannery let herself in. "So, I couldn't decide between mini-quiches, mini-egg rolls, and crab rangoons, so I just brought all three." Flannery slid a huge platter of the finger foods onto the kitchen table.

Zarah had to laugh. "Couldn't be because they're all your favorites, could it?"

Flannery shrugged. "I brought a bunch of movies, too."

"Please tell me you brought more than just those old black-and-white murder mysteries you like so much."

Flannery gave her an exaggerated glare. "It's called film noir, as you well know. And no, after all the grief I got last time when I suggested one, I didn't bring any. I brought all those romantic comedies *somebody* gives me for my birthday and Christmas every year."

Though Flannery's affected tone indicated dislike for the romantic comedies, Zarah took no offense over the reference to the DVDs she'd given Flannery over the years to augment her large library of classic films. Most of what Zarah picked out for her were old and in black-and-white. They just weren't mysteries.

"I think Stacy and Lyssa volunteered to bring games." The oven timer beeped, and Zarah turned, grabbed an oven mitt, and pulled two pans of brownies out of the oven—her mouth immediately started watering. She set them on cork trivets on the counter to cool for a few minutes before cutting. "I just hope they don't decide to play that charades game again. I hate that game."

"You hate any game that makes you the center of attention or in which people are watching you." Flannery crossed the kitchen and lowered her face to just over one of the pans of brownies. She closed her eyes and inhaled deeply. "Mmm. You know I can put some brownies away, but were two huge pans of them really necessary?"

"One pan has nuts; the other doesn't. A few of the girls don't like nuts in their brownies."

"Right. But did you really need to make two boxes of each? You know you're going to be eating these for days to come. And you're the one who mentioned going back to the gym recently."

Zarah waggled her finger at Flannery. "No, I have a plan. Whatever is left over gets put in sandwich bags and sent home with people. That way, I can enjoy one or two tonight, but I don't have to deal with having them in the house or taking them to the office."

Flannery lifted the edge of the aluminum foil from her tray and pulled out an egg roll. She hopped up to sit on the counter beside the refrigerator. "Isn't your quarterly senate report coming up soon?"

"Thursday, as a matter of fact."

Flannery seemed to struggle to swallow the bite of egg roll she had just taken. "And you volunteered to have girls' night at your house this month, knowing that it was going to be the weekend before the senate report is due?"

Zarah nodded. "Yes. I'm actually ahead of schedule on it this time. Of course, I had a lot of extra time on my hands the last few weeks."

"Extra time. . . ? Zarah, you were in the hospital with pneumonia!"

Flannery shook her head and took the last bite of egg roll. "It's no wonder it's taking you so long to recover from this, if you're not getting the rest you need."

Zarah shrugged and pulled a table knife out of the silverware drawer. "It was either work on the preliminary draft of the report or go absolutely insane with nothing to do for weeks on end. You were the one extolling work the other night. I like my job, and I enjoy the time I spend doing it."

"You make it sound like I don't like my job, which you know is not true."

"And you make it sound like I'm the only person in this room who brings work home." Zarah looked pointedly at the smart phone clipped to Flannery's belt.

Flannery covered the thing with her hand as if Zarah's glare might harm it. "I turned the sound off, you'll be pleased to know. Besides, in the publishing industry, pretty much everybody takes Friday night off."

"Mmm-hmm. Unless you have a book signing event or a book-launch party or some other kind of appearance for one of your authors." Zarah winked at her friend then turned and started cutting the brownies.

Flannery reached over and pulled one of the plain brownies out of its pan before Zarah had even finished cutting all of them. "Why doesn't anybody ever show up on time for these things?"

"Because only complete dorks like me ever show up on time." Zarah reached into the cabinet above and pulled down two stoneware plates, one light blue and one dark purple—stoneware Kiki had given her from her own collection. Zarah herself usually ate from paper plates. But she promised herself that as soon as she had a dishwasher that actually got the dishes clean, she would start using the stoneware for more than just when she had guests. She quickly arranged the brownies on each plate.

"Yeah, you're probably right. You *are* a dork." Flannery reached for another brownie, but Zarah twirled, whisking the plates out of

Flannery's reach. "Hey! I wanted one of those!"

Zarah set the plates on the table. "Well, that's what you get for calling me a dork."

"You started it."

The doorbell rang. Zarah glanced at the clock on the back of the stove—6:49. "Someone's early. Why don't you go see who that is while I put the plates and cups and stuff out?"

Flannery hopped off the counter, wiped her fingers on the dish towel hanging by the sink, and exited the kitchen muttering.

Even though someone else had signed up to bring plates, cups, plasticware, and napkins, Zarah always put some out just in case the person didn't show up or forgot to bring them or didn't bring enough.

She turned to greet the earliest late arriver. "Stacy, it's good to see you. How was your week?"

The petite real estate agent tossed her abundant, silky, dark hair over her shoulders. "Fantastic. In less than twenty-four hours, I helped our new member buy a condo just off Hillsboro Village. We looked at two places last night—one in my building and one in the Village. He made an offer on the second one, and the seller accepted it today."

Zarah hastily turned to pull the pitcher of iced tea she'd made earlier out of the refrigerator. She did not dare look at Flannery, afraid what her own expression might reveal to an outsider.

So Bobby had bought a condo. He was settling in a lot faster than she'd expected, although she shouldn't be surprised. He had always been very decisive. He knew what he wanted, and he went after it wholeheartedly.

Over the next half hour, twenty other young women showed up. Zarah wasn't sure she liked the fact that the monthly ladies' night gave the appearance of excluding the single mothers; however, as they had excluded children from the gathering, that made it hard for the single moms to participate. But she worked with them to plan their own events as well. And for the monthly singles' group gathering, Zarah always found a few girls from the youth group who were willing to provide child care. She wished she could do it for this function as well, but it was hard to get them to do it once a month—twice a month had proved impossible.

The guests, who all came bearing food, didn't have to be told to help themselves. And they were so familiar with Zarah's house that she didn't even try to direct traffic. Truthfully, they'd probably outgrown her house. But she was centrally located, and no one else would volunteer to have it at her house. She would have asked Flannery to help with the hosting responsibilities, but though Flannery called what she lived in a condo, Zarah called it a rabbit warren.

She really wanted to go look up the Web site for the condo complex that Stacy said Bobby had bought his condo in to see if they had descriptions—and, even better, floor plans—for their condos online. Had he become the kind of person who would pay through the nose for a prestigious address and little living space, or was he still the same laid-back guy with a taste for contemporary design?

And what had he thought of Stacy?

No. She was not going to do that to herself. His presence was bad enough; the last thing she needed to do was lead herself further into jealousy and insecurity by trying to imagine which girls he was attracted to and wondering if he ever compared them to her the way she had compared every man she met in the past fourteen years to him.

"Seriously, congrats, man."

Bobby caught himself on the stair railing as Patrick's huge paw slammed into his shoulder. "Thanks. I was really happy to learn that the sellers are willing to close in fifteen days instead of thirty."

The door from the parking garage stairs led out directly onto Second Avenue. Bobby glanced up and down the main drag of Nashville's entertainment scene. Though the names on several of the clubs, restaurants, and honky-tonks had changed, it didn't really look much different than it had last time he'd been down here, ten years ago when he'd attended the Air Assault School at Fort Campbell and had come down a couple of times and met Mom and Dad for supper here. It was cleaner—but the sun hadn't finished setting yet, so that might change by the time the night was over.

Patrick grabbed his arm and started dragging him right across the middle of the street. Yep—the Old Spaghetti Factory was right where he remembered, smack in the middle along the main drag of Second Ave. Patrick gave his name at the front desk then led the way into the massive lobby and bar area to the left of the entrance. This early on a Friday evening, it wasn't too crowded yet, and they found a grouping of old royal blue velvet armchairs and sofas where they could wait for the rest of the guys to arrive.

"So tell me." Patrick lowered himself into his chair. "How long have you and Zarah known each other, and what did you do to her to make her not want to have anything to do with you?"

Bobby tried to get comfortable in the lower-than-standard wing chair while considering how to answer.

"I'd say she hates you, but I don't think she's capable of hate." Patrick leaned his elbows on his knees and clasped his hands in front of him. "But she sure is going out of her way to avoid you. I thought she was going to have a conniption-fit when she realized you were going to be in the group she was originally assigned to lead Wednesday night at Bible study."

Bobby still couldn't figure out exactly how to answer his friend without giving away more information than either he or Zarah would want anyone to have.

"Look, dude. You and I go back a ways. But you've been gone, and Zarah's been here. I've known her since college. She helped me get through my history classes. I wouldn't have been academically eligible to play my junior year if it wasn't for her. So if there's a choice to be made, I'm gonna have to choose her."

Dread rummaged for a foothold in Bobby's soul. "So I take it the two of you are more than just friends."

"Yeah. I thought you were supposed to be the smart one." Patrick cocked a grin at him, but his eyes remained serious. "Zarah is like my little sister. She's had enough trouble in her life, so I'm drawing a line. If there's something between the two of you that's going to hurt her, you're going to have me to answer to."

A smile started to wedge itself between Bobby's lips, but he clamped them together to stop it, wondering if Zarah knew she had such a ferocious defender in Patrick. "Zarah and I. . .knew each other years ago, in New Mexico, when I was stationed at White Sands under her father's command. We. . .well, we were close, but then it ended and we went our separate ways."

Movement caught his attention, and he looked around to see a few of the guys he'd already met arriving with a few he didn't know. "We'll discuss this later," he murmured to Patrick as he leveraged himself out of the sinkhole of a chair to greet the new arrivals.

Shortly thereafter, their table was called, and they followed the hostess through the dining room, past the Pullman car—which was already full of diners—and to the back of the room where multiple tables had been pulled together.

Bobby chose a seat near the middle of the table, though he knew wherever he sat, he'd be limited to what he could hear and with whom he could talk due to the high ambient noise level in the restaurant already. Though he'd been cleared medically, his years on active duty—with guns, explosives, helicopters, Humvees, and other extreme sources of noise—had damaged his hearing to the point he noticed it, especially in public settings. He usually did well enough in large groups—but lower-pitched voices were harder to hear than higher.

With eighteen men at the table, several appetizers were ordered, but Bobby limited himself to one piece of the cheese bread—and very carefully passed on the dish of shrimp, spinach, and artichoke dip, careful not to come into contact with any of the drippings on the sides. Having his hands break out in hives right before playing laser tag would be no fun.

"Not having any?" Ryan asked, taking the dish from him.

"Allergic to shrimp."

"Really? Tough luck, man." The former marine glopped some of the dip onto his small plate. "Is that all shellfish or just shrimp?"

"Just shrimp. But I don't like most seafood." Bobby folded his hands in his lap to keep from reaching for the plain, freshly baked bread on the small cutting board in the middle of the table. He loved bread, and he could make a meal just off that loaf. But as he would be having spaghetti—with spicy Italian sausage and meat sauce—for supper, followed by the complimentary scoop of spumoni ice cream for dessert, and as he had not yet made the time to stop by the YMCA to join so he could start working out daily, he didn't need the additional carbohydrates. He'd have to go at it hard at laser tag later to justify what he'd already be consuming.

After the usual round of get-to-know-the-new-guy questions, multiple conversations struck up around the table. Bobby joined in the talk of the University of Tennessee game from last Saturday—finding it ironic that the local team in the same athletic conference, Vanderbilt, was never mentioned, even though several of the men at the table worked for either the university or the medical center.

But he loved it. In Los Angeles, there were so many different universities—and it was hard to find anyone to talk football with. Although at one company he'd infiltrated, there had been a large group of USC fans and another group of UCLA faithful. Bobby had truly been able to lose himself in his undercover persona during the week leading up to the big rivalry game, as he staunchly hoped UCLA would beat their rival.

It had been at the sports bar, watching the game with those two factions of co-workers that one of them, having had too much to drink, let slip the piece of information Bobby needed to close the case.

". . .the kind of nun all the boys would be in love with."

He frowned. Obviously he'd missed something.

Ryan must have noticed his expression. "You've met Zarah Mitchell, right?"

Bobby gave a terse nod.

"We were just wondering why she's never had a boyfriend—not one any of us has ever seen her with, anyway—and saying she's probably the kind of girl who would have become a nun if she'd been raised Catholic. She just doesn't seem all that interested in relationships."

If only they knew. He'd thought her cold and distant the first time he met her, but once he'd cracked that barrier of fear and low self-esteem, he'd found her to be funny, warm, and passionate—about life, about history, about people she loved.

"For a while, we wondered if she might be gay"—Ryan leaned closer to Bobby and lowered his voice—"because a few of us worked up the nerve to ask her out, and she said no. But then one of the girls who's gone through a bunch of breakups and always cries on Zee's shoulder about it afterward said that Zarah told her she'd almost been engaged once but the guy walked out on her. And you know the worst part of it?"

Bobby tapped his front teeth together, biting off words before they could escape. He shook his head.

"Zee's father kicked her out of the house anyway—kicked her out for dating a guy when the guy had just walked out on her. Of course, that's just a rumor, and I don't know how much faith to put in it. I've never heard Zee mention it herself. But, I mean, if that's true, it could explain why she shies away from relationships."

Okay, first of all, Bobby didn't like the fact Ryan called Zarah *Zee*. Second, General Mitchell had told Bobby Zarah chose to leave early to get settled in at Vanderbilt before the summer school session started, even though it meant she'd missed graduation, at which she'd been slated to give the salutatory address, which she'd practiced on him for weeks beforehand. Third, Bobby was starting to wonder if he was the biggest idiot in the world for believing the man, who'd never had a kind word to say about his daughter.

Chapter 13

As soon as the Wednesday morning briefing ended, Bobby returned to his office and closed the door. Before he could make investigation assignments to the team members Carroll had assigned to him, there was one very important thing he had to do.

Two thick files sat atop his in-box. He'd hoped it would take much longer than just a week to secure the subpoenas and then for the financial institutions to comply with the release of records. But there sat copies of the raw data on the bank accounts of Dennis Forrester and Zarah Mitchell.

He should probably wait for the forensic accountant's findings instead of wasting his time digging into them, only to discover he'd misinterpreted something and jumped to wrong conclusions—especially with everything he'd learned about Dennis Forrester. The file containing the man's financial records was enormous.

Bobby pulled the thinner of the two folders toward him. Zarah's life—at least the pecuniary part of it—lay here in his fingers.

His hands shook slightly as he set the folder in front of him on the desk-blotter calendar and opened it. Bank statement. Credit report. Home mortgage. Life insurance policy. Investments.

Home mortgage first—the most innocuous of the documents.

He scanned the copy of the contract and the loan documents. She'd gotten a really good price on her house—and made a 25 percent down payment. Impressive. According to the company holding her loan, she'd never missed a payment; in fact, she paid five days early every month, rounding the payment up to the next highest hundred. And she'd gotten a fifteen-year loan instead of twenty or thirty years.

Credit report. Had to be the highest credit score he'd seen in six years of conducting investigations like this. Even his credit, which lenders and banks considered to be excellent, wasn't that good. One credit card on which she charged fifty to a hundred dollars a month and then paid off immediately. She'd paid her student loan off in five years instead of the ten she'd been given to do it. No car loans, meaning she'd most likely paid cash for her car when she bought it.

He grinned. That little blue Honda—pristine outside and inside—was just like her. Practical, understated, looking good for its age, and perseverant.

Life insurance policy. Five hundred thousand dollars. . .twenty-year term, set up when she was twenty-five years old. Odd. She hadn't gotten very good advice on that one. Universal would have been much better for her instead of one on which the rates would skyrocket once she turned forty-five. Wait. Her *grandparents* were her beneficiaries? He could understand why she wouldn't name her father and stepmother in the policy as the recipients of the money should she meet an untimely end, but her *grandparents*? What about her older sister. . .oh, what was her name?

The phone beeped. He jerked, heart hammering from the shock of the loud sound in the otherwise silent office, and hit the flashing INTERCOM button. "Yes?"

"Special Agent Patterson, Captain Carroll would like to see you in his office."

"Thank you, Julie." Bobby closed the folder and pulled himself together—straightening his tie, buttoning his suit coat. He grabbed his notebook-style organizer and headed for the stairs.

He stepped out into the hallway on the third floor just as the elevator dinged and opened.

"You get called to the principal's office, too?" Chase Denney stepped out of the elevator and fell in step with Bobby.

"Yeah. Any idea what's up?"

"None whatsoever."

Julie waved them in when Bobby knocked on the open door to her office. "Captain Carroll's waiting for you." She jerked her head over her left shoulder and picked up her ringing phone.

Chase motioned for Bobby to enter ahead of him. *Chicken*, Bobby mouthed.

The other agent grinned and followed him into their boss's office.

"Oh, good, you're both here." Captain Carroll came around his desk and leaned against the front edge of it. "Since the two of you are the specialists at covert infiltration, and because you've both agreed to serve as trainers for other agents—as well as local police departments who wish to make use of the program—I'm sending you away."

Bobby frowned and looked at Chase—who frowned back at him. They both turned back to the captain.

"The FBI is offering a week-long intensive-training session at Quantico in a few weeks, and we've been offered two spots. Y'all are taking them."

Once again, Bobby exchanged a glance with Chase—who didn't look any more certain about this than he. "Captain Carroll, I'm possibly going to be closing on a house in the next ten to fourteen days, which means the inspection, final walk-through, and actual appointment for closing."

Chase seemed to take courage from Bobby's speaking up. "And my kids have soccer and other stuff going on, and I'm needed to chauffeur them around town in the evenings and on weekends."

Captain Carroll held his hands up in front of him, palms out. Bobby had never noticed before that his left ring finger, bare now, had what looked like the permanent impression of a wedding band around it. White, with graying brown hair and blue eyes, and anywhere in age from late forties to late fifties, the captain was nondescript enough to do well in undercover work. That had presented a problem for Bobby a couple of times in his UC days—being recognized by someone and called by the name he'd used in a previous assignment. It hadn't blown the current case in either instance, but it had come close.

"You're going." Carroll raised his thick eyebrows, expression austere. "Get your personal affairs settled. You fly out the first Sunday in October. It's going to happen, so best be prepared. That is all." He gave a brisk nod then turned his back on them to pull something out of the lateral file behind his desk.

As soon as Bobby realized he'd pulled his jaw forward, putting his bottom teeth in front of the top, he forced himself to relax. No need in betraying his annoyance over the command. Aside from the fact that he was eager to close on the condo and get moved in, he really had no reason to not look forward to the opportunity for some intensive training with the FBI. Besides, having a week away, focused on covert infiltration, could help him figure out how to work with Zarah, to rebuild those burned bridges without creating false impressions or expectations.

Back in his office, the file containing Zarah's financial information stared at him from the desk blotter. With a sigh, he sank into the chair and turned to the computer, where he typed her name and social security number into the search engine. Whatever he was going to learn about her, he was going to have to do it sooner or later.

Whether he liked it or not, she was part of this investigation. Her life would have to be examined on the microscopic level. He and his team would look at each piece of her life, everything she'd ever done. They would treat her as a suspect, look at her from every angle, including the angle that said she was guilty of this crime.

It was going to happen. So he'd best be prepared.

Zarah set aside the second half of the still-warm roast beef sandwich and corrected three typos in the sentence she'd just typed one-handed. Picking up dinner from The Frothy Monkey on her way home had been a great idea. Stopping to take the time to eat it before jumping back into the report might have been an even better idea.

Before leaving the office, Dennis popped his head in and encouraged her to get some rest tonight. His laughter had trailed him down the hall on his way out. She'd only stayed an hour after that, knowing she could work more comfortably at home in her pj's. And with coffee. Lots and lots of coffee.

Around three in the morning, eyes—and stomach—burning, Zarah slid the clip in place on the final presentation folder. She'd e-mail the reports to each member of the senate committee after the meeting—well, to each of their secretaries—but for the meeting, they liked to have a hard copy of the report in their hands as she went through each piece of it. She'd spend all of next week responding to e-mails and phone calls as they came across things in the report they wanted more information on or didn't understand, most likely items she planned to discuss with them a few hours from now.

She took a shower, hoping the hot water would ease the muscles cramping between her shoulder blades. It didn't help, but at least now she could sleep a few minutes later.

At 5:45 a.m., she dragged herself out of the bed and, after doing the stretches given her by a physical therapist many years ago after a car accident, she flipped on the light in the small walk-in closet and went to the end of the rack and pulled out the wine-colored suit. She bent to retrieve the dark gray peep-toe suede pumps with the patent trim and bow details.

She hung the suit on the shower-curtain rod and spritzed it lightly with citrus-basil scented body spray, then turned the bottle toward herself. The image in the mirror when she faced it didn't make her happy. Flannery constantly bemoaned her fine, straight hair and said she envied Zarah's thick, naturally curly mane. If possible, Zarah would trade with her friend in an instant. Everyone said late-1980s styles were coming back in vogue—but she seriously doubted that several-inch-high bushed-out curls would ever make a comeback.

After half an hour and tons of product, she managed to get her hair under some kind of control—and to try to hide the fact it was unevenly multicolored, with reddish highlights on one side and blondish highlights on the other. Actually, the blondish highlights were starting to look more whitish gray than blond. Maybe she needed to take Caylor up on her offer to teach her how to color her own hair.

She wolfed down two pieces of whole-wheat toast and drained what was left of the coffee from last night—not as good reheated in the microwave as fresh, but better than no coffee at all—then put on her makeup and dressed.

Midtown traffic at a quarter of seven in the morning wasn't too bad, and the clock in her office showed 6:54 when she walked in. She put a final copy of the senate report on Dennis's desk then walked down the hall to the aptly named map room to return the maps she'd taken home to scan last night.

An hour later, she barely had time to stop by and exchange good mornings with Dennis and ask him if he had any last-minute changes to the report.

"Would I do that to you?" He smiled at her in an indulgent, fatherly way. At least, it was the way in which she'd always wished her father had smiled at her.

She shook the thought from her head. "It's not that I expect you to have any changes; it's only that I want to make sure you haven't found anything that needs to be changed in an eleventh-hour review of the document."

"Ah. It's because you suspect that I don't actually read your report until the night before you're going to give it. I see."

"No, it's not—" She stopped. From the amusement in Dennis's brown eyes, she'd stepped right into his trap.

"Zarah, the report is perfect, just like you."

She rolled her eyes. "We're in big trouble if the report is just like me. They're going to find flaws and imperfections all over the place."

Dennis stood, came around the desk, and took Zarah by the shoulders, as if to shake her. "How many times have I told you not to speak that way in front of me? I have known you for ten years, Zarah Mitchell, and I can tell you beyond a doubt that you are one of the most wonderful people I have ever had the honor of knowing. You are my right hand—and my left hand, most of the time—and I don't know what I would do without you."

Zarah blinked rapidly against the burning moisture pooling in her eyes. After fourteen years away from her father's influence—and many of those years spent in counseling—it was so easy for her to fall into self-deprecation whenever anyone praised her. But to be called *perfect*—no one had ever called her that. In fact, her father had always pointed out the ways in which Phoebe was perfect and how Zarah could never be like her older sister.

"Remember, if you aren't oozing confidence when you walk into that conference room, those senators will tear you to pieces. So" he nudged her chin up with his fist—"buck up and remember who you are. You are Zarah Mitchell, PhD, assistant director and senior archivist of the Middle Tennessee Historic Preservation Commission."

"And your right hand." Zarah took a cautious deep breath. With her head angled up, she had to look down her nose at Dennis, who was already almost two inches shorter than she, but with heels on, she towered over him.

He laughed, squeezed her shoulder, chucked her under the chin, and returned to his chair. "Yes, my right hand. Now, you'd best be on your way. Don't want to be less than half an hour early, do you?"

Zarah checked the pendant watch. "Goodness, I didn't realize how late it was getting. Hopefully I'll see you this afternoon, boss. Depends on how many questions the newbie has for me."

Dennis waved in dismissal. "Go. Remember—confidence."

She left the building humming "I Have Confidence" from *The Sound of Music*—great, that would be stuck in her head for the rest of the day now. She laughed and checked to make sure she had everything in the car she needed for the meeting, then got in and headed for Legislative Plaza.

After setting up her laptop on the podium and testing the connection to the projector, she placed the vinyl-covered reports at nine places at the first of two raised, semicircular tiers of desks. She then sat in one of the spectator seats below and closed her eyes, asking God to give her genuine confidence and calm and to help the meeting go well. She prayed for each of the senators by name—except the new one, for whom she prayed generally, too.

"Excuse me, I hate to interrupt. I'm Todd Warren—I'm looking for the Middle Tennessee Historic Commission presentation."

She opened her eyes at the masculine voice. . .and then blinked again. Instead of middle-aged and looking bored to death, the man who hovered in the doorway couldn't be much older than she—and his arrival a full five minutes before the meeting time gave him the air of eagerness.

Zarah stood and walked to the end of the row of theater-style spectator seats, extending her right hand. "Senator Warren, I'm Zarah Mitchell from the MTHPC."

The young senator's mouth dropped open slightly as he took her hand. "*You're* Dr. Mitchell? I expected some old, frumpy-looking librarian type. Not someone young and beautiful." His face flushed deep red. "I mean, it's very nice to meet you, Dr. Mitchell."

Zarah's face felt as hot as his looked. "I'll even the score and say you're not the only one who's surprised. You're not at all what I expected, either."

Senator Warren released her hand and wandered up onto the stage behind the first crescent-shaped table. The room always reminded her of a courtroom, with the senators sitting above her, judging her.

"I know." Senator Warren ran his fingers along the top of one of the high-backed leather chairs. "Most people still expect my great-uncle when they hear *Senator Warren*. He passed away suddenly nine months ago, and I decided to run for his seat in the special election. Helps that the district is more than half filled with relatives." He grinned at her, showing lines around his mouth and eyes that hinted he might be a little older than she'd first guessed. But his sandy brown hair didn't show any signs of graying, so she probably wasn't too far off her guess of mid- to late thirties.

"When I found out I was going to be on this committee, I went to the state library and pulled the records of the last few meetings and listened to excerpts from them. I have to say, I'm fascinated by what you do, Dr. Mitchell."

She stood beside the podium, gripping the edge of it. "Thank you, Senator Warren."

"Please, it's Todd."

Shaking her head, she looked pointedly at the nameplates that showed where each senator was to sit during the committee meeting. None of them bore the senators' first names. "We keep things rather formal. As Senator Taylor likes to point out—we all worked hard to get into this room."

Senator Warren had very white teeth, shown off nicely when he smiled. "Very well then, Dr. Mitchell. I have tons of questions—but I don't want to take up everyone's time asking you about stuff they all probably know because they've been coming to these meetings for years. I would love to come by and see your facility—get the five-dollar tour, you know—and maybe go for coffee so I can pick your brain a little bit."

Her heart pounded like a drummer boy sounding the command to charge in the heat of battle. Had the young, good-looking new senator just asked her out?

No. He'd asked her to get him up to speed on what he'd need to know going forward with the committee. But that didn't mean she couldn't enjoy herself at the same time. "Yes, I think that sounds like a great idea."

Wouldn't Flannery be proud?

Chapter 14

Please don't make me have to come get you this morning.

Bobby kept his eye on Zarah even as he moved about the large Sunday school classroom, meeting new people and exercising his memory in greeting by name those he'd met before. Though he knew it would not endear him to her, he determined before arriving this morning that he would make sure Zarah did not separate herself from the group once the lesson began.

Something seemed different about her today. And it wasn't just that she'd pulled her hair back into a cluster of curls at the back of her head, leaving just a few long curlicues loose at her temples and around the nape of her neck. Nor was it the fact that she wore a skirt that barely came below her knees, showing off tanned, shapely calves and ankles above a pair of low-heeled red shoes with a cutout that showed a couple of her pale pink toenails.

No, there was something in her expression, a glint of self-confidence in her eyes he hadn't seen before—well, he'd seen it before, just not in a very, very long time. Maybe it had been her recent illness that had made her seem more like the downtrodden teen he'd known.

Lyssa Thompson slipped her hand through the crook of his elbow. "Hey, there. I hear congratulations are in order."

134

Bobby's arm tingled—and not in a good way. He turned, dislodging her proprietary grip. "Congratulations?"

"On buying a condo. I'm so jealous. I love that building. I actually put a bid in on a one-bedroom when it first opened, but the bidding went way higher than I could afford. Stacy didn't give us the details. What did you end up getting?"

Yep, the guys had been right last week. Lyssa Thompson was like kudzu—once she took root, it would be nearly impossible to get away from her. "I'm under contract for one of the two-bedroom-with-study, panoramic condos."

Lyssa couldn't be more excited for him—she loved those units, would *simply die* to see the interior of one of them.

A familiar laugh drew Bobby's attention away from the babbling young woman beside him. His insides went all soft, like cheese fondue—then hardened like the crusty residue left at the bottom of the pot at the end of the party. Zarah stood with a man Bobby was pretty sure he hadn't met yet—about six-foot, maybe 190, short brown hair, nondescript profile—and she *touched his arm* when she laughed again.

Bobby forced himself to relax. Just because he'd decided that maybe he'd been wrong to believe what General Mitchell had told him about Zarah didn't mean he had any right to be jealous when she flirted with another man.

He did suddenly remember something he needed to talk to Zarah about, though. As soon as Lyssa took a breath, he took his opportunity. "Will you excuse me, please?" He inclined his head and moved away before she could say anything else and made his way to Zarah.

The guy she'd been talking to wandered off—to be surrounded by several females—and Zarah turned, coffee carafe in hand, looking for anyone who might need a refill.

She blinked a couple of times when she saw him, and her lips thinned slightly before she smiled at him. "Bobby. Good to see you this morning. Can I get you some coffee?" She lifted the carafe between them.

"No, thank you. I saw you giving out tickets earlier. I meant to e-mail you earlier this week, but I kept getting distracted." Actually, he'd dismissed the idea of e-mailing her so that he'd have an excuse to start a conversation with her.

"Oh, yes, I have your ticket." She turned and stepped over to the welcome table and grabbed her purse from the chair.

"That was what I wanted to talk to you about. You see, something's come up. A co-worker is having an office party on Friday night, and I really feel like I should go—you know, new guy in the office and all. Be a good way for me to get to know some of the other folks I work with."

Zarah straightened, eyebrows raised. "Oh. Okay. I can refund your money and either sell the ticket to someone else or get a refund from the school."

"Actually, I was hoping you could exchange it for me—and get two additional tickets—for the Saturday matinee. When I told my grandparents about it, they decided they'd like to go, and I think they have some other friends who are going to the Saturday afternoon show. So I thought I could go with them instead."

He watched her expression carefully. Mamm had mentioned that Trina and Victor Breitinger had said they'd be attending the show Saturday afternoon. . .with Zarah. Chase's invitation to a get-together at his house this Friday had made the perfect excuse to go to the matinee, when he'd have a better chance at talking to Zarah.

Zarah's brows raised even higher, her blue eyes widened. "Oh. . . well, okay. Yes, I can get those Saturday tickets for you. But I won't be able to get them until Thursday evening when I'm out there for my class."

"Where's your office? I could pick them up from you Friday around lunchtime."

"We're just south of downtown on West End." She gave him directions and he frowned, as if trying to picture them in his mind, even though he knew exactly where the Middle Tennessee History

Museum and the attached MTHPC offices were.

"I think I can find that pretty easily. And I have to go to the state library to do some research Friday afternoon, so I could just swing by your office on the way there." The archivist had told him that the library's copy of the report Zarah had given to the senate committee would be available for him to look at by Friday.

An invitation to go to lunch, since he'd be stopping by her office around that time anyway, was on the tip of his tongue, but he clamped his teeth together. No need to push his luck.

He reached for his wallet and pulled out thirty dollars and handed it to her. He held it so that she couldn't take it without her fingers brushing his. Though no bolt of electricity struck him when her fingers made contact with his, the back of his neck tingled at the memory of the last time he'd touched her hand—holding it as they walked around the mall in Las Cruces after a dinner of corn dogs and french fries. He'd picked up the engagement ring that afternoon—before she arrived at the mall—and considered proposing then. But he'd already planned everything for her eighteenth birthday: dinner at the Double Eagle restaurant and a starlight stroll around the plaza in Mesilla, culminating in the down-on-one-knee proposal in the bandstand at the center of the plaza.

But she'd run away. Or had she?

"I'm leaving a couple hours early on Friday, so try to be there before two o'clock." She gave him a smile that wasn't as strained as her initial greeting.

"I'll do that." He took his cue to leave when Flannery came in the door. But he kept half his attention on Zarah the remainder of the morning.

Last week, after Zarah had finished filling out the roll sheets, she'd left the room and been gone the rest of the time. This week, when Patrick called everyone to the chairs—set up in rows instead of the big circle now that attendance was back up to around sixty—Zarah handed her Bible and purse to Flannery, who used them to save her a seat. Bobby smiled and sat with Ryan and the other guys he'd bested at laser tag a week ago.

Zarah didn't know if it was her imagination, wistful thinking, or paranoia, but she couldn't shake the feeling that Bobby had been watching her ever since he'd entered the Sunday school room earlier this morning. She'd avoided looking at him, so she couldn't be sure, but she had the uncanny sensation she was under constant surveillance.

And what was with him wanting to come by the office to pick up the tickets? She'd wanted to suggest he just get tickets at the door on Saturday—so far, though the presales of the tickets were good, none of the shows were sold-out. But he hadn't even given her the chance to say she'd get them for him and wait for him and his grandparents before the show Saturday. Of course, he couldn't know she was going to be there Saturday—could he?

Zarah looked down at the open Bible on her lap. Kiki and Lindy Patterson. Of course Bobby knew Zarah would be there Saturday. And it had probably been Lindy Patterson's suggestion that Bobby go on Saturday, when Zarah wouldn't have the buffer of fifteen or so people from the singles' group.

She couldn't back out without disappointing Kiki and Pops—and having to tell them why she wasn't going. Truth be told, she was curious to observe Bobby away from the dynamics of the singles' group—away from the adoring females who flocked to him, or at least couldn't keep their eyes off him as soon as he walked into a room.

Before she realized it, Patrick started the closing prayer. She'd missed the lesson, worrying about Bobby—and promised herself as she closed her eyes for the prayer that this would be the last time it happened.

She murmured, "Amen," along with everyone else.

"Before y'all leave, I have an announcement I'd like to make." Patrick's voice froze everyone in place.

Zarah frowned. Whenever he was going to announce something, he usually discussed it with her ahead of time.

"Stacy, you want to join me?"

As the petite brunette stood and made her way up the aisle between the rows of chairs, Zarah's insides lurched. No. This couldn't be what she thought it was.

Sure enough, Patrick put his arm around Stacy's shoulders. "Last night, I asked Stacy to marry me, and believe it or not, she said yes."

Zarah smiled and clapped along with the applause and cheers that broke out through the crowd of singles, just so she wouldn't appear out of place. But she mourned inside. She and Patrick had worked long and hard to build this singles' ministry. He'd been pulling away for a while now, and she couldn't deny she'd suspected he and Stacy had feelings for each other. She just couldn't believe things had progressed so far.

She'd seen it happen before. As soon as one high-profile member of the group "coupled up," it seemed like everyone else felt like they needed to—which only created problems. The new relationships often created jealousy among the others and hard feelings between the couple if they broke up.

"Why didn't you tell me?" Flannery hooked her arm through Zarah's and leaned close, her voice low.

"Because I didn't know." Zarah struggled to keep her expression happy.

"You didn't—you mean Patrick didn't tell you before everyone else?" Shock hung from Flannery's words and filled her light brown eyes.

Zarah shook her head, closed her Bible, collected her purse and sermon journal, and stood. "Apparently he didn't feel I needed to know before anyone else."

"But. . .but. . .it's going to change everything, isn't it? I mean, they'll leave and go to the Nearly Marrieds/Newly Marrieds class, won't they?"

Frustration gurgled in the pit of Zarah's stomach. "I don't know." She smiled at the people who turned at her less-than-whispered statement then grabbed Flannery's arm and dragged her to the end of the room away from the coffee and doughnuts.

"I don't know what they'll do because, obviously, I'm not important enough to even know that they were dating, much less getting to the point at which marriage was even on the horizon." Zarah hugged her Bible and sermon journal to her chest.

"But you and Patrick have always been close. I mean, I grew up with him, and you know more about him than I do."

"Welcome to the world of being me. I'm important only when people need me to do something but the last one they think of when it comes to anything else." Zarah wished the words unspoken as soon as they left her mouth. Nothing like sounding bitter and jealous and immature upon hearing a friend's good news.

"Oh, sweetie." Flannery flung her arms around Zarah, apparently not minding that Zarah's arms—still holding her Bible and journal close—pressed into her stomach.

Zarah wanted to draw comfort from Flannery, wanted to be able to shake off the sense of dread Patrick's announcement had wrought. But she couldn't let go.

Flannery ended the hug and stepped back. "We need to call Caylor and hash this out. Can you do coffee this afternoon?"

"No, I—" If she didn't talk to Flannery and Caylor about it and try to figure out why she felt this way, she'd compartmentalize it, not deal with it, and end up back in therapy again. She didn't have time for therapy. She had time for coffee with her two best friends. "Yes. If Caylor can make it, let's get together with her for coffee this afternoon."

"Are you still going to go to lunch with the group? I think it'll be good for you—after all, everyone's going to be looking to you more and more for leadership now."

Eighty pounds of responsibility dropped onto Zarah's shoulders, but she found a smile in spite of it. "Gee, thanks for reminding me."

"Come on, shake it off. Everything will look different after worship."

Zarah walked down to the sanctuary with Flannery but parted ways with her when she saw Pops enter the auditorium alone.

She wound through clusters of people milling at the back of the large room and finally caught up with him about halfway down the outside aisle.

"Hello, granddaughter." He reached his arm around her waist and gave her a squeeze.

Zarah leaned into his strength for a moment. "Hello, Pops. Where's Kiki this morning?"

"Ah, she's down in the nursery, keeping the babies. Want to keep your old grandpa company this morning?"

"Love to." She slid into the pew he motioned toward just as one of the associate pastors called them to order and gave the opening prayer.

After the organ prelude and the choir's beautiful a cappella call to worship, Zarah stood with the rest of the congregation to sing the first hymn. But as soon as everyone started singing, Zarah closed her eyes and reveled in listening to Pops sing the bass line of each hymn. As usually happened when someone sat near him who didn't know him, the young mother in front of them turned around during the greeting time and asked him why he didn't sing in the choir.

"Oh, I'll leave that for the young folks," he said, and he winked at Zarah when the woman turned to greet someone else. When he'd retired after fifty years as a minister of music—the last twenty of those being here at Acklen Ave.—he'd made the choice not to be involved in the music ministry, allowing the new minister to establish himself and his way of doing things without everyone looking to Pops to make sure it was okay.

Even though she tried to concentrate on the sermon, her mind wandered. Patrick and Stacy. The singles' group. Bobby. Senator Todd

Warren. Flannery and her list of potential dates for Zarah.

That last thought brought a smile to Zarah's lips. She looked up to her right, bringing her focus onto the stained-glass window depicting Jesus healing the lame man.

All right, Lord. I give up. I can't handle any of this on my own. That's clear. You seem to be throwing a lot of stuff at me right now, and I'm guessing You're once again trying to teach me that the only way I'll get through it is to depend on You. So forgive me when I fail to trust You and turn everything over to You. Because we both know I will. Please, strengthen my faith so I can make it through these trials.

She was startled out of her prayer when Pops stood and opened his hymnal for the closing hymn. Zarah almost laughed when the organist played the intro to "Trust and Obey." One point to God for showing her His sense of humor.

After the closing prayer, Pops put his arm around Zarah and kissed her temple. "You being social with the young folks today?"

"Yes, sir. I thought I'd go to lunch with them today." She wrapped her arms around his waist and gave him a squeeze. "My love to Kiki."

"And hers to you. Now you'd best go, or you probably won't get a seat." Pops shooed her away.

Zarah laughed but didn't want to admit how true his joke could be. On a few occasions when she'd been delayed leaving church, by the time she'd arrived at the restaurant, the rest of the group had already ordered and hadn't thought to save a seat for her, even though she'd told them she was coming.

Oh, well. It was usually easy enough to pull up an extra chair.

"Zarah. Zarah Mitchell!"

She stopped and looked around for the man calling her name. The large foyer behind the sanctuary roiled with well-dressed people, most of whom Zarah had never met in the fourteen years she'd attended this church. Not because it was overly large, but simply because she was in the singles' group. And they didn't have much contact with any other groups in the church.

The associate pastor of adult ministries waved over the heads of several people between them. Zarah raised her hand in response and made her way around to him.

"Hey, Pastor Ben. What's up?"

"I had hoped to catch you and Patrick together this morning, but it looks like he's already slipped away, so I'll shoot him an e-mail this afternoon. Pastor Joe would like to set up a meeting with you two sometime this week—probably Tuesday or Thursday evening—to discuss the singles' ministry with you."

Her heart thumped. In the eight years she'd been a leader in the singles' group, never once had the senior pastor taken an interest in them—except when a delegation from the singles' department had met with him six years ago to ask that the singles' department be made part of the adult ministry instead of the youth ministry. Since then, they'd worked with Ben.

"I can't speak for Patrick, but I can't meet on Tuesday or Thursday, unless it's after nine o'clock—I teach those nights. Tomorrow or Wednesday before or after Bible study would be the best days for me."

"Pastor Joe can't meet tomorrow—Monday's his day off. I'll have to see if he thinks he can make time for it on Wednesday. I'll shoot you both an e-mail once the time is firmed up."

"Can you tell me what the meeting is about?" Unable as she was to control her reactions, she hated being blindsided by anything.

"Um. . .no, I'd better leave that for Joe to tell you both." Pastor Ben gave her a compulsory smile. "I'll be in touch."

"Okay." She didn't move for a few moments after the associate pastor walked away into the thinning crowd. Her insides writhed, eliminating the hunger pangs she'd had just minutes ago.

When she arrived at Sam's Sports Grill, they were still in the process of pulling tables together, so she was certain to get a seat. Still wondering why the pastor wanted to meet with them, Zarah sank into the chair nearest her once the tables were finally in position to accommodate the twenty-some-odd people.

It wasn't until she looked over her right shoulder to take the menu from the waitress that she realized she'd sat right next to Bobby Patterson. He gave her a benign smile when their eyes met then immediately turned his attention to his own menu.

Her breath caught in her throat—and triggered the first coughing spell she'd had in almost a week. She excused herself and fled to the restroom.

Flannery entered a few seconds behind her. "You okay?"

Zarah nodded and pressed a wad of paper towels over her mouth. Once the coughing subsided, she tossed those towels and grabbed fresh ones to dab at the perspiration on her forehead and at her streaming eyes.

"I couldn't believe it when Bobby went around to sit by you. I was sure you'd see him coming and move down to where I'm sitting."

"I wasn't paying attention." Zarah's voice came out raspy. She told Flannery about her all-too-brief conversation with Pastor Ben leading to her distraction.

"Maybe they're finally increasing the singles' ministry budget like you and Patrick have been asking for the past several years."

Zarah hadn't thought about that. "Maybe you're right. Or maybe Patrick already told Pastor Joe he's getting married, and they're going to dissolve the singles' ministry entirely."

Flannery turned to face the mirror and fluffed her hair. "I don't know why you automatically assume everything is going to be bad."

"Because it usually is." Zarah checked to make sure her mascara hadn't run. "Come on. They'll place their orders without us if we don't get back out there."

"Want to move down to my end of the table?"

"That would be pretty conspicuous, don't you think?"

"Yeah, but then you wouldn't have to sit by *him*."

"I think I can bear it for an hour or so." And she didn't want him to know how much his nearness unnerved her.

But when they rounded the corner, the chair to Bobby's left—her chair—wasn't empty. Lyssa Thompson tossed her bleached-blond hair over her shoulder, wrapped both hands around Bobby's arm, and threw her head back and laughed.

Really, Zarah just couldn't take having her place at the table stolen on top of everything else today. Not only that, but she didn't want Bobby to get hurt by being the rebound from the breakup Lyssa had cried to her about on the phone less than two weeks ago.

Zarah marched right up behind the chair and cleared her throat.

Lyssa looked up with a little squeak. "Oh, Zarah, you scared me."

"I need my chair back, Lyssa." Zarah's pulse pounded so hard, she could feel it in the tip of her nose. Normally she would have avoided the confrontation, taken her purse from where it hung off the back of the chair, and moved. But this wasn't a normal situation.

"Is this your chair? I thought it was empty." Lyssa batted short, stubby eyelashes at her.

Zarah smiled at the bald-faced lie. "Nope, not empty." She kept smiling as Lyssa slunk back around to the far end of the table—across from Flannery—to the chair she'd been in before Zarah had gone to the restroom. Zarah resumed her seat and draped her napkin across her lap.

"Thank you." Bobby's whisper tickled her ear, and his shoulder pressed against hers.

"For what?" With as close as he was, she dared not turn to look at him. She opened the menu instead.

"For standing your ground."

She risked turning to look at him when the contact between their arms ended. He winked at her.

And with that one gesture, she was seventeen years old again, staring in wonder at the handsome young soldier who was the first person to ever notice or take an interest in her.

Was it possible that, after all this time, she could excavate beneath all the hurt feelings, the anger, the bitterness, and find that her love for Bobby remained as strong as it had been fourteen years ago? Or was she only setting herself up for an even greater heartbreak when he disappointed her again?

Was she strong enough to find out?

Chapter 15

While spending a couple of hours talking to Caylor and Flannery Sunday afternoon—about Patrick's engagement and the singles' group, not about Bobby, not yet—had helped Zarah sleep better the next couple of nights, by Wednesday afternoon, anxiety over what Pastor Joe wanted to talk to them about weighed on her mind again.

"Dr. Mitchell?"

She tore her eyes away from the artifacts on the specimen table and looked at the graduate-student intern. "I'm sorry, what did you say?"

"I think I identified one of the soldiers in this photo, and I hope you can confirm it for me."

Zarah moved around the corner of the table so she could see the intern's laptop screen.

"I found him in a couple of the photos from that new group of Battle of Franklin pictures we just got. I thought I recognized him, and when I pulled up the Stone's River photos, sure enough, I found a couple of images of him there, too. Except he was identified in those." She pulled up the other images for comparison.

Zarah examined the images—grainy at the level of magnification needed to see the soldier's face. "I do believe you're right, Felicity. Good job."

"Dr. Mitchell." Another of the interns came into the room. "I'm back with that box of letters and journals the state library and archives was restoring for us, just like you asked." He set the large box on the end of the long, wide, underlit specimen table.

"Great." Zarah slipped on a pair of white cotton gloves and opened the box. "Oh, good, they sent a copy of the microfiche along with it. Excellent—that means one of you can start typing them in from the microfiche while someone else works at scanning the originals into the computer in the documents room for the visual database."

Adam groaned. "Tell me again why the Tennessee State Library and *Archives* doesn't do that for us?"

"Because that's why we exist—to research, document, and preserve items of significance to the history of Middle Tennessee. Anything to do with the government goes to them; everything else comes to us. They're just helping out while Danica, our document restoration expert, is on maternity leave."

Zarah glanced at the wall clock. "But you don't have to worry about it today. Go ahead and wrap up whatever you're working on and knock off a few minutes early. Adam, tell Jonah and Amberleigh, please."

"Sure thing. Thanks, Dr. M." Adam bounded out of the room.

Felicity finished what she was doing, shut down the laptop, and stowed it in the cabinet, which Zarah locked behind her.

She didn't make it a habit to let the grad students leave before five, but they'd gotten a lot accomplished so far this week—and Zarah didn't want to stay much longer herself.

She straightened the stacks of photos of the state's centennial celebration she'd been staring at all afternoon, turned off all the lights, and locked the room.

The meeting with Pastor Joe wasn't until five thirty, and it didn't usually take more than ten minutes for Zarah to get over to the church from here, even at five o'clock, but she left early anyway. No point in sitting around here stressing.

She pulled into the church parking lot seven minutes later. She had time to go home and change clothes—but the dress pants, silk tank, and short-sleeved jacket she wore were as comfortable as anything else in her wardrobe. Plus, appearing pulled-together and professional was never a bad thing.

Though the lingering late-September heat nearly made it unbearable, Zarah sat in the car, eyes closed, mind running through every eventuality she could imagine, until she heard the unmistakable rumble of Patrick's truck pulling into the space beside her.

She climbed out of the car, bringing her leather carryall with her. She might not need the notebook and pen she planned to take out for the meeting, but she couldn't leave the bag with the laptop in it in the car for several hours. Her life was on that computer.

"Have a good day today?" Dressed in his usual work boots, khakis, and solid-color polo shirt with his company logo over his heart, Patrick grinned at her.

She had to smile back—if for no other reason than that she couldn't imagine him in a tuxedo. His getting married would be worth it just for that spectacle. "We got a lot accomplished today. You?"

Patrick launched into the details of the house he was renovating, which took the entire walk to the pastor's office.

"He's on the phone," the secretary said, "but he'll be—"

The office door opened, and Pastor Joe stepped out. "I'm ready. Come in, Patrick, Zarah. Veda, ask Ben to come in, please."

"Yes, sir." The secretary picked up her phone and dialed an extension.

Patrick motioned Zarah to enter ahead of him. It was only the second time she'd ever been into the senior pastor's office. It was just as big as she remembered, and even though three walls were lined with floor-to-ceiling bookshelves, several stacks of books sat on the floor near his desk.

"Let's sit at the table."

Zarah followed the minister to the table at the far end of the room and had just sat down when the associate pastor arrived.

"Ben, close the door, will you?" Pastor Joe picked up a legal pad from his desk and carried it over to the table.

Zarah sank onto the edge of one of the chairs and pulled it close to the table, setting her own notebook and pen out. She pressed her palms to the tops of her thighs, trying to control her nerves.

As soon as everyone was seated, Pastor Joe started. "I asked the two of you to come because you're the tacit leaders of the singles' Sunday school class. Patrick, I believe you've been teaching the class for several years now?"

"Eight, sir," Patrick confirmed.

"And Zarah, you've been providing administrative support—record keeping and outreach, is that correct?"

"Record keeping, outreach, event planning, mentoring, pretty much anything that's needed."

"Very noble." Instead of complimentary, Pastor Joe's words sounded condescending. "You may not know, but the senior ministers recently attended a church growth and membership conference. One of the topics discussed at the retreat, which we've been scrutinizing since we came back, is that of the singles' ministry and how it doesn't mesh well with the rest of the church. It sets unrealistic and, frankly, unchristian examples for young people in the church. We are a family-oriented church. We want our young people thinking about building families."

Zarah's skin prickled with heat; her insides froze into a solid block.

"We understand you have provided leadership with good intentions, but the ministers of the church have decided unanimously that changes are in order to better integrate the unmarried members of our church into the congregation."

"You're just going to change things—without even asking the people affected by these changes if they want them or not?" The words had come out of Zarah's mouth without conscious thought or effort.

"It is the duty of the ministers of the church to ensure that the members are being ministered to in the best way possible."

"But isn't it your duty to find out in what way those members *want* to be ministered to?" Zarah gripped her pen so hard the clip bit into her palm.

"Zarah, just listen to what they have to say—I think you'll like it."

She stared at Patrick, wondering what alien had invaded his body.

"Now, as I was saying. . . We will combine the young marrieds and the post-college, twentysomething singles into a new Young Professionals class. This will take the place of the Nearly Married/Newly Married class—so they'll be integrated into it as well. They will continue to meet in the large room that currently houses the singles' Sunday school class." Pastor Joe looked up from his notepad. "Patrick and his fiancée have agreed to teach that class. Then we'll have the Single Again/Single Parents/Divorce Care class. They'll meet in room 301A."

The last room before the youth wing of the education building. They'd never be able to hear their lesson over the music and noise the teenagers made on Sunday mornings.

"We have wonderful teachers lined up for that class, too. A couple who've both been through divorce and are now happily remarried." Pastor Joe leaned back in his chair and looked at Patrick and Zarah as if that was all he had to say.

"And what about those of us who are over thirty but who aren't qualified for the Single Again class? What are we supposed to do?" She tried to keep the anger and hurt out of her voice, but it didn't work.

"Oh, yes. We will encourage those people to integrate into one of the wonderful classes we already have for people of that age group. If they insist that they want to have a class of their own, I have a couple lined up, ready to teach it."

"A couple? A married couple?" Zarah leaned forward and clasped her hands atop her notebook. "Is there a particular reason why you're not looking for someone from within the singles' group to teach it?"

KAYE DACUS

"Yes, as a matter of fact. Because the ministers feel that a married couple provides a much better example. They can give unmarried people something to strive for, something to want to model their own lives after. The couple I have in mind are in their forties, so they're right in the same age range. But they've been married for twenty years, so they'll be able to start steering the singles onto the right path. They've already got a lot of ideas for activities and small group Bible studies they want to do, if the older singles decide they want to go that route."

Dumbfounded, Zarah could only stare at the pastor. Surely the next thing he was going to say was, *Just kidding—we're actually increasing the singles' ministry's budget because you've been growing and doing such a good job of ministering to your members.*

"Sir, when we talked about this," Patrick said, "my understanding of the reason for the change is to better integrate the singles into the church—not to try to make them feel like being single is wrong. Did I misunderstand you?"

Pastor Joe frowned, looked down at his notes, then back at Patrick. "Did I make it sound as if being single is wrong?"

Zarah joined Patrick in nodding.

"That's not what I meant—what I meant is that it's important that we help the unmarried folks in our congregation see that staying single isn't always the best path for their lives. That marriage and building a family are the biblical model of Christianity."

"In whose Bible?" Zarah blurted out. "Not the Bible I've read in which Paul encourages unmarried people to stay unmarried so that we can better serve God. Not in the Bible in which Jesus was unmarried. Not in the Bible in which the apostles all abandoned their wives and children to fend for themselves so they could go out and spread the gospel."

Patrick rested his hand on her shoulder, ceasing her torrent of words but kept his gaze on Pastor Joe. "I think what Zarah is saying, which I agree with, is that not everyone is called to marry or have

152

children. Just like not everyone who is currently unmarried is called to stay single." He turned to look at Zarah. "And what Pastor Joe is trying to do is to make sure that the unmarried people in the church don't feel quite so isolated from the rest of the church family anymore—and we'll be better able to minister to the singles by being able to focus on topics and issues that are more specific to those within the new classes."

"Yes—yes, Patrick. That's what we were going for." Pastor Joe beamed at him. "Zarah, I'm sorry if my awkward explanation offended you. We want to better integrate everyone into the church family."

Zarah's pounding heart began to return to a more normal pressure and rhythm. "May I make a suggestion, then?"

"Yes, please." Pastor Joe's head bobbled like one of the large-headed sports figurines on the shelf behind him.

"We're going to need that class for the median singles—the thirty- and fortysomethings who don't really fit in anywhere else. We aren't going to fit in with the married people our age—who mostly have young kids, and with whom we don't have a lot in common at this stage of our lives. We need to be able to explore issues we face on a daily basis—issues that stem from being single, from living life alone, from wondering what it is that God wants us to do when it comes to relationships. And I think the best person to teach the class is someone who's been through that. Someone who's lived life as a single adult, not someone who's been married their entire adult life."

"Do you have a suggestion?" Pastor Joe asked.

She shook her head. "Not off the top of my head."

"Then let's give the couple who've volunteered to teach it a try. They seem eager to work with this group."

Grudgingly, Zarah conceded. "Okay."

"Will you work with us through this change, Zarah? Having you on board, the leadership you'll be able to provide, will be key to make the transition smoother."

Still not happy about it but seeing no alternative, she nodded.

Patrick squeezed her hand again. "Thanks, Zarah. This is going to be a good change. And by splitting up the group, it'll be a lot less work for you."

Anger, sadness, disappointment, and a sense of betrayal cramped her stomach. Where was she, personally, going to fit into this new structure? What would happen to her ability to mentor the younger single women—would they even let her near them if she was such a bad example of Christianity because she was still unmarried? They'd effectively taken away her ministry—her source of joy—without even asking her how she felt about it.

She had a lot more she wanted to say on the subject—especially to Patrick, who wasn't one of her favorite people in the world right now—but she swallowed the words. She pulled her hand away from his and looked at the pastor with raised brows. "Is that everything?"

"I believe so. The change will take place the first weekend in October."

Good. She wouldn't be here. She'd be in Washington DC.

That job at the National Archives suddenly sounded much better than it ever had.

Bobby pulled into the church parking lot, surprised to see Zarah's car. He'd heard she didn't usually come for supper.

A few feet from the main entrance, he stopped when the door flew open and Zarah barreled out—and almost ran him down.

"Whoa! Easy there." He reached out and grabbed her shoulders to steady her.

"Sorry." Patches of bright red painted her cheeks, and tightness pulled her mouth into an angry pucker.

"What's wrong?"

She shook her head, eyes closed, as if whatever had her upset was too foul to repeat aloud. "It's. . .nothing." Crystalline tears welled in her blue eyes.

Bobby pulled her out of the pathway to the door and led her over to sit on the low wall surrounding one of the trees. "Talk."

She raised one shoulder in a half shrug. "Apparently I'm a bad example to all of the younger single women in the church."

"I'm trying to follow you here, but I'm having a little trouble." Bobby pulled his handkerchief out of his inside coat pocket and handed it to her. "Wanna start from the beginning?"

Zarah dabbed the corners of her eyes then clutched the cloth in her fist. She started slowly, but as she warmed to her subject, her eyes flashed and her tone became vehement. Bobby listened in astonished silence as Zarah related what she'd just learned from the pastor.

"I'm certain he didn't mean he thought *you* were a bad example to the younger singles. He'd be insane to think so."

"But that's the thing. . .in a twisted way, that's what he was saying: I'm a bad example to them simply because I'm not married—and because I've never dated."

A slow smile caught the corners of Bobby's mouth. "Never?"

She looked at him—and finally seemed to realize to whom she was talking. For a moment, he thought she might run away. But then she released a halfhearted chuckle. "Not since I've been here, no, not really. You aren't supposed to know that, though. According to Flannery, the best way to deal with you is to make you insanely jealous over the thought of all the handsome, wealthy, successful men I've dated since we broke up."

"We'll get back to that in a minute. But as to what the pastor said about the singles' group, do you know the couple he said wanted to teach the older singles' class?"

"He didn't say who it was. Only that they were in their forties and have been married half their lives, so don't know what it's like to be single."

"And you're going to write them off just because they're married?"

"No—I'm—no, that's not—" Zarah huffed and rolled her eyes. "That's not what I'm saying."

"Oh, so you're saying God couldn't possibly have called this couple to minister to the singles?" He let just enough sarcasm slip through into his tone that, hopefully, Zarah wouldn't take offense.

"Of course not!" Her mouth twisted in wry frustration.

"Then what are you saying?"

"I just think it would have been nice if they could have discussed it with us and let us help make the decision. We're not children, to have someone else decide how our Sunday school class or Bible study should be run." Zarah twisted the handkerchief around one long finger.

"And you think because you're not being asked to teach the class that they think you're a bad example?"

"Are you being purposely obtuse?"

He hid his smile. At least now she wasn't so dejected and weepy anymore. "No. I'm just having a hard time understanding why you believe they think you're a bad example of a Christian simply because they want to restructure the singles' ministry so that they can meet our needs better. You said the pastor apologized for not being clear with what he said."

"He said that married people are a *better example* to singles. That obviously means he thinks that people like me aren't a good example."

Bobby couldn't think of anyone who was a better example of Christianity to the young single women than Zarah. He wished more of the ones in this group took their cues of behavior from her. "I think he didn't do a good job of thinking through his explanation. I seriously doubt Patrick would have been on board with this if Pastor Joe truly felt that you—that someone like you—isn't a wonderful example for others in the singles' ministry."

"Oh—and that's another thing!" Zarah jumped up and turned to shake her finger in his face. "Your friend Patrick is a jerk."

"Whoa, there. Hold on." He captured her accusatory hand between his to keep her from poking him in the eye. "I agree. Patrick was wrong for not telling you all of this ahead of time. I can't defend him or his choices. But don't take it out on me."

She yanked her hand away and sat with a huff. "I enjoyed working with the younger women, trying to mentor them and help them figure out that being single is okay, that their whole identity doesn't have to be wrapped up in who they're dating. I liked planning the group activities and being there to make sure everything ran smoothly. I liked providing all of the administrative work so no one else had to deal with it. I liked helping lead small groups in Sunday school and Bible study. From what Pastor Joe said, this couple he has lined up are going to want to implement their own ideas for activities and Bible studies."

"Maybe this is God's way of making you slow down a little bit. You are a wonderful model of what it means to be a single Christian woman; anyone would be crazy to think—or say—otherwise."

Her cheeks glowed pink and the corners of her mouth trembled as if trying to fight off a smile.

"I know I've only been back a couple of weeks, but from what I've seen and what I've heard, you have a tendency to run yourself ragged for this group of. . ." *Ingrates* sounded a little too harsh. "You put out and put out and put out and don't seem to get anything in return from most of the people in the singles' group—except disregard."

She cocked her head and frowned at him. "I get the joy of knowing I've ministered to others."

"Zarah, they ignore you unless they need you to serve them coffee or orange juice or bring them a Bible or something. Maybe this is God's way of saying it's time you let someone else take over doing that and just rest for a while. Let people get to know you in some other capacity than as a servant—and I don't mean that in the good sense of the word."

"There's nothing wrong with serving others."

"There is when you allow people to treat you like a doormat." Now he was starting to get riled. How could she not see the way people treated her?

"I don't think you've been back long enough to make that judgment, Robert Oliver Patterson."

Warm ooey-gooeys dribbled through Bobby's chest at Zarah's use of his full name. "Maybe I haven't, but I know you pretty well, Miss—*Doctor* Zarah Victoria Mitchell." Just how well, he didn't want to admit. He still hadn't compiled the complete profile on her, but right now, he probably knew more about her than she knew about herself.

"Yeah, well, I know you pretty well, too, and I know you have a tendency to see things the way you want to see them. Anyway"—she pressed the handkerchief back into his hand—"I'm not supposed to be carrying on a civil conversation with you. I'm supposed to raise my chin and look the other way."

"Is that what Flannery told you to do?" He tucked the hankie back into his pocket.

"It was in an article she e-mailed me about what you're supposed to do when your ex comes back into your life." She turned and started digging in her big leather bag. "I'm supposed to make you jealous, too, by making sure you happen to run into me while I'm out on a date with some drop-dead gorgeous hunk."

All she had to do was talk to another man one-on-one and that made him jealous enough. "And was there anyone in particular you're planning on going out with to make me insanely jealous?" He thought through all the men in the singles' group he'd met so far. He couldn't imagine her going out with any of them—and several of them had admitted at that guys' night out a couple of weekends ago that they'd asked and she'd said no.

"Flannery has a list." Zarah finally found what she was looking for and pulled her hand out of her bag with her fingers wrapped around her keys.

"A list?"

"Yeah, authors, agents, business associates." Zarah's cheeks turned a little pink again.

"And do you want to go out with them?"

She shrugged. "I don't know any of them."

"Is that why you haven't dated since. . .moving to Nashville? Because you didn't know anyone who asked you out?"

"Oh, I've been out on a few dates. I've just found it. . .easier not to do that." Her expression sobered. "I think it's better for me if I don't date."

He turned sideways to face her. "Really? Why's that?"

Her eyes followed several people as they walked into the building. "Because that way I don't have to put someone though. . .through. . . well, through a whole lot of pain and suffering."

"You think that having a relationship with you is going to cause someone a whole lot of pain and suffering?" He reached over and took her hand in his. "I can tell you, that isn't the case."

She pulled her hand away from his, stood, slung her bag over her shoulder, and backed a few steps away from him. "Flannery asked me Sunday why I always expect things to turn out badly. It's because they do. Just look at us, Bobby. You know, in a way, I'm glad you wised up and walked away. If we'd stayed together, it would have been the worst mistake of our lives."

Tears once again swimming in her eyes, Zarah lingered a brief moment longer then dashed to her car and drove away.

"I'm glad you wised up and walked away."

She thought *he* had walked away from *her*? Of course that was what her father would have told her to get her to leave for college without even trying to say good-bye to him.

Bobby stood and dusted off the back of his pants before returning to his car. He'd head back to the office and get a couple more hours of work put in on completing Zarah's profile. Now, more than ever, he wanted to get her name cleared from the suspect list as soon as possible—so he could start rebuilding their relationship without that hanging over them.

She might assume things always turned out badly. But he had enough optimism for both of them.

Chapter 16

At ten o'clock Friday morning, Bobby ushered the two agents assigned to his case into his office, followed shortly thereafter by the unit's forensic accountant.

The time had come to discuss Zarah with his team.

He handed folders to the two men and one woman now sitting in the chairs they'd rolled in from the furniture storage closet next door. Four people in his tiny office made it nearly claustrophobic, but he didn't want to do this out on the floor where anyone could hear their conjectures, suspicions, and conclusions.

Bobby quickly went through the relevant details of Zarah's life: born in Georgia when her father was stationed at Fort Benning. Had lived in four different states and two foreign countries by the time she graduated from high school in New Mexico. Finished her BA in history at Vanderbilt in three years, then her master's and PhD in historic preservation at James Robertson University by the time she was twenty-five. Started working at the Middle Tennessee Historic Preservation Commission part-time when she was a graduate student, full-time after she finished her doctorate. Taught history as an adjunct professor at both the community college and JRU every semester since finishing school herself. Had been promoted to assistant director and senior preservationist two years ago.

"Now that you know the basics, I'll turn this over to Jill so she can review the financial records for us."

"Thanks." The middle-aged woman scooted forward in her seat. "If you'll turn to page ten of the dossier, you'll see my summary of Mitchell's financial records. There are a couple of unusual findings, though nothing irregular that I could find."

Bobby flipped to that page of the report, though he almost had it memorized by now.

"Dr. Mitchell has an unusually large life insurance policy for someone so young who is unmarried and has no children. That, combined with the fact that it's a term policy that will expire before she's sixty leads me to wonder why she would have chosen such a policy.

"Next, you'll see that she has a very large savings account—in addition to a few other large investment products, like CDs and money market accounts. From what I can tell, there have been no unusual or one-time large deposits to these accounts—but what is she socking away all this money for? She purchased a house five years ago. She paid off her car more than eight years ago. She paid off a twenty-year student loan in less than eight years."

Jill dipped her head and looked at Bobby over the rim of her readers. "If I didn't know any better, I'd think I'm looking at the financial records of someone who was putting her affairs in order."

"What do you mean? Affairs in order for what?" Gage, the younger of the two agents, asked the forensic accountant.

Instead of answering the young man, Jill kept her gaze on Bobby. "There's something going on in this woman's life to lead her to believe that she needs to get everything wrapped up before she's forty years old—because she's on track to have her house paid off by then. Either she's planning for a very early retirement, or there's something else going on. I know it's not my job to try to profile anyone, but I'm just telling you what the numbers are telling me—and they're telling me something's off about this woman. No one in their early thirties has financials like this."

Bobby cleared his throat—twice. What *was* Zarah socking all that money away for? "We'll look into that. You said there were a few things that caught your attention?"

"Yes. Seven years ago, over the course of about six months, Dr. Mitchell purchased eight airline tickets. Within a week of each of those, her bank account showed restaurant and other charges in Houston, Texas. No hotel charges, though. So I cross-referenced this suspect's file with the other suspect in the case. . .Forrester. Not only did Forrester already own several properties in Houston—including a small boutique hotel, at which I believe Dr. Mitchell most likely stayed during her trips there, as many of the restaurants she charged meals at are near it—but during the six months that Mitchell made these eight trips, Forrester made several additional real estate transactions in Houston. His accounts show that he made three trips to Houston during corresponding dates when Dr. Mitchell was there."

Bobby's heart sank. She'd traveled with her boss? What sway did that man hold over her? What had he dragged her into?

"She has also made several trips to northern Virginia and Washington DC throughout the years, and there have been some crossovers with Forrester's accounts there as well."

Bobby's stomach churned the longer Jill talked. If he didn't know Zarah—or believe he knew her based on what he'd *known* of her— he'd be as suspicious of her activities as the other three people in the room appeared to be. The fact of the matter was that he was making some pretty big assumptions about her from things she'd shared with him a decade and a half ago—almost half their lifetimes. A lot could change in that many years, especially for someone as eager to please others as Zarah was.

Once Jill finished her overview of Zarah's financial records, she left the room. Gage and Milligan shoved the extra chair out into the hallway and leaned forward on the edge of Bobby's desk.

"So, what do you say? Sounds like she's involved in one way or another with this Forrester's real estate schemes. Where are his records?" Milligan shrugged out of his suit coat and rolled up his sleeves.

"Why do you believe she's involved?" Bobby rocked back, remembering too late that the spring was loose. He caught the edge of his desk to keep from flipping backward out of the chair.

"Right now, it's all circumstantial," Gage said, frowning over the page summarizing Zarah's financial information. "But it does point toward her involvement."

"Involvement in what?" Milligan demanded. "We haven't seen Forrester's records yet. The only thing she might be involved in is possibly some real estate transactions in Houston seven years ago."

"Well. . .and involved with Forrester. I mean, they have been traveling together."

Bobby bit his tongue so hard it made his eyes water. But it was either that or punch out Gage. And he didn't think it would look good at his ninety day employment review to have to explain why he'd decked a subordinate.

"Again, circumstantial," Milligan muttered, buried in the dossier. He flipped back to the opening pages of the profile. "There isn't really much in here about her family. Other than her father's being in the army, what else is known about her family?"

Bobby crossed his arms. "She has one sister—older. Her mother died when Z—Dr. Mitchell was eight years old. Cancer. Mitchell left home at eighteen and moved to Nashville. Her grandparents live here, and she is close with them. Her father, now a three-star general, has been at the Pentagon since 2001—survived the 9/11 attack." He'd been surprised to find that tidbit of information on the man who'd ruined his life.

"Any info on the whereabouts of the sister?" Gage asked.

Bobby turned to his computer and pulled up his saved search for Zarah. Backtracking through her information, it only took him a couple of minutes to find the sister's birth certificate and—

"Well, this could explain why Dr. Mitchell made so many trips to Houston. The sister, Phoebe Mitchell, died there six and a half years ago. Official cause of death. . ." The text on the screen stabbed through him. "Official cause of death is overdose of prescription pain medication. Ruled suicide. Apparently she was being treated for cancer, though."

Oh, Zarah. Not your sister, too.

"So the mother and sister both had cancer? Could that be why Mitchell is putting her affairs in order, as Jill said?" Milligan asked. "What if Mitchell has found out that she has cancer—or the gene for it? There are some kinds of cancers that are genetic."

Bobby's hands drew into fists. Not Zarah. God wouldn't let that happen. Not to her. Not now, not when he could see the chance of eventually having her back in his life.

"I don't know." Gage drew out his words as if weighing each one before speaking it. "I have a hard time believing that anyone who is so careful with her own money would be involved in any kind of fraud. Besides, if Forrester was involved in some kind of real estate fraud in Houston, Mitchell's accounts don't show any evidence that she derived any financial reward, either from him or from the transactions."

"Secret or off-shore accounts we didn't find?" Milligan postulated.

Gage shook his head. "Why would she keep so much money in these accounts if she had some secret stash elsewhere? Why not keep just a nominal amount in her regular accounts and transfer all the rest of this to her secret stash? No, once her savings account grew to the maximum level, it looks like she started investing in CDs and money market accounts. Someone who has off-shore accounts wouldn't leave this much just sitting around."

Bobby cheered slightly. The kid was right—and Bobby had investigated enough financial fraud cases to back up the statement.

"Unless she's someone who expects her accounts to be examined and created this kind of financial trail to throw us off."

On the other hand, Milligan could be correct. There were some people who were savvy enough to plant evidence to point toward their innocence. Could Zarah be one of them?

"If she does have a more-than-professional relationship with Forrester, he could have accounts set up for her that we don't know about yet." Gage frowned as he looked from Milligan to Bobby. "When are we going to get the full profile on Forrester?"

Bobby pulled his mind back from the whirlwind of conjecture and speculation about Zarah. "Jill told me it would probably be the beginning of next week before she finishes analyzing Forrester's financials." He rubbed the back of his neck. "Let's reconvene next Wednesday after the weekly unit briefing. Until then, keep researching the background of the real estate and contractor companies involved before and after the injunctions and sales of the land tracts the MTHPC has been involved in over the past ten years."

"Yes, boss."

"Yes, sir."

Gage and Milligan moved the extra chairs back out of Bobby's office. He stood and closed the door behind them. He needed time to think. . .and pray.

"Dr. Mitchell, you have a guest in the museum."

"Thanks, Debby." Zarah hung up the phone and blew out a nervous breath and grabbed the last file she needed to take home this weekend. Ever since leaving church Wednesday evening, her conversation with Bobby hadn't stopped running through her head.

And now she would have to face him again—one-on-one, with no buffer of other people around. She stuck the file into her bag, flung it over her shoulder, and turned the office light off.

"I don't believe it."

She turned at Dennis's voice. "Don't believe what?"

"Well, when you said you wanted to take a half day today, I figured you meant you'd be leaving at three thirty or four o'clock." Dennis looked at his tasteful, but expensive, watch. "It's barely one thirty."

"Yep—and there's nothing you can do to make me stay, either." Zarah grinned at him, even though nerves continued to riot in her stomach at the thought of Bobby waiting for her downstairs.

Dennis's left brow raised. "Really?" He chuckled. "You know I wouldn't do that to you. Have a great weekend, kiddo." He turned to go back into his office. "I hope you're not taking more than ten or twelve hours' worth of work home with you."

"Only about eight." She patted the leather carryall. "See you Monday."

At the bottom of the stairs, she took another deep breath and squared her shoulders before opening the AUTHORIZED PERSONNEL ONLY door into the museum. She cut through the Tennessee Centennial exhibit to get to the front counter where Debby, who served both as the admissions cashier for the museum and an administrative assistant for Zarah, sat working on the computer.

But no Bobby.

Zarah paused, confused, then continued on to the desk. "Where. . . ?"

Debby looked up. "Oh, he's wandering around the museum. I didn't charge him for admission, since I figured he wouldn't be here long enough to justify it." The middle-aged woman winked.

"Thanks for that." Zarah hefted her bag onto the raised counter and pulled out the envelope containing the three tickets for Bobby. "I'll be back for this in a minute."

" 'Kay." Debby went back to her work.

Zarah turned and scanned the main area of the museum that covered more than five thousand square feet. At his height, Bobby should have been easy to spot—but she didn't see him. She headed toward the Pre-statehood Room, then on into the Founding of Nashville exhibit. Still no Bobby.

The Early Frontier Room led to the largest exhibit at the back of the building—the Civil War Room.

The fluttery feeling returned full force at the sight of Bobby standing under the portrait of Zander and Madeleine Breitinger and gazing up at her ancestors.

"Who were they?" Bobby asked without turning around.

"My great-great-great-grandparents." Zarah wasn't sure why she felt the need to speak in a tone just above a whisper, but she was pretty sure speaking at full volume would have sounded almost vulgar in this moment.

Bobby finally turned, a slight smile easing his face which, with all of its angles and planes, could be quite severe. "I can't wait to hear this story."

"Okay—trade places with me so you can have the full effect." Zarah pulled Bobby's sleeve and took his place under the image, which she displayed with her best Vanna White impression. "This is Zander and Madeleine Breitinger, my ancestors. As with many people from that era, they were not born in this country but had been brought here by their families when they were very young. Zander's family, the Breitingers, and Madeleine's aunt and uncle, who took her in when she was orphaned as a baby, all settled just north of Nashville—in what is now known as Germantown. . . ."

She watched Bobby's expression carefully as she got further into the story she knew so well and had recited so many times. He stood stock-still, hands clasped behind his back, eyes fixed on the image, a slightly bemused expression on his handsome face.

"With nothing left, and no hope that Zander would ever return, Madeleine agreed to return to Germany with her aunt and uncle." Zarah's voice cracked—and Bobby's eyes locked with hers.

"But that's not the end of their story," he said softly. "You like happy endings, so you wouldn't have chosen this couple's picture to display if they didn't somehow have a happy ending."

Zarah raised her left brow—a little something she'd picked up from Dennis—and cocked her head. "Really? You know most stories like this have tragic endings. Remember the letter quoted in Ken Burns's *Civil War* series?"

"The one that was on the soundtrack you used to make me listen to over and over and over and over and then he died in battle right after he wrote it?"

The teasing lilt in his voice coaxed out the smile she'd been trying to hide. "Yes, the letter you could quote to me verbatim shortly after we met—before I ever made you listen to that soundtrack. That had a tragic ending."

"But this story doesn't. So get on with it." He waved his hand in the air as if a TV director instructing someone to wrap up a segment.

Zarah heaved a put-upon sigh. "Fine. But I don't know if you're going to like how this ends, coming into it with such a preconceived notion. Madeleine returned with her family to Bavaria, but she left her heart behind in Tennessee. . . ."

She ignored Bobby's smug expression when she got to the part about Madeleine's inability—or unwillingness—to find a man who could replace her husband, and the knowing wink when she got to the part about Karl Alexander's leaving for America.

"With a map drawn by his great-uncle, Karl made his way to where the farm had been. Expecting to find a pile of burned-out rubble obscured by more than fifteen years of overgrowth, he was shocked to find a large white farmhouse looking exactly the way his mother and great-uncle and great-aunt had always described their home—"

"I hope I'm not interrupting something important."

Zarah jumped—almost dropping the photograph of Karl Breitinger—and Bobby whipped around as if ready to defend himself.

Senator Todd Warren trailed a finger along one of the artifact display cases and came to a stop closer to Zarah than she was comfortable with.

Under the pretense of putting the smaller picture back where it belonged, she stepped away from him. "Senator Warren, I. . .wasn't expecting you. Did I forget an appointment?"

There had been no appointment. She wouldn't have forgotten something like that. Not even with as distracted as thoughts of Bobby and the brouhaha over the singles' ministry had made her this week.

"No. I was in the neighborhood and thought I'd stop by for that five-dollar tour followed by coffee you promised." Todd Warren flashed his megawatt smile at her, all the while looking strangely out of place standing here, in her favorite spot in the building.

"Dr. Mitchell," Bobby said behind her, and she gratefully turned to face him—but almost wished she hadn't when she caught the severe set to his massive jaw. "Obviously you have important things to which you need to attend, and I really should be getting back to work. So if I can get those tickets from you, I won't keep you any longer."

No. Why, when everything had been going so well, did something have to happen to ruin it again?

Maybe it was a sign. Maybe she and Bobby just weren't meant to be.

Then why, just moments ago, standing here under the softly smiling faces of her ancestors, had she believed that she could have her own happy ending, just like she used to dream?

She pulled the envelope out of her jacket pocket and handed it to him. "I'll—" Should she forewarn him she'd be there tomorrow? Why—to have him decide to not go? "Thank you for going to the trouble of coming down here to pick them up."

Bobby gave a curt nod to both her and Senator Warren and marched out of the room.

Zarah tried to borrow some of his starch for her own spine. She plastered on a smile before turning to face the senator. "Senator Warren, I'm sorry you came all this way just to be disappointed. I was actually on my way out. But we can go up to the front desk, and Debby can pull my schedule up on her computer so we can set an appointment for sometime next week."

Before she could get Todd Warren to leave, Zarah had to agree to letting him take her out for lunch instead of coffee, followed by a personal tour of the museum and offices and labs upstairs. He even said he wanted to see the artifact storage and preparation rooms in the basement.

Even though Debby's desk now separated them, he lingered over shaking her hand. "I'll see you next Wednesday, Dr. Mitchell. And maybe then I can convince you to call me Todd outside of the committee chamber." He winked at her, then at Debby, before making his exit.

As soon as the door shut behind him, Debby let out a soft wolf whistle. "My goodness, Dr. M., it doesn't rain, but it pours. I had high hopes when the first young man came in here looking for you, but then when another one came in asking after you, I knew my prayers had finally been answered."

"Your prayers?" Zarah picked up her bag from the counter.

"Yeah—my prayers that some handsome young buck would come sweep you off your feet. Looks like I've been praying a little *too* hard." Debby chuckled, still looking at the door.

Zarah slung her bag onto her shoulder and rounded the desk. "Well, at least now I know who to blame when they don't work out."

The door closed behind her on Debby's laugher. Zarah's smile faded in the bright sunlight. Why did she always assume things would take a turn for the worse?

Because they usually did.

She paused, hand on the car door's handle. No. She didn't want to live her life that way.

"Lord, You've helped me overcome my pessimism before. Help me to be open to all opportunities and to see the good in those around me." *And to believe my heart when it says Bobby and I have another chance.*

Chapter 17

$\mathcal{E}$scape and quiet beckoned beyond the sliding glass doors. Bobby nodded in greeting to a couple of co-workers who leaned against the deck railing but moved quickly beyond them, around the corner of the house. He sank onto the top of the steps leading down into Chase and Michaelle Denney's backyard and leaned his elbows heavily against his knees.

At the end of the day, he had no clarity, no certainty, no lessening of his confusion over the data presented him this morning by the forensic accountant or from the questions raised by Gage and Milligan afterward, further compounded by the way his emotions overrode everything else when he was near Zarah as she told the story of her ancestors and the intense jealousy that flared up when Senator Warren arrived.

If Chase hadn't stopped by his office to give him directions here tonight, Bobby would still be in his office running the background search on State Senator Todd Warren.

"Bobby, dude, what is up with you tonight?" Chase lowered himself onto the step beside Bobby with a groan.

Bobby turned to look over his shoulder at his fellow agent but couldn't find the strength or energy to sit up straight. "Sorry—I'm being a rotten guest. I probably should have just gone straight home tonight."

"You've been like this all day. Something's obviously bothering you, and I have a feeling it has something to do with the meeting you had with your team this morning. And you were in a pretty foul mood when you came back from that lunch meeting."

"I almost married her, you know."

"Married. . .who?" Chase turned and leaned against the stair railing.

"Zarah Mitchell—Assistant Director and Senior Preservationist at the Middle Tennessee Historic Preservation Commission. And number-two suspect in my investigation."

Chase let out a whistle. "You said you knew her, but—she's your ex? Does the captain know?"

"No. And unless I'm certain it'll compromise the case, I don't intend to tell him."

"Do you think she's guilty?"

"No." Bobby sighed. "At least I don't *want* to believe she's guilty. But there are enough questions about her—legitimate concerns over some of her background and activities and finances—that I can't be 100 percent certain."

"What do you *know*? What are the facts?"

Bobby ran through Zarah's basic profile, including some generalizations about her financial information.

When he finished, Chase waited a long moment before speaking again. "What does your gut tell you?"

"That she's innocent. But that's my quandary—do I feel that way because I still harbor romantic feelings toward her after all these years?"

"How did you meet this woman?"

Bobby glanced up at the stars, then closed his eyes. The image of the general's home—that big, expensively appointed house—came clearly to mind. "The general I served under at White Sands invited the members of the team I was attached to over to his house for Thanksgiving dinner. There was this beautiful young woman who appeared to be part of the catering staff; and, since I didn't really fit in with the officers who were there, I made my way to the kitchen and offered to help out so that I could flirt with her. Even after I found out she was the general's younger daughter, I couldn't help myself."

Bobby pulled out his wallet. From the pocket behind his credit cards, he withdrew a frayed, rumpled photo and handed it to Chase. "I have carried that picture around with me for more than fourteen years."

Chase held Zarah's senior picture up to the light coming from the house's windows. "Wow. I can see why you were interested." He handed the picture back.

Bobby pressed it between his palms. "Zarah was a senior in high school when we met—seventeen years old. So not only was she off-limits because her father had forbidden her from dating enlisted men, but she was underage, as well. I should have run—not walked—away. But I didn't. I couldn't. I knew from that first afternoon we spent together working alongside the hired caterers in her father's kitchen that I was supposed to marry this girl."

"So you kept seeing her?"

Bobby nodded. "Yeah. Since they lived over the mountain in Las Cruces, it was easier than if they'd lived on base. It was expected that soldiers would either go over into Las Cruces or down to El Paso or Juarez during off-hours. Zarah's older sister, Phoebe, attended New Mexico State and lived on campus. Zarah had a car, and we would meet at Phoebe's dorm so that Zarah didn't have to lie to her father about where she was going when she left the house. She was so concerned about that—she hated the fact that she couldn't be completely honest with her father about our relationship. So she did whatever she could to make sure she could be as honest as possible with him."

The appetizers Bobby had managed to get down half an hour ago turned sour in his stomach. "Why she felt like she owed that horrible excuse for a father anything. . ."

"Her father?"

"Yeah. . .she told me some of the things he said to her—privately, of course, never in public. The more kind things were that she was worthless and wouldn't amount to anything."

Chase breathed a sigh. "He said that? To her?"

Bobby nodded slowly. "Phoebe, the older daughter, could do no wrong, apparently. Zarah could do nothing right. She was so timid when I first met her, but after we'd been seeing each other a couple of months, she started coming out of her shell. She has a dry sense of humor that took me by surprise when she first started letting it show. I wanted to do everything I could to show her that everything her father said about her and to her was wrong, that she was smart and beautiful and very, very important. I think I was the first person who ever told her she was beautiful."

"I'm surprised she didn't have boys lined up."

"With a father like hers? No, she was too shy and self-deprecating. High school boys don't know how to deal with that." Bobby arched his back, and it popped in a couple of places. "We started seeing each other secretly in December. In May, she was graduating from high school, the salutatorian of her class—she was going to give a speech at her graduation and would get physically ill whenever she thought about it."

He smiled. "She practiced that speech so many times with me, I can still remember most of it—and I couldn't even be there to hear her give it at the ceremony. I was on duty. She'd been offered a scholarship to several colleges, including Vanderbilt. She'd told me her grandparents—her mother's parents—lived here in Nashville. I knew that if she could get away from her father, away from his verbal and emotional abuse, she'd continue growing into the person I saw the potential for. But I also didn't want to take the chance of letting her move here without a guarantee that she wouldn't go off and fall in love with someone else."

"So you proposed?"

"I planned to. I scraped together enough money to buy an engagement ring with the smallest diamond in it you can possibly imagine, and planned, with her sister's help, a special date for the night of her eighteenth birthday—the day after her high school graduation."

That day—May 19—came into such clear focus in his mind's eye that he could almost reach out and touch the general's desk.

"So what happened?"

"That morning—of the day I was going to propose—the general ordered me into his office. He told me Zarah had confessed to him about our relationship because she wanted to get out of it, wanted to break up with me, but didn't know how to. He said he'd sent her away for her own protection—for protection from me—and I was to have no further contact with her."

"So how long did you wait until you saw her again?"

"Fourteen years. I didn't see her again, didn't have any contact with her, until a couple of weeks ago, right after I got back to town. I ran into her at a church-group party." The memory of the expression of horrified astonishment on Zarah's face even as the beans slopped over the side of the pan in her hands brought a guilty grimace to Bobby's face.

"Don't tell me you believed her father's explanation."

"At the time, I was so hurt and angry at the idea that she could have told her father about us, I hate to admit it, but I did believe him." Bobby rubbed his thumb against the soft edge of Zarah's picture.

"And now?"

"He had to have learned about us from someone else. We were discreet, but Las Cruces was a small city."

"She's still single after all these years?" Humor laced Chase's deep voice.

"Yes—and apparently hasn't really dated since. . .us." But was that because she still carried a torch for him or because she'd been involved with Forrester for the past ten years? Somehow, he just couldn't see it. Not Zarah. Not with her boss.

"And you're still in love with her."

Bobby sat up straight. "That sounds more like a statement than a question."

"You carry her picture around with you fourteen years after you broke up. I'm just using deductive reasoning." Chase shifted position. "She still goes to church?"

"Heavily involved in leadership of the singles' group at the church I grew up in." Bobby slid the photo into the pocket of his denim shirt.

"Does she wear a lot of expensive jewelry? Drive a fancy car? Live in a big house?"

Did she wear any jewelry? Just that long gold chain with the big pendant that she toyed with and looked at occasionally. No rings, no bracelets. Last Sunday, when she'd had her hair pulled up, she'd been wearing small diamond earrings. Very classy, but not overly expensive or in the least flashy.

Her car. That little Honda had to be at least ten years old. . . . He smiled over the memory of driving her home that first night. And he knew exactly how much she'd paid for that house—his condo cost almost twice what she'd gotten the house for.

"No, no, and no."

Chase sighed. "Sounds to me like there's a reason God has brought this woman back into your life. I believe it's so you can prove her innocence and keep her from being brought down by whatever's going on where she works."

He stood, using Bobby's shoulder to push himself up. "Look, Patterson. In a case like this, with the circumstantial evidence that points to her guilt, we would typically go after her with all guns blazing, hoping to get her to turn evidence on her boss—and if not, to at least convict her of something, even if we weren't sure she's guilty. You know how it goes—captain and director want cases closed and people convicted. I truly believe this has all fallen in your lap because you've been sent here to protect her."

Bobby turned sideways and looked up at his co-worker. "So I'm her guardian angel, is that it?"

"Something like that. Clear her name and then marry the poor girl. You've made her wait way too long already."

The last few notes of "Seventy Six Trombones" echoed through the auditorium, nearly drowned out by the applause of the opening-night crowd.

Zarah once again found herself trying to move farther down the pew-style seat to keep Mr. Big-time Author from pressing his arm against hers. She wasn't certain if it was his constant invasion of her personal space that bothered her or if it was the fact that Flannery had invited him to come tonight without warning her—or if she was overly sensitive to the situation because of the incident with Bobby and Todd this afternoon.

One thing was certain—she and Flannery would be having words.

The college's small marching band struck up the song again as the players came out on stage for the curtain call. The minor characters first, in groups, then the more important characters.

Finally, when the audience was already in a near frenzy, Caylor and the actor portraying Harold Hill's sidekick stepped forward. Zarah jumped to her feet with a whoop. Flannery stood and pressed her fingertips to her lips and let out a piercing whistle. More than half the audience stood and cheered and whistled for them, too.

The two students portraying Marian Paroo and Harold Hill made their bows, to a fully standing ovation.

"I think this is the best performance they've done yet," Flannery yelled over the din.

"I think you're right."

After the directors came out and received flowers, Harold Hill jumped back up on stage and led the audience in singing "Seventy-Six Trombones."

Zarah sang along at the top of her lungs, safe in the knowledge that between the band, the microphoned actors, and everyone else in the audience singing, no one could hear that she couldn't carry a tune in a bucket.

Laughing, she and Flannery collapsed back onto their seats while the nearly full house dispersed, crowding the doorways.

One of the single moms from the Sunday school class leaned around Flannery and squeezed Zarah's hand. "Great idea, Zarah. Thanks so much for suggesting it. The kids had a ball!"

"I'm so glad you could come." Zarah squeezed the woman's hand, happy in the secret pleasure of having paid for the three kids' tickets herself instead of taking the money from the Sunday school class's Fun Fund as she'd led her to believe had happened.

To Zarah's left, Mr. Big-time Author pulled out a small notebook and scribbled something in it. "Story idea?"

He nodded. "They strike at the most unusual times."

Like during one of Caylor's best scenes, when he'd spent five minutes writing, the sound of his nubby pencil's scratching on the paper rasping Zarah's nerves like a cheese grater.

"Look." He turned sideways on the pew and addressed both Zarah and Flannery. "I hope you don't mind if I bug out on y'all tonight, but I've got some great ideas flowing and I really want to get home and get them written down before I lose them."

"Sure, no problem—"

Flannery elbowed Zarah. "Oh, must you go so early?"

" 'Fraid so. When the muse calls, I must obey." He held his hand over his heart and bowed, which looked rather ridiculous from a seated position. He stood and tucked the small notebook into his shirt pocket.

Zarah stood and extended her right hand. "It was great to meet you. Good luck with your book."

He pressed her hand between his. "Luck has nothing to do with it, mademoiselle. 'Tis blood, sweat, and tears."

Zarah sat again, and he leaned over her to press his cheek to Flannery's and give an air-kiss. "Lunch next week?"

"I'll check my schedule tonight and shoot you a text." Flannery watched him wend through the crowd until he disappeared, then turned narrowed eyes on Zarah. "You can't possibly tell me you don't like him."

"Like him? I think my left arm is chafed from where he kept rubbing up against me."

"Oh yeah. I should have forewarned you—he's not really big into the idea of personal space. Sorry. But you'll go out with him if he calls and asks, right?"

If it were a choice between him and Todd Warren, she'd choose Mr. No Personal Space. But she already had a date, of sorts, set up with the toothy senator. "I suppose so. If he calls and asks me out and I don't already have plans."

"That's my girl."

"Yeah, well, next time I'd appreciate a little forewarning before you show up with one of the guys off your list."

Flannery grinned shamelessly. "But where's the fun in that? You'd just say no."

"I might surprise you and say yes."

They discussed the highlights of the performance while the auditorium cleared.

"Think we can get to her now? They should still be out in the lobby area." Flannery looked over her shoulder toward the doors.

"Yep. I don't want to miss getting an opening-night picture of the three of us together with her still in her costume." Zarah powered on her digital camera, already loaded with tons of pictures of the performance.

She followed Flannery into the lobby. The biggest crowds were around the students who'd been in key roles. Only a few people stood around Caylor, who beamed and hopped up and down when she saw Zarah and Flannery. She excused herself and jogged toward them and threw her arms around both of them at the same time.

"Wasn't it fantastic? Oh, I'm so glad you could come tonight. It was perfect. Only a couple of little errors, and I doubt anyone even noticed." She babbled for a few more moments. "Did you bring your camera? We need a picture."

"Yeah, so twenty years from now we can compare it to what you *actually* look like as a fifty-year-old woman." Flannery looked pointedly at the special-effects makeup that gave Caylor an aged look and the streaks of silver in the big red Gibson-girl wig she wore.

Caylor called a student over to take the pictures. They took a few normally posed shots, then started acting silly—those were always the best shots, even though Zarah hated the attention that making faces and standing in silly positions drew.

"So really, how did it go? Really? Honestly, now."

Zarah and Flannery exchanged a glance. Flannery winked. "Honestly? You were flat on both of your solos, and your fake Irish accent stinks."

Caylor leaned so far back when she laughed that Zarah was afraid the wig might fall off. But it survived, and Caylor straightened, arms wrapped around her stomach. "Ouch. Laughing and corsets don't go together."

"You're wearing a corset?" Zarah reached out to feel Caylor's waist. Caylor had looked much slimmer than usual on stage, but the last couple of times she'd run into Caylor on campus or seen her at what was becoming their regular Sunday afternoon coffee, Caylor's clothes had looked like they were hanging on her.

"It's not a true corset. It's one of those long-line bustier bras. Only way I could fit into this dress without my top tummy roll showing. Can I borrow a pen?" She reached for Zarah's purse and pulled one out and promptly used it to scratch her head through the wig. "So who was that beautiful man sitting next to you tonight, Zarah?"

"You—you could see him?"

"Sure, during the curtain calls and when everyone was singing and the house lights were up. So, who is he?"

"He's one of Flannery's author friends."

"And. . . ?" Caylor raised her eyebrows, creating even more wrinkles in her artificially wrinkled forehead.

"And what? He had to go home because his muse called and told him he was out past his bedtime or something."

Flannery made a sharp sound in the back of her throat. "That's not what happened. He got an idea and wanted to get home to write before he forgot it. You understand that, don't you, Caylor?"

Caylor, who'd had six romance novels hit national bestseller lists before she switched to writing sweet and inspirational romances, shrugged. "I don't know. If I'm out and an idea for a scene strikes, I write it down in my notebook and then go back to what I'm doing."

"See?" Zarah hooked her arm through Caylor's. "He wasn't any more interested in me than I am in him."

"No, he's just not still in love with someone who broke his heart half a lifetime ago." Flannery crossed her arms. "You saw him today, didn't you?"

"Him?" Zarah tried to affect an innocent expression. "Him who? Senator Warren? Yes, I saw him this afternoon."

The astonished expressions on both Flannery's and Caylor's faces were worth knowing she'd have to tell them the full story now.

One good thing about Bobby's coming home and Senator Todd Warren's intrusion into her life: now *she,* Zarah Mitchell, was the one with man problems to talk about instead of always listening to Caylor or Flannery talking about their dating issues.

Hopefully tomorrow she'd have a chance to see if Bobby's coming home would bring other good things back into her life. Like his respect, admiration, and love.

Chapter 18

Trina paced the square layout of the first floor of the house—from kitchen to dining room to living room and into the entry hall, pausing at the front door each time she passed.

Lindy had sounded agitated on the phone—and that was so unlike her friend. Lindy could be high-strung and was very excitable but rarely anxious or worried. Not when her son had been in Vietnam nor when her grandson had been in the Middle East.

"Will you sit down already?" Victor looked up from his book when she entered the living room again. "Your wearing out the varnish on the floor isn't going to make her get here any faster."

"Something's wrong. I know it is. Why wouldn't she tell me on the phone whatever it is? Why did she have to come tell me face-to-face?" Trina stopped and straightened the already-straight books stuffed into the bookcase behind her husband.

"I'm certain there's a reasonable explanation that doesn't warrant—"

"Greeley has cancer—*she* has cancer!" She grabbed the back of the wingback chair in which Victor sat as though he had not a care in the world.

"Has she gone to the doctor recently?" Victor removed his reading glasses and twirled them with his hand.

"No—not that she told me. But maybe she didn't want me to worry—"

The doorbell rang. Ignoring the arthritic ache in both knees, Trina bolted for the front door. The square frosted glass in the top half of the door revealed Lindy's tall, trim figure.

Trina flung the door open. "What is it? Are you all right? What can I do for you?"

Lindy's face registered her surprise. "Do for me? What are you talking about?"

Trina ushered her into the house. "Just tell me straight out. I can take it. Are you sick? Is it cancer?"

Lindy threw her head back and laughed, showing all her teeth—and she had lots of prominent ones. "I'm not sick. No, Greeley isn't sick, either. No one in the family is sick as far as I know. I shouldn't have sounded so mysterious over the phone obviously." She grabbed Trina's hand and started past the stairs toward the passageway to the kitchen.

In the living room, Victor looked up from his book. "Mornin', Melinda."

"Good morning, Victor. I'm just going to take Trina to the kitchen so that we don't disturb you." Lindy pulled Trina into the kitchen and slid the pocket doors shut behind them.

Knees aching, Trina sat down at the kitchen table. "What is going on?"

As if it were her kitchen instead of Trina's, Lindy filled the kettle with water and put it on the stove then retrieved two teacups from the cabinet to the right of the stove and two teabags from a canister on the counter.

"You remember our little project?"

Trina shook her head, frowning. "Project?"

"Our grandchildren." Lindy leaned a hip against the cabinet.

"The setups we're supposed to be doing? I haven't been able to get Zarah nailed down for a date in October for us to have the family cookout."

"I haven't been able to get a date out of my grandson, either. But that's what I wanted to talk to you about."

The kettle whistled, and Lindy stopped to pour the steaming water into the cups and carry them to the table.

"Go on, please." Trina took her cup and saucer and set it on the table for the tea to steep.

"I told you Robert has purchased a condominium over near Hillsboro Village and that he hopes to move by the end of the month." Lindy dunked her bag repeatedly in her cup.

"Yes. Do you think that will create more of a problem with trying to set him up with one of our granddaughters?"

"Perhaps. But I have reason to believe that you and I may not have much to worry about." A coy grin danced around Lindy's wide mouth.

Her earlier anxiety gone, curiosity took a foothold—cautious curiosity, though, as Trina still couldn't be certain how much Bobby had told his grandmother about his prior relationship with Zarah.

"Because Robert has been working such long hours, I volunteered to do his laundry for him this weekend so that he could get some rest and start packing what he's had to use since he's been living with us."

Trina pulled her teabag out of the cup and added two sugar cubes to it. "Very thoughtful of you to ask instead of just doing it."

"I know. I thought so, too." Lindy squeezed out her teabag and set it on the saucer before adding four sugar cubes to her cup. "Well, having always had boys and men in the house, I learned a long time ago to check the pockets before putting anything in the washer. And in the pocket of the shirt Robert was wearing last night, I discovered this."

Trina looked down at the object Lindy slid across the corner of the table toward her. She gasped.

"Recognize it?"

"Recognize it—I have the eight by ten hanging on my wall in the hallway." She picked up Zarah's senior picture. The white edges around the image were no longer white but smudged, not sharp but soft, almost featherlike, indicating years of handling. She turned it over and recognized Zarah's handwriting on the back. "*To my one and only. Love, Z.*"

Trina looked up at Lindy—who regarded her with narrowed eyes.

"There's something you haven't told me about your granddaughter and my grandson, isn't there?"

"Zarah asked me not to tell anyone. Not even you." *Especially not you.* Trina looked again at the picture. Though smiling, Trina recognized the emptiness in Zarah's eyes—the emptiness that had been almost overshadowed by pain when she'd arrived, unannounced, on their doorstep to tell them her father had kicked her out of the house and she had nowhere else to go. Between the emotional trauma inflicted on her by her father and that of having the man she thought was the love of her life walk out on her, Zarah had seemed unlikely to ever recover. But she had.

She fingered the soft edge of the photo and then looked up at Lindy again. "Wait—you said you found this in Bobby's shirt pocket? A shirt he was wearing just yesterday?"

Lindy nodded, eyes bright with excitement. "He told me that he knew Zarah when he was stationed in New Mexico and that they didn't part on good terms. But I read what she wrote on the back of that picture, which leads me to believe he meant they broke up after dating for a while."

Breaking up was putting it lightly.

"But I can only assume that if he's still carrying her picture around with him all these years later, he must still have feelings for her. Has Zarah said anything to you about him? I know they've seen each other several times, as they're in the same Sunday school class."

Trina took a few sips of tea to give herself time to formulate an answer that wouldn't reveal any secrets. "She mentioned running into him at the singles' party before Labor Day. She hasn't really said much else about it." Not that she could repeat, anyway.

'"Well, he's going with us to see that musical this afternoon. I understand Zarah is going with y'all?"

"She is."

"Well, then, we'll just have to watch them to see what happens and how they act around each other. And maybe, with a little hint here and there, it won't be long until they realize they're still in love with each other and"—Lindy waggled her eyebrows—"I can almost hear the great-grandbabies crying now."

Chapter 19

$\mathcal{P}$eople in their midthirties who complained about feeling old only needed to take a ride in the backseat of their grandmother's Cadillac to feel twelve years old again. Of course, Greedad had offered to let Bobby sit in the front seat so he'd have more legroom, but Bobby wouldn't hear of his grandfather trying to get in and out of the backseat. So he folded himself into it instead.

Of course, if Mamm hadn't gotten back from running her errand just in the nick of time, Bobby could have ridden in comfort in Greedad's truck. But now they'd help the parking situation by arriving in only one vehicle. At least, that's how Mamm had convinced him to ride with them—by complaining of how little parking there was on campus.

As soon as she put the car in park—in what did turn out to be a very small parking lot—Bobby jumped out and opened her door for her.

She slipped her arm through his. "My grandson, the gentleman."

He shaded his eyes to look up at the massive columns extending the full height of the three-story building, lining the deep front porch. "This is the building the auditorium's in?"

"Yes, sir." Mamm tugged his arm to get him moving. "When we were in school here, it was where they held graduation and other all-school assemblies. Now there are far too many students for that—they hold those events over in the field house."

"It's hard to believe that all these years later, you still live within five minutes of your alma mater." He ascended the front steps ahead of his grandmother and opened the door for her.

"Thank you, dear."

The doors opened into a large foyer, which made the perfect theater-style lobby. He fished the tickets out of his shirt pocket and handed them to the young woman standing at the double doors leading into the auditorium.

"It's open seating, so please feel free to sit wherever you'd like."

"Thanks." He turned and waited for Mamm and Greedad to enter ahead of him. If the room hadn't already been half filled with senior adults, he might have been able to pick out Mamm's best friend. But it had been so many years since he'd seen Katrina Breitinger that he couldn't trust his memory.

"There they are."

Bobby looked in the direction of Mamm's wave. "Seems like they got here early enough to get good seats."

Mamm grabbed his hand and pulled him through the clumps of people impeding the aisles. The woman with the salt-and-pepper hair and a very prominent nose came out into the aisle and hugged Mamm like she hadn't seen her in ages, which Bobby knew wasn't the case. They'd seen each other on Thursday for their regular coffee date.

"Trina, Victor, you remember my grandson Robert."

Zarah's grandparents greeted him enthusiastically.

"And this is Celeste Evans. Her granddaughter is a professor here at JRU and is in the play." Mamm pulled forward a petite lady with white hair in a short, very modern style.

"Just call me Sassy. Everyone does."

He applied a cautious amount of pressure in returning Sassy's handshake; she was so tiny and frail-looking. "It's very nice to meet you, Sassy."

"Why don't you go on in, Robert. That way you won't have to be surrounded by all us old folks." Mamm waved him toward the pew Trina, Victor, and Sassy had stepped out from to greet them.

He started edging his way toward the end—and realized someone else was already sitting on the other end of the somewhat short pew.

No, not someone. Zarah.

He scooted the rest of the way down and, when she didn't look up from her program when he stood right beside her, he tapped her shoulder.

She finally looked up. Anxiety, chagrin, and pleasure all flashed through her blue eyes. "Hey."

"Hey, yourself. Move over. I want to sit on the end so I can stretch my leg out in the aisle if I need to."

With Bobby pressed as far against the pew in front of them as he could manage, Zarah slid down the bench, leaving him plenty of room at the end.

He sat, nearer to her than to the arm of the pew, then leaned closer—he could smell the fruity aroma of her hair. "I think you left something out when I told you I was going to come today with my grandparents."

"I. . .I didn't want you to change your mind." She once again kept her eyes pinned on the playbill.

Oh, if only she knew how much he wanted to spend time with her—and how bad an idea that was for his objectivity when it came to the case.

"So, that was State Senator Todd Warren." Bobby followed her lead and pretended to be more interested in reading the program than in looking at her.

"Yes. He's new on the committee I report to quarterly for the commission. At the last meeting, he asked me if I would give him a tour of the facility, since he'd never seen it."

Todd Warren. Thirty-seven years old. From the biggest town in the smallest senatorial district in the state—a district filled with his family, from what Bobby had been able to pull quickly from the Internet. The state elections board had investigated his campaign for allegedly tampering with the election, but Warren and his election committee had been exonerated—possibly because the judge was a fishing buddy of the former senator, Warren's great-uncle.

Bobby didn't trust him. But whether that had to do with his investigator's instinct or his jealousy, he couldn't be certain. And until he could figure that out, he didn't want to raise any red flags at work by initiating a background check on an elected official of the state. No matter that he was smarmy and had obviously made Zarah uncomfortable.

"So, what's this musical about?"

That succeeded in getting Zarah to look at him. "You've never seen *The Music Man?*"

He ducked his chin and raised his eyebrows. "Zare—think about it. Think about what you know of me and what my movie preferences are. Have you ever known me to willingly watch a musical?"

"It's been a long time. Things change."

"Certain things don't." Like how absolutely beautiful she was. "So, what's it about?"

"The musical does a pretty good job of explaining itself. I don't want you to lose the joy of learning the story as it goes along. I will tell you, though, it has one of those dreaded happy endings."

He leaned closer, so that his arm pressed lightly against hers. "Which reminds me, you never did finish telling me that story yesterday."

Goose bumps appeared on Zarah's arms. Bobby smiled. He loved that he still had that effect on her. He straightened, putting a little space between them again.

"Ah, Dr. Mitchell, imagine running into you here."

A vaguely familiar, short man with silvery dark hair and heavy dark eyebrows slid into the pew in front of them and leaned one knee on the seat.

"Dr. Forrester. I hoped you'd find the tickets I left for you yesterday."

Bobby's heart sank at the way Zarah's face lit up when greeting her boss. Could he, too, illicit the goose-bump reaction from her?

"Yes, thank you for that. I brought a couple of people from the city arts council and one of the theater reviewers for the paper. And who is this?" Dennis Forrester turned his professorial gaze on Bobby.

"Oh. . .sorry. Dennis Forrester, this is Bobby Patterson." She turned to Bobby. "Dennis is the president of the Middle Tennessee Historic Preservation Commission—my boss. Dennis, Bobby is an agent with the Tennessee Criminal Investigations Unit."

Bobby stood—towering over Forrester—and shook the man's hand. How could this man, with his earnest gaze and clean-cut, everyman appearance, be the same person who, on paper, looked like the mastermind of a huge real estate scam?

"It's nice to meet you, Dr. Forrester."

"And you, Agent Patterson." Forrester turned his attention back to Zarah. "I just wanted to thank you for your thoughtfulness and tell you that if you paid for those tickets, I'll be very unhappy."

Bobby sat down in time to see Zarah grin at her boss unrepentantly. "I'll never tell."

Forrester reached across the pew back separating them and tweaked Zarah's chin. "What am I going to do with you?"

"You could always fire me, I guess, as I'm stubborn, hardheaded, and don't listen to you."

Dennis tapped his forefinger against his lips as if seriously considering her suggestion. "No, that wouldn't do. I'll think of something fitting. I guess I could make you stay in DC longer than a week, just to get you out of my hair."

Bobby's head snapped around to Zarah, whose smile faded inexplicably.

"John would probably love to put me to work for however long you'd allow him to have me." The teasing lilt was gone from her voice, though she worked hard to keep her tone light. Had Forrester's suggestion that he might want her gone for a while really hit her that hard?

At the front of the auditorium, the orchestra began their warm-ups.

"I guess that's my cue to return to my seat. Agent Patterson"—Forrester held out his hand again, which Bobby shook—"so nice to meet you. Make sure our Zarah behaves herself—and that she didn't sneak any work in here with her." Forrester winked at Zarah and departed, just as someone else came along wanting the seat.

Dennis Forrester. Genuine guy—as he appeared? Or master manipulator? The sooner Bobby could get to the bottom of those questions, the better—for Zarah's sake and for his own peace of mind.

Zarah raised a shaking hand and covered her eyes. She'd almost blown everything by blurting out that Dennis might just lose her to the National Archives if he wasn't careful. She was of half a mind to cancel the interview. But she couldn't pass up this kind of opportunity.

"When do you leave for DC?" Bobby asked.

"A week from Sunday. I'm on loan to the American History Museum for a few days to help them sort through a bequest they received of memorabilia and artifacts from a family that lived in this area for generations." She glanced over her shoulder to make sure Dennis was out of earshot. "And I have a job interview with the National Archives while I'm up there."

Bobby looked like he'd been sucker punched. "A. . .job interview in DC? I didn't realize you were interested in leaving Nashville."

Goose bumps ran up and down her body again, and she shivered involuntarily at the disappointment in Bobby's tone. "I'm not. I want to stay here more than just about anything. But it's a once-in-a-lifetime opportunity just to get an interview with them. Of course, I'd have to get a second job just to afford rent up there."

"But you have—" Bobby stopped, jutting his jaw forward as if using his bottom teeth to catch words before they escaped.

"I have what?" She so wanted to run her finger along that jaw, just as she'd done years ago. But she didn't have the right. And even if she did, this wasn't the place for that kind of public display of affection.

"You have your house you could sell. Stacy told me you got it for a steal and that she's been trying to convince you to sell it because you could get more than twice what you paid for it. That's a pretty profit."

"But still not enough to afford something in DC or its suburbs."

The house lights lowered and the room went dark—thanks to the blackout blinds covering the three-story-tall windows that ran along the left side of the auditorium.

As familiar as Zarah was with this particular musical—and she'd seen this cast perform it once already—her attention focused more on Bobby and his reactions than on what was happening onstage. In the beginning he seemed to enjoy it; but as the story unfolded, he didn't react the way he should—the way everyone else in the audience did.

About halfway through the first act, Bobby's hands lay fisted atop his thighs. But at the end of the first act, when Marian Paroo tore the page out of the journal that would provide evidence of Harold Hill's guilt before giving the book to the mayor, Bobby crossed his arms.

The house lights rose, and when Zarah turned to look at Bobby, to ask him what he thought, she caught sight of a scowl before he quickly rearranged his expression into a smile and unfolded his arms.

"I'm almost afraid to ask you what you think of it so far."

Bobby glanced at the stage and then back at her. "The performances are great. Your friend—Caylor?—isn't really Irish, is she?"

"No. She spent a year in Britain—England, Ireland, and Scotland—working on her master's degree. She's always had an ear for accents, but she came back sounding like she'd grown up over there." Zarah curled the card stock program in her hands. "But what do you think of the story?"

Bobby pressed his lips together—making them almost entirely disappear. "Honestly?"

She nodded. "Honestly."

"It bothers me."

"Bothers you? In what way?" With Kiki having left to go to the restroom with Sassy and Lindy, Zarah turned sideways, leaning her arm against the seat back.

"Well. . .this Harold guy, he's a con man." Bobby's expression indicated this should be enough explanation.

But Zarah wasn't quite following him. "Right. That's who he is at the *beginning* of the story. I don't want to give away the ending, but most stories are about someone who needs to go through some kind of change—a metamorphosis—and grow into a better person. So they have to start out with flaws."

"Flaws? Zarah, the man's a criminal." Bobby nodded, red-faced, at the few people who turned at his raised voice. He turned to face her, his knee touching hers. "I'm just saying that I've had lots of experience with men like that over the past several years. They don't change their ways."

He looked so earnest, so concerned over the plight of the fictional people Harold Hill was in the process of swindling, that Zarah wanted to reach out and hug him. Instead, she leaned back a little. "It's called willing suspension of disbelief. You should try it."

Bobby ducked his head, a grin forming. "Fine. For your sake, I'll try to enjoy the rest of the play—I'll try to forget that master manipulators never stop trying to manipulate people." He reached over and squeezed her hand.

Zarah swallowed convulsively. One thing she'd never forgotten over the years was the feel of Bobby's hand around hers, the way it completely enveloped hers. Even though the contact ended quickly before Bobby stood to stretch, Zarah couldn't stop thinking about it for the remainder of the performance.

During the curtain calls, Bobby stood with everyone else and clapped politely. And when the lead actor once again leaped back up on the stage to direct the audience in singing "Seventy-Six Trombones,"

Bobby remained standing but clasped his hands behind his back, jaw jutted slightly forward, looking like he was fighting with himself to keep from checking his watch.

Zarah—mouthing the words today, rather than expose her tone deafness again—didn't bother hiding her smile. If he'd tried to suspend his disbelief, he'd failed. Oh well. He never had been a big fan of fiction—whether books or movies or TV.

As soon as the song ended, Kiki put her arm around Zarah's waist. "We're all going over to The Cheesecake Factory at the Green Hills Mall for supper and would love it if you and Caylor would go with us—to keep Robert company, as he rode over with his grandparents and would be stuck with just us old folks otherwise."

Miss the opportunity to spend more time with Bobby—more time to see if she could figure out what she felt about him, what their future might be? And for Caylor to meet Bobby and start getting to know him? "I'd love to go. And I'm sure Caylor will, too. That's one of her favorite restaurants."

"Wonderful. We'll meet you over there, then."

Zarah followed Bobby out of the pew. "Why don't you ˮ

"Dr. Mitchell, I'm glad I caught you. I wanted to introduce you to my guests." Dennis came around and cupped her elbow to propel her forward, eliminating her chance to ask Bobby if he wanted to ride over to the mall with her.

"I guess I'll see you at the restaurant." Bobby's face had gone strangely blank—almost cold—at her boss's interruption.

"See you there." She watched him make his way through the crowd to catch up with his grandparents even as Dennis started the introductions. Odd. She hadn't remembered Bobby as the jealous type, but he'd definitely shown that tendency a couple of times just in the past two days.

She endured the small talk with Dennis's acquaintances, glad to know that the writer was going to give the performance a glowing review in the weekend-wrap-up section he wrote.

KAYE DACUS

Ten minutes later, she found Caylor in the lobby and told her the plan for supper. "I couldn't believe it when I saw you sitting beside a *gorgeous* man once the house lights came up. I almost fell over when I was doing my bow. I've been dying to ask—who is he? Where did Flannery find him? And does she know any more like him?"

Zarah laughed, even as heat flooded her face. "Well. . .he and Flannery grew up together—same schools, same church—but she didn't find him for me. I found him for myself—when I was seventeen."

"When you were. . .oh. *Oh.*" Caylor's perfect, full lips fell open wider than Zarah had ever seen. "You mean—*that* was Bobby Patterson? And you were *sitting next to him*? Oh my goodness. Please tell me he's going to be at the restaurant."

"He's going to be at the restaurant."

"Then what are we standing around here for?" Caylor grabbed her arm and dragged her down the hall to the room that served as the women's dressing room. She yanked her wig off then grabbed a pot of cold cream and slathered it liberally all over her face.

Zarah found a metal folding chair and carried it over beside the table at which Caylor sat, wiping the cold cream and stage makeup off.

"Can you unzip me?"

Zarah complied. Within just a few minutes, Caylor was back in her street clothes and—with just a bit of powder, mascara, blush, and lip gloss—ready to go.

"Why don't you ride over with me—parking's always a mess at the mall on Saturdays." Caylor hung her costume on the rolling rack, set the wig onto the foam head form, and grabbed her purse from one of the lockers along the back wall.

"Okay."

"Great. Because I want to hear how you came to be sitting beside him today."

Zarah told Caylor everything her friend didn't already know about Bobby—from their talk Wednesday night to his visit to the museum yesterday, as well as his reaction to Senator Warren's untimely interruption. But even having to circle the parking lot at the mall a couple of times until someone finally pulled out of a parking space didn't give Caylor any time to ask questions.

The restaurant was much more crowded than Zarah had expected for four o'clock on a Saturday afternoon. The hostess led them back to their grandparents' table—a round table which had room for only five people.

"They had to separate us to two tables, Zarah," Kiki said. "Robert is at another table just there." She pointed to the bank of booths to her left.

Zarah turned around and Bobby waved from the end unit. Zarah looked back at her grandmother. Kiki's expression seemed a bit too innocent to be believable.

She grabbed Caylor's arm as Caylor moved toward the booth. "I'm sitting next to *you* not *him*," she whispered.

"As if I'd embarrass you like that." But from the guilty grin on Caylor's face, the romance novelist had been planning to do just that.

Bobby stood as they approached the table—hoping Zarah would choose to slide into the seat he'd just vacated?

She slid into the empty seat across from him. "Bobby, this is Caylor Evans, one of my best friends."

"Nice to *finally* meet you."

"Likewise." He shook hands with her, an amused frown crinkling his eyes. "How tall *are* you?"

Caylor laughed. "Without heels, I'm six feet tall. But"—she looked down at her feet—"I like my fancy shoes."

Zarah hadn't noticed until he mentioned it, but in her high-heeled sandals, Caylor was almost the same height as Bobby.

Caylor slid in next to Zarah, who used the menu to shield her once-again burning face at Caylor's emphasis on *finally* getting to meet Bobby. As if Zarah talked about him all the time.

Caylor advised them on certain menu items, and they all agreed to order something different and exchange tasting samples.

Once they'd ordered and the drinks had been served, Caylor folded her arms on the table and leaned forward. "So, Bobby, what did you think of the performance?"

Zarah cringed. Would he sugarcoat his reaction to it for Caylor's sake?

"The performances were great, from what I could tell—but I have a limited experience with live theater. Your accent was spot-on." Bobby added artificial sweetener to his iced tea.

"Ach, ye ken the Irish accent, do ye?"

He smiled. "I had a good friend out in California who was from Limerick. Your accent sounded a lot like his."

Caylor beamed. "I spent a few months in Dublin when I was working on my master's degree. My next-door neighbor was from Limerick." She reached across Zarah for the salt and shook it over her small beverage napkin before placing her glass back down on it. Zarah did the same—to keep the napkin from sticking to the glass once it got damp from the glass's condensation.

"So other than my accent, what did you think of the performance? Don't beat around the bush, Agent Patterson. I've heard you can always be counted on for your candor."

"Are you sure you want to know my candid opinion of the musical? I've already said I liked the performances."

"But I have a feeling there's more you aren't saying."

Bobby's gaze flicked to Zarah. She shrugged. If Caylor was going to press for his real opinion, who was Zarah to keep him from giving it?

"Who was your favorite character?" Caylor prodded.

"Well. . .in the beginning I had high hopes for the girl—Marian?"

Caylor nodded. "My character's daughter."

"She seemed to be the only person in that town who had any sense whatsoever. But then when she fell for that man's charms, I lost all respect for her."

Zarah's careful focus on Caylor's face was bountifully rewarded by

Caylor's unguarded, surprised reaction. "What?"

"So I'd have to say the anvil salesman—though he was a royal jerk—was my favorite character when all was said and done. Because even though his motivations were selfish, he wanted to see justice done."

Caylor looked at Zarah. "He's joking, right?"

Zarah grinned and shook her head. "Nope."

Bobby pushed his tea back and leaned his elbows on the table, hands clasped. "What is it with women and con men, that they just can't resist them?"

"Con men?" Caylor took a moment to process the appellation. "Ohh. I think I know what you're getting at. It's the same kind of fascination as with 'bad boys'—I see it all the time with my students. Instead of going for the nice, steady, quiet, studious boy, they go for excitement, believing they can reform him. Then, one of two things happens: Either she gets her heart broken when he doesn't change his ways, or he does change and becomes a quiet, steady guy, and she leaves him for the next bad boy to come along."

"So which of those two scenarios happens to the characters in this story?" Bobby leaned back as the server brought their food. Caylor didn't answer until after she'd said a quick blessing for them.

"That's the best thing about romances. You can close the curtains at the kiss and leave the reader—the audience—with the fantasy of a happily-ever-after ending." Caylor cut off a chunk of her Chicken Costoletta, dumped it onto an unused bread plate, and handed it to Bobby.

Zarah decided to try another tactic. "He went and faced his accusers, and they forgave him. So why shouldn't he have a chance at a new life? Doesn't everyone deserve that chance?"

The intensity in Bobby's eyes when he looked at her sent goose bumps scurrying all over her again. "He only went before his accusers in *that* town. What about all the other people he scammed in all those other towns? The ones he bragged about? They'll never get justice."

Somehow, Zarah had the feeling Bobby was no longer talking about the musical but about something much more personal. And she inexplicably feared his quest for bringing someone to justice had something to do with her.

Chapter 20

$\mathcal{B}$obby stared at the forensic accountant. "What do you mean, 'his financials are clean'?"

"I mean Dennis Forrester's financials are clean. I've examined everything, every account, every real estate transaction. It's all legal, all aboveboard. I'm telling you: There is no evidence of any illegal, illicit, or even questionable activity that I can find." Jill dropped the thick file on Bobby's desk. "I've included a list of several individuals and businesses Forrester has conducted real estate transactions with. Maybe that will be helpful."

Bobby rubbed the back of his neck. "Thanks, Jill."

She gave him a sympathetic grimace and left his office.

So Dennis Forrester was clean. While that might make his job and the investigation more difficult, it also meant it would likely be much easier to prove Zarah's innocence if he could determine that no one at the commission was involved.

"Hey—I just saw Jill leave." Gage entered the office and dropped into the spare chair. "Tell me she finished Forrester's financials."

"She did." Bobby rested his hand on the folder.

Milligan came in, pushing a chair in front of him.

"Close the door, please."

As soon as Milligan settled into his seat, Bobby filled them in on what Jill had told him. "So we need to move from box one to box two." He turned his chair to face the whiteboard on the side wall of the room.

In the very middle of the board was a green box with Dennis Forrester's and Zarah's names written in it. A larger red box around the green one contained a few dozen names of known associates and business contacts—of Dennis Forrester's. Not even Gage and Milligan had been able to find anyone Zarah was connected to who might be involved in the scam.

They went through each name one by one, having split them evenly among the three of them to start the background research. Milligan, who had the best handwriting, made notes on the board—and started a third box surrounding the first two, in which he wrote the names of people and businesses connected to those in box two, but not to Forrester or Zarah.

Bobby leaned—carefully—back in his chair and took in the scope of what was taking shape on the board.

"What're you thinking, boss?" Gage looked up from the paperwork he'd strewn about him—on the floor, on Milligan's chair, and on Bobby's desk.

"I think we're casting too wide a net. We need to look at anyone who is currently or has been previously employed by the commission. Interns, part-timers, too. Whoever is behind this has access to detailed information about how the commission works. They also have to be able to somehow work the system to keep stringing the commission and the judicial system along so that the injunctions stay in place long enough for the value of the land to drop."

Milligan moved down to the right end of the board and drew a new, small box. In it he wrote *MTHPC*. He drew a second, larger box around it. "Who do they work with to halt construction on these land parcels? Where does their funding come from?"

"The courts, the city council, and the state senate," Bobby answered automatically.

Milligan erased the single framing box and drew three separate boxes, connected to the first with lines, writing *Courts, City Council,* and *State Senate* in them. "Now we need the names of everyone they deal with in those three places."

"I'll take the state senate committee." Now Bobby wouldn't need to think up an excuse for running a full background check on Senator Warren.

"I'll take the city council," Gage volunteered.

"And I guess that leaves me with the courts." Milligan wrote his name in the orange box.

"Since I'm out of town all next week, let's reconvene on Friday afternoon and see where we are." Bobby turned to put the folder containing Dennis Forrester's financial information into the lateral file behind his desk.

As soon as his agents left, he turned to the computer and typed *Todd Warren* into the search system.

He hadn't mentioned it Saturday, in talking about the musical with Zarah and Caylor, but the character of Harold Hill reminded him powerfully of Todd Warren—not just because the kid playing the flimflammer had looked something like the state senator. Or was it merely because the way that the fictional con man flirted with the pretty, naive piano teacher had been very much the same way Warren had flirted with Zarah?

The computer started spitting back tons of information—much of which Bobby had already found online in his brief search of the public Internet over the weekend. While it worked, he accessed the state government's Web site and found and printed the list of the senators who served on the committee that oversaw Zarah's agency.

On the left-hand end of the whiteboard, he wrote each of the nine names, four of them in each of two columns, and Todd Warren's name in a separate third column with plenty of space for writing notes on all of Warren's suspicious activities he was certain to find.

He reached for the ringing phone without looking at it. "Patterson."

"Agent Patterson, this is your mother."

For a moment, Bobby didn't comprehend what he heard. "Mom? Hey—you're back from New York?"

She laughed. "We told you we were coming back on Wednesday morning."

He looked at his watch. A few minutes before twelve. "How was the dog show?"

"Fabulous. It was so wonderful to see everyone. And of course getting to spend a couple of days at Niagara Falls is always the best part of that kennel club's show." She talked about several people from the dog show circuit Bobby was certain he'd never met in his life. He sank into his chair. Wednesday. Noon. His stomach growled. Lunchtime.

He popped upright again, the chair squealing in protest at the sudden movement. Zarah's lunch with Warren—that was *today*.

"Bobby? Are you still there?"

"What? Oh. . .yeah, Mom, sorry. What did you say?"

"I asked if you'd like to come over for supper tonight."

"Tonight. . . ?" He couldn't miss the possibility that Zarah would be at church tonight, that he might find out how the lunch went. "I have Bible study tonight. How about tomorrow night?"

"Okay. Come over after work. I might actually get industrious and cook."

The idea brought an amused sense of dread. "Maybe we can order Chinese instead?"

Mom laughed. He'd missed that sound more than just about anything else in Nashville. "Chinese it is. We'll be looking for you tomorrow evening, then. I love you, son."

"Love you, too, Mom." He hung up the phone and eased back in the chair, propping his right foot on the open file drawer of his desk.

As much as he hated to admit it, the real estate fraud couldn't have originated with Senator Todd Warren—not only was he new to the committee, he'd only been a senator a few months.

Bobby stood and picked up the blue marker. He drew an arrow

down from Todd Warren's name and wrote *Delbert Warren*. Perhaps the seat in the senate wasn't the only thing Todd Warren's great-uncle Delbert had handed down to him.

While he didn't hold out her chair for her—the way Bobby would have—State Senator Todd Warren did have the manners to wait until Zarah was seated before he sat across the table from her.

"Too bad they don't have a patio. . .it's such a nice day outside, and I never get a chance to get out and enjoy it," Todd commented as he picked up his menu. "I bet you get to work outside a lot, with as much on-site work as the commission does, right?"

"Not really. As the assistant director of the agency, I'm pretty much stuck in the office all the time now. I work with the artifacts after they come back in from the field."

"What do you recommend here?" Todd didn't look up from his menu when he asked the question.

As Todd had pleaded his status as newcomer when he called to confirm lunch—but cancel the tour of the museum—yesterday, Zarah had suggested Amerigo. "You can't go wrong with whatever the special of the day is—or anything from the menu. This is one of the best Italian restaurants in town."

He asked her a few more questions about specific menu items before the waiter came back to take their orders.

As soon as the waiter was gone, Todd propped his elbows on the table and gazed across the table at Zarah. His scrutiny made her uncomfortable, not because it was inappropriate but just because she wasn't used to having someone—particularly a handsome someone—pay such close attention to her.

"I feel like I know so much about you, yet you've never asked the first question about me," he said finally. "Feel up to a game of twenty questions?"

Zarah smiled, grateful he'd finally broken the silence. "Actually, I think I've pretty much got you figured out."

Todd's left eyebrow arched up gracefully. "Really?" His tone of voice added: *Prove it*.

"Well, you grew up in the aptly named Warren, Tennessee. You went to UT, where you were in a fraternity—either Phi Kappa Psi or Sigma Nu—majored in PoliSci, and were involved in the Student Government Association. . .you were definitely an officer, perhaps even president. After UT, you went to law school at Vandy and interned in the state senate. You wanted to be in the senate by the time you were thirty-five, so you started with the local school board at home, then moved up to other positions until your great-uncle died and you ran in the special election to fill his seat. . .right?"

Zarah smiled at the dumbfounded look on Todd's face. "How did you know all that?"

For a moment, she thought about fibbing but then laughed. "I did a little research on you after the committee meeting. It's amazing how much one can learn about someone else out there on the Web. And what wasn't there, I filled in with my imagination. So was I right about the fraternity?"

Todd nodded. "Sigma Nu. And I was president of the SGA my senior year. Wow. I'm impressed—you *researched* me. I guess I shouldn't be surprised since research is what you do for a living. Okay, so maybe you do know more about me. I don't even know where you grew up, just that you moved here fourteen years ago for college."

And how had he come by *that* piece of information? "What do you want to know about me?"

"Where were you born?"

Zarah looked up and smiled at the waiter as he refilled her iced tea. "Georgia. My father was stationed at Fort Benning at the time."

"Ahh, so you're an army brat."

Zarah nodded and shrugged. "I guess so."

"So you've lived lots of different places? I never even left the state of Tennessee until I went to college, and we took a trip over to North

Carolina. Where all have you lived?" Todd leaned forward as he talked, obviously intrigued by the topic.

How many times had she answered this question? "Georgia, Germany, Texas, Maryland, Belgium, New Mexico, and now here."

Their conversation was interrupted when the waiter arrived with their food. Zarah had ordered her favorite salad, and Todd exclaimed over the size of the serving of pasta he'd ordered.

Before picking up her fork, Zarah momentarily closed her eyes and sent up a word of thanks to God. When she opened her eyes, she noticed Todd looking at her, his fork halfway to his mouth.

"What?" she asked.

"Were you just praying?"

"I was." She raised her eyebrows, challenging him about whatever he was going to say next.

Todd took his bite, wiped his mouth, then said, "Oh. I didn't know—hadn't pegged you for a church goer. But I respect that. I go to church with my parents whenever I get home."

"How often do you do that?"

"Once or twice a month. I feel like it's important to remain connected with the community I represent. So I go to the church I grew up in and see all the people who put me where I am today. . . . I guess it's my way of remembering where I came from—to keep me humble, as you put it."

"So you must be very close to your parents, then." Zarah impressed herself by keeping her tone light.

"Yes, of course. I come from a very close-knit family. I've got two older brothers—or didn't you see that in your research?" His eyes twinkled as he teased. "Most of both of my parents' families still live in and around Warren. Is your family nearby?"

Zarah shook her head. "My father and stepmother live in Alexandria, Virginia."

"Do you get up there often to see them?" Todd added a copious amount of salt to his fettuccini.

Zarah looked down at her salad to keep her distaste from turning to disgust at the display of sodium excessiveness. "Not often. But I hope to see them while I'm up there for work next week."

"Any siblings?"

"Two half brothers. The older is twenty-three and in graduate school in Massachusetts. The younger is twenty and in college at the University of Virginia."

"Half brothers, so your parents are divorced?" Todd looked around the restaurant, waved at one of the servers, and pointed to his glass to indicate that he needed a refill.

Zarah was surprised he hadn't snapped his fingers to get a server's attention. His gesture was borderline imperious, but she supposed in the position he held, he was used to getting immediate attention.

"My mother passed away when I was eight." She hoped the tone of her voice clearly indicated she didn't want to talk about this subject further.

"Sorry to hear that." He tagged the waitress with an impatient glare as she refilled his tea.

Zarah waved her off from refilling her own glass. "No, thank you, though."

"So, tell me about this piece of property in East Nashville. How did you find it to begin with? Isn't that all residential over there?"

Finished eating, Zarah folded her linen napkin and laid it on the table. "It is. This strip of land is right on the Cumberland River, and it's where several houses and businesses were destroyed in the flood. The insurance settlements cleared this summer, and when the owners all decided to sell out and the buildings were razed in preparation to auction the land, we had the opportunity to send out a field crew to see if there was anything of historic value on the land. The crew ran across what looked like an old stone battlement wall—just like up at Fort Negley. There are records of an entrenchment along the river, but nothing about an actual fort being built there. I've seen pieces of the masonry they uncovered, though, and it looks like more than just an entrenchment—which would have been temporary and not reinforced with stone and brickwork walls. There may have been a substantially sized wall or fort there."

"What if you can't find anything other than just pieces of a wall? Those houses that were there had all been built in the late eighteen hundreds, and I'm sure that since there was a minimall there, lots of things have been built and torn down over the years. What if all of your evidence is already gone?"

Zarah raised her eyebrows and sighed. "It's worth finding out, isn't it?"

By the look on Todd's face, she could tell he wasn't convinced, but she decided to let it slide for now. She wasn't a lobbyist, and she didn't want him making decisions on her requests based on their having a personal relationship. That's why going out with him had been such a bad idea.

"I know what you're thinking," Todd said. "I can see it in your face. Give me a little credit. I can make prudent decisions without letting personal relationships color my judgment. But what I want to know is this: If I ever decide not to support a project of yours, because it's what the committee has decided or because I feel like it's in the best interest of the community, will you hold it against me personally? Or will you be able to separate our personal and professional relationships?"

That was the crux of the matter, wasn't it? Zarah didn't know if she'd be able to separate herself emotionally from her work—and she wasn't certain she wanted to have a personal relationship with Todd Warren. "I'm not sure."

"I'll tell you what. Let's just take this one step at a time, okay? Today we're just two colleagues having lunch. Maybe, pretty soon, we can be two friends having dinner and going to a movie. . .maybe this Friday night?"

Zarah shook her head. "I'm not sure—I don't think so. Look, I have enjoyed lunch, but I'm not certain that it's a good idea, ethically, if we see each other outside of the committee chamber again." She reached for her wallet when the waiter brought the check.

"Put that away," Todd chided. "This is my treat."

"Thank you, but that wouldn't be appropriate." She placed her cash in the check folder and glanced at her watch. They hadn't been here quite an hour yet.

Todd's face bore an expression of injured confusion when she looked up again.

"Please understand, I appreciate your interest in the commission and our work and that you're willing to take time to find out more about what we're doing. But I couldn't bear the thought that our developing a personal relationship might do something to harm either the commission or your career. The last thing either of us needs is some opponent raising questions about whether or not one of us made decisions based on us having a personal relationship and not on what's in the best interest of the commission or the state."

Todd stood when she did and held out his right hand. "I do understand, and I can do nothing other than respect you for your integrity."

Zarah placed her hand in his, and he clasped it tightly. "Thank you for lunch, Senator Warren."

"I guess I'll see you in about three months, then."

Zarah nodded and started backing away. "Yes. . .three months. Thanks, again. 'Bye."

Outside, she handed her valet ticket to the attendant and pulled money out of her wallet for a tip while she waited for her car to be brought around. She took a deep breath and exhaled slowly. It was a good thing Todd was putting his portion of the bill on a credit card and that the waiter hadn't even come to pick it up before Zarah left the table. She knew she could be in her car and gone by the time Todd got finished paying.

What *had* she been thinking? Developing a personal relationship with someone on the committee was a bad idea, yet she'd let Todd badger her into this lunch—even after he'd canceled the tour of the facility. But if she hadn't agreed to the meal and he'd been offended, would that have set him firmly against her and every proposal she ever brought before the committee? She knew she had several people on Capitol Hill—the state archivist and state historian, for starters—who would always be on her side. The senators, however, could never be depended on to decide the same way twice. It all came down to money.

Zarah sank into the seat of her car with a sigh and pulled away from the building just as Todd came out the front door. Something about the interest he'd shown in the East Nashville property didn't sit right with her. She wasn't sure why, but there was something in the tone of his voice when he'd questioned her about finding evidence—or not finding it—that set off a warning in the back of her mind.

Bobby had access to all kinds of research tools. Maybe he would be willing to look into Todd Warren for her, if for nothing else than to give her peace of mind before the next committee meeting.

Yes, tonight at church, she would ask Bobby if he could look into who Todd Warren was and what his true agenda might be. Not only would it be helpful to her, the request would hopefully set his mind at case and quench his jealousy.

Not that she minded Bobby being jealous over another man showing interest in her. It meant he still cared. Didn't it?

Chapter 21

The classroom echoed the snap of the light switch. Zarah looked up from arranging the name tags on the welcome desk, for which the sunset blazing in through the windows had provided plenty of light. Patrick raised his hand in a tentative wave.

"Thanks for agreeing to meet me early tonight." She set the stack of plastic-laminated tags on the table and motioned toward one of the small circles of chairs still set up from Sunday school three days ago.

"I'm sorry I didn't have time to talk Sunday."

"And that you've been avoiding my calls for the last week?" She smiled at him as she took one of the chairs, but she wasn't going to let him off the hook.

"And that I've been avoiding your calls." Patrick sat a few chairs away and leaned forward, propping his elbows on his knees. "I know why you want to talk. It's because I've been keeping stuff from you."

"Stuff." She pressed her lips together and nodded. "Yeah, that's one way of putting it."

"I'm sorry. I kept Stacy and me a secret from the class because I didn't want to see the problems we had last time a pair who had leadership roles started dating. It took us forever to rebuild from that."

"I can understand your wanting to keep it private from the group—but from me?" Zarah toyed with the long gold chain of her pendant watch. "I don't understand why you didn't feel you could trust me."

Patrick's head snapped up. "No—Zarah, no. It didn't have anything to do with whether or not I trust you. You're like a sister to me. I didn't tell you because. . .well, because every time I started to, it just felt weird. Like I was letting you down or something. Ever since you taught that series in Bible study on finding contentment in our singleness, I felt like I'd be disappointing you if I told you I was lonely and wanted to get married."

Zarah covered her mouth, horror-stricken. "Oh, Patrick. I never— *never*—wanted anyone to feel. . . I'm so sorry. The one time I muster up the courage to teach, and I screwed it up. I've got to explain, to let everyone know I didn't mean it that way."

Patrick reached over and patted her knee. "I think I'm the only imbecile who interpreted it that way, Zare. Don't stress yourself out over it. It was stupid of me. I should have at least taken you aside and told you before announcing it to the whole class. Stacy was furious with me when she found out I hadn't done that. That's why she didn't come to class Sunday—she was too embarrassed and told me she couldn't face you until I'd made it right."

"You make sure she knows that she has nothing to be embarrassed about." Okay, she'd made it through that part of the confrontation. She took a deep breath, steeling herself for the next part. "Now, about the meeting with Pastor Joe last week."

Patrick hung his head again. "I got no excuse. That's totally on me. When Stacy and I went to Pastor Joe to tell him we're engaged so we could schedule some pre-wedding counseling sessions with him, that's when he told me about this idea he'd come back from the pastors' conference with. I thought it would be great but—well, I wasn't sure you'd like the idea. So instead of telling you myself, I thought you might take it better coming from the pastor. I didn't know how badly he'd mangle the telling of it, though."

Zarah wasn't sure if she should be hurt over these two clear instances that Patrick didn't trust her or touched by the fact that he didn't want to do anything to hurt or disappoint her.

"Think you might could see your way clear to forgiving me for being such an idiot, Zare?"

Whenever Patrick turned on his good-ol'-boy charm, Zarah couldn't deny him anything. "Of course, I'll forgive you. I just hope that, in the future, you'll see your way clear to trust me to be able to handle anything that's going on before it happens and blindsides me."

He stood and grabbed her up into his arms in an almost-suffocating bear hug. "I promise."

"Thanks." She steadied herself by grabbing the back of a chair when he released her.

"Is everything okay?" A timid voice came from the door.

Zarah turned, then crossed the room to give Stacy a hug. "Everything's fine." She stepped back and held the petite woman by the shoulders, generating as serious an expression as she could muster. "Of course, I'll be praying for you, Stacy. You're going to need all the prayers you can get to put up with Patrick."

Stacy and Patrick both laughed, and a warm feeling settled in Zarah's chest. As others meandered in, some from the supper downstairs, some from work, Zarah greeted each one with a growing enthusiasm for the ministry and the new opportunities everyone—the new teachers, the students, and she—would have for further growth.

Movement at the door caught her eye, and her excitement flagged. She might be in for a long night after all. Walking in with Flannery was a somewhat good-looking man Zarah had never met before—and his stance and body language made it obvious he wasn't *with* Flannery. Which could only mean one thing.

"Zarah, you're here already." Flannery diverted over toward the welcome table, pulling the stranger with her. "Zarah Mitchell, meet Jack Colby."

Zarah's jaw almost hit the floor. Flannery had been talking about Jack Colby, an associate publisher at the book publishing company where Flannery worked as an editor for years—and she had something of a love/hate relationship with the man. She loved that he could get her requests and projects pushed through. She hated that he questioned her decisions, especially about acquisitions, regularly.

For some reason, Zarah had always pictured him in his late forties or early fifties. Not the mid- to late-thirtyish guy she now shook hands with.

"Flannery's told me so much about you that I asked her if I'd ever get the chance to meet you. So she invited me to come. I hope you aren't put out with either of us." Jack Colby's blue eyes twinkled, and the dimple in his chin deepened.

"I'm just frightened to know what she's told you about me." Zarah cast a glare at her friend.

Flannery rolled her eyes upward and feigned a look of innocence with one index finger touching the corner of her mouth.

Jack laughed. "Nothing bad, I assure you. She did tell me you're working on a book about your great-grandparents. I'd love to hear about that."

Zarah took a fortifying breath to keep from slugging Flannery in the arm. "They're my great-great-great-grandparents, and it's personal research, not a book."

"Jack, it's a book. And it's a great story. I keep telling her she either needs to publish it as creative nonfiction or get our friend Caylor Evans to help her fictionalize it." Flannery looked down and pulled her smart phone off the clip on her belt. "Excuse me. I've got to take this."

Flannery was hindered from leaving the room when someone else tried to enter it at the same time.

Zarah's insides gave a little lurch. Bobby's smile faded when he looked down at Flannery—who glared up at him.

Oh dear. She was going to have to speak to Flannery, get her friend to stop acting like a mother tiger defending her cub. If Zarah really had a chance to work things out with Bobby, having Flannery continue to treat him with open hostility wasn't going to help.

"I would love to look at what you have so far and let you know if it's something worth trying to get published. Sounds like Flannery is pushing you in that direction."

Zarah reluctantly tore her gaze from Bobby and returned it to Jack. "Flannery is somewhat biased when it comes to the quality of what I've written. She's heard me tell the story aloud several times. She hasn't read what I've written—which probably reads more like an article in a historical journal than a book. Besides, why would anyone want to buy a book about my ancestors?"

"If it's a compelling story, it could reach a good base of customers. Especially if we sent you on a media tour of all the big broadcasters." Jack stroked his chin as a man who had a beard might do.

From the corner of her eye, Zarah kept tabs on Bobby's whereabouts and progress into the room. Right now, he stood in a group of men, with several women hovering around outside the group, heads together, whispering.

"A media tour? Now I know I don't want to get published. I'd never be able to do something like that." If she angled like this. . . She took a step to her left and turned slightly—now she was in Bobby's line of sight, if he'd just look in this direction.

"Aw, all of our authors say that when they're first getting started. But once they get out there and get a taste of the attention of the media—especially the national media—they find themselves liking it more and more." Jack reached into the inside pocket of his suit coat. "Tell you what. Why don't you give me a call, and we can set up a time to get together for lunch or dinner and talk about this further. I hate to ruin something like this by talking business."

Zarah slipped the card into an inside pocket in her carryall and handed him one of hers. Flannery chose that moment to reappear. She beamed at Zarah as Jack took the card.

Jack looked like he wanted to ask Flannery whom she'd been talking to, and Flannery looked like she wanted to tell him. Zarah started backing away, taking a glance across the room to gauge Bobby's position and whether she could get to him without being obvious as to her intention.

Of course, Patrick would choose that moment to holler for everyone to take a seat. Disappointed, Zarah took one last look toward Bobby over Flannery's shoulder.

Their gazes locked. A slow smile spread over Bobby's face. Heat exploded in Zarah's face, and her lips trembled with the effort of controlling her responding smile. She glanced down, then back up again.

Bobby winked at her before moving off to the large circle. Still smiling, she adjusted the straps of her carryall on her shoulder. But the smile melted almost as quickly as it formed. No matter how she felt about Bobby, allowing him to fall in love with her when he didn't know the truth about her wasn't right. He deserved to know. He deserved the opportunity to walk away sooner rather than later, when the revelation of the truth would be devastating.

She should tell him tonight.

"We should go find seats."

At the flat tone of Flannery's voice, Zarah turned to look at her—and was surprised by the frown on her friend's face. Zarah cocked her head and gave her a questioning look.

Flannery shook her head. "Later."

Somehow, she ended up sitting between Flannery and Jack. Though he personally didn't make her uncomfortable, the idea that Flannery had brought Jack to meet her—as in *meet* her—made her squirm in her seat.

As he had done Sunday, Patrick explained the changes that would take place in the Sunday school structure. She bowed her head when Patrick led the opening prayer. *Lord, thank You so much for allowing me the honor of serving You here for so many years. I'm not sure exactly what it is You want me to do next, but please help me to graciously step aside so You can raise up the next leaders and so that others can enjoy growing closer to You through serving in this wonderful ministry.*

Give me the right words with which to tell Bobby about me—and the strength to handle it if he decides to walk away. Ame—

Oh, and Lord, please help me figure out how to tell Flannery I don't want her trying to set me up anymore. Amen.

Patrick started to wind up his introduction of the last chapter of the book. Bobby quietly excused himself to refill his water. He timed it just right. The last drops of water in the pitcher dribbled into his cup while everyone in the big circle numbered off to split into small groups.

Zarah moved off with group three. Bobby swigged the ounce of water and tossed the paper cup in the trash bin before joining her group. Thankfully, the overly groomed guy in the overly expensive suit with the overly white, overly straight teeth went into a different group with Flannery. Bobby didn't know if he should be annoyed or amused at Flannery's continued attempts to find someone for Zarah and thus make him jealous.

The chaotic flurry of moving chairs and figuring out who would sit where gave Bobby the opportunity to maneuver through the small group until he was right where he wanted to be—next to Zarah.

A cute pink flush glowed in her cheeks when she looked up and realized it was him. He so wanted to grab her hand and run off with her to a place where they could be alone, where they could talk through everything that had happened between them.

He opened the study book on his lap and slowly flipped through to the last chapter. He wanted to clear the air between them, but to what point? Just how honest could he be with her right now?

Although she did a great job of leading the discussion, Bobby couldn't concentrate on it. The case kept interfering. He found an old bulletin in his Bible and started writing down thoughts and questions that would not leave him alone, angled carefully so neither Zarah nor the guy to his right could see what he was actually writing down.

Whatever problems Zarah'd had last week with the changes to the Sunday school structure and the wording the pastor had used to explain it, the expression of contentment on her face during Patrick's reminder tonight nearly rendered Bobby speechless. Just when he'd thought he'd seen her at her most beautiful, she managed to surprise him. He hoped she and Patrick had worked everything out—he didn't want two of the most important people in his life at odds with each other.

Would Zarah initiate the conversation, or did she leave it up to Patrick? Bobby wanted to believe Zarah had grown into a woman who would stand her ground and meet conflict head-on. Of course, he also still worried that she had been so browbeaten as a child that any man with a strong personality would be able to steamroll right over her and manipulate her into doing something she didn't want or believe in.

He looked down at the last questions he'd written. *What does T. Warren want from Zarah? What lengths will he go to get it?*

"You guys may not know this about me, but I don't do well with changes."

Bobby looked at Zarah, then around the circle as the people in the small group smiled, chuckled, or guffawed at her blatantly obvious statement.

"But one of the main things I took away from this chapter is that God doesn't necessarily put us in places of ministry permanently. I also believe He challenges us in the areas in which we're weak—be it change, patience, grace, hospitality, or whatever area in which He knows we'll have to grow stronger in our faith to be able to face the challenge."

She looked around the group, her gaze resting on Bobby longest. "Last week, I was reminded by someone that sometimes instead of being called into a position of ministry, God might be calling us into a period of rest, a time when we can regroup and allow ourselves to be ministered *to* instead of constantly ministering to others. It's also a time to learn to refocus on our individual walk with God. It can actually be an exciting time, to be finished with one ministry and trying to figure out what God has in store for us next—because there are so many possibilities and usually so many things God wants to teach us during that time, if only we'll be open to it."

He grinned at her. So she had been listening to him last week.

The discussion continued along in that vein. Bobby continued writing questions, turning the order of worship every so often to make use of all the margin space. Though he hadn't been dragging his feet by any means, ever since he walked in this room tonight, a sense of urgency made him anxious. He needed to close this case as soon as he could.

Zarah closed them with prayer. Patrick made a few more announcements. For safety's sake, Bobby was about to leave with just a quick good-bye to Zarah, but she stopped him by laying her hand on his arm.

"Can we. . .will you. . . ?" Zarah pressed her lips together, frustration gleaming from her blue eyes. "There's something I need to talk to you about—and a favor I need to ask you. Do you have time for coffee?"

"Sounds serious." He tucked his Bible and the study book under his left arm.

"It is." She couldn't—or wouldn't—meet his gaze.

Bobby's heart sank. Something she needed to talk to him about? *Please, Lord, don't let her confess to being involved in the fraud. I don't think I could handle that.* "Sounds like this might not be the best conversation to have on an empty stomach. I missed supper tonight, and I've been craving Mexican food all day. How about that taco place over on the corner of Edge Hill and Villa Place?"

She nodded. "Okay. I'll meet you over there." Her mouth quirked up in a half smile, but then she looked away again, cheeks pink.

"No problem. See you at the restaurant."

He had to admit it. That woman confounded him sometimes. Last week, she'd practically cried on his shoulder after the meeting with the pastor. This week, when he'd first seen her, she appeared flirtatious and willing to consider giving a relationship a shot. . .then she acted nervous and embarrassed around him.

Which one was the real Zarah? Rather than stay here and be swarmed by the Stepford girls, Bobby nodded his good-byes and left the room with haste.

"Bobby?" The feminine voice echoed in the hallway.

He cringed and turned around. "Yes?"

Flannery stalked toward him. "I need a moment of your time." She stopped a few feet from him, tossed her blond hair over her shoulders, and crossed her arms. "I want to know what you think you're doing."

"Excuse me?" He mirrored her stance.

"When I first met Zarah fourteen years ago, she was one of the most fragile, broken people I'd ever seen. There were times when I didn't know how she managed to get up and go to class, she was so defeated and wounded. You did that to her."

Bobby's gut wrenched, imagining Zarah in such a state. "I didn't—"

Flannery held up one hand. "Zarah seems to have put that behind her. It's obvious she still has very strong feelings for you. And that's why I want to know what you're doing."

"Are you. . . ?" He dropped his arms to his sides. "Are you asking me what my intentions toward Zarah are?"

She gave a one-shouldered shrug. "If you want to put it in such antiquated terminology." Moving a few steps closer, right into the edge of his personal space, Flannery poked him in the sternum with her sharp index finger. "If you hurt her. . .if anything happens and she ends up broken and defeated again. . ."

Flannery glanced over her shoulder as if checking to make sure what she said next wouldn't be overheard. "I know you're some big-wig agent with the state criminal investigations department. But I know people. I have connections you would never imagine. All I have to do is pick up the phone"—she patted the device clipped to her belt—"and I can ensure the rest of your life is miserable and not worth living."

Bobby would have laughed—but for the suspicion that Flannery might actually be telling the truth. If he remembered correctly, her mother was Italian, from New York. Though he hated using ethnic profiling and stereotypes, he wouldn't be surprised if what she said was true.

Of course, he could arrest her for threatening an officer of the law but decided to let it pass. . .this time. "My, uh, *intention* toward Zarah is to see if we can clear the air, put the past behind us, and move on to rebuild a new relationship as adults. Whether that relationship is friendship or something more remains to be seen."

Flannery's expression softened slightly. "And do you want that relationship to be more than friendship?"

He couldn't believe he was having this conversation with her. "I see potential for that, yes. But I'm not going to push her into something she's not ready for or doesn't want." Not that he could right now anyway. Not while the case was still active, and not while there was the possibility she might be about to confess something to him tonight that would put him in the position of being the broken, wounded one. If Zarah was involved. . .

No, he couldn't think that way. She wasn't involved. She couldn't be involved. She didn't know the first thing about deceit and treachery— except what her father had taught her the day he'd changed both of their lives forever.

He left the church and drove over to the Edge Hill area, just beyond Music Row. The development of what had been mostly rundown residential properties before he left Nashville continued to amaze him. As did the issue with parking in this area of town. Seemed like nowhere he went had adequate parking.

He finally found a space—and an old, small, silver Honda Civic squeezed into a tight space just a few down. He waited for her, leaning against the trunk of his late-model black Dodge Charger.

Zarah paused to zip up her ivory leather jacket. "It's getting chilly out here." She grinned. "I love fall."

"I remember. That's one of the first conversations we ever had—how fall is your favorite season." He refrained from putting his arm around her, his hand on the small of her back, as they walked toward the restaurant.

"And summer is yours. California must have been ideal for you." She reached for the door handle, but he was too quick for her. She glanced up with a grateful smile, then entered ahead of him.

"It was, in some respects. But there were many, many reasons I didn't like it and wanted to come back home." He caught the hostess's eye and raised two fingers over the heads of the large party milling about in the entry. She waved them forward.

"Sorry about that," she said when Bobby and Zarah caught up with her. "We had a birthday party descend on us unexpectedly. Would you prefer a table or a booth?"

"Table." Bobby glanced down at Zarah, who'd said it at the same time, and winked. "Jinx."

"He's too tall to sit at a booth," Zarah explained to the hostess. "He kicks me constantly."

Warmth settled in Bobby's gut. She said that as if no time had passed since the last time they'd been alone together in a restaurant. *God, please don't let her be involved.*

The hostess found them a table in a corner where it wasn't too noisy and handed them each a menu. "Enjoy your supper."

"Thanks." Bobby didn't bother opening the menu. He knew exactly what he wanted.

Zarah opened the menu and started reading it. "Wow—these are some of the most unusual tacos I've ever heard of in my life. Thai shrimp. New Orleans po' boy. Lamb gyro. Unless I'm reading this wrong."

"You're not reading it wrong. Those are all tacos."

"Whatever happened to beef and cheese?" But the amusement in

Zarah's tone indicated she didn't mind the lack of traditional Mexican dishes on the menu. "You know, I'm not very hungry. I think I'm just going to have the chicken tortilla soup."

Silence fell until after the waiter took their order and brought their iced teas.

Zarah added two packs of artificial sweetener to her unsweetened tea. Bobby sipped his—not as sweet as they usually made it, but not bad.

He allowed her to finish stirring and taste it. "So, what is it you wanted to tell me?"

"How about the favor first?"

"Okay."

"I had lunch with Senator Todd Warren today." Zarah ran her thumb and index finger up and down the beveled edges of her glass.

"Right." The sound of the man's name coming off Zarah's tongue grated on Bobby.

"There's something about him that doesn't quite sit right with me." Zarah launched into some of the details of her conversation with the senator. "It made me wonder why he'd ask questions like that. He's taken a rather unusual, personal interest in. . .the commission and the work I'm—we're doing there."

Had she told him the story of her ancestors when she gave him the guided tour of the facility? Had her face glowed the same way when telling him the story as it had when she'd related it to Bobby? He tried to shake the jealousy off. "Was that all?"

The food would arrive right then, cutting off Zarah's response. As soon as the waiter left and Bobby said a quick blessing, he asked his question again.

"Well, he asked me out—on a date. Dinner and a movie."

No comfort food in the world would salve the mental and emotional wound knowing Zarah had gone out with Warren again would cause. "And what did you say?"

"I told him I thought it would be inappropriate for us to have a personal relationship outside of the committee. I don't want it to raise ethical questions for either of us."

His heart did the Snoopy dance, pumping extra hard once as if giving an emphatic *yes*! "So what is the favor you want to ask?"

"I know you're already extremely busy at work, and I wouldn't want to generate any more work for you. And if this is something that would be wrong or unethical for you to do, you have to say no. Okay?"

She looked so earnest he almost laughed. Instead, he employed his emotion-free interrogator's mask. "Okay."

"I wonder if you might look into Todd Warren for me. See if there's any reason I should be concerned about the amount of attention he's showing me—the commission."

Emotionless. Interrogator. Unflappable. Yeah, right. Bobby fought the smile trying to break through. "I think I can do that for you." No reason she needed to know he already had a pretty thick file of information on the senator.

"Thank you." She smiled at him, but it didn't linger when she looked down at the minipot of soup she'd been stirring since it had arrived.

"You're welcome. Now, about that other thing you wanted to tell me. . . ?"

"I—it can wait. Let's just enjoy our dinner. I'll tell you some other time."

The pain and vulnerability in her voice wouldn't allow him to let it rest, though. "I'd really like to know what it is."

Zarah set her spoon down—he hadn't seen her take a bite of the soup yet—and folded her hands against the edge of the table. "Last week, I told you I haven't dated because I don't want to hurt anyone."

"I remember." Right after that, she'd said she was glad he'd wised up and walked away. He needed to tell her what really happened. But he'd let her have her say first.

"Bobby, I never expected you to come back into my life. I hoped and prayed for a time that you would, but then, after a lot of therapy, I put that behind me. I moved on with my life."

"So you're saying that you don't want a relationship with me because—what?—it would cause you to regress or something?"

Tears welled in Zarah's eyes. What was going on here?

"No, that's not it at all. I don't want a relationship with you because I don't want to cause you pain and suffering."

"You said that last week, and I'm still not sure—"

"Stop. Please. Just let me say this." Zarah took a deep breath and dabbed at the corners of her eyes with her napkin. "I think it would be better for you in the long run if you move on from me, if you look for love somewhere else."

"What if I don't want to?" Who was she to tell him he shouldn't love her?

"Bobby, I don't want to break your heart when I die in a couple of years."

Chapter 22

By the time Bobby finished signing all the paperwork, his hand cramped and the profit he had made on his condo in Los Angeles was gone. But he had his own place now, and could schedule the movers to bring his stuff as soon as he got back from Quantico.

He shook hands with the mortgage broker and gladly accepted the keys to his new place from the real estate agent. Though he really needed to get back to work, anticipation ran too high. Instead of driving northwest of downtown, he drove south, used the key card to get into the gated parking lot, and found what was now his very own detached two-car garage. He pulled up to the door and used the touch pad beside it to activate the electronic opener. Nice and clean; not even any oil spots on the sealed-concrete floor.

He didn't have all day to admire the garage. Closing the door behind him, he crossed the driveway to the nearest entrance into the building. The elevator opened as soon as he punched the call button; and when he stepped out onto the fourth floor, a sense of excitement bubbled in his chest. The only thing that would have made this perfect would be Zarah at his side.

Zarah. He shook his head. His heart still ached over her fear that she might one day develop the same cancer her mother and sister had.

The revelation last night had taken him so completely by surprise, he had not known how to react. Unfortunately, he was pretty sure Zarah had taken his consternation the wrong way, from the haste of her departure shortly thereafter.

He'd have to figure out some way to make it up to her. Once they both got back from DC, once he closed the case, he would figure out how to reassure her it didn't matter.

Empty of the previous owners' furniture and decor, the condo seemed even more spacious than he remembered. As promised, two garage door openers sat on the near end of the kitchen counter. Even though he'd just done the final walk-through a couple of days ago, seeing it now with the keys in his possession made him like it all the more.

He could not wait to see Zarah's reaction to it.

He stood in the middle of the living room and looked through the rounded wall of windows past his balcony to the panoramic view of midtown and downtown Nashville. His view—even if, structurally, he couldn't knock down the wall in the kitchen to see it. Nevertheless, it was his home.

As soon as he walked back into his office twenty minutes later, Chase appeared at the door.

"How did it go?" Chase leaned on the doorjamb.

Bobby held up the keys still in his hand. "It's all mine."

"Congratulations. Be sure to call me when you're ready to have people come over to help move the furniture and unpack boxes. I'll be sure to avoid your phone call."

"Don't worry. I've done this often enough—and have so few things—that I don't usually invite anyone over until everything is unpacked and the place is ready to be seen." Bobby tossed the keys into his desk drawer and moaned at the sight of his in-box, with several new, thick files piled on top of what had already been overflowing the plastic tray. He picked up the top file and started flipping through it.

"So, Sunday. Do you want me to come pick you up so we only have to deal with one car at the airport?"

Tossing the file containing background information on one of the senators onto his desk, Bobby sank into his chair. "Naw, my grandparents already offered to drop me off. Besides, Green Hills is way out of your way. Thanks for the offer though."

"If you change your mind, just let me know." Chase nodded toward the stacks of files on Bobby's desk. "I'll let you get back to it then."

"Thanks for that." Bobby rolled his eyes.

Chase's laughter lingered behind when he left.

Bobby reached for the five new files still sitting in his in-box and spread them out side by side atop the other clutter already on his desk. A few years ago, a sting operation had been conducted to uncover a group of senators who had been taking bribes as well as violating other ethics regulations. Since then, files had been kept on all of the state's elected officials. In a way, it made Bobby's job easier because he didn't have to start the research from scratch. In a way it made it harder because he didn't know which files were up-to-date and which had not been touched in a while. But it was a good starting point.

Bobby dived into the work, wanting to get through as much as he could before the Quantico trip. He was well into the fourth file and a second legal pad when his cell phone rang.

"Hey, Mom. What's up?"

"Just wondering if you're still planning to come over for supper tonight. I wanted to wait until I knew you were on your way before ordering the food, but I wanted to make sure you were actually coming since you're not here yet." His mother's voice held a note of amusement.

Bobby looked at his watch, shocked to find that it was almost six thirty. Using the legal pad as a placeholder, he closed the folder. "I'm leaving right now. Order me a couple extra egg rolls, please."

"Oh, I'm ordering a dozen. Whatever you and your dad don't eat tonight, he'll eat for breakfast tomorrow. We'll see you in a little bit."

Bobby returned the phone to the holster on his belt, rolled his sleeves down, buttoned the cuffs, and shrugged into his suit coat. If he had been able to think about anything other than the house closing this morning, he might have thrown a change of clothes in the car. Now he didn't even have time to run by Mamm and Greedad's house to change into something more comfortable.

One advantage of having lost track of time—rush hour traffic had almost dissipated by the time he hit the interstate in downtown. He lucked into a parking space not too far from the midrise building just off Division Street. The concierge at the front desk greeted him with an air of friendly snobbishness. Bobby kept his smile to himself until the elevator doors closed. The man needed to go to Los Angeles if he wanted to intimidate guests the way they did out there.

The hallway and the building's top floor had such good soundproofing, Bobby couldn't hear himself breathe. It was actually kind of creepy. He didn't mind so much the occasional sound of neighbors coming and going, even though he was pretty sure with his corner unit, farthest from the main stairs and elevator, he wouldn't hear much. Here, he couldn't even hear the doorbell when he pressed the button beside his parents' door.

But it must have rung—his mother flung open the door and pulled him inside, drawing him into a hug.

"So good to see you." Mom ushered him into the enormous, luxurious condominium.

Bobby squeezed his mom's shoulder. "You act like you haven't seen me in months. It's only been a little more than a week."

"Yeah, well I still haven't gotten over not getting to see you for a couple years back when you were in the army. Or when you were hiding out in California."

"I wasn't hiding out. I was working." He'd been making something of himself before he came back to face everyone who'd only known him as the kid who had to enlist in the army instead of go to jail—for something he hadn't actually done.

"You're here now, and that's all that matters. How did the closing go?"

"Just like a closing should go. No problems. Went by and looked at the place."

"Can't wait to see it. When you get ready to decorate, call me, and we'll go shopping."

"Beth, leave the boy alone." Andrew "Tank" Patterson joined them in the entryway. He shook his son's hand and squeezed his shoulder. For a man almost sixty years old, Tank Patterson could have passed for much younger. So could Bobby's mother.

He would never be able to make up for the pain he had caused them when he, along with two of his friends—the judge's son and the mayor's son—had been arrested after the other two boys decided to rob a convenience store while they were all three out one night. Mom and Dad had warned him that those boys were no good. But because they were the captains of the football team, Bobby had thought it better to stay on their good side rather than to cross them.

Even though his parents had believed him when he told them he wasn't involved in the robbery, the fact that he had lied to them about where he was going and whom he was going with had hurt them deeply. And the fact that the mayor's son and the judge's son had not only blamed it on Bobby but also gotten off scot-free had hurt him deeply.

"When is the food going to get here? I'm starved." Dad shoved Bobby in the back to propel him into the grand, wide-open living space. The huge, flat-panel TV was tuned to one of the sports channels. Though the TV was muted, it only took one glance to figure out his father had been watching a show previewing the professional football games coming up on Sunday.

Bobby asked his mom about the dog show they'd attended in New York and used the time to try to transition his brain from work mode to family mode. After about fifteen minutes, their phone beeped twice. Dad told the concierge to send the delivery guy up. A few minutes later, the three of them stood in the pristine, mostly unused kitchen, opening boxes to determine what was what. Mom had ordered enough food for at least six people—well, six normal people. But she knew her husband and son well. He and Dad could put away a lot of food.

At Mom's request, Bobby and his dad pulled down several serving dishes which she proceeded to dump the food into. It took a couple trips to get it all to the dining room table, which Mom had already set with some of her nicer plates and flatware.

After Dad asked the blessing, they all dived in with relish. In the middle of serving a heaping spoonful of Szechuan beef onto his plate, the inevitable question came up.

"Have you met anyone special at the singles' group?"

Rather than the exasperated look he wanted to respond with to his mother's question, Bobby figured he might as well go ahead and tell them everything. "Do y'all remember back when I was stationed in New Mexico and I mentioned I'd gone out on a couple of dates?"

His parents both nodded.

"Well, I wasn't entirely forthcoming." He told them the full story of meeting Zarah, secretly dating her, all the way up through his buying an engagement ring for her.

"Why didn't you tell us any of this?"

The hurt tone in his mother's voice knifed through his chest. "Because I didn't want you to tell me I was too young to be thinking about getting married. Even though I loved her and was certain we were destined to be together, I was worried that if something happened and it didn't work out, I would've disappointed you once again."

Dad reached over and rested his hand on Bobby's shoulder. "Son, you know there is nothing you can do that would make us stop loving you."

Emotion pressed at the back of Bobby's throat. "I know. But I was twenty years old then and still trying to figure things out for myself." He finished the story, including his doubts about what General Mitchell had told him.

"What happened to this girl? Have you heard from her?" Mom's eyes looked suspiciously moist.

"Actually, she's one of the leaders of the singles' group at Acklen

Avenue Fellowship." He told them about running into her at the cookout at Patrick's house and everything that had happened since then.

"Mom, she said something last night that I wasn't sure how to respond to. Her mom died of ovarian cancer when she was eight, and her sister was diagnosed with it seven years ago. Zarah told me one of the reasons she has shied away from relationships since we broke up is because she's afraid that if she's diagnosed with cancer, it'll cause too much pain for the person she's with."

"Sounds to me like she might be more afraid the person she's with will leave her and cause *her* pain if that happens." Dad reached for the bowl of fried rice and glopped more onto his plate.

"Yeah, I thought about that." Bobby pushed his plate back. He had eaten nearly as much as he could, and already more than he should.

"Did you ask her if she's been tested? Has a doctor told her that this is a definite eventuality?" Mom asked.

"She said there's some kind of genetic test for it that she got done a few years ago. The results showed she didn't carry the gene that typically caused that type of cancer—and she had taken her sister's medical records with her so they could compare the results."

Mom didn't say anything for several long moments. "Her fear is understandable. Unfounded, but understandable. Are we to understand from this story that you're thinking about a possible future with this young woman?"

"I want to try it, yes. But there's a complication." He told them about the case.

"You can't date her while you're investigating something to do with the place where she works. But what about after that?" Dad reached for another egg roll.

"After that, if she is willing, I want to give it another shot."

"Good. But, Bobby, you have to tell her about the investigation. Even if it turns out that it has nothing to do with her whatsoever, if she finds out from someone else that you investigated her at all, it could create problems." Mom pulled the plate of egg rolls away from his father and pushed it toward Bobby.

He took two of them. "Don't worry. I'll tell her." When the time was right. Like maybe when their first child graduated from high school. Or college.

"The way things looked on Saturday made me wonder if you and Bobby Patterson have patched things up."

Zarah should've known Kiki had an ulterior motive when she'd called and suggested Zarah drop by for tea after Thursday night's class. But she couldn't deny the truth of her grandmother's observation. "The more I'm around him, the more I'm coming to believe he didn't mean to hurt me back then. I'm still not sure exactly what happened; all I know is that since he's been back, I've had a strong feeling that we could work things out. . .as long as he doesn't get freaked out by the whole cancer thing."

Kiki groaned. "When are you going to believe what the doctor told you? You don't carry the gene for the cancer. You're more likely not to get it than you are to get it. It's almost like you want to get cancer because that would show that you're more like your mother than your father."

Zarah stared at her grandmother, opened her mouth to protest, and then closed it again. Deep in the recesses of her soul, Zarah knew her grandmother was right. Ovarian cancer was the legacy her mother had passed to Phoebe—the only legacy she had had. Not inheriting the gene that caused it meant that, on a genetic level anyway, Zarah was more like her father than her mother. "You're right. I need to let go of that fear—the fear that I'm anything like him. He is my father. And holding on to that fear from the way he treated me in the past is not going to help me heal our relationship in the present."

Kiki turned to pull the whistling kettle off the stove, but not before Zarah caught her skeptical expression. "Do you want to work things out with Bobby?"

"Maybe. . .if I can be sure he's not going to hurt me again."

Kiki handed her a cup and saucer before sitting down with her own. "I wish I could take that away from you."

Frowning, Zarah looked down at her teacup, then back up at her grandmother. "Take what away from me?"

Kiki released a little chuckle. "This certainty you have that every man you cross paths with is eventually going to hurt you."

"You sound like my therapist. That was one of the things we worked on all those years—trying to get me to admit that I think every man is like my father. But I know they're not—there's Pops. I know Pops would never hurt me." She startled when two large hands settled on her shoulders and squeezed them gently.

"And I'm glad you know that, little one." Pops leaned down and kissed her cheek. "I could never hurt you. You're one of my favorite people in the world. One of the brightest, smartest, most successful, most beautiful people in the world." He ambled over to the stove to fix himself a cup of hot chocolate. "That young man would be lucky to get you."

"You know we want nothing more than to make sure you're happy and well provided for." Kiki reached across the corner of the table and took Zarah's hand in hers. "You know we would love to see you marry. But we don't want to see you hurt any more than *you* want to, so guard your heart. Just don't build such a high wall around it that no one can get in."

"Don't worry, Kiki. I've had my fill of both being hurt and being alone. I'm ready to put the past in the past and start building a new future."

"And might part of that future be in Washington DC?" Pops dumped a handful of mini-marshmallows into his hot chocolate and joined them at the table.

Zarah sighed. "I don't think so. I don't know. It's a wonderful opportunity for someone like me—no, make that for anyone. But I can't help feeling that even though going on the interview is the right thing to do, neither that job nor moving to Washington DC is what God wants me to do. Whether that's true or whether that's me trying to guard myself against disappointment, I'm not sure. All I know is that for me to move forward, to have a happy life, I have to give whatever opportunities come my way a try and not automatically assume nothing good can come from them."

Pops grinned at her. "What you're saying is that you're trying to become more of an optimist like me instead of staying a pessimist like your grandmother."

Zarah shrugged even as the corners of her mouth crept up. "I'm very proud not just to look like my grandmother but to *be* like her. So I thank you for the compliment. But yes, Pops, I am going to try to live more by your favorite motto, 'Seize the Day,' than by my own personal belief that everything's going to turn out bad."

With midterms to write and papers to grade at home, Zarah didn't stay long at her grandparents' house, even though she really wanted to. Her cell phone started ringing as she pulled into her own driveway. Rather than risk dropping it while juggling everything else she needed to carry inside, she turned the car off and answered the phone.

"Hello?"

"Zarah, it's your father."

Her heart hammered. She'd left him a message more than a week ago to see if it might be possible for them to get together while she was in DC. After so long, she hadn't expected a return call. It wouldn't have been the first time. "Dad? It's good to hear from you."

"I got your message that you're going to be in town next week. Your stepmother and I can meet you for dinner next Friday night." He gave her the name of a restaurant on King Street in Alexandria near where she would be staying. "We'll be there at eight o'clock. The reservation will be in our name."

Hot tears pressed the corners of Zarah's eyes. "I look forward to seeing you there."

After a brief, businesslike good-bye, her father hung up. Zarah squeezed her eyes tightly shut and wiped the few tears that escaped to her cheeks.

"Thank You, God." What more of a sign did she need than that to confirm God was pleased with her new attitude toward life? Which meant, as soon as she got back from DC, it was time to see if she could make things work with Bobby.

Chapter 23

$\mathcal{Z}$arah leaned her head against the window and let the white blanket of clouds below the plane fill her vision while her mind wandered. Actually, it didn't wander as much as dwell on Bobby. She hadn't seen or talked to him since the fiasco of a dinner Wednesday night after church. Even though she'd promised Kiki and Pops—and herself—that she was going to turn a new leaf and not live with the worry she might one day be diagnosed with a fatal disease, his whey-faced reaction to her explanation that ovarian cancer ran in her family hadn't boded well.

A touch on her arm startled her. "Excuse me, miss. We're landing—would you replace your tray table?"

"Sorry." Zarah lifted the plastic tray and locked it into place on the back of the seat in front of her. She rolled up the copy of the *American Heritage* magazine she'd brought to read but hadn't even opened and returned her gaze out the window. Gray clouds and rain obscured the familiar landmarks of the Virginia countryside that would have indicated their close proximity to Ronald Reagan Washington National Airport.

South of the city lay Quantico, the training facility for the FBI—and where Bobby would be all week for a training seminar.

A week in which they were forced apart, in which communication with each other would be almost impossible would be good for both of them. They'd both have time to think, to pray, to figure out exactly what it was they each wanted.

As soon as the plane landed, Zarah called Kiki and Pops to let them know she'd arrived safely. Half an hour later, she pulled her suitcase off the luggage carousel and headed for the Metro station. She hopped the Blue Line south and got off two stops later at King Street. Thankfully, her hotel was less than a block from the Metro station—even still, she was pretty much drenched by the time she made it up the steps and into the front door.

Dennis's frequent-guest account with the hotel got her upgraded to a junior suite—which she appreciated, since she'd be here for almost a week. She took the elevator to the seventh floor, found her room, and collapsed on the sofa in the sitting room. She'd thought about taking the trolley down to the Fish Market Restaurant on the other end of King Street for supper, but getting soaked after several hours of traveling put the kibosh on that idea—especially since it was still raining steadily out there.

As soon as she got her second wind, she took her suitcase into the bedroom and unpacked, hanging her suit on the hook inside the closet door. She'd need to touch it up with the iron before bed. Even though she was now convinced she shouldn't accept the job if they offered it, showing up at the interview in a rumpled suit still wouldn't be a good idea.

After a long, hot shower, she dressed in comfy knit pants and a JRU sweatshirt and called room service. Twenty minutes later, her crab-cake burger with sides of fries and apple coleslaw arrived. The server set the meal out on the dining table in the outer room of the suite, and she tipped him well before retrieving a soda from the minibar.

She didn't take extravagant trips on her vacations. She might as well treat herself when she could.

Though she opened her laptop and got online so she could

download her e-mails and pull up the work she needed to get done this week, Zarah couldn't concentrate on it. Instead, as soon as she finished her sandwich, she picked up her cell phone and checked the time. Ten o'clock here, which meant nine o'clock in Nashville. She pressed and held the three. CALLING FLANNERY McNEILL scrolled across the small screen of her phone. Carrying the plate of fries with her, she crossed to the sofa and snuggled up in the corner of it.

"Hey, girl. I was starting to get worried about you." Flannery's voice sounded anything but worried.

"I know. I meant to call earlier. But it was raining when I got here, so taking a shower—and then getting something to eat—took precedence." Zarah related everything that had happened on the trip, from the young woman who'd never flown before whom she assisted at the Nashville airport to the very cute Scottish guy she'd helped find the Metro station at Reagan National.

"No, Flan, he was headed into DC instead of into Alexandria."

"You still could have tried to get his number or e-mail address or something—if not for you, for me."

"Believe me, this guy was most definitely not your type."

"That scruffy, huh?" Flannery made a disappointed noise in the back of her throat.

"Yeah—long hair, ripped jeans that looked like they could have used a good wash. . .typical vagabond hipster."

Flannery sighed. "Ah well. Keep your eye out for me, though. You have a picture of me on your phone to show, right?"

Zarah nearly choked on a french fry from laughing. "I'm not here to shop for a boyfriend for you."

"Speaking of boyfriends—"

"Were we?"

"You brought it up. Anyway, speaking of boyfriends," Flannery continued, "what is going on with you and Bobby Patterson?"

Zarah returned the plate of fries to the table and paced the length of the room to the large windows overlooking the Masonic monument to George Washington. "I don't know what's going on with us. I told you what happened at dinner Wednesday night. That's the last I've heard from him."

"I really don't see him as someone who'd get scared off by this phantom idea you might one day get cancer. He's in a high-risk job, too, you know."

"It's not that high-risk. He investigates white-collar crimes, not violent offenses. It's not like he's out there chasing down guys with guns. According to him, he does most of his work behind a desk." For which she thanked God. "He doesn't even carry a gun. He has one, but he keeps it locked in a gun safe in his office."

"Right. Look—" Flannery interrupted herself with a yawn. "It's getting late up there, and you need to get to sleep. What time's your interview tomorrow morning?"

"Nine fifteen. Which means I've got to be out of here by eight, just to make sure I have enough time to get there and collect myself. Hopefully it won't be raining. I'd hate to have to pay fifteen or twenty bucks for an umbrella in the hotel gift shop."

"Better that than looking like a drowned poodle when you get there."

"I know."

"Tell us, Dr. Mitchell, why you're interested in working at the National Archives." For the past week, the phone had rung at random times with Flannery on the other end, asking Zarah random questions she might face in the interview. She had not dared tell Flannery she'd already decided not to take the job if it was offered.

Zarah launched into her answer to that question.

"You're getting better. That almost didn't sound rehearsed. You know, Caylor is really the one who should be coaching you on this— she's so much better at acting than you or I."

"Why do you think it sounds only *almost* unrehearsed? Believe me, I've driven Caylor as crazy as I've driven you about this."

"You'll do fine." Flannery yawned again. "I'd better let you go. Call me—wait, I'm in a pub board meeting all day tomorrow. Leave me a message when you get finished tomorrow, and I'll give you a call back as soon as I'm free."

"Sounds like a plan. Thanks, and good night."

" 'Night. Good luck. I'll be praying for you."

Ending the call, Zarah checked the battery status on her phone and decided to go ahead and plug it in to charge overnight. She also got out her MP3 player and plugged it into the clock beside the bed, scrolling it to her instrumental music playlist.

After setting her supper dishes and tray out in the hallway, Zarah slipped into bed, taking along with her the new Tennessee history textbook she'd received to review. She didn't make it past the first page of the introduction before falling asleep.

The chiming of her cell phone woke her what felt like minutes later. Her eyes burned, and a sense of tight heaviness filled her chest—as it had every morning for the past five months, though today was the worst it had been in a couple of weeks. She wrote it off to the stress of traveling, crawled out of bed, and started getting ready for her day.

Rather than deal with her hair—as rain still pattered against the windows—she pulled it back into a loose bun, leaving the few curls that escaped to bounce around her temples, ears, and nape. Once finished with everything else, she pulled out the ironing board and pressed her pants, jacket, and blouse. She finished it off with the understated emerald-and-diamond jewelry Kiki and Pops had given her for her thirtieth birthday—earrings, necklace, and bracelet—and with her heavy carryall over her shoulder and blue-and-tan-patterned trench coat over her arm, she headed downstairs for breakfast.

Over a belgian waffle topped with raspberries, boysenberries, and blackberries, Zarah tried to find anything of interest in the newspaper, but set it aside after a few minutes. The nice thing about dining in a hotel: She wasn't the only person seated alone.

Earlier than she needed to, she headed for the gift shop to purchase an umbrella, then stopped in the lobby to shrug into her coat before heading out to the Metro station. Like most of the women she'd observed in this area, she wore comfortable black leather mules to walk to the Metro and from the Metro to the Archives. Once there, she ducked into the women's restroom and changed into her gray suede pumps.

She checked in with the guard at the main desk, then waited for her escort to take her into the "Authorized Personnel Only" area of the building. After submitting to a thorough search of her bag and inspection of her laptop, Zarah followed the secretary through a maze of corridors to an elevator.

By the time they arrived at the conference room, Zarah was so turned around, she wasn't certain she was still in the same building she'd entered—and wished she'd stuck with the comfy shoes.

The people on the committee interviewing her seemed bored with the process and uninterested in anything she had to say. Obviously, she wasn't the first candidate they'd seen.

About an hour in, one of the men asked, "Dr. Mitchell, in your own words, why do you want to come to work here?"

The speech she'd memorized and rehearsed so many times with Flannery and Caylor formed in the back of her throat. But she stopped and swallowed. Why should she continue to put herself and these people through such prolonged agony?

She closed the folder in front of her containing the job description and other information about the archives. "You know what—I'm really not that interested in coming to work here. I thoroughly appreciate your interest in me—you have no idea how much this opportunity means to someone like me. But to be perfectly honest, I don't want to live in Washington DC. I don't want to leave a job I love and the place I adore. Not even for a prestigious job like this."

Standing, she extended her head to the chairwoman of the committee. "Thank you so much for your interest, and I am so sorry I wasted your time."

The woman stared at Zarah's hand, astonishment elongating her face. "But. . .but. . .you were one of our top candidates. Dennis Forrester himself highly recommended you—grudgingly, because he doesn't want to lose you. But he said he didn't want to hold you back, either."

Zarah pressed her lips together to keep her smile in check. "Again, I am terribly sorry I wasted your time. But this isn't the right job for me. I'm confident you'll find someone who'll not only be a good fit for the job, but who will actually enjoy living and working here. It's just not me."

The committee chairwoman stood and shook Zarah's hand. "Thank you for being so honest with us up front. If you ever change your mind"— she handed Zarah a business card—"please call me personally."

"Thank you." Zarah pocketed the card and thanked everyone else in the room. The same secretary who'd walked her in walked her out.

Outside, cracks formed in the clouds and streaks of blue broke through and pushed them apart. She slipped back into the mules, stuffed the pumps into her bag, and pulled out her phone.

After a couple of rings, a man answered.

"Hi, John. It's Zarah Mitchell. You said to call you whenever I'm ready to meet up. I'm about fifteen minutes away. I can entertain myself for a good long while if you don't have time this morning."

"Hi, Zarah. Good to hear your voice. I'm about to go into a meeting. Is it still raining out there?"

Zarah looked up at the sky, now more blue than gray. "Nope—it's clearing up and looking like it's going to be a gorgeous fall day."

"Excellent. How about I meet you down at the Star Spangled Banner around noon and treat you to a picnic lunch out on the Mall?"

"That sounds great. And it'll give me a couple of hours to explore—I haven't seen the museum since the renovations a couple of years ago."

"Enjoy yourself—I can't wait to hear what you think of it. I hope you brought your laptop with you."

"I did."

"Check in at the security desk and have them call down here. You'll still have to go through the screening, but they shouldn't give you a hard time about having the computer with you once we clear it up for them."

"Thanks, John. See you in a little bit."

Rather than hurrying—like everyone else on the street in a business suit—Zarah took her time walking up Constitution Avenue. Before entering the museum, Zarah pulled out her phone and took a picture of the exterior of the building—catching it at just the right angle so that the Washington Monument could be seen over the far corner of the building, making it look like a steeple attached to the museum. She typed out the text message, LOOK WHERE I AM—WISH YOU WERE HERE!, attached the photo, and sent it to Caylor, Flannery, Dennis, and Kiki. (Pops didn't like receiving text messages on his phone but would look at them on Kiki's.) She then remembered her promise to Flannery and left her a voice-mail message.

After clearing security, a much less rigorous process here than at the Archives, she set the phone on vibrate-only mode and lost herself in the exhibits—those she'd seen many, many times and those that were new. In fact, she allowed herself to become so enthralled with the redesigned layout and collections that she lost track of time and didn't make it to the spectacular new display for the Star Spangled Banner until several minutes after twelve.

"You didn't have to dress up for me, you know."

She turned at the familiar voice. "Hi, John." She accepted his handshake. "Good to see you."

"Hard to believe it's been almost four years since you've been up here. What do you think of the changes?"

Zarah turned in a slow circle, taking it all in. "It's like a totally different place. I loved it the way it was, but this is breathtaking."

Even though just one of many curators at the museum and probably someone who'd had nothing to do with the actual layout or design changes, John beamed like a proud papa. "Thanks. Come on. I promised you a picnic lunch on the Mall. Though"—he looked her up and down—"dressed like that, I should probably take you next door to the Atrium Café in the MNH."

"Vendor food on the Mall will be fine."

John, a stout man in his fifties, grinned like a kid. "Good. I've had my fill of the café food. We've been busy preparing for next year's exhibits and special events, so I've spent the last couple of weeks down in the dungeon without getting out at all during the day. But let's go back down first so you can drop off your stuff."

The difference between the public spaces and the private collections labs and offices couldn't have been more vast. Down here, stillness permeated every corner—as did a lingering smell of antiquities, Zarah's favorite smell in the world.

She set her bag down under John's desk in the small office he shared with another curator beyond an artifact storage room. They went back up to the Flag Hall and out onto the Mall on that level.

"So why are you so dressed up? Did you have a job interview or something this morning?"

Zarah squinted against the bright sun and didn't turn to face her colleague.

"You did! Tell me—wait. Was it that job over at the Archives? Zarah, you'd be great at that. . .and so close we'd be able to consult you whenever we wanted."

"I'm not going to get the job." She told him about the interview and how she'd ended it.

John handed her a hot dog loaded with sauerkraut and mustard, along with a bag of chips and a bottle of water. "Too bad. You know if anything ever comes open in our division, we'd love to have you come work with us."

Two major agencies in her industry telling her in less than four hours that they wanted her. She turned and looked around at the museums and monuments visible through the nearly naked trees lining the National Mall. Every historian, archaeologist, and anthropologist dreamed of coming to work here, didn't they?

She thought of the grandeur of the remodeled American History Museum compared to the somewhat poorly lit and definitely poorly funded MTHPC museum. Sometimes embracing change was a good thing. But sometimes. . .

"Thanks, John. But Nashville is my home—the place where I'm supposed to be. And I don't really ever see that changing."

Chapter 24

$\mathscr{B}$obby pulled the suitcases out of the trunk of the rental car while Chase dealt with returning it. Five nights on a too-short, too-hard hotel bed made Bobby dream of the soft—though still too short—bed that awaited him tonight at Mamm and Greedad's house.

And next week. . .his own super-plush, pillow-topped California king-size bed in his own place. Ah—what bliss that would be. A major splurge item, the bed had almost filled the bedroom area of his studio apartment in LA. But in the new place, the bed would fit with plenty of room to spare for him to get some more furniture and even put a chair or small sofa or something in the room.

"All taken care of." Chase came back, tucking the rental receipt in his shirt pocket. "Let's get out of here."

"Agreed." Bobby pulled up the handle of his suitcase and dragged it along behind him, only too glad to get out of this place. Though the training had been invaluable, it should have been a couple days shorter.

More than three hours early for their flight—having skipped the last session so they wouldn't have to fight quite so much of the Friday afternoon traffic—they discovered they couldn't check in yet.

"Let's grab something to eat." Chase looked up and down the main terminal. "Down there."

The small café served Italian food—not something Bobby really wanted on his stomach right before flying a couple hours. He settled for a small caesar salad. He had one protein bar left from the box he'd brought with him, which would help tide him over until he got back to Nashville and found a fast-food place with a drive-through window open late.

Chase pulled out his pen and notebook and started bouncing ideas for possible training sessions the two of them could develop and teach at the TCIU—both locally in Nashville as well as statewide. Once the food arrived, Bobby took over as notetaker and jotted down several more ideas.

They checked in, finally made it through security, and found their gate. Bobby walked over to one of the convenience stores and got a bottle of ginger ale and a pack of peanut butter crackers. Flying hungry was worse than with something down there. If motion sickness medication didn't knock him out for a couple hours—and leave him loopy for several more hours after that—he'd get some of that, too. But he'd had to rely on ginger ale this trip—not wanting to drool on Chase's shoulder on their flights.

When he got back to the gate, Chase stood at the check-in counter, looking stressed. Bobby joined him. "What's going on?"

"Flight's overbooked. They're trying to find people who'll agree to stay overnight, take a flight out tomorrow." Chase rubbed his palms over his face. "If I miss another one of Michael's soccer games, Michaelle is going to kill me."

Bobby leaned onto the high counter and caught the airline attendant's attention. "How many people do you need to give up their seats?"

"I have three, I need one more. We'll give a hotel voucher, and we have a gift card that's good at several restaurants down in Alexandria, along with a two-hundred-dollar airline credit that will be applied to your next flight with us."

"I'll do it." Bobby pulled out his ticket and driver's license and handed them to the woman. "I can take a flight out tomorrow just as easily as today."

Chase looked like he was about to melt into a puddle on the floor. "Are you sure?"

Bobby nodded. "I'm sure. You just think about getting home to your wife and kids. Don't worry about me." He accepted the paperwork—including the page with the discount code for the hotel and the gift card. He looked down the list of restaurants on another page she handed him.

"Hey, there are several restaurants on King Street that I've actually heard of and always wanted to try." He grinned at Chase. "See, there's a silver lining. It's another night in a hotel—a nice one, this time—but I may get some four- or five-star food in exchange."

Chase laughed and shook his head. "Have fun, man. But not too much. I don't want to feel like I missed out on something."

Bobby gathered up all the paperwork and his carry-on and headed down to the baggage claim area to where he'd been told to collect his suitcase. Once he did that, he wasn't exactly certain where to go.

He stopped an airport porter. "I'm trying to get to this hotel in Alexandria." He showed him the page. "What's the best way? Cab? Does the hotel have a shuttle?"

"Take Metro. Blue or Yellow. To King Street exit. Take trolley to hotel." The man's heavily accented English made the words difficult to decipher.

"Blue or Yellow Metro to King Street station? Thank you." Now, where did he find the Metro—ah, a sign. "Thanks again." He'd deal with figuring out how to transfer from the train to the trolley once he arrived at the correct station.

He found the train, almost got onto one going the opposite direction, figured it out, and got off just as the doors started to close, then found the correct train. He barely had time to catch his breath before the doors opened at the King Street station.

The trolley stopped at the corner of the block containing the hotel.

He navigated carefully through the steady flow of people walking the wide, brick sidewalk, obviously out for a night on the town.

Perhaps a bit of exploring would be in order before settling on a restaurant. If his suspicions were correct, nightlife in this area didn't get started until after nine or ten o'clock on a Friday night, and most restaurants would be open past midnight. He checked in; even with the discount voucher from the airline, the price of a standard room made him cringe. But he never knew when he'd be back in this area again. Might as well enjoy it.

He wished he had Zarah's phone number programmed into his phone. He'd call her and see if she was anywhere nearby so they could meet up.

The quality of this hotel far exceeded the one they'd stayed in down in Triangle, Virginia. It smelled better, too. He left his suitcase standing by the closet in the small but well-appointed room.

He lowered himself to sit on the edge of the bed, groaned in bliss, and fell back to stretch out on it. Under the thick white comforter lay a mattress he could live with.

Exploring? Who'd come up with the idea of doing anything other than staying put the rest of the night?

Zarah hopped off the trolley when it stopped practically right in front of the restaurant. She stood for a moment on the wide sidewalk, gazing up at the front of the building. A red-brick Georgian row house in a previous life, the building housing the restaurant rose three stories above the street, with black box windows sticking out on either side of white double doors, carved masonry work surrounding them.

"He would choose the most expensive place on the street," she murmured. Her stomach lurched. She hadn't allowed herself to dwell on it this week, but for the first time in almost five years, she would see her father and stepmother.

Steeling herself for the encounter, she took a deep breath, adjusted her wool wrap around her shoulders, and pushed the door open.

A few couples waited in the hostess area. Zarah walked up to the Queen Anne-reproduction hostess stand. "Hi. I'm meeting someone here. The reservation is under Walter Mitchell."

"Table for three?"

Zarah nodded, pulse pounding at the base of her throat.

"Right this way, please. The rest of your party is not here yet, but we will bring them back as soon as they arrive."

"Thank you." Zarah followed one of the hostesses through the dining room, past the bar and the grand piano, to a table along the far wall of the room. She couldn't see the main entry into the dining room from here, but if she watched carefully, she should be able to see them coming before they were right on top of her.

The soft jazzy piano music didn't do anything to allay her anxiety. Every clank of silverware against china, every laugh, every time someone moved, catching her eye, Zarah flinched and looked around. She read through the menu four times before she began to comprehend it. She didn't touch the glass of tea she'd ordered for fear that, with the way her hands were trembling, she'd spill it down the front of the black Audrey Hepburn–style dress she'd borrowed from Caylor for tonight.

Where were they?

She lifted the antique gold pendant watch. Ten minutes past eight. Maybe they got caught in traffic on the Beltway. Friday night traffic in this area could be almost as bad as rush hour.

"Ma'am, would you like a basket of bread while you're waiting?" The waiter leaned forward at the waist, but the rest of his body stayed stiff, formal.

Her mouth tried to form words but no sound came out. She cleared her throat. "Yes, please."

"Very good."

Zarah kept her eyes trained on the menu, not wanting to look up and witness everyone staring at her and whispering about the pathetic woman sitting in the expensive restaurant alone.

Movement caught the corner of her eye. Heart hammering, she looked around. It was—not them. She looked at her watch again. Thirteen minutes after eight.

The waiter brought a basket of warm sliced bread and dinner rolls. Zarah thanked him and reached for a slice of what looked like sourdough. She spread the soft whipped butter on it and set it on the bread plate in front of her.

Well, that had occupied her hands for all of twenty seconds. Now what?

She pulled a corner of the bread off and put it in her mouth. Swallowed it. Did it again. Looked around as more movement caught her eye. Not them.

Finally, when her watch read almost eight thirty, she reached into her small black purse and pulled out her cell phone. Since her table was rather well blocked from those surrounding her, she didn't bother getting up, just dialed her father's cell phone number.

It rang once. . .twice. . .three times. He wasn't going to—

"Hello?"

"Dad? It's Zarah."

"Zarah?"

The surprised tone of his voice took her aback. "Yeah. . .um, I'm calling to see about what time you expect to be at the restaurant."

"At the. . ." Her father paused at the sound of a muffled female voice in the background. "Oh, was that tonight?"

Zarah held her breath to keep from bursting into tears. After a few seconds, she regained a measure of control. "Yes. I'm here at the restaurant waiting for you."

"Chad has fall break this weekend and came home, so we drove up to Boston to surprise Brice and spend the weekend. We'll reschedule for the next time you're in DC."

Which might not be for another four or five years. Zarah wasn't exactly certain how to respond.

"Was that all?" Her father's voice came through the phone, sharp and demanding.

"I'd hoped we could. . .reconnect. I wanted to tell you about my promotion at the Historic Preservation Commission. I had a job interview earlier this week here at the National Archives. The people at the American History Museum told me they wanted me to come work with them. Those kinds of things."

"Don't pin your hopes on any of those. The National Archives and national museums don't hire people like you. They hire people who've excelled in their field, who've become nationally known for their knowledge and expertise."

The nine-year-old who still resided in Zarah's soul wanted to find the farthest, darkest corner, curl up, and hide. But then the thirty-two-year-old woman reasserted herself. If her father knew anything about her, he'd understand that she, Zarah Mitchell, *was* becoming nationally known for her knowledge and expertise. "I told the Archives I didn't want the job, even though they told me I was one of their top candidates."

Her father sighed. "Was there something important you called about? You're interrupting our family time."

Because she didn't count as family. The righteous indignation of seconds before deflated. "Just checking about dinner."

"Which we have already discussed."

"Okay. Enjoy your weekend with the boys." Try as she may, she couldn't keep the thin, reedy tone out of her voice.

" 'Bye." The line clicked dead.

"Good-bye." Zarah squeezed the phone in her hand until it bit into the skin. *"Guard your heart,"* Kiki had said. But she'd believed that her father's call last week setting up this dinner was a sign that God wanted to restore all her relationships, wanted to give her back everything she'd lost in her life.

Lord, I don't understand. Tears welled in her eyes.

She couldn't cry. Not here. Not in front of all these people. If there was one thing she'd learned from her parents, it was to never show anything but a positive facade in public.

Why couldn't they choose me for once? Love me?

Shielding her eyes with one hand, Zarah lowered her head as if intently studying the menu. The text blurred and swam before her eyes, but she refused to allow the gathering tears to fall.

"I AM your Father."

The words reverberated through Zarah's mind and heart. Not in the booming voice of James Earl Jones, but in a soft, gentle voice—a voice like the first rain of spring.

"I chose you. I love you."

Zarah fought against the sobs that gathered in the back of her throat. *But I want to be loved here, in person. I want my father to love me.*

For a long moment, only the sounds coming from the nearby diners and the tuxedo-clad man at the piano filled her ears. Then, someone laughed—and sounded almost just like Kiki.

Kiki and Pops loved her more than life itself—definitely more than she deserved. When her father had kicked her out of the house, had it been God's plan? His plan to get her away from a father who had never even liked her and instead put her in the arms of her grandparents, who wanted nothing more than to love her unconditionally?

But why couldn't her father love her? And if her father couldn't love her, that didn't bode well for any other man's being able to love her.

A red rose appeared, hovering over the menu below her still-watery eyes. She blinked a few times to clear the mirage—but it didn't disappear, only came into clearer view.

She pulled her hand away from her forehead and let her gaze follow the stem of the rose to a large, masculine hand, up a long arm, and to an extraordinarily square jaw.

"Bobby."

Chapter 25

When Bobby had seen the name of this restaurant on the list of those that would accept the gift card he got at the airport, he had no idea how expensive or fancy it would be. But once he entered the dining room and looked at the menu, he'd decided to stay.

Good thing, too.

Zarah's face pinched with the effort to keep from crying when she looked up at him. He laid the rose on the table and took hold of her hand as he sat in the chair across the corner from her.

"How did you know I was here?" Anguish thickened her voice.

"I didn't. I'm actually supposed to be on a plane flying back to Nashville right now, but it was overbooked." With his free hand, he reached into his interior jacket pocket and fished out his handkerchief for her, though she didn't really need it as she seemed to be keeping her emotions under control for the moment. "I agreed to fly out tomorrow so my co-worker could fly back tonight and be at his kid's soccer game tomorrow."

A fresh wave of emotion stole some of Zarah's control. Her hand convulsed in his, and she held the handkerchief up to cover her nose and mouth, eyes squeezing shut.

"I came in and got a table across the room—and then I saw you sitting here by yourself. I thought you were waiting for someone; and when you made that phone call, I realized your. . .party wasn't coming. So I decided to invite myself to join you." *Please, God, don't let it have been a date. Not on top of her interviewing for a job up here.*

"It was my. . .my. . .my f–f–father."

He had to lean closer to hear what she said. Movement caught his eye—a waiter approached the table. Bobby held up his hand and shook his head. The waiter diverted to another table.

"Your father?"

She nodded, and her face pinched up again. But still, no tears escaped.

"Do you see this rose?" Bobby picked up the long-stemmed, de-thorned flower. "I stole it from the vase of roses on the piano. But then I left the pianist a big tip."

Zarah released a sound that was half sob, half laugh. "You brought me a rose on our first date. I think you stole that one, too."

"Sort of. I picked it from a rose bush I saw on my way to pick you up at your sister's dorm." He smelled the rose then laid it on the table again. He turned Zarah's hand faceup in his and traced the lines of her palm with his free hand. "Can you tell me what happened tonight?"

She opened her mouth, frowned, then shook her head. "Not here." Her voice crackled.

"Did you order dinner?" He reached for his billfold.

"No."

He placed a couple of bills on the table, stood, and reached for Zarah's wrap, marveling at how someone could be so statuesque and strong and yet so fragile at the same time. He settled the thick shawl around her shoulders, waited for her to retrieve her purse and the rose, and took her hand to lead her out of the restaurant.

"Sir, sir—is everything all right?" A woman who must have been the floor manager chased them into the hostess lobby.

Bobby settled his arm around Zarah's waist. "She's not feeling well. Everything was fine, thank you."

The contrast between the warmth of the building and the cool autumn night outside made Bobby long for the continual warmth of Southern California. Really, though, he couldn't bring himself to miss anything else about it.

Zarah shivered beside him. Ignoring his own discomfort, Bobby draped his topcoat around her shoulders and drew her into his side.

To his dismay, she burst into tears. Not just a few jewel-like droplets on her cheeks, but sobs that wracked her body, interspersed with raw, rasping breaths.

Disregarding the flow of people on the sidewalk, many of whom slowed or paused to stare at Zarah, Bobby guided her up the block to a side street, where he pulled her out of the main flow of traffic. Sheltered from prying eyes by a half-story staircase on the side of a furniture store, Bobby turned and pulled Zarah fully into his arms and let her cry herself out.

"Why can't he love me?"

Bobby thanked God he held Zarah in his arms so she couldn't see his expression. "Your father?"

She nodded against the base of his throat.

Anger—no, fury gushed molten hot through Bobby's veins. But just as she'd controlled her emotions in the restaurant, he tamed his now. "Tell me what happened."

"I. . .a few weeks ago, when I made my travel reservations, I called and left a message for my father, letting him know when I'd be in town and that I would like to get together with him and my stepmother for dinner one night." She took a deep breath and dabbed at her cheeks with the handkerchief, but she didn't lift her head from where her forehead rested against the junction of his shoulder and neck.

"I didn't hear anything until last Thursday." She made a rueful sound. "I'd been at Pops and Kiki's house, and Kiki and I talked about you and me, and about how I needed to let my walls down but still keep my guard up. I promised her I would. And on my way home, my father called. Told me to meet them at that restaurant at eight o'clock tonight." Her voice hitched.

He rubbed his hand in a circle on her back and waited for her to continue in her own time.

When she did, her voice came out as a deep, but frail, rasp. "When they hadn't shown up by eight thirty, I called. Their younger son, Chad, came home from UVA for a long weekend, so they decided to drive up to see the older son, Brice, in Boston."

She coughed, a deep, wrenching sound. He redistributed his weight to keep both of them balanced. He needed a gym, a boxing ring, something. Rage against Zarah's father grew so palpable inside him, his skin tingled.

But when she told him what happened next, what her father had said in response to her telling him about the job interview, he had to release her for fear of squeezing her too tightly and injuring her.

At first, she looked hurt by Bobby's abandonment of her. But when he started pacing between her and the alleyway behind the building, she seemed to understand his need to burn off some of the manic energy brought on by his strong reaction to her story.

"He said. . .he said I was interrupting their—their family time."

If Bobby turned and saw fresh tears streaming down her cheeks, he wasn't certain he would be able to control himself any longer. Good thing General Mitchell was in Massachusetts.

"But I'm their family, too, aren't I?"

He turned, walked back to her, and took her by the shoulders. "No. No, you're not their family."

The little hope in Zarah's face vanished.

"You're not their family because they don't deserve you. They've made their position perfectly clear. They are not worthy of your consideration, of your thoughts, of another single tear." He took his handkerchief out of her hand and dried her cheeks with it. "You have a family. You have parents—Trina and Victor. You have sisters—Flannery and Caylor. You have"—he floundered a moment—"Dennis."

Zarah laughed, a glorious, if tentative, sound. "Who's like an uncle."

"And you have everyone in the singles' group, who looks up to you and depends on you and loves you." *And you have me,* he wanted to add. *I love you.*

He held Zarah's wonder-filled gaze a long moment. "General Mitchell may be your flesh and blood, but that doesn't make him your family."

Zarah stared at Bobby. At his words, something inside of her clicked, like an ancient, rusted padlock unlocking for the first time in living memory. Everything she'd ever talked about with her therapist suddenly made sense.

"What did he say to you?"

Confusion drew lines across Bobby's high forehead. "Who?"

"My father—General Mitchell. What did he say to you that day?"

Bobby's gaze flickered back and forth between hers. "That's not a conversation for an empty stomach."

Zarah pulled up her watch. "It's almost ten o'clock. There's a café in my hotel that's open twenty-four hours."

Bobby pulled the pendant out of her hand. "It's a watch. I've been wondering why you were always playing with this necklace."

"It was my great-great-great-grandmother's watch." Her hand tingled when he placed it back in her palm.

"The one in the picture at the museum?" He put his arm around her waist and started walking back toward King Street.

"Madeleine Breitinger."

"You don't look anything like her, you know." He looked down and winked at her.

"I take after Kiki's Greek ancestors, apparently."

"You never did finish telling me Madeleine and Zander's story. I'm still waiting for my happy ending."

A shiver passed through Zarah's body that had nothing to do with the cold breeze that hit her in the face as soon as they turned onto King Street. Rather than mention the happy ending she still waited for, Zarah launched back into Madeleine and Zander's story, finishing it as they reached the hotel's front steps.

"Though she never returned to full health, with Zander always at her side, the last five years of Madeleine's life were the happiest she'd ever known."

"See, there you go. A happy ending."

"A happy ending."

Bobby opened the front door for her. "So what happened to Karl?"

Zarah chuckled and stepped into the hotel lobby. "He went to college, fell in love, got married, and had a happy ending."

"You and your happy endings."

"Everybody's entitled to one." She led him to the hotel's café.

Rather than order a heavy meal so late at night, Zarah ordered a slice of quiche with a fruit salad on the side—to go along with her super-giant-sized caramel mocha latte. Bobby's roasted lamb gyro came with a huge plate of french fries.

"Looks like the kitchen is trying to clear out leftovers from the dinner rush." Bobby scraped a wad of mayonnaise out of a ramekin, added an equal amount of ketchup to it, and swirled it into a pink concoction with one of the fries.

Zarah watched in disgusted fascination. "That's new."

"What—oh, the mayonnaise. I picked that up from a buddy in Iraq."

Halfway through her piece of quiche and starting to feel sated, Zarah redirected the conversation. "Speaking of when you were in the army. . .what did my father say to you?"

"The morning after your graduation, he came to me and told me that you'd admitted to him we were secretly dating, that you wanted out but didn't know how to tell me—because you were afraid of me. He told me I was to have no further contact with you—that you didn't want it." Bobby polished off the last bite of his sandwich. "What did the general tell you happened?"

"The morning of graduation day, he woke me up at five o'clock in the morning by throwing a suitcase on the end of my bed. He said he'd found out about us, that I'd been sneaking around and lying to him, and that I was no longer welcome in his house. He gave me two hundred dollars and told me I had until noon to pack up whatever I could carry and get out of the house. If I went to Phoebe, he'd stop paying for her college. I packed up as much as I could and went to the lady next door and asked if she could drive me to the bus station."

"She just took you? No questions asked?"

"She didn't like my father very much. She believed I was running away—and I let her believe that. I knew if I could get to Nashville, I at least already had a place at Vanderbilt. And I had my mother's address book, so I knew my grandparents were here—at least, I hoped they were still here."

"But what about graduation—your salutatorian speech? You worked so hard on that." Bobby leaned back and laced his fingers over his flat abdomen.

She shrugged. "Survival was more important to me at that point in time. All I could think of was getting to Nashville."

"So was that all the general told you?"

If only. "No. He said that you'd told him about us because you were afraid he was going to find out some other way and it would ruin your career. He said you apologized to him and told him you would do anything he asked to keep you in his good graces."

"So he made you think I chose my career over you. And he made me think you didn't want to see me—that you'd chosen college over me." He sat forward and captured her hand in his. "Can't you see now how he doesn't deserve for you to waste another thought on him?"

Tingles crawled up Zarah's arm from the small circles Bobby made on the inside of her wrist with his thumb. "I worked with a therapist for years, and one of the main issues we worked on was forgiveness. The way he treated me was wrong, but I have to forgive him. We both have to forgive him for what he did to us. Or else it will stay with us forever."

"We'll work on it together." He squeezed her hand then released it. "I promise."

The server came by and refilled Bobby's coffee. He took his time doctoring it with skim milk and artificial sweetener. "How did he find out? About us—if I didn't tell him and you didn't tell him, who did?"

"I started wondering if what my father told me about you was true seven years ago when Phoebe died. In the letter she wrote me before she. . ." Zarah always had a hard time calling it what it really had been. "Before she committed suicide, she admitted that she couldn't live with the guilt of what she'd done. She was the one who told my—the general about us, and she'd never forgiven herself for getting me kicked out of the house. She wrote that she believed the cancer was God's punishment and that she didn't deserve the kindness, forgiveness, and love I'd shown her during my trips there to visit her while she was going through chemo. So she decided to die rather than continue to live with the guilt."

Bobby's jaw dropped. "Phoebe ratted us out?"

Zarah nodded. "Apparently our father suspected something was going on—for two sisters who hadn't spent time together growing up if we could help it, I was going out to campus to 'visit Phoebe' far too often. He cornered her and told her he'd stop paying for everything—college, car, allowance—unless she told him the truth about who I was seeing behind his back. She'd always been Daddy's girl—more than she was ever Zarah's sister—with the way he set us up against each other."

Shaking his head, Bobby picked up his coffee cup but didn't drink from it. "That's got to be tough, finding all that out when it was too late to talk to her about it."

"Too late to talk to her, but not too late to forgive her. What bothers me more is that she died not realizing that the cancer was just something that happened because of her genetics, not a punishment from God." Zarah couldn't help her lips from twisting into a wry smile. "And it's not too late for me to realize that even if I don't develop cancer, it doesn't mean I'm going to turn out to be anything like my father."

Bobby grinned at her. "That's my girl. You know, even if you got cancer, it wouldn't change the fact that. . .well, it wouldn't change how I feel about you."

Zarah's face burned. "Thank you. I appreciate your saying that."

"I'm not just saying it. I mean it." He punctuated the soft but emphatic statement with a serious expression.

She finished off the tepid last sip of her latte and stretched her back, which popped in a couple of places. She couldn't handle any more deep thoughts or conversation tonight. "What time does your flight leave tomorrow?"

"Eight in the morning. Yours?"

"Ten. So I guess we're not on the same flight." That would have been *too* convenient. She reached for the check to have it billed to her room, but Bobby stopped her, pressing her hand flat on the table.

"Dinner's my treat."

"But I can expense it."

"I know. It's still my treat." He tucked the cash into the black padded folder. "Walk me to the door?"

"Okay." She flung her wrap over her shoulder and handed Bobby his overcoat before following him out of the restaurant. She wished he'd take her hand or put his arm around her again, but he folded the coat over his near arm and walked a respectable distance to her side.

Just before the main doors, Bobby took her elbow and diverted her to a deserted sitting area.

"Zarah, there's something I need to tell you. I've been—"

But what he had been, he apparently couldn't say. His voice cut off and he stood there, his eyes searching hers.

How many years had she dreamed of this? Dreamed of standing close to him, gazing up into his eyes again, believing she might get that happy ending after all?

"You've been what?"

"I've been. . .thinking about you and praying for you ever since that day. Look"—he pulled his billfold out again—"I've even carried your picture around with me since. . ." Frowning, he started searching every compartment in the small wallet. "Where is it? It was here—I've kept it here ever since I left the service."

The despair in his voice almost brought her another round of tears, but Zarah acted quickly to remedy that.

"Here." She grabbed his phone from his belt holster, figured out how to activate the camera feature, and put her arm around his waist. She snapped a few pictures until she got one in which they were both smiling and both centered in the frame. "Now you have a new picture of me."

He looked at the picture a moment longer, then returned the phone to its place. He settled his big hands on her shoulders. "You know, your father isn't the only one who doesn't deserve you."

"Hmm." She chuckled. "I know."

He still looked like he had something he wanted to tell her, but then he shook his head and the moment passed. "I should really get going."

"Probably. You have to be at the airport in just a little more than six hours to get checked in." Tentatively, she reached her hands out and settled them on his waist—just so they'd be in position when he hugged her good-bye.

He would hug her good-bye, right?

"Zarah, I—oh, never mind." He leaned toward her.

She moved forward and met him halfway. Their lips met. All the emotion and hesitancy of a first kiss, yet imbued with the longing, the passion that came from a love put on hold. A love that had lingered over the years. A love that remained strong despite her father's worst intentions at ending it.

A love that was meant to be.

Chapter 26

He's been acting funny since he got home yesterday, and now I think I figured out why." Lindy Patterson motioned with a nod of her head across the church vestibule to where her grandson stood on the perimeter of a knot of the singles—with Zarah Mitchell by his side, looking up at him with rapt attention as he bent to say something to her privately.

"I've only spoken on the phone with Zarah since she returned, but I was surprised to see how happy she looks this morning, given what happened with her father Friday." Trina gave Lindy a pointed look.

Lindy clucked her tongue and shook her head. "That poor girl. But they were both in Washington. What if. . . ?" She cast a significant gaze at their grandchildren and then looked at Trina again.

"He hasn't said they saw each other, has he?"

"No. Has she?"

"No." Trina crossed her arms. "One of us needs to find out. Look—Zarah's walking off with Flannery. Now's your chance to corner Robert. Tell him we'd like for the six of us to go to Sunday dinner together."

"Done." Lindy thrust her Bible and sermon-notes book into her best friend's arms and hurried over to catch her grandson before he followed the dissipating singles' group out the door. "Robert!"

He turned at her high-pitched call, grinning. "Hey, Mamm." He even bent down so she could kiss his cheek.

"I was just talking to Katrina Breitinger. She suggested our families go for Sunday dinner together. We saw you and Zarah chatting, so we thought the two of you might like to join us."

He put his arms around her and lifted her off the floor with his hug. "Nice try, Mamm. But Zarah and I already have plans."

"Really?" Lindy bit her bottom lip in excitement.

"Really. We're driving down to the Sam Davis House in Smyrna for some special exhibit they're doing down there this weekend. But thanks for the thinly veiled offer."

"So are you two. . .have you worked out your differences?" Lindy took his proffered arm as they made their way to the back of the foyer.

"Pretty much. There's still one or two things we need to talk about before we can really figure out where it's going, but we've managed to clear up a lot of things about the past so that we can move beyond them."

She squeezed his arm. "Oh, I keep forgetting something."

She reached into her handbag and withdrew the picture of Zarah she'd found in his shirt pocket a few weeks ago.

A smile of mixed pleasure and relief painted his face. "Where did you find this?"

"In your shirt pocket that one time you let me do laundry for you."

"And you had it in your purse because. . . ?" He ducked his chin and raised his eyebrows—the same way his father had always done to get under her skin.

"Because I put everything important in my pocketbook. That way I won't lose it." She pressed the photo into his hand. "Now, you know if there's anything I can do. . ."

"I know. But not right now, thanks." He glanced over the top of her head. "I think you need to go tell Mrs. Breitinger what I just told you, though. She looks fit to burst."

Lindy glanced over her shoulder then laughed. "You're right. I'll go set her mind at ease. You kids have fun this afternoon."

"Thanks, Mamm."

Lindy returned to Trina and told her everything.

Trina's blue eyes took on a triumphant gleam. "I have only one thing to say."

"What's that?" Lindy asked.

"Dum-dum-da-dum."

Trina's off-key rendition of the "Wedding March" echoed in Lindy's head for the rest of the day.

Chapter 27

$\mathscr{A}$fter a wonderful afternoon on Sunday with Bobby, touring the Sam Davis house and grounds, then lingering over coffee, Zarah poured herself into work. Dennis insisted she didn't need to put in eighty hours this week to make up for the forty—or more likely sixty—she'd missed last week, but her guilty conscience wouldn't let her leave earlier than seven every evening. So when Bobby called Friday morning and insisted she meet him for lunch, she figured she could allow herself the indulgence.

She arrived at Chappy's a few minutes before Bobby, which was good, since the hostess gave her an estimate of fifteen to twenty minutes for a table. Everyone standing near the door shivered and mumbled when he came in—as they did whenever anyone opened the door and allowed the cool autumn breeze in.

Bobby joined her and gave her a squeeze around the shoulders with one arm. They chatted about their week—about the hours they'd put in since getting back from DC.

At the table, Zarah didn't even bother to open her menu. The server arrived with the water pitcher and asked them for their drink orders.

"Tea," Zarah echoed Bobby. "And could you go ahead and put in an order of fried green tomatoes for us?"

"I sure can, darlin'." The waitress winked at her and hustled off toward the kitchen.

"Really? Fried green tomatoes?"

"Have you ever tried them?"

"Uh. . .when have you ever known me and tomatoes to play nicely together?"

"You have to at least try them. They're fabulous. I got hooked on them a few years ago when I went down to Baton Rouge to speak at a Civil War symposium at LSU. And the ones they have here are actually better than the ones I had down there."

"Okay. I'll try them. But I'm reminding you now that I don't like tomatoes."

After they gave their lunch orders, Bobby returned the conversation to what she'd been saying before they were seated. Zarah explained as much as she could about her job, without going into great details so she wouldn't bore him.

The appetizer arrived. Zarah picked up the small plate the waitress set in front of Bobby and put one of the fried disks of deliciousness onto it for him.

He eyed it speculatively.

"You promised you'd try it."

With narrowed eyes, he cut a miniscule piece from the lightly battered slice of tomato. "You know I'm only doing this for you."

Her heartstrings zinged. "I know."

He carefully scraped the morsel off the tines of the fork with his teeth and closed his eyes while he chewed. His face eased from wrinkled nose and puckered lips to grudging acceptance. "It's not as bad as I expected."

Zarah speared the biggest slice and put it on her plate. "So you like it?"

"I didn't say that."

"Thank you for trying it."

He whirled his hand in front of him and bowed as best he could. "Your wish is my command, milady."

"Ha! I'll believe that when I see it." Zarah closed her eyes in sheer pleasure as the spicy, crispy, juicy tanginess filled her mouth. She quickly finished that piece and went for a second slice.

Before she could ask Bobby more specifics about his job, he went back to what they'd been talking about when the appetizer arrived. He only paused when the waitress brought them their main dishes. And like a dog with a bone, he picked up right where he'd left off after the server departed.

Zarah ate as best she could while trying to answer his questions.

He got through his food a lot faster than she could. "How much evidence do you have to have before you can go to the judge for the injunction?"

Zarah swallowed the bite of salmon she'd just put in her mouth. "You know, lunch with you had sounded like a really good idea, but I didn't realize before I got here I'd be getting the third-degree about my job."

Bobby grinned shiftily. "Sorry. I'm interested in how your job works."

"I know. You asked me about it quite a bit on Sunday at lunch, too. I guess if I'm going to be hanging out with you, I'm going to have to get used to this new aspect of your personality—Bobby the Interrogator." Truthfully, she didn't mind, so long as they spent time together.

"Hanging out. Is that what we're doing?" Bobby put his fork down and lifted his tea glass.

"It must be—because you haven't responded to any of my attempts to talk about what happened last Friday night." She pushed her plate back and leaned her folded arms against the edge of the table.

"You mean the whole thing with you ruining a perfectly good handkerchief by wiping all your mascara off on it?" He winked at her.

"Yes, that's exactly what I mean. Which reminds me to ask: Has anyone told you recently how old-fashioned you are? A handkerchief? Really?"

"Hey, now—my dad and grandfather both carry handkerchiefs. They have all their lives. It's a proud tradition in our family. And I haven't seen you complaining about them when you've used mine."

"Yeah, well. . ." She grinned at him, even though her heart pounded. "Why did you kiss me, Bobby?"

"Because I wanted to."

Obviously. She'd wanted him to, also. "But what did it mean? I can't do this cat-and-mouse, shades-of-gray thing. I have to know what's going on with us. Where do you see this going?"

Bobby straightened his tie and took another gulp of tea. "I want us to be together."

"As friends?"

Bobby glanced up and accepted the bill folder from the waitress. He slid a credit card into it and set it on the edge of the table for when she returned.

"Did I say that?" He rested his arm across the table and beckoned with his fingers for her hand.

Zarah placed her hand in his. "So then, what?"

"Dating is a perfect way to be together, don't you think?" He lifted her hand, leaned forward, and kissed it.

Bliss made her head soar, her heart run laps in her chest. "I think that's possible. If I recall, that's how we were together the first time."

"But let's not make it a big deal—you know, at church or. . .or with our families. I'd like to keep this private, just for us, for a little while." Bobby lowered his chin, his forehead crinkled up in that worried, questioning, little-boy-innocent look she couldn't resist.

"Okay." But no, she didn't really understand. If they were dating, they were dating. "Let's not do like Patrick and Stacy and keep it such a secret that it creates hard feelings for the people around us." Several people—young women—had stopped coming after Patrick's engagement announcement.

The mention of Patrick turned the conversation to their new Sunday school class. Zarah agreed with Bobby that the couple teaching it had done a great job—though she really hadn't been able to pay much attention to the lesson with Bobby sitting beside her.

"Anyway, back to you and me," Bobby said. "I guess Flannery and Caylor have heard everything that happened. And that I'm going to have to get used to them knowing pretty much everything about me." He pulled off a frustrated expression—sort of.

Zarah laughed. "I know how to be discreet and share only what I want them to know. Besides, I don't kiss and tell. Unless it's really bad. Or funny."

Bobby signed the receipt and then helped her into her jacket. "And you've been kissed so many times, you've figured out which stories to tell?"

"Okay, so, no, I haven't. But it's somewhat of an unwritten rule with the three of us, that we don't share a lot of personal details about our romantic relationships. Enough, but not everything." He held the door to the entryway open for her, and she went through, then held the exterior door open for him.

"Good. I'll still be able to look them in the eye." He put his arm around her shoulders and gave her a squeeze. "I've got to run. Meeting at two."

"Am I still supposed to come over tomorrow to help you unpack?"

"If you want to. I thought it would be a good way for us to spend time together talking."

"And for you to get some free manual labor."

"Yeah. That, too. Come anytime after eleven in the morning." He hit the remote button to unlock his car. "See you tomorrow."

The one-armed hug and no other sign of affection upon parting didn't define *dating* to Zarah, but she would follow his lead. "See you tomorrow."

She hadn't been back in her office five minutes when the phone beeped. "Hi, Debby."

"Hey, Zarah. There's a Mr. Todd Warren here to see you."

She groaned. "Okay. I'll be down in a minute." Annoyed that he'd broken his promise to stay away, Zarah pulled her hair back and secured it with a clip before heading downstairs.

Todd stood near the front door, staring out at West End Avenue. Interesting. She'd had to hunt Bobby down in the museum a few weeks ago. Todd obviously couldn't care less about the historical treasures contained in this building.

"Senator Warren, what can I help you with?"

Todd turned and gave her a tight smile. "Is there somewhere we can talk privately?"

"My office." She motioned him to join her.

As he seemed disinclined toward small talk, she didn't try to initiate any on the way upstairs. Having just finished several projects, her desk and office were unusually neat and organized.

"Please have a seat." Zarah rounded her desk and sat in her chair.

Todd took the guest chair closest to the door in the small room.

"Now, what can I do for you?" She tried to sound as pleasant—but professional—as possible.

"I wanted to let you know that the committee's vote is going to go against you."

Zarah's heart paused, then restarted with a crashing beat. "What do you mean?"

"I'm talking about the East Nashville project. I know you have your heart set on digging up that land to see if there's an old fort there, but the committee isn't convinced by the evidence you presented in your report. They'd like to avoid any more public controversy over this."

"This is because of that editorial in the newspaper last month, isn't it?" She dug her blunt fingernails into her palms to keep herself from overreacting.

"Partly. Look, your department and the committee have a clean record so far—nothing that's created any kind of public outcry or protest. Until now. Zarah, what I'm saying is that it would be in everyone's best interest if, when you go back to the judge next week, you would agree to have the injunction dropped and let the auction take place."

"Or?" Anxiety sparked through her limbs. She crossed her arms just to keep them from trembling.

"Or. . .the committee will have to start a serious reevaluation of the commission's projects and funding." Todd stood, a faux-sympathetic expression marring his handsome face. "I'm coming to you as a favor, because I feel like we have a connection. Nothing is set in stone yet. I know this is a blow to you, but in the long run, you'll see it's for the best."

She had a strong feeling she wouldn't.

Bobby stared at the reports in front of him in horrified silence. These numbers couldn't be correct. He glanced up at Jill, who nodded, and then looked back at the paperwork in front of him.

"How was the account hidden?"

The forensic accountant launched into an explanation of networked and offshore accounts the likes of which Bobby would never understand.

He rubbed the back of his neck. "You're certain it's his?"

"Positive."

"And the judge?"

She nodded. "Definitely connected. Numbers don't lie."

He might be sick. "Thanks, Jill."

"I figured you'd be thrilled to finally have a solid lead."

"Oh no. I'm grateful to finally have a defined target for the investigation. I just hadn't expected it to be *him*."

"None of us did."

"You'll keep this quiet, right? With a judge involved, too, if this got out. . ."

"Believe me, this is not information I'm wanting to pass on to anyone. I'm the soul of discretion. Good luck." She left the office as quietly as she'd arrived a few minutes ago.

Bobby called Gage and Milligan to join him. The joy that had lingered since lunch with Zarah evaporated faster than a drop of water on asphalt in August.

The two agents that comprised the whole of his investigative unit joined him in his office less than five minutes later. He filled them in on the newest wrinkle in the case.

Gage let out a low whistle. "That's a pretty big wrinkle."

"I'd say about the size of the Rocky Mountains," Milligan added, pale and looking as if he, too, felt like he was going to be sick.

"Obviously this information cannot leave this office. We'll continue with all aspects of the investigation that have given us any hint of a lead, just so we don't tip our hand. But I think it's time we start *quietly* questioning some folks. This is one of those times when we need to have an ironclad case before moving on the suspect. Given how well hidden these accounts were, he obviously has resources we never suspected, and he could easily slip through our fingers."

"Where do you want us to start? The historic commission?"

Bobby rocked back in his chair. Zarah should be questioned—and not by him. But he had to tell her about the investigation first. "Let's start with Dr. Zarah Mitchell. The two of you call her on Monday and see if she can meet with you early next week. I believe she's scheduled to go to court about the injunction Tuesday morning, so it might be better to wait until after that—just to be respectful of the restraints on her time."

Gage and Milligan exchanged a questioning glance. Gage spoke for them. "You said you know her. Wouldn't it be better if you questioned her? She'll be more comfortable with you."

"No. We have to make sure that there is nothing a defense attorney can use against us—such as conflict of interest in the questioning of a potential material witness. The two of you can gather information without the subjectivity of a prior knowledge of Dr. Mitchell." And if she weren't having the women from the singles' group over for Girls' Night tonight, he'd do it as soon as he could get out of this office. But it would have to wait until she came over to help him unpack tomorrow.

Shortly after Gage and Milligan left his office, Chase knocked and let himself in before Bobby could issue an invitation.

Chase closed the door and sat.

"Hey, Chase. Come in and have a seat." If anyone could help him regain a positive outlook on this case, it would be Chase. Except. . .

For the first time since Bobby had met the other special agent, Chase wasn't smiling.

"What's wrong?"

"I met Michaelle at Chappy's for lunch this afternoon."

"Really? What time were you there? I didn't see you."

"I know. But I saw you." Chase rubbed his chin, creating a rasping sound. "You remember that talk we had at my house about you and this girl from your past?"

"Yeah—and I'm still grateful to you for listening to me and helping me clarify some of my thoughts and feelings." Bobby chewed his bottom lip, concerned over Chase's somber air.

"I think you didn't hear me correctly at the end of that conversation. I said to close the case and *then* get back together with her." Chase leaned forward and braced his elbows against his legs. "I know you're a man of faith, and I know you have a sound knowledge of scripture. So I know you know that we're told as Christians not to do anything that creates even the appearance of evil—of misconduct or unethical practices."

"Right. We can't be seen together in public."

"From what you've told me, the last time you tried dating her in secret had devastating results. Do you really want to do that to her again?"

Agonizing hollowness sucked the air out of Bobby's lungs. "No.

I can't do that to her again. You're right." He stood and held his right hand out toward his friend and colleague. "Thank you for caring enough about both Zarah and me to confront me. It couldn't have been easy."

Relief practically dripped from Chase's expression. He bounded out of the chair and pumped Bobby's hand. "I only hope you'll repay the favor if it's ever warranted."

"I hope it won't be."

"So do I."

Bobby left the office shortly after Chase departed, taking the most recent file from Jill home with him, unwilling to leave it in his office—even in his locked file cabinet.

The condo, with boxes in every corner and space where furniture would eventually go, wasn't the relaxing environment he hoped it would be soon. But he wouldn't have been able to relax tonight anyway. He powered up the laptop, got online, and ordered a pizza before navigating his way through the cardboard jungle to his bedroom to change clothes.

He had to imitate a hurdler to get to his phone when it rang, silently reprimanding himself for leaving it in the office.

"Hello?"

"Dude—you coming tonight or what?"

"Mack? I—" Bobby looked at his watch. Seven thirty. "No. I'm not going to make it. Something came up at work." Understatement of the millennium.

"Okay. We'll catch you next time."

"Thanks, Patrick." He ended the call and tossed the phone on the desk, then sank into the chair to put on his trainers.

The file lay there in the middle of the rustic oak desk, staring at him, daring him, accusing him. Rather than think about the issues it raised, Bobby ripped open the top of the nearest box labeled OFFICE and started unpacking.

Six hours—and four antacids—later, he dropped into bed,

physically exhausted. He'd unpacked and organized the entire office, including setting up his personal files in the bottom three drawers of the tall filing cabinet that matched his desk, leaving the top drawer for any sensitive information he might bring home from work.

The accusatory file lay locked in it right now.

He turned and stared at the glass door leading to the curved wrap-around balcony. Two choices lay before him like a fork in the road. He could put things on hold with Zarah until he completed the investigation—meaning charges filed and arrest warrants served. Or he could pull himself from the case, hand it over to someone else, and risk his career and reputation.

He lost something either way.

Sleep did not come. Around seven o'clock, he dragged himself out of the bed, donned sweats and an army T-shirt, and went down to the fitness room to use one of their treadmills, since his still needed to be assembled. Running helped organize his thoughts and boosted his energy level—for the first four miles. He stopped at six miles, returned to the condo, and took a long shower.

Though he didn't usually indulge, today warranted coffee. But which box contained the coffeemaker?

Eight boxes later, he'd found both the machine and the carafe. Now. . .coffee grounds. He rummaged through the bags of groceries sitting on the pantry floor and finally unearthed the pound of store-brand breakfast blend he'd picked up the other day "just in case."

He pulled the eggs and bacon off the top shelf of the almost-empty fridge. In which box had he seen the skillet?

With no other options, Bobby sat on the kitchen floor to eat his breakfast. Would his life be as easy to organize as his condo?

At precisely eleven o'clock, a knock sounded on the door. Bobby rinsed the plate and set it on the paper towels spread beside the sink, then quickly dried his hands before opening the door.

Zarah's hair bloomed in a pile of haphazard curls from the top of a clip at the back of her head, and even in faded jeans and a James

Robertson University long-sleeved T-shirt, she was a splendid sight.

"Come in." He opened the door wide and stepped aside for her to enter.

"I brought you something." Her blue eyes twinkled, and she pulled her left hand from behind her back to reveal a basket—loaded with cleaning sprays and powders, rubber kitchen gloves, and scrub brushes and sponges in a variety of sizes. "Happy housewarming."

Of course, she would bring a gift. *Thanks. Just compound the guilt.* "I appreciate it, but you know you didn't have to."

"I know." She held the basket out toward him until he took it from her.

He carried the basket into the kitchen and put it under the sink for now. Taking a deep breath, he straightened and turned to face her. "I need to tell you something."

His words echoed in Zarah's voice, and they gaped at each other for a long moment.

He inclined his head. "Ladies first."

"Senator Warren came to see me yesterday."

Okay, she definitely had his attention. He paced the kitchen while she told him about Warren's suggestion she back off the injunction next week before the judge.

Another wrinkle. And exactly what he needed to make his decision.

"So, what do you think?" Zarah prompted when he didn't respond at the end of her story.

"I've been investigating the MTHPC." Um. . .not exactly how he'd meant to tell her, but fatigue wreaked havoc with the logic center of his brain.

Zarah grabbed the edge of the counter. "What?"

He told her about the assignment, the choice he'd had to take it or pass on it, and the reason he'd chosen to handle it himself. "I took the case to protect you—to clear your name and make sure no one could place any blame on you."

"You. . .you investigated *me*? How much—what did you look at?" Patches of bright pink flamed in her cheeks.

"Total background and financial records check. Our forensic accountant reviewed your financial records. I only saw the final report with her conclusions and a few pieces of the raw data. I handled your background check. I didn't want anyone else doing that. It felt like enough of a violation with me doing it."

Her throat worked as if she was having trouble swallowing. "*Violation* is a good word." She rubbed her forehead. "But I guess you had to do what you had to do. And have I been cleared or are you going to arrest me?"

He wanted to go to her, to draw her into his arms, to take back everything he'd just said so she wouldn't be ill-disposed toward him from the information he'd dropped on her. "You've been cleared. Way cleared."

"That's good to hear. And do I get to know anything else about the investigation?"

"Don't drop the injunction. Unless you truly feel it's the right thing to do."

She nodded but didn't respond.

"As for the continuing investigation, you have nothing to worry about for yourself."

Zarah knelt down and started pulling dishes out of the box on the floor beside her. "You sound like there's something else you want to tell me."

He crossed the kitchen in two steps and crouched beside her, staying her hands by wrapping his loosely around her wrists. "Zarah, until I finish this investigation. . ."

Comprehension, followed by understanding, filled her sky blue eyes. "You have to put us on hold to avoid the appearance of a conflict of interest."

He sat hard on the tile floor, shocked at her easy grasp of the situation. "We can still be around each other—I mean, we do go to

282

the same church and our grandmothers are best friends. I don't think we can avoid each other. But as far as dating. . .I am so sorry. If I'd known—"

She pressed a hand to his mouth. "You still would have taken the case, because you are a man of integrity who wants to see justice served. I don't want you to ever compromise your values and ethics because of me. We did that before—lied and sneaked around—and it didn't turn out well, when we could have waited a few months until the time was right." She gave him a gentle smile. "I've waited fourteen years. I can wait a little longer."

"I don't know how much longer I can stand to wait. I want to marry you." Mortification burned his neck and face. He hadn't meant to blurt that out.

She rubbed her thumb over his lips. "I'll pray even harder that your investigation ends quickly."

"I don't deserve you."

Her hand moved, and she trailed her fingertips along his jaw. "I know."

Chapter 28

Ooh, he makes me so mad." The door into the screened porch slapped shut behind Flannery.

Zarah dragged her gaze from Bobby to Flannery. The blond bombshell clasped her hands in front of her and shook them as if throttling someone. Zarah had thought inviting Flannery to come to the cookout today—the cookout that seemed to have been painstakingly planned by her grandparents, Sassy, and the Pattersons and scheduled for a Saturday when Zarah, Caylor, and Bobby could all attend—would be fun, so that Flannery wouldn't feel left out. Now, she wondered if it had been the right choice for Flannery.

"Who?"

"That. . .that *man*. That Jamie guy." She threw a dirty look over her shoulder toward the house. "He's the short one who came with—oh, what's her name, the redheaded lady."

"Maureen."

"He calls her Cookie. *Cookie!* Can you believe it? Why not *dollface* or *babycakes*?"

Zarah's laugh turned into a snort. "That's rich, coming from you. You call your grandfather Big Daddy. I think Cookie is a cute grandma nickname."

"Yeah, well, if Big Daddy could have been here, he would have shown that Jamie character what's what."

"You know, you didn't have to come today."

"Well, it's your fault for inviting me. You and Caylor." Flannery crossed her arms and put on her best pout face.

Zarah rolled her eyes and returned to staring through the screen toward the men gathered around the grill on the other end of the large porch that stretched from both sides of this screened portion to wrap around the entirety of Melinda and Greely Patterson's large Victorian.

Her gaze met Bobby's. For a delicious moment, the world stood still. Then Pops said something to Bobby, and he broke eye contact.

"How's the not-having-any-contact thing going?" Flannery spoke in a low tone.

"It's been two weeks since he told me. He's putting in so much overtime on the case that it's doing a fair job of keeping us apart."

"Is he going to stop coming to church, or are the two of you going to alternate weeks as to who'll be there and who won't?"

"No—nothing like that. We're going to continue with all of our normal activities and get to at least see each other that way. We just can't officially date until"—Zarah glanced around to make sure no one would overhear her, and, seeing no one near their secluded spot in the screened porch, still lowered her voice—"he finishes his investigation."

Not running to him and throwing her arms around him as soon as she'd arrived at the Pattersons' house an hour ago for the multi-family cookout had been torture.

The door from the kitchen slammed, making them both whirl around. Caylor stomped toward them, tea sloshing over the rims of three red plastic cups. "Next time y'all want something to drink, you're going in to get it yourselves. I thought I'd never get away from Mr. Science Guy."

"Which one is that?" Zarah took one of the cups from the fuming redhead. She didn't really need to ask. If Jamie was the short one, Mr. Science Guy had to be—

"The tall one with the curly hair and the pimply neck. I know, that's a horrible thing to say, and I'm sorry"—she looked up at the ceiling—"but I didn't think he'd ever stop talking about the theoretical physics experiments he's involved with over at Vandy."

Yep. Zarah had pegged him as Vanderbilt University type.

"What I want to know is how it's Zarah who managed to be the first one of the three of us to snag a hot guy when she's the one who never dates. She kisses one frog, and he turns into a handsome prince. I've kissed a pondful of frogs, and all I have to show for it is a past full of toads." Caylor twisted her face into a comically pained expression.

Zarah laughed despite the longing eating away at her. "I haven't managed to snag him yet. Remember, we can't date—"

Flannery waved her hands dismissively. "Yeah, yeah, yeah. You can't date until he closes his investigation, blah, blah, blah."

Zarah tried to shush her, reaching to cover Flannery's mouth, glancing around to make sure no one would hear.

Flannery pushed Zarah's hands away, but she did lower her voice. "You have the guarantee that as soon as he *does* close the case, he's going to be knocking on your door."

Zarah arched a brow. "Or maybe I'll be knocking on his."

"Ooh-la-la, a modern woman." Caylor fanned herself with her hands, as if about to faint. "Flannery, I think we finally have had an effect on our dear Zarah."

The kitchen door opened again, and Kiki joined them. "Zarah, dear, may I steal you away for a moment?"

"Sure." She excused herself from her friends and followed Kiki out of the screened portion of the porch opposite from where the men supervised the grill.

Kiki lowered herself with a groan and popping knees onto the white slat porch swing. She patted the seat next to her.

Zarah joined her. "What's going on?"

"I'm worried about you, Zarah. I noticed you and Bobby have not exchanged a single word since you got here. I don't think I've seen the two of you in the same room together." She took Zarah's hand in hers and stroked the back of it. "Is everything all right between the two of you? You haven't had a spat, have you?"

Zarah grinned at the old-fashioned *spat*. To set her grandmother's mind at ease, she explained the situation, though revealing as few details as possible and asking Kiki not to share it with anyone but Pops—and leaving out the part about having been under investigation herself originally.

Kiki hugged her neck, her broad smile once again in place. "I'm so happy it's not something more serious than that. Pops and I will pray continually for a quick solution to Bobby's case."

"Kiki, have you and Lindy actively been trying to push Bobby and me together? It seems like you've taken a bit too much interest in our relationship. Before the DC trip, you were always asking me about him, mentioning his name, or telling me something Lindy said about him."

"I told you before I just want to see you happy. And I could see that you'd be happy with Bobby Patterson." She kissed Zarah's cheek. "Now, go back and enjoy the young folks' company."

When Zarah returned to the screened porch, Flannery and Caylor pounced. "What was that all about?"

She told them. "I knew my grandmother had been a little too interested in the progress of my relationship with Bobby ever since he came back to town."

Caylor narrowed her eyes. "And my grandmother has been a little too anxious to mention her friends' *unmarried* sons and grandsons to me. She told me she'd given a friend of hers permission to pass along my Web and e-mail addresses to this woman's son—who's in his late fifties! Can you imagine?"

Flannery shuddered. "Sounds like you two have a problem."

"Yeah? What's that?" Caylor asked.

"Grandmothers who fancy themselves your very own Cupids. Imagine—back in the old days, they would have just hired a matchmaker and been done with it."

Caylor cocked her head as if giving the idea serious thought. "You know, a matchmaker isn't that bad of an idea."

"Uh. . .remember Mr. Science Guy inside?" Flannery tapped her knuckles against Caylor's head as if knocking on a block of wood.

Caylor pulled the corners of her mouth down in a grimace. "Oh yeah. Sassy does suffer from extremely bad eyesight. Seems like her judgment is going, too." Caylor looked toward the sky again. "I know, God. I'm sorry. I'm a horrible, awful, judgmental person."

Zarah couldn't hold back any longer. She threw her arms around her friends' necks and drew them close for a hug.

Caylor gasped; Flannery laughed.

"What brought this on?" Flannery asked in her right ear.

"I don't know how I would have gotten through the last fourteen years without the two of you. You're closer than best friends—Bobby was right. You're my sisters."

Bobby turned from the sight of Zarah's sudden three-way hug with Flannery and Caylor, a sense of contentment merging with sadness. He wanted to be the one she hugged so tightly and publicly.

Seeing her here with her grandparents and best friends made him ache to be able to be at her side, to experience everything with her, not just observe her interactions.

"Robert, right?"

Oh no. The advertising guy. "Bobby."

Jamie O'Connor—short, too groomed, and overdressed for this casual family function in slacks and a button-down oxford shirt—set his cup on the porch railing. "They said you know that blond chick— Fanny, I think they said her name is."

Bobby barely kept himself from spewing his tea through his

nose. He swallowed it and coughed to clear the little bit he'd inhaled. "*Flannery*, not Fanny."

That was rich. Fanny. He couldn't wait to tell Zarah. . .he could probably do it at church tomorrow.

"Oh, I guess I didn't hear it right when we were introduced. Anyway, what can you tell me about her?"

Some embarrassing stories from junior high school, which she wouldn't appreciate. Her penchant for protecting her best friend.

He glanced down the porch. Zarah, Flannery, and Caylor now sat at the table in the screened-in, gazebolike area of the porch behind the kitchen. What would Flannery want him to share with a stranger— one she'd watched with mild distaste in her eyes not an hour ago?

"She's an editor at one of the book publishers in town. She grew up here." He shrugged, hoping to give the impression he didn't know much more than that.

"An editor? Do you know what authors she works with?"

A question he could answer honestly. "No clue."

"Hmm. . ." Jamie leaned against the porch railing, eyes narrowed with speculation as he looked toward the other end of the porch.

"Robert! James!" Mamm's voice carried from the kitchen door.

"Guess we're needed."

"Food's almost ready," Zarah's grandfather said over his shoulder. "They probably want you to help set up the tables out here."

Bobby nodded and went inside—through the living room so he didn't have to walk past Zarah.

With the help of Jamie, the gangly scientist, and Gerald Bradley— the scientist's grandfather—end-to-end folding tables lined the stretch of porch between the grill and the screened-in portion.

Somehow without looking at each other, Zarah and Bobby managed to find seats at opposite ends of the long table. Mamm eyed him with concern, but thankfully, she didn't say anything.

Greedad and Victor Breitinger carried the sheet pans of steaks and chicken over from the grill and served each person individually before placing the pans, with plenty of meat remaining, on the table. Other dishes were passed around—from left to right, as they'd always done at Mamm and Greedad's house.

Talk and laughter continued long after everyone finished eating—until Greedad remarked upon the time and that the football game would kick off in a couple minutes.

Everyone filed through the kitchen, scraping off their plates into the garbage before setting them into the large, farmhouse-style sink.

"Now—everyone *out of the kitchen*. I refuse to have anyone in here working while there's fun and fellowship to be had elsewhere in the house." Mamm blocked the sink and shooed everyone from the room.

Bobby followed his grandfather into the family room where the University of Tennessee game appeared on the supersized television.

"Ladies, if you aren't interested in the game, I'd love for you to join me in the sitting room." Mamm carried one of the large pitchers of iced tea with her into the other room.

Zarah cast a glance in Bobby's direction before following their grandmothers from the room. He tried his best to get lost in the game, but the radar in his brain tuned to Zarah wouldn't let him. When he heard her offer to refill the tea pitcher, he pushed himself up off the sofa and carried his cup toward the kitchen as if getting more to drink.

"I thought you came in here to refill the tea pitcher." He kept his voice low, trying to avoid any prying ears.

Zarah turned from the sink where she held a plate under a trickle of water. "I just can't help myself. I see a sink full of dishes, and it's like there's this little switch in my brain that needs to see them washed before I can walk out of the kitchen."

He pushed up the sleeves of his favorite waffle-weave thermal sweatshirt. "I'll help."

She turned and held the scrub brush in front of her like a sword. "I don't think that's a good idea."

"Zarah, it's just us. We already know as soon as this. . .whole thing is over, we're going to be together. Besides, no one can see us."

"God can. Bobby, we promised we'd only see each other in group settings, only around other people, and not in a way that would lead to the appearance that we're dating. I'm not breaking that promise again. I know that unlike my fa—unlike the general, God will forgive me if I screw up and break a promise. But if I purposely flirt with temptation, if I don't avoid being alone with you, how can I live with myself?"

An image of a young man in a bowler hat and spats danced through Bobby's memory. "I'm just like him."

Zarah lowered the scrub brush. "Like who?"

"That con man from the musical Caylor was in. The traveling salesman who went from town to town and manipulated people into doing something against their nature for his benefit. That's what I was just trying to do to you. I wasn't thinking about anything other than what I wanted. I didn't think about how it would affect you—or even what God would want me to do. Just about my own gratification."

"Don't beat yourself up. We all slip up occasionally. That's why it's good to have others around us to keep us accountable."

"Why do you always have to be right?" He backed toward the door. "I'm sorry. Maybe this time apart will be good for us. It'll allow me time to grow up and start acting like the man you deserve instead of the boy who deserted you."

"Whether you feel like you deserve me or not, you have me—or you will. Eventually. Just hurry up, okay?"

He blew her a kiss and bowed. "Yes, ma'am. Oh. . .and will you do me a favor?"

"What's that?"

"Put the dish brush down and go back and be social with everyone else. Do you really want your grandmother—or mine—coming in here and seeing what you're doing?"

Zarah laughed. "Okay. Just let me finish this one—"

He started back toward her.

"All right!" She turned the water off and reached for a towel to dry her hands. "I'll be right behind you as soon as I refill the tea pitcher."

Exiting through the dining room to go see what the other women were doing before calling it an early night, he ran into someone in the dark dining room.

She grabbed his arm for stability. "Robert?"

"Mamm?" He reached out and clutched her elbows to keep her from falling over.

"What is going on? I thought you and Zarah worked things out. Why aren't you talking to each other?"

He explained in as few details as he could, swore her to secrecy, then kissed her forehead. "So you have nothing to fear. You and Katrina have been successful with your matchmaking."

Mamm made an appalled sound in the back of her throat. "I'm certain I don't know what you are talking about."

"And I'm certain you do." He gave her a squeeze, then moved toward the front hall to retrieve his leather jacket. "My grandmother, the matchmaker."

Chapter 29

Zarah jumped when her desk phone rang. Over the past four weeks, her patience had worn thin, she hadn't slept well, and every little noise startled her.

She picked up the receiver. "Yes, Dennis?"

"I need to see you in my office, please."

"Coming." She hung up, glanced in the mirror hanging on the side of her file cabinet, and walked away with the vision of dark circles, tired eyes, and pale cheeks indelibly imprinted in her mind. It was only Tuesday, and she already found herself wishing for the weekend. If she wasn't careful, if she didn't figure out a way to get a few restful nights' sleep soon, she'd probably get sick again.

No matter how strong her conviction had been a month ago when she told Bobby she could wait however long it took him to finish his investigation, she wasn't sure how much longer she could hold out. Not only was she suspicious of everyone she came in contact with outside of the commission, but she couldn't stop thinking about Bobby and dreaming of their future together.

That brought a slight smile. The future she dreamed for them now was quite different from the future she'd dreamed for them at seventeen.

She knocked on Dennis's door before opening it.

"Come in, Dr. Mitchell."

Formal title? He had someone in there with him. She straightened her shoulders and pinched her cheeks to try to raise a little color in them before opening the door.

"Dr. Mitchell, I believe you know Special Agent Patterson of the Tennessee Criminal Investigations Unit."

Zarah's heart soared, and she drank in the sight of Bobby dressed in a charcoal gray suit and looking more deliciously handsome than she remembered.

But as quickly as her elation came, it vanished. Bobby was *here*—in Dennis's office. That meant. . .

She didn't want to speculate, so she cut off that train of thought as she sank into the spare chair. Dennis and Bobby both regained their seats.

"Agent Patterson asked me to have you join us to let you know I've recalled Glenn Vaughan from the field so he can question Mr. Vaughan about the riverfront property."

Zarah looked from one to the other. Since Bobby had informed Dennis of the investigation into possible fraud connected with the commission, Dennis had been nearly beside himself trying to help Bobby in any way he could to find the culprits.

"You are Mr. Vaughan's direct supervisor, aren't you Z—Dr. Mitchell?" Bobby had his notepad out.

"I am. He's an archaeologist who works for us as basically an independent contractor. He works in the field but comes in twice a week to report on his activities and bring in his findings so we can analyze them in the labs here."

"How would you rate his work?"

"He seems to do a good job. He's discovered quite a few promising pieces at the riverfront property." She searched Bobby's face—that handsome, beloved face—for any sign of what he was thinking, but either they'd been apart too long and she'd lost the ability to read him, or else he had developed the skill of hiding any shred of emotion or reaction.

Dennis's phone buzzed. "Yes, Debby? . . .Thank you." He returned the handset to the cradle. "Mr. Vaughan is on his way up."

Zarah tucked her hands under her thighs and rocked back and forth slightly. She glanced at Bobby, but he kept his gaze cast down on the notebook in his left hand.

She jumped at the knock on the door.

"Come in," Dennis called.

Glenn Vaughan, a slight, nondescript man in his forties, paused and eyed Zarah and Bobby. "I'm sorry, I didn't mean to interrupt."

"You're not interrupting. Come in and shut the door behind you." Dennis motioned him to the only remaining chair in the room. "Glenn, this is Special Agent Patterson from the Tennessee Criminal Investigations Unit. He's here to ask you a few questions."

Zarah watched Glenn Vaughan's face carefully as Bobby asked him about his background and experience. A line of perspiration formed across Glenn's forehead. Her heart sank. A sign of guilt?

Guilt of what?

"Mr. Vaughan, have you ever accepted money to falsify your reports and submit items stolen from protected federal and state land to the Middle Tennessee Historic Preservation Commission?"

Zarah clenched her teeth together to keep from showing a reaction.

"I. . .I don't know what you mean."

"Did you, on the night of October 18, enter the grounds of Fort Negley illegally and take pieces of brick and masonry work which you tried to pass off as archaeological finds from the property the commission is currently contracting you to examine?"

Zarah closed her eyes a moment. How could she not have known? She'd remarked upon the similarity between what Glenn had sent to be studied and the stone and masonry work at Fort Negley. How could she have been so naive?

"I. . .I think I need to contact a lawyer."

Bobby stood. "You can call one from the police station after they book you. Glenn Vaughan, you are being arrested for desecration of county property, with other charges pending." Bobby recited the Miranda rights as he escorted the archaeologist from the office.

Zarah stared at Dennis. "Glenn Vaughan? Taking bribes to make us think there was something of historical value on the East Nashville property?" She pressed her fingers to her temples, trying to alleviate the forming headache. "Did you know?"

Dennis ran his fingers through his steel gray hair. "I suspected—and told Agent Patterson."

"Why didn't you tell me?"

"I didn't want him to know he was a suspect. They've had him under surveillance for several weeks now. That's how they know about Fort Negley."

Her stomach twisted. "I cannot believe an archaeologist would agree to such. . .treachery against such a significant historic site."

"You'll need to bring the rest of the team in. I'll explain to them what happened, but unfortunately, the aftermath of this will fall on you. The agents will question each team member to find out if any others were involved. With those who were not, you will have to put together a new team. Put Justin and Reina in charge. Their field projects are on hold until the spring, so they can head up the team to go out and see what's actually been done on the East Nashville site. When they tell you what they've found, I'm going to depend on you to help me prepare a report for the Metro Council and the senate committee. This is going to wreak havoc with our funding for next year."

"Yes, sir." She stood, almost surprised to find her legs would support her weight.

"And Zarah?"

"Yes?"

"It's almost over. Very soon, we'll be able to get back to doing what it is we're supposed to be doing around this place. And that's preserving history, not making it."

As soon as Bobby returned to his office from the downtown police station, where Glenn Vaughan was even now being booked, he called Captain Carroll's office.

Julie answered the phone. "Yes?"

"Is everything set for the meeting with the director this afternoon?"

"He'll be here at two, and he said he's anxiously awaiting your report. He's ready for this case to be closed."

"Aren't we all? Thanks, Julie." He disconnected, then called Gage and Milligan. They spent the rest of the morning reviewing every detail, every fact of the case. Shortly before noon, the state district attorney's office called to tell Bobby they had his warrants ready.

He sent Gage and Milligan to lunch, then went and stood over the fax machine in the common area outside his office while copies of the arrest and search warrants slowly printed. Once the transmission ended, he jogged up the stairs.

Julie sat at her desk eating a sandwich. "Go on in. He's been expecting you."

"Thanks." Bobby knocked on the open door.

"Finally." Captain Carroll left his lunch of what looked like leftover Italian on his desk and moved around to the small conference table.

Bobby closed the door and joined him. They started collating the copies of the several warrants—those which they needed and those which needed to be sent on to other regional unit offices.

After the warrants were straightened out and the necessary copies given to Julie to fax, Bobby reviewed everything for the meeting with the director. Captain Carroll helped him refine a few areas but deemed everything ready.

"He'll be here in less than an hour." Carroll stood. "Let's be on our toes with everything. I'll call the regional captains and get the ball rolling there so you can finish what we talked about."

"Yes, sir." Bobby took the warrants back to his office—where Gage and Milligan waited, looking for all the world like two fathers-to-be sitting in a maternity ward waiting room.

He gave them the warrants they needed for the tasks they were assigned and sent them out.

At 1:55, he gathered up all his files and paperwork and headed back to Captain Carroll's office.

The director, who had apparently just arrived, turned upon Bobby's entrance into the office. "Agent Patterson, isn't it?"

Bobby shook the man's hand. "Yes, sir. Thank you for taking the time to come in today. I know the week before Thanksgiving can be hectic."

"Not a problem. I can always make time to come by when we're ready to close an investigation."

Bobby and his two direct superiors sat at the table. Captain Carroll nodded for Bobby to start as soon as they were all settled.

"Captain Carroll explained to me that it is not usually necessary for a special agent in charge to review the entire case and his investigation methodology. However, since I'm new to the unit and we're all still trying to get to know each other and how we work, the captain and I wanted to review everything just to be sure we're all on the same page. He suggested calling you in, sir, since you do have an interest in the case."

The director gave a swift nod. "I appreciate the consideration. I have been reading your updates with interest, and I am very impressed by how thorough your investigation has been."

"Thank you, sir." Bobby looked down at his notepad to refresh his memory on how he wanted to start this briefing. "As you know, when we first opened this investigation, we initially focused on the director and the assistant director of the Middle Tennessee Historic Preservation Commission. We pulled background and financials on both of them and began our investigation. . . ."

He reviewed the investigation methods, including the forensic accountant's involvement, and what they had learned in general. "We also pulled all of the financial information for the commission. It was at this point in the investigation we started seeing some transactions that raised flags for us. So we went deeper as well as broadening the scope of our investigation."

As best he could, he described verbally what was still drawn on the whiteboard in his office in concentric, overlapping, and arrow-connected boxes and circles. At one point in the investigation, Milligan had joked that the board was starting to look like a very complex game of Six Degrees of Kevin Bacon, as they had discovered a multitude of layers of interconnectedness amongst the parties involved.

Bobby paused when a buzzing sound drew the director's attention away from them. The director pulled out his smart phone and read a message. The skin around his eyes tightened and he pressed his lips together, shoulders stiffening. Bobby threw a questioning glance at Captain Carroll, who urged him to continue.

"As we looked deeper into the commission's financial records, we began to notice what looked like connections between several large donations to the commission and private real estate transactions by the commission's director, Dr. Dennis Forrester."

"Are you telling me"—the director leaned forward—"that Dennis Forrester was using the commission for—for what?—for laundering money?"

"That was what we wanted to find out, sir." Avoiding any mention of Zarah, Bobby described their renewed investigation of Dennis Forrester, his relationship with the MTHPC, and his several and varied real estate transactions over the past three years that seemed to relate with some of the red flags in the commission's financial reports.

After an hour, Captain Carroll called for a break and asked Julie to bring in coffee. Bobby excused himself; and as soon as he cleared the office door, he made a dash for the nearest restroom. He braced his hands against the edge of the counter and took a few deep breaths before leaning over to splash water in his face. The first hour had been the easy part of the report. He did not look forward to what was coming next.

Collected once again, he returned to the captain's suite. Julie handed him a bottle of water on his way through her office.

When they resumed their seats at the table, the director seemed even more uptight than he'd become after receiving the text message earlier. But he entreated Bobby to continue, so continue he did. He talked about the genuine leads as well as some of the rabbit trails their investigation had followed in the wake of discovering what looked like evidence pointing to Dennis Forrester's guilt.

"But once we realized the connection between the financial irregularities in the commission's accounts and Dennis Forrester's real estate transactions were not connected, we had to redirect our efforts."

The director reeled back in his chair, face slack with shock. "You are certain it is not Dennis Forrester? All the evidence you discussed so far seems enough to convict him of embezzlement or money laundering."

"That's what we thought, too, sir. So we kept digging."

As Bobby talked about the long, tedious weeks he'd put in on the investigation, some of the stress from them began to lift. Soon this would all be in the hands of the state district attorney.

Soon he would be able to get on with his own life. A life that included Zarah.

Now he was coming to it—the most difficult part of concluding this investigation. "Since the last update I submitted, there have been several breakthroughs in the case. Because of a suspicion that one of the field researchers at the commission might be involved, we placed him under surveillance. He was booked at nine o'clock this morning on charges of defacing public property, trespassing, and falsifying state documents. Other charges are pending."

Bobby stole a glance at Captain Carroll, who gave him an almost imperceptible nod. He turned his gaze back to the director. "But I imagine you already know that, Director Vaughan, as I assume someone else in your family sent you a message a little while ago informing you of your nephew's arrest."

The director blanched, his eyes swinging between Captain Carroll and Bobby. "My. . .my nephew was involved in this?"

"Yes, sir. Once we were certain of his involvement, the other pieces started falling into place. You did a good job of hiding the money and eliminating the paper trail, sir—and setting Dennis Forrester up to look guilty." Yes, Vaughan had been good. . .but Bobby, with his own future on hold, had been spurred to be better.

"As we speak, agents from this unit are serving an arrest warrant on your brother-in-law, Judge Doddridge, as well as executing a search warrant on the judge's home. A team from the Memphis division is searching your home and office there, and a team from the Knoxville office is searching your chalet in the Smoky Mountains—the one I expect you never thought any one would track down. The state district attorney's office is working with the FBI to seize your domestic and international bank accounts."

Bobby stood and pulled the last warrant from the folder atop the pile he had brought with him. "And I am executing this arrest warrant. Samuel Vaughn, I'm placing you under arrest for bank fraud, conspiracy to commit fraud, bribery of public officials, and money laundering."

Even though it wasn't a public, walk-of-shame-in-handcuffs kind of arrest, none had ever been so satisfying to Bobby. He now faced an even greater mountain of paperwork, but rather than a chore, it would be a joy, knowing the release he now had.

Though there were hours yet to go today, as soon as he got back to his office, he closed the door and pulled out his cell phone. He scrolled through the address book until he found the entry he wanted and pushed the CALL button.

His insides twanged like a bowstring at the female voice that answered. "Hello?"

"Flannery, it's Bobby. I need your help."

Chapter 30

$\mathcal{S}$o much to do, so little time.

Bobby glanced at the clock. Not quite midnight. He looked at his desk. Reports and follow-ups, mostly finished, yet still a daunting amount to be accomplished. And until it was all done. . .

After the arrests and searches on Tuesday, his team had dived into sorting through all the seized information while he wrote the reports and briefs—those usually required after arrests were made, plus a few extra pieces necessary due to the involvement of Director Vaughan.

Today—wait, was today still Wednesday?—all four of the local news broadcasts had led with the breaking news of the "major sting operation" that had brought down a local judge and the director of one of the major law enforcement agencies in the state.

"Don't answer any questions from anyone—not even people you know. Once the reporters find out that you're the agent in charge of the investigation, they'll try to get information from anyone connected with you."

Bobby forced his gaze back to the unit's public affairs officer. He'd brought down CEOs of major corporations out in California and never had to be briefed on how to act and what not to say.

The spin manager slid a memo across the desk toward him. "Here are the approved talking points. Everyone has a copy of these. But I suggest screening your phone calls carefully—both here and at home as long as this case is making news. Since you're going to be at the court-house tomorrow, which is likely to be a circus, make sure you're very familiar with these before you get there."

Bobby hoped his raised eyebrows gave the appearance of interest. After getting only three hours of sleep yesterday, tonight wasn't shaping up to look much better. But if he and his team could plow through everything in the next few days, they might all actually get to spend Thanksgiving with their families next week.

"You'll review this with your team? I've e-mailed the memo to everyone but just wanted to review those points with you, as the team leader."

He nodded his heavy head. "I'll go over it with them tomorrow morning."

She yawned. "I think that's all I needed to tell you, then."

"Thanks." He turned back toward his computer, anxious to finish his paperwork so he could go home and get back to the personal projects he wanted to get finished before next Thursday.

At two o'clock in the morning, he e-mailed the last report to Captain Carroll—who'd gone home hours ago—and shut everything down for the night. He wished he could take a few hours of comp time in the morning and sleep in. But he had to be at the DA's office at nine to be briefed before heading over to the courthouse for the preliminary hearings in General Sessions Court—something that could last all day, depending on when the case was called.

At the condo complex, he pulled his car into the garage—and almost nodded off as soon as he cut the engine off. He forced himself to take the stairs up to the fourth floor instead of the elevator; he had to get some kind of physical activity in today.

After twice trying to unlock the door to the condo with the remote for the car, he finally made it inside. The keys slipped out of his hand and landed with a *thunk* on the wood floor. He left them there—and dropped his briefcase beside them so he wouldn't have to search for them in the morning. By the time he got to the bedroom, he had his coat and tie off and his shirt unbuttoned. He kicked off his shoes, and his belt whipped from the loops of the waistband of his pants when he yanked it off.

He dropped face-first across the bed and would have stayed there for the next several hours— but remembered something he had to do tonight.

Groaning, he pushed himself up and shuffled to the spare bedroom where he'd moved the boxes he hadn't yet unpacked.

A stubbed toe and a pile of frustration later, he found the box he needed—at the bottom of a stack in the back of the closet, naturally. Rather than take the time to go get a pair of scissors or a knife to cut the tape, he ripped the cardboard. Digging below his yearbooks, the scrapbook his mother kept for him through his high school football career, and a box containing photos from most of his overseas postings, he found what he was looking for. He wedged the shoe box out, opened it to make sure it was the right one, then carried it to the front hall, where he set it on the floor beside his briefcase and keys.

He returned to the bedroom and changed into pajama bottoms before climbing into bed. He barely lifted his head when he reached over to make sure his alarm clock was set. His last coherent thought was to pray the case came up early on the docket and that the judge could see enough probable cause in all three arrests to bind them over for trial.

"Happy Thanksgiving, Dr. Mitchell."

Zarah looked up from the computer to find all four of her interns crowded in the doorway of her office. She waved them in. "I'm pretty sure I remember that Friday was your last day. So what are you guys doing here the day before Thanksgiving?"

Amberleigh rolled her eyes as she perched on the edge of one of the chairs. "Dr. M, it's 'y'all' not 'you guys.' You've lived here long enough to know that by now."

Zarah laughed, though a memory twinged. She'd always teased Bobby about saying *y'all* when everyone in New Mexico said *you guys*. "I'll try to remember that and adapt accordingly."

"We just wanted to come by and tell you how much we enjoyed working here this semester." Felicity perched on the wooden arm of Amberleigh's chair. "This was my third internship, and I've never learned as much anywhere else as I learned here."

Amberleigh, Adam, and Jonah nodded.

"So we wanted to give you this." Felicity turned and Adam drew from behind his back a large gift bag, which he handed to Zarah.

She took it, surprised at the weight. "You guys—*y'all* didn't have to give me anything."

"We would have done it last week before we left, but we needed to wait until after you turned in our evaluations, just so nothing looked fishy," Jonah said.

Zarah let out a rueful laugh. "Yeah, we've had enough fishiness around here recently."

"Go on, open it!" Amberleigh bounced in her seat.

"Okay." Zarah set the tall purple and black abstract-design gift bag on the floor and lifted out something flat and heavy wrapped in lavender tissue paper. The paper fell away under her hands to reveal. . .the back of a wood-framed stretched art canvas. She turned it over. "Oh, my. . ."

The oil-painted portrait of Zander and Madeleine Breitinger's wedding picture trembled in her hands. Madeleine's blue eyes danced; Zander's dark blond hair shone as if kissed by the sun. Emotion clogged Zarah's throat.

"We know how much the story of your ancestors means to you," Adam said in a low voice. "You've worked so hard to make sure we learned everything we could this semester, so we wanted to make sure we gave something that would reflect how much your mentorship meant to each one of us."

She had to blink back pools of moisture before she looked up at them. "How in the world did you do this?"

"Jonah's mother is an artist. She came in and took some pictures of the enlarged photo downstairs and painted it from that." Felicity beamed.

Zarah stood and hugged each one of them. "You'll never know how much this means to me. Thank you."

"My mom attached one of her cards to the back. She said for you to contact her before you frame it. She can hook you up with a friend of hers who does framing."

Long after the students left, Zarah stared at the portrait, standing up against the wall at the back of her desk.

She owed her existence to Zander and Madeleine. She owed her belief in the power of love to hold strong over years of separation to them, too. She just hoped God wouldn't make it as difficult for her and Bobby to find their happy ending as it was for her great-great-great-grandparents.

She glanced around the office, the joyful interruption the first high point in a week. Since Glenn Vaughan's arrest last Tuesday, everything and everyone at the commission had been discombobulated. And when the news of Bobby's case broke—leading each of the local news broadcasts Wednesday and filling much of the front page of Thursday's paper with the splashy news that the director of the Tennessee Criminal Investigations Unit had been arrested by one of his own agents, along with the judge who'd handled all of the commission's cases for the past three years—she'd been nearly as shocked as everyone else in Nashville.

Bobby had looked good on TV—at least, the fleeting glimpse she'd seen of him as he entered the courthouse Thursday morning for the arraignment hearings.

Dennis had been closeted with the Metro Council or senate committee for most of last week, and everyone had looked to Zarah for guidance—and information. The guidance she could give. The information. . .she was still a little sketchy on the details herself.

She sighed and turned back to the new information on Zander's regiment the archivist from the state library had sent over a few days ago. Losing herself in more research into her great-great-great-grandparents' lives had been the only distraction she'd found to keep her from thinking about Bobby constantly in her spare time.

Her phone rang. Her heart leaped, then plummeted at the familiar number on the caller ID screen. She reached for it and tucked the handset between her shoulder and ear.

"Hi, Caylor."

"Hey, Zare. How are you holding up?"

She leaned back in her chair. "As well as can be expected."

"Have you heard from him yet?"

"No. I imagine he's hardly left the office in the past week."

"And you've been patiently waiting?"

"As patiently as possible." Zarah pushed her heavy curls back from her face. Every time the phone rang, every time someone knocked on her office door, her hope soared only to come crashing down when it wasn't Bobby. "I only hope he can clear it up before Thursday."

"I hope so, too. Of course, I'm not sure how I feel about having dinner at your grandparents' house and having to watch the two of you be all lovey-dovey with each other."

They discussed Thanksgiving—for which her grandparents always included Lindy and Greeley Patterson along with Sassy and Caylor. "Could you have imagined last year that Bobby would not only be back in your life this year but that you'd be anxiously awaiting the day when the two of you can officially start dating?"

"Nope. I figured it would be like the previous years—eating too much food on Thursday at Pops and Kiki's house and then playing card games the rest of the afternoon. Then on Friday, watching movies and eating desserts all day with you and Flannery."

"And what's to say we can't still do that? Just bring your man with you—if he can come. If not, Flan and I will try to get your mind off him and on to Cary Grant and Gregory Peck and Robert Mitchum and Dana Andrews and maybe, if Flan leaves the room, Frank Sinatra and Bing Crosby and a little *High Society*."

"Yes, listening to you and Flan bicker about whether we're going to watch film noir or musicals is definitely one of the highlights of my Thanksgiving weekend." Zarah checked e-mail one last time—nothing that couldn't wait until after the holiday. She turned off the computer.

She stood and crossed to the window to check if it was still raining. "I hate that it's dark so early this time of year."

"Hmm. . . ? Oh yeah."

"Are you even listening to me?" She transferred her phone from hand to hand, ear to ear, to get her jacket on.

"Sorry. Just got a text from Flan. Want to go grab a bite to eat?"

"Sure. How about DaVinci's Pizza over on Hayes? I've been craving their blue cheese and spinach pizza recently." Probably because she'd had a few slices of it when she'd taken the interns over there for lunch on Friday.

"Sounds good. Are you getting ready to leave the office?"

She glanced at her watch. "Yeah. It's only four thirty, but everyone else left at noon today. So I'll lock up and head on over there."

"Okay. I'll text Flan to let her know."

The local pizzeria, nearly empty when Zarah arrived, filled up pretty quickly as people left work at the nearby hospitals and office buildings, surprising for the evening before Thanksgiving.

They demolished the large pizza in short order, then each ordered dessert—Snickers pies all the way around.

"You realize," Caylor said around a mouthful of candy bar bits, caramel, cream cheese, and piecrust, "that we're ruining our appetites for desserts Friday."

"Not hardly." Zarah licked a smear of caramel off the back of her spoon before plunging it back into the sticky pie. "I have never met a slice of lemonade icebox pie I couldn't eat. And I have two of them in my freezer, just waiting for us."

Flannery's phone beeped. Zarah and Caylor looked at each other, shook their heads, and rolled their eyes. She read whatever message it was and then—to their complete and utter astonishment—turned the phone off and dropped it into her purse.

"I told everyone I was taking the rest of the weekend off, that I would be out of touch until Monday morning." Flannery dived back into her pie with gusto.

Zarah dropped her spoon and applauded. "Good for you. And I'm sure your grandfather and parents will appreciate it, too."

Caylor harrumphed. "I think everyone driving between here and Birmingham tonight will appreciate it."

"Hey, I've been hands-free with the phone ever since I got the new car."

"Yeah, because you needed a car that doubles as a phone." Caylor winked at her.

"Well. . ." Flannery wiped her mouth and tossed the napkin on the table. "It's almost seven, so I'd better be hitting the road—I told Big Daddy I'd be at his place by seven thirty to pick him up."

"He doesn't mind traveling so late?"

"He didn't have much of a choice—the church decided not to move their Wednesday services to Tuesday this week, so he had to be there to conduct prayer meeting."

"I thought he was supposed to retire this past summer."

"They asked him to stay until they found a replacement." Flannery dug in her huge bag and came out with some cash. "I think he's finally realized that until he tells them what his last day is, they're not going to start seriously looking for another pastor."

Caylor took Flannery's cash, added her own to it, and stuck it in the bill folder. Zarah added hers as well, and they donned jackets and headed out to their cars.

"Drive safely." Zarah hugged Flannery.

"You know I will." She hugged Zarah and Caylor. "Happy Thanksgiving."

They echoed the sentiment.

After a quick stop at a drugstore to pick up batteries for her digital camera, Zarah headed home.

She glanced at the dark front porch. "I've got to start remembering to turn that light on."

But at least the living room light was on.

Wait—she never left lights on inside when she left the house. Maybe she'd just forgotten. She stuck the pack of batteries into her carryall and hefted it out of the front passenger seat, finding her house key before getting out of the car so she didn't have to fumble for it in the dark overhang of the small front porch while loaded down with the briefcase and the gift bag containing the portrait.

As soon as she touched the key to the dead bolt, the door moved.

Her heart leaped into her throat. A light on inside, the front door not latched. Something wasn't right here.

She ran back to the car as quietly as she could, got in, and locked the door.

Trembling, she yanked her phone out of its pocket in the bag and called the one and only person she could think of.

"Zarah?"

"Bobby—I think someone's broken into my house." Even to her own ears, her voice sounded shrill.

"Are you there, right now? You aren't in the house, are you?" The smooth calmness in Bobby's voice soothed her raw nerves.

"No—the door is unlatched and there's a light on inside. I'm sitting in my car with the doors locked."

"Do you see any unfamiliar cars?"

She jerked around, looking side to side and behind her. "No. I recognize all of my neighbor's cars."

"Okay, if it is a break-in, they probably aren't there anymore. I'm in my car right now. I'll be there in less than five minutes. You just sit tight. Don't get out of your car until I get there, okay? Promise me."

"Don't worry. I'm not budging."

"Good. Now. Tell me about your day."

As a tactic to both calm her down and keep her on the phone until he drove up, it worked. She was just getting to the Snickers pie when headlights flashed in her rearview mirror. Even though she recognized his car, she didn't unlock her door until she saw him climb out.

They both hung up at the same time. Bobby gave her a quick hug. "I'm glad you called me."

"You're the only cop I know."

"In this context, I guess *cop* works. Now, I want you to get back in the car and lock the door until I come out and give you the all clear, okay?"

She did as told, gripping her cell phone in her hand, ready to click SEND on the 911 she'd dialed.

A few long moments later, the front porch light blazed on and Bobby stepped out and motioned her in.

Leaving everything but her keys and phone locked in the car, she joined him on the porch. "Well?"

"You have to see it for yourself." Bobby pushed the door open and propelled her in with his hand on her back.

She took a deep breath and stepped over the threshold. She'd thought she was prepared for whatever she might see.

The sight that faced her knocked the wind out of her. She staggered back—right into Bobby's solid chest. Rather than a wrecked living room, missing electronics, or vandalism, she beheld a virtual forest of photos.

Hanging from the ceiling from fishing line were dozens, maybe even hundreds, of pieces of paper. Pieces of photo paper on which were printed blown-up snapshots of Zarah and Bobby together.

She walked from picture to picture, joy tingling in every nerve in her body. Their trip to White Sands National Monument. The day they went hiking in Aguirre Springs. The dinner with Phoebe and her boyfriend. The photos they'd taken themselves, just messing around with Bobby's camera whenever they were together.

Turning, she found Bobby only a few feet behind her. "You did this?"

He nodded. "I had a little help—from Flannery and Caylor. I gave all the pictures to Flannery, and she spent several hours scanning and printing them for me. Caylor met me over here this afternoon to let me in—and then made sure you wouldn't come home until everything was ready."

"Flan and Caylor—they knew about this?" Laughter bubbled up from Zarah's toes. "The text message Flan got at supper—that was you, wasn't it?"

"Guilty." He looked around the room. "I've carried the box of these pictures around with me everywhere I've been since I left New Mexico. I was so angry over the whole situation, yet I couldn't bring myself to get rid of any of them."

He closed the distance between them, pulled her into his arms, and kissed her.

Zarah wrapped her arms around his neck and clung to him with every ounce of longing she'd borne for the past fourteen years.

The kiss ended, but Bobby didn't let go; neither did Zarah.

"Is it finally over?" she whispered.

"My part is. All that got me through the last week was this—my plans and preparations for tonight." He finally eased his hold and led her over to the sofa.

Zarah sat. Bobby knelt.

Her heart raced, and even her hair trembled in anticipation of what might be coming next.

"I know we have a lot of work to do on our relationship. We have a lot of years to make up for, a lot of getting reacquainted to do before we can join our lives together. Are you willing to take the time we need to do that?"

She nodded, now uncertain of where this conversation was going. "I'm willing to commit however much time it takes."

He cleared his throat and tried to smile. "Fourteen and a half years ago, I wanted to ask you a question." He pulled a small velvet box from his pocket. "I can't believe God has given us another chance, but this time, I'm not going to let you get away."

She couldn't breathe, couldn't swallow, couldn't do anything but look into his eyes.

"Zarah Mitchell, will you do me the honor of marrying me?"

Unable to speak, she nodded, leaned forward, and kissed him—then grinned at the momentary haziness in his gaze when she pulled back.

He opened the ring box to reveal a beautiful emerald-cut diamond in a platinum setting. Taking her left hand in his, he slipped the ring on her finger. It was a little tight, but she could get it resized.

"Don't you like it?" Concern edged his voice.

"Oh—I love it." She threw her arms around his neck and hugged him, then sat back again, looking at how the ring sparkled in the lamplight. "It's just. . .I don't know. I thought. . .maybe. . .since you'd bought a ring for me back then. . ." She shrugged. "This is perfect. Thank you."

A slow smile spread over his face. He reached into his other pocket and pulled out another, slightly larger jeweler's box and handed it to her without a word.

Frowning, Zarah opened the box. A gold open-work heart pendant with a small diamond suspended from the top point sparkled and twinkled at her.

"I wanted to give you an engagement ring that represents who we are, the love we rediscovered for each other now." He moved to sit beside her, took the box, and removed the necklace from it.

Zarah turned her back to him and lifted her hair from her neck.

"I had this pendant made from the ring I bought for you then. I wanted it to serve as a reminder to both of us that no matter what happens, love remains the constant that will see us through it." He kissed the back of her neck.

Hand covering the pendant—which rested over her own heart—Zarah turned to face him again. "Thank you."

"For what?" Bobby caressed her cheek.

"For giving me my happy ending."

Kaye Dacus is a graduate of Seton Hill University's Master of Arts in Writing Popular Fiction program. She is an active member and former vice president of American Christian Fiction Writers (ACFW), serving as the online course coordinator. Her *Stand-In Groom* novel took second place in the 2006 ACFW Genesis writing competition. Follow her at kayedacus.com.

OTHER BOOKS BY KAYE DACUS

Stand-In Groom
Menu for Romance
A Case for Love

If you enjoyed

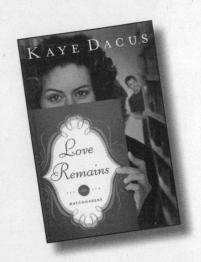

Love Remains

then read

The Art of Romance

coming Spring 2011